Silent Music

Julian Wolfreys

Published by:
Triarchy Press
Station Offices
Axminster
Devon
EX13 5PF
United Kingdom
+44 (0)1297 631456

info@triarchypress.net
www.triarchypress.net
Second Edition, November 2014

Print ISBN: 9781909470415

Contents

Prelude

It is said that the dead are the most demanding of our love. We are defenceless and delinquent in the face of them. Yet even the most beloved of ghosts is reticent, never to be seen when the sun is brightest, the sky bluest. The merest breeze coming off the sea might give you to recollect a face, a look, another place not unlike this, but nothing more than the slightest of traces returns. All we have is the memory of a voice; a whisper in the silence of a sound we no longer hear, but merely imagine was just there. Or, in the absence of the beloved's face, there is just that feeling of having recently been seen, watched. I had the sense I was looked at. Observed, I turned to nothing, save for the memory.

A look, a final glance. A last gaze; what else is there?

Sitting here, before the light goes, I am looking at a photograph of you. At the piano, smiling, knowing the applause, silent and therefore invisible in the photo but obviously there, the appreciation is for you. The music has ended, remaining a memory, a silent music you once had called it, that small space between the last note and the first pair of hands closing together. The photograph, a close-up, head and shoulders; a nimbus of light, a halo of golden hair rendered white in the spot, your eyes their bluest, radiant, looking over, not seeing, the lens into the unseen. You are gazing as if blindly at all those faces looking toward you. Head held to one side, as you often did, in public, in private.

Faintly embarrassed, as if surprised, that others could be so taken with you. Though no more than twenty-four or twenty-five at the time, laughter lines appear strongly at the corner of those eyes, your bluest, oceanic eyes, their colour signs, ciphers of a calm, a depth in which is carried every secret. As with so many other photographs, I was not the one to take it; had I been, I would not have seen you so; I would not have seen you at all; but here, in photographs such as this, I see you again as if you were there; I see you as I saw you when you were not looking at me but turning elsewhere. Looking at you now, I can see that you were unaware of my gaze then. So, I fancy myself your ghost, your only phantom looking on unseen, lovingly. In that world, I am the memory you barely realise. And so you remain.

I, and the others, we must have been off to the right of the image, on your left as always. Where were they looking? I no longer remember. Toward the audience, perhaps? At you? What had been the song? Or was it something without words? All the questions miss the point, they miss you, precisely who you were; irrelevant, they simply detract. The photograph though protects you from the questions, from all interrogations. Nobody asks. Nobody says, *what was she like or tell us who she was.* They respect what they think of as my privacy, trust to me to let them in just enough. That's sympathy for you, even now, after all this time. You are kept secret, then. You withdraw behind the image; just like this photograph. I know your face, its contours, what they reveal, how they might be read, the turn of mouth, the tilt of the head, the other small signs, all the little ghostly flickers, about to disappear, captured in the instant of transition. But all at once you are there, and secret at the same time; you remain hidden, except to me.

I knew you for a short while. All too brief a time. At the time, during its measure, it seemed as if it might go on forever. There was, I do not think I exaggerate, a glimpse of the eternal in what we shared. But eternity lasted not long enough. A few months shy of seven years. Seven years, save for three months, twelve, thirteen, perhaps fourteen weeks. I could count them of course, I could work it out to the day, but that kind of thing is for others, for those who like evidence, details, those dull enough, unimaginative enough, brutish enough to believe the biography is the be all and end all. For those who would like, but do not dare to ask, *how did it end?* Them? For them, nothing could be easier. I could give them the facts, just the facts, along with other details determined by their objective accuracy. *She was born*, I would say, *here* not *there*, and she…. But no, I cannot bring myself to say that. At the end, that was told to me by another, our mutual friend. She had to deliver that terrible sentence. The event itself, or what I know of it, if pushed, I could tell what I was told, at first delivered with care, shared shock and horror, then shortly after, I'm very sorry to inform you. I was not there, though I found out not that long after…after; after what, what should I call it? The event, as I just did? Why do I find it hard, impossible to say? Why do I search for, and use words, as if they were a picture frame enclosing emptiness, silence, loss? Or is this, the act of saying, too easy? You would tell me, wouldn't you? I wish you would. I wish you could. Give me the word for what remains unspoken, the nameless act, a short moment for which all words are obscenities.

Those who never wanted to know were the ones I had to tell. Like a ghost, I had to relive in my imagination for others, betraying their lives in one irredeemable instant, a few minutes to last a lifetime, irreversible. The ones who want to know though, who like facts with which to anchor loss, as though it were a balloon seeking to escape gravity, leave earth's orbit, disappear upwards; those who would see the photo and confusing the who and the what, would ask what you liked, what you enjoyed doing; they are the ones who would politely, tastefully, with just enough embarrassment of their own to signal a proper sense of gravity, offer condolences as if it had just happened: oh, I'm so sorry. You know, the kind of thing one says when accidentally knocking

over a cup, just at that moment, as though this unspeakable
event had just occurred and was no longer in the past, nearly
thirty years ago, a generation. Such inquisitors, all solace
and consideration, want life stripped bare nonetheless; they
want you naked. They want me to bare myself as I present
you to them. What is it in people, tell me, please, if you can?
They want some clues that give them the real you, to sum
you up, by stripping the mystery of you down to a few short
lines, whats, hows, whys, captured in the tabloid fact of the
compact biography. They think, knowing me—but they don't,
you would interrupt—that they have some insight into you;
but then they think they have me in a nutshell. How you
would laugh at the very idea.

I know what the others would say, our friends, a small
group, a family in more than blood or definition, the four or
five friends, more than friends; and then your family, your
other family as you would like to say. Our friends knew you,
and that is enough, it is more than enough. It is enough that
there are just a few, we few. There can be no more; this would
be unthinkable. I will for the time of telling struggle to keep
the larger world at bay.

For now though, no one around this evening, I am alone
with just the photograph. There are so many photographs.
All the boxes ranged before me, kingdom of ghosts, of the
past. This is just the first to come to hand. There you are:
your hair, flaxen, shining, woven intricately, finger thick braids
entwined, embracing, though, of course, a fugitive strand
insinuates itself down one side of your face, as you smile; no,
you are laughing, absolute joy; one earring visible, shimmering
in the artificial light, silver; a favourite pair, hand-made by
a mutual friend as a present from me to you, a surprise one
Christmas: leaf earrings, larger leaf below smaller, delicately
tooled blade; and on the reverse, fine, hidden script: in
aeternum. Te in aeternum amabo. I had this inscribed in what,
in all seriousness you used to call my dead language. Now it
returns in silence just for you, in your wake, trailing after you.
Inadequate words, words giving away their only secret, which

is that they give nothing away, being inadequate. You sit, laughing in the light, brightly alive, your dress, one you loved so much, coffee brown, horizontal bands interrupted by dark blue horizontal lines, and, against the broad brown bands, small cream leaf motifs. You appear briefly in the world, only to retreat. Of the world, unworldly.

Though I have not opened any of these boxes for nearly thirty years, though I have not dared to, coward that I am, self-recriminating all the while, having left you alone in the darkness when I know how much you loved the sun, how much your hands, your eyes, your golden, sunbright hair looked so alive in the full light of day, I recollect, in holding this image to me, a child in the dark holding a precious possession long thought lost, that you liked to write on the reverse of photos. Usually the date, the place or venue; and occasionally, as if the photograph were a private post card, from you to me, shared just between us, there you would write something; in German, English, Swedish; your own words, a phrase we would share as if it were our own; or otherwise, a quotation, something you had learned, a sentence from a book. Turning this over I find my memory has not betrayed me. The date: März 31.83. Now everything comes back, from this last public photograph, the last spring, the last concert, as it turned out. So much returns, too much, all at once too quickly. I focus again, concentrate, for you had left me some words here, risking everything in this, now thirty year-old note, as if you could have known, as if you were calling to me; as if you knew you would have to call on me. You risked everything on this quotation: 'The work of love in recollecting the one who is dead is the work of the most disinterested, free, and faithful love'. It is signed: A. For your name? No, you never did that. For the author then, someone you had read. Who, I cannot recall but I hear your voice, I hear in the silence the sound for which I have longed. You're coming back. There you are. Let's begin.

I Endless Summer

1. Overture: A Meeting (July 1976)

Where to start?

A phone call last summer, a call nearly thirty years arriving. Or a first day at a new school, it must be forty years ago. A feeling caused by hearing a piece of music for the first time, returning through the decades, or recalling what now seems like an entire life, no longer one's own, on seeing a photograph, which, amongst the hundreds, thousands of others, captures the whole...the whole what? We feel as if we're watching one of those movies punctuated by songs. The tune, the words, they're supposed to have significance, or to open a door for us, even though everyone we're looking at, everyone in whose lives we've become temporarily involved—it is as if all of them have only the most precarious, tenuous claim to our interest. The song, shorthand for a life, a feeling, a moment of crisis or sublime realisation, is there to draw us in, to help us overcome the distance, taking us to the heart of something, everything else. Everything else: words are supposed to substitute for that everything else, but they remind us, tatters that they are, that they are not this vague collocation we call 'everything else', just shreds and patches. Threads of memory, itself a woven screen on which we see as in a haze, until the moving image slows down, the focus tightens, the frame freezes.

Memory is a tricky thing, a fickle thing. It is nothing very much. It is nothing we can hold or touch, though it can touch us; and yet it is also an empire of ghost tales, over which no one but the phantoms have sovereignty. Coming when they come, we have no choice but to give them our attention, our allegiance; there is no higher court of appeal. Ghosts are capricious, cavalier in their indifference. We are moved by whim, the caprice of the other. What the spectre of a memory tells us was a beginning and what we then find we remember might not have been any such starting point at all. Where does that leave us? With an instant, an occasion, which serves to start the recollections going. Perhaps the memory that creeps up on us, giving us pause, is more reliable than the one we believe we choose. We don't know; we cannot tell. I have no idea. But if we have the feeling that the memory causing us to respond in an apparently immediate, let's call it an emotional way—that might be the one, not the other, more calculated reflection, conscious, deliberated, measured out so as to protect or keep a distance between us and... what, exactly?

How much memory do we have? How much do we store? How much can we bear? The burdens of memory are many, and at times unbearable. As unbearable as they are unburiable, a friend had once quipped. Sounds, sensations, tastes—are these mnemonics of a sort, not letters adding up to or standing in for words, but something...much more touching? The spirit's lexicon I am tempted to say, small ghosts, children of Mneme moving through and leaving their mark on you. They tempt and prod, tease and demand. Here we are, at the edge, on the verge, waiting to cross a threshold I am not sure is even the right door. I am caught in a pause, suspended by that experience of not knowing exactly which moment I want, no which I need, and which, faithless as it is, will push me into committing myself to telling the tale, as I had found once that I had, without knowing it, committed myself. To you.

So, if memory tells me anything at all, it is that a beginning is a departure from the path we had thought we were pursuing. Everything is comfortable, habitual, mechanical even. We walk around pursuing daily chores safe in the absence of thought; we drive through our lives carelessly in automatic. Until a roadblock, causing us to swerve, to brake hard. Forced into a detour, without a path or road, no map for where we are going, we are caused to take a new direction, or an unanticipated one at least, an old path given a new perspective. It's not like taking a wrong turn, so much as, entering a curve in the road, coming round the bend we confidently believe ourselves to be driving into, we find that we are no longer at the wheel; we are not in control, and there, there in front of us, in the headlights, there comes the future, unplanned for, unprogrammed. It is there, waiting, but accelerating in our direction. It's there; to come, and coming at the same time, probably as blindly confident in believing it knew the road as well as we did. Neither driver had anticipated the encounter; no one ever does; and despite looking in all directions, no one ever sees that event coming. Changing paths, changing lanes, changing directions, changing lives, a game changer, everything up in the air. Only afterwards, in the memory, is the belated realisation of the weight of significance that we come to assign the inconsequential, in that haunting experience of the invisibility of the obvious.

Are you the story I want to tell? Or your part in another story? Both involve me, so perhaps this is my story. I don't yet know. What I do know is that all the stories meet in the memory of you, in the memory of you that returns to me. No, that's dishonest, inaccurate. Not 'memory' singular, even though every memory is singular, different from every other; but memories—memories of you. I cannot ask you what your memories are. That's impossible. Even if this should not be my story, though for a while your story and mine were involved in one another's, I still have the burden of memories, the responsibility of remembering for you. I have to do justice to you, the memory of you. In your name, justice has to be done.

~~~

And there you are, in this memory. That voice, the handshake. It is always your voice first, doubtless because this returns most frequently in those interminable waking hours. Do I wake, thinking I have heard you call? Or do you start to speak, shortly before I realise it is just before three in the morning. So, your voice, your hand that day, initial unsuspecting intimacies haloed in light, too much light to see much else, though light enough to realise intensely the proximity of another. So much light it might as well be dark. No. Back up, rewind. Before these, I recollect—what? What am I seeing in that light, when at the time, I could see nothing? When did I become aware that you were moving towards me, that someone was moving in my direction? It was a warm afternoon, no, hot, oven fired, glazed that endless summer. Nearby the susurration of willows, gently complying to the drying motions of the air, a quiet murmur still making its way through all the other sounds, laughter, voices, lots of voices, music from somewhere nearby, further away the sound of engines. Above, below, steam and propeller. Low throbbing hum of life, inconsequential music of the day, the everyday unaware as yet that it was soon to be breached. A field, some fences, trees and tents, stalls here and there, buildings nearer, institutional, further away, residential. Bodies in the heat, occupying, reshaping the spaces in between. In remembering all of this, feeling the light, hearing as it seems the random mix, in which laughter sits nearest the surface, memory's hook that draws me in, I know that the clichés are inevitable, even as they multiply.

High up—I looked briefly, still not quite back in the everyday, thinking about the previous hour recently concluded—a small aircraft, single propeller, looking like the model it doubtless was, a small kit plane for some enthusiast. Blue to white that sky, crayoned in around the gold balloon, the kind always remembered as a summer of the past not the present, in which there is the merest trail of cloud, not even worth the name really. Distracted, sunglasses stained with sweat, thirsty, I looked from the sky to my feet, for no reason other than that this was one of those moments when I found myself becoming gathered back into the pleasing anonymity of being just one more person at a social event, rather than a particular focus. Light, warmth, sound; a general summer happiness everywhere around, on a day which, even were it not for a special moment—and they are rarely special for everyone—would be 'one of those days'. The ones remembered as being warmer, brighter, lasting longer, as if a window had been opened, granting a glimpse onto what infinity or eternity should be like. No, it was not everyone's special day; it was not even, in that instant of distraction and quiet reflection, a special day for me as yet.

Kate, James, Graeme; they had wandered off in different directions. James was over by the beer tent, its triangular bunting flapping unenthusiastically against the canvas of an awning on which a banner proclaimed 'probably the best beer tent on the Island'. The joys of a small life lived large. James's back was a great map, an unknown territorial patch of dark sweat causing his tee-shirt to cling, his shaved head shining, smaller sibling of the larger sun. Looking around, I saw Kate talking with a couple and their child. Parents eager, I imagined, for their surely unique and undoubtedly gifted daughter to take up a musical instrument, the violin or mandolin, having just witnessed Kate's dexterity with both; I am equally certain though that neither would have mentioned accordions, melodeons, or the various squeezeboxes Kate also played. It was always possible to tell how serious someone's intentions were when it came to those unwieldy and definitely strange contraptions out of which some people produce such enchantment; my Island magic, Kate would say, her accent seeming to be marked by some burr or twang, just below the surface of a flawless diction, hinting not at the regional but as if she was inhabited by another from some other place: a voice that held a past life. If they asked how long it took to learn to play Bach on an accordion, it was easy to see that they meant business, Kate had once told me. This couple—he looking vaguely uncomfortable in a tie and tweed jacket despite the temperature, she having walked out of a Laura Ashley catalogue, both obviously subscribing to all the right magazines—did not mean business. I smiled, knowing that Kate's politeness now would mean a rebarbative comeback or put down later this evening in the Harbour Lights.

Graeme, I couldn't see at first. Having just moved away from everyone after playing, I felt, almost inevitably, the need to reassure myself that they were there still. Then I remembered the water contraption. The volunteer sits in the seat over which is suspended a bucket full of water. If someone hits an attached target with a ball and not the person sitting in the seat, the bucket tips, the sacrificial victim getting a drenching. Sometimes repeatedly, depending on aim, or a matter of will, on the part of the participant throwing. Graeme had volunteered to be next up in the seat. Looking over in the direction of the playing fields' entrance, where the car park had overflowed onto the grass, there was a large, beet-red man of overgrown proportions in every way, a muscular arm, expansive mutton chop whiskers, and a faded plaid shirt rolled to the elbow, pulling back to release a certainly accurate ball: Graeme's father, George. Cricket ball cheeks, a deep cherry expanded, the wire wool of the grizzled sideburns moving with them in the execution of the delivery. Had Fred Truman pitched instead of bowled, it might have looked much like this. This could be a long afternoon for Graeme. I smiled. Then

— Hello.

Brought back to myself suddenly, I turned my head around to the left, in the direction of the sun. For a moment I was unable to see very much because of the brightness.

— eh…

— Don't you speak? You sing okay.

— I'm sorry, what? … Hello, I'm sorry, I'm always like this…

I became aware of a smile while this was being said, an accent, not heavy, but definitely announcing this still semi-silhouetted figure as being from further afield than the British

Isles; I was aware also of light through hair, golden hair, gold, gold fired, as the features pulled into focus.

— You're always speechless?

The question was both gently mocking, a little scornful, but also completely innocent.

— No, I'm sorry…

— You keep saying that. Is that your name? I'm Anna-Margaretha, Annagreth.

— Hello. I'm Benedict.

— The bass player called you Ben.

— Yes, people, friends, call me that.

— Is that not short for Benjamin?

— Yes, also; I mean, it is but I'm not. Not Benjamin. I'm Benedict.

— Yes, you said that too. You do repeat yourself, don't you? Benedict. *Benedictus*. It means 'blessed'. May I call you Ben?

— Certainly, of course.

Pausing again, there was that brief silence of yours that opened always into quiet laughter, as Annagreth's smile, Anna's face, your eyes were now fully in focus. I returned the smile. Her hand, I realised, was raised; long fingers, delicate tapers, short nails, a single silver ring on the smallest finger. Taking the hand blindly, my eyes tired in the sun were looking into hers. I understood that the grip was firm, the palm cool.

There we were.
There you are.

There you are in memory, before me again, in that instant, which, in the telling now takes longer than its real counterpart, then. In recollection the vision seems to hold, time on pause, a moment suspended rather than trapped. I want to recall whether or not the impression then seemed an age or over in the blink of an eye, but this is impossible to decide. Now and then, but not now, not really, though perhaps more real than the reality: you—she—both of you, both of me, both of us.

— You may call me Anna.

May. Not can; may. Grammatical correctness, precision, with just a hint of permission being granted, a gift given, as you now appear to have been, in memory, or in the manner of my recollection at least. Looking for a way to move beyond the initial contact, wanting to dispel the awkwardness that seemed to have settled, at least in me, I suggested we get an ice cream, or perhaps something to drink. Walking towards the ice cream van, its line showing no signs of decreasing, we began to talk more freely, about music in general, about the set Graeme, James, Kate and I had just played. Annagreth, Anna, was a pianist and organist, the first by training, the second because her father was organist and Kapellmeister in Lübeck *in the Marienkirche. The North of Germany, you know? The home of Marzipan.* Her sister, Heike, who would be visiting soon, was a singer; theirs was a musical family. And, amongst other things, they sailed, *Kieler Woche, just like Cowes Week.* Children ran past as we walked. Teenagers, not that much younger than me or the others in the band, moved in different directions, towards or away from this booth or that stall, from or to tent, parents, teachers. A small, uncaring, happy world of habit and occasion was taking place around us. Small joys, lived large, so few seeming so many, knowing and being known in the comforts of casual acquaintance, a communal familiarity not yet overly familiar. The odd word of compliment—nice show, good set—tempered by an inevitable 'a bit loud', met me as we walked.

Arriving at the back of the line, I knew by now that Annagreth, Anna, had recently arrived in Cowes to be German Assistant at the High School, and that she planned to spend the next year there; she had come from Germany a few weeks earlier with her mother and sister, to find a place to stay, and had wanted to get here for the summer, I want to get to know my new home, rather than arriving at the beginning of the school year. Our talk entwined, words crossing one another, tangents, questions, mutual interest, politeness relaxing into the first signs of friendly unguardedness in the heat of the late afternoon. This late July afternoon, one of a seemingly endless family of drouthy days that overcooked year, distilled summer, the air touched us, folding us into its quietly enervating hold. The world that day was brightness: invisible, ineluctable force, the clarity of light balanced against a muffled gauze of sounds, a commingling of scents and other odours that could only be described as smells, pungency with floral or acid top notes: grass, the occasional strongly scented flower, slightly burned meat, and when the wind shifted the faint trace of a car starting, or, fainter yet, the sea.

Ice creams bought, cans also of something far too sweet, and not at all capable of calming a thirst, we walked back across the playing field, dried, brittle grass piercing sharply once or twice the canvas of a deck shoe as the grass became more unkempt, to a less densely populated spot nearby a windbreak row of Elders, separating the school grounds from the neighbourhood of bungalows, curving down the slight incline of the hill, looking out over the Solent. Nearer to the trees, their voices became more prominent, human noises muted, just a little. The flowers of the Elders had begun to diminish, the berries begun to form, though not as yet fully ripened, fully black. Time, then, seemed anything but precipitate.

— These trees are supposed to protect us from evil spirits. If you cut an Elder down it's supposed to release one, but it's also a source for herbal remedies and medicines. You can make drinks, teas and cordials from it, and the wood is hard so it has been used to make musical instruments.

— But, if you make an instrument from it, you have to chop it down, no? So won't that release the evil spirit? Or will the instrument be haunted? I should not like a ghost under my fingers.

There was that slight mocking tone again, an undercurrent or resonance, one which became so familiar, one in which there was no harm because affection, as I learned, tempered sharpness always. I hesitated to ask if she had enjoyed the performance, so danced around various topics, until she asked if I wasn't curious about whether she'd enjoyed the show. Smiling for a moment, I looked away, before saying I had wondered, but did not want to seem…I paused, as I so often did, for the right word, looking across the fête, which was bustling, an independent life form, self motivating, spinning on through a perpetual summer's day. It was always easy enough to write a lyric, come up with a hook, find the right way of fictionalizing a life and get to the heart of the matter in under five minutes. Unformed language is messier. The ends, when there are any, fray; words are already fragments, orphans, homeless, looking for some shelter.

— I thought you were all good, and good together, you play well, no, not just technically, but with feeling, *ja*.

A pause. A criticism, or a search similar to my own, words being just out of reach?

— but you need something…*wie sagt man? Leim?* Can you say 'glue' for this?

Glue was good; yes, glue was what we needed still, something that bonded us at the edges, the corners, between one point and the next. I turned back; looking directly at her said

— I think you're right. Perhaps we need a pianist.

— *Quatsch*!

This, in a deeper register, her head pulled back, amused, her chin, tucking itself toward the neck. Already there in this first hour of acquaintance, I had begun to notice gestures, inflections, attitudes in miniature that form someone's carapace, all the little half remembered motions by which we are given a what to go with a who and which give us also reasons for thinking about that person in a way we wouldn't even imagine when it comes to anybody else.

— You're having, making fun with me.

— No, not at all; Kate—that's our violinist…

— and she sings…

— yes…

— and plays accordion…

— yes…

that smile broadened, the eyes glinted just a little more
— and *mandoline*…

This last word retained its German tone; there was a
musicality to it, with its long vowel sounds and final, breathy,
almost whispered, dying 'e'. A fall, a grace note. I felt myself
breathe in slightly too emphatically, as again, Annagreth,
Anna, found spaces in what I was about to say, occupying
those gaps, but not insistently, not with impatience.
— what I was going to say…

I carried on, perhaps a little too hurriedly, aware at that
moment that the shadow was creeping round, a deep, dark
promise of illusory cool approaching us behind, and that my
face felt suddenly tanned, was burning a little perhaps; what
I was going to say, was that Kate can play the piano, but gets
restless, likes to move around, so yes, we've all talked about
this, but it's difficult finding the right person; or anyone for
that matter. There had been one person, Martin, I offered
pointlessly, always giving too much information, he had
just come out of the army, but he was too lazy to learn the
material properly. And he had queered the pitch by going out
with James's then girlfriend while she was, apparently, still
seeing James.
— Queered the pitch?
— A metaphor from cricket; to make a mess of things.
— Cricket. A game in which nothing much happens for a
long time, no? And is not to be understood.
— Not unlike life.
— Ooh, that is serious. You are a serious young man!

The subject of the band dropped, or was caused to drop
as, halted in our cautious circling of one another, we became
aware of a shadow, and with that a presence.
— It's getting on for five, bugger. Do you want to help
pack the stuff so we can go eat before we have to set up at
the Lights, or are you going to sit here for the rest of the
afternoon, trying to chat someone up? He's hopeless at it you
know, he always starts telling 'em useless things. I bet he's told
you about the trees; don't let him get on to the birds, though

by then you'll have fallen into a coma, doubtless. Hallo, by the way, I'm Graeme; aren't you going to introduce us then, bugger?

Most of Graeme's sentences included the word 'bugger', not as a statement of disbelief, frustration, or exasperation, but as a generic pronoun of sorts, which, when uttered in that broad, almost 'stage' southwestern rural accent as if he'd never got over being an extra in some amateur dramatic production of a Thomas Hardy novel, laid heavy emphasis on the 'r' most of us are too lazy to pronounce.

— I'll be right there Rog, this is Anna-Margaretha, Annagreth, Anna …

I realised my apparent idiocy in the face of Graeme at offering three names for the same person.

— Annagreth, this is Rog … Graeme, he drums.

— You got three names or is he stammering?

— No, my given name is Anna-Margaretha, but this becomes Annagreth or just Anna.

— Well, I suppose I've got two names, but I'm Graeme anyway, or Gray.

— I know, I saw; I heard. What then is 'rodj'?

This would have been a long, and not entirely edifying explanation, certainly not something suited to a first conversation. *Just what we call him*, I said, too quickly, with an emphatic glance at a clearly amused percussionist, accompanying an irritability not unlike that when attempting to swat away a buzzing insect, the annoyance remains indifferent, attracted even to the exasperation. Certainly the question, phrased as it had been with the query directed towards not the name but the entity, was one that others had asked for some time, without having ever proposed an answer. Their emphasis though had been not on the name but on the person. Graeme occupied a space at angles to what the rest of us thought of as the real world. I switched tack quickly, as Graeme stood there with that predatory grin he reserved for moments of others' embarrassment or when meeting an attractive woman, the smile preface to any further less subtle incursions; it was nice to have met, sorry we couldn't talk longer—*has he asked to see you again; 'course not*—this, Graeme, pushing the advantage of discomfort with the pressure of playfulness; all the while the shadows extended, and on Annagreth, Anna's face—why had I introduced her not as Anna, but as Annagreth and Anna-Margaretha?—a smile, her eyes on me; Graeme, again I can hear her voice, I hear your voice, with the Elder leaves' soft sonorous sleepy murmur: *Graeme*, you said, talking to him, looking at me, amusement at the edges of your mouth,

— did you say you are setting up somewhere else? Are you playing again? Tonight? Here, in Cowes, or somewhere else?

— At the Harbour Lights, down on the water, along The Parade. Nine tonight, two sets. It's free; I'll buy you a drink; bring your mates. I'll buy 'em one n all.

He grinned ever more knowingly, looking at me

— I'll tell the others you'll be over directly, right? We're to start without you? Right-o, lazy sod.

— Why not, it must be your turn by now. Look, I do have to go; I'm sorry, we have to pack up, set up before the pub opens, do a sound check. It'd be good if you could come down, perhaps we can talk more then. About pianists.

— I'll try and be there by eight.

At that, we began to walk back. There was still much activity across the school grounds, but it showed signs of beginning to come to a slow, desultory end. Diminution might be the better word. Diminuendo; ending with a whimper, rather than a bang.

Magic can often turn sad; it carries in it its own brand of melancholy. Though the warmth of the day was as yet unabated, there was the impression of, if not a chill, then something no longer unalloyed. Like those late summer afternoons, when we know the sun is trying, but doesn't have the heart. Or when, as if turned too high, some toy oven with a too bright bulb, it bakes the world too hard, too brittle, daylight lingering a little too long, before the shadows turn

to washed out mute colours, draining, leeching everything
that had been vibrant, long before the night gets fully under
way with the greyness of an untimely, premature, perennial
twilight. Or those late September days, only experienced at
seaside resorts, when the first squall sets in, anticipating later
autumn, the last tourists hovering uncertainly by a bus shelter,
all sandals and plastic ponchos, a supermarket carrier bag,
much used, for sandwiches, tissues, and, vainly, a tube of
sun cream. A dog barked, as a too strident, too tired mother
spoke a little too intemperately to a too tired, too agitated
child. Not quite enough, yet too much at the same time. The
world of that afternoon had begun to list, exhausted under
its own weight. It was time to pack, to leave, before ennui
gathered into something indefinable, though with a soured
note, a dissonance or aftertaste, perhaps, apprehension of the
impossibility of remaining in the day.
— Tonight then, maybe.
— *Vielleicht das nächste mal.*

~~~

I am looking at a photograph of you, another that brings
back the end of the day, end of season feeling, a point of
transition; perhaps it is just the thought of German glue, of
lime, limning, quick lime, caught in a snapshot of emotion,
in between places, moments, times, always on the verge, on
an edge, a boundary: liminal—suspended there…and here.
I know there are other photographs you would have liked
more, but there is, in this, something true to your spirit,
as I remember it, as it haunts me, as, I think, without false
memory or nostalgia, it haunted me then, in that first time of
meeting. A close up, looking up; there you are, sitting at the
piano, on a stage somewhere, blue light describing diagonally
an upward trajectory, fanning out triangularly behind you.
The lacquer of the piano shows blue too, the silver of the
microphone and its grille also tinted similarly, and your
shirt, one sleeve buttoned the other having come undone,

azure—the sky that day—shading to cerulean, or is it the colour of lapis lazuli? I have no word for that colour, which touches me so closely, which haunts with the drained intensity that colours dreams, through which we seem to see and after which we struggle. Too much blue, playing the blues, blue everywhere, blue, blue my love…that absurdly cheesy song, one you liked, but which, with its insistent harpsichord interjections, you would insist on playing or better yet, Joni Mitchell's 'Blue'; but yes, blue everywhere, mostly in your eyes. Looking into your eyes that day; your eyes don't reveal their colour in this otherwise blue photo; they are shaded, guarded. You are not playing. It must be a moment between songs. A rest, a pause, a silence, your left hand pulls the microphone closer to your mouth, smallest finger and thumb steadying it from beneath; your right hand shades your eyes, looking away, up and off to your right, lips parted slightly about to speak, thinking the response, clearly a riposte, and your eyes narrowed, bridge of the nose and brow wrinkled, your chin beginning—again—to pull itself in. Everything, everyone, is poised, in that moment, waiting for what you, Annagreth, Anna, Anna-Margaretha, are, were going to say.

2. First Act: James (August 1973)

— The next one's a slower number, 'Little Wing', you can all get smoochy.

— Yuuuuuuh.

This from the audience, a 'regular', a punter of our acquaintance, bane of the soundman's existence.

— it's particularly heart rendering; anyone you want to dedicate this to?

This last throwaway comment, on mic, to me, arriving with that viscous grin, too many teeth, cheeks too full. That moment when one finds oneself the centre of attention, but not for the usual reasons. Some people appear to be in on a secret. Some people: closest friends, the ones who make the jokes, giving me a hard time from love, as I would any of them. Public, exposed, naked, I feel this unreasonably; after all, why? What has happened exactly? A pleasant, if overheated afternoon made more so by a chance encounter; an hour of trivial happiness defying definition, perhaps not worthy of that. So what do I say, or do I say nothing? Flustered, eyes cross the room, playing for time, not playing but for time, tuning, pretending to, and finding that, drawn, I am looking to the very place I least had wanted to, at the heart of the matter, as though an other person's eyes drew me. Is that a smile? A smirk? Having to be quick now, I remark…

— I didn't know we were doing 'Leila' tonight.

— Yuuuuup.

— Judge won't be at any rate.

...This from Graeme, and I begin, aware of laughter from behind me, four simultaneous bells, Dopplershaped, phaseshifting, hanging from gossamer, something floats into the air, sound taking flight, shaping to the image in the mind's eye, anticipating, perhaps desiring, other sympathetic resonances of which, as yet, no one had any idea, least of all the guitarist.

But this still remains to come. Four years into a future already underway, prelude to the act. After all, whether characters in the play, or those who think themselves to be telling the story, we find ourselves communicating incommunicability. We find that we butt up against the incommunicable, our lips poised, wanting to find a place in the silence. For now therefore, rewind once more, retreat further, searching for a different beginning, one at least that leads you and I to here. Shape another, give someone else a voice now that mine hesitates, and yours remains silent.

~~~

The arrival of Norman Stanley Fletcher and the West Indian Cricket team for a three test series were in many ways the highlights of the year. By the end of the summer, those who cared about such things knew that starting a test series at the Oval rather than concluding it there could only herald disaster for English cricket. For some, such events took precedence over the UK's half-hearted entry into the EEC. As did the release of *The Dark Side of the Moon*, as much an end as it was a beginning. Memory decides on these events retrospectively as being of much greater personal significance than others having what might be called greater historical heft. Memory is right, history wrong. History is a monster of order, facts mere henchmen, thugs to corral and coerce. How we place ourselves, and those around us in relation to the past

is partly the way we come to understand how we get to where we are now, hitchers on the side of the road, even though we lack the thread of our own stories until they're picked apart; we lack the detail that comes at us rapidly. Follow any clew, pull on any thread in memory's skein, and everything promises not merely to unravel but to multiply, leading you, being pulled along, not pulling at all. One thread only or too many to count, we find ourselves entangled, undone, ravelled up in our very own snares, the ones we never knew we were weaving. Each thread vibrates; each holds a small clear bell to sound the significance of the moment, bringing to us the otherwise mute and silent traces of particular places, events, people. History's facts are only significant in that we find ourselves involved. Royal engagements, Cod Wars, a new London Bridge, none of these mean as much as moving from a city to an island, if, as I had done, you are the person being moved, uprooted, starting a new school, sixth form. And if, in having moved, I find this bright, large stranger, bald, beaming, occupying more than mere physical space. He is standing there, silhouetted in the afternoon sun.
— I'm James.

Imagine him here, someone whose initials—*BJW / JBW*—I will come to realise are mine, something shared by chance, one the graft or palimpsest of the other, opposites attracting with the force of similarity in a place that seems the very end of the world on a late summer's day, yet one more when sea and sky conspire, glass and canopy of lead tending to gunmetal, to extinguish summer's proof. An overexposed snapshot, the light is bruising, the past not a truth in being fact but a truth I've been searching for; as good a turning, if not a starting point, as any. From out of all those disputatious, querulous details that vie for attention there emerges a voice, name and light. Light is important, potent, its tenor, its mood gives experience to the memory of place, it triggers the remembrance of what moves us to recall. That august grey, tending to oatmeal in tone and density, with those hues of weighted shadow, poised above, behind, surrounded us, enfolded us in that first conversation, casual and without direction as it was. Drifting, we drifted, it seems now. I no longer remember the words with any clarity. But in this moment of weight and drift the world became uninhabited, and so focused. Most of the time, where we are is almost as uncertain as when we are; where and when make the who over, little adjustments in course tending to greater transformations in the soul, as memories and echoes of endless voices merge without coalescing. Briefly though, there are those points of time, when memory, like a hidden doorway opens, makes possible an opening onto an avenue leading to a future no one can begin to fathom. *Overture*.

That Monday, on which anxiety transferred itself as if by personal magic to the atmospheric density of the small world, the lumpen canopy was provided a counterpoint in this tall, tending to corpulent, shineheaded figure. Not a skinhead, a shinehead. James's skull was shaved scrupulously and, as I was soon to find out, kept daily in its light bulb nudity. That head shines in memory, whenever memory presents me with an empty space, or dark screen, whenever I struggle to recollect with any precision, or when confusion stirs up, muddying, the often too rapid succession of dancing scenes. James stands out from the dark, lighting the track, providing co-ordinates, clearing the path. Always off to one side, but mapping the route, keeping everything moving steadily while buoying everyone from underneath. A rolling wave, an always ready wit, James steadied the world for others in a manner he could never accomplish for himself. It is because he is there that memory appears. Every time I find I have to start again, whenever I think I cannot say, do not want to say, what lies beneath, James shines.

Except for the odd stage wig, and some were very odd, his head was always free of hair, as he would have it. He explained one day the reason, an incident a couple of years before at Stamford Bridge. Standing with his father, John, a man who wore a theatrical substitute for hair as part of his profession, in the terraces, James had felt his head give way, the lights go out with a blinding flash, as a broken bottle, hurled indiscriminately but with malice, found contact. Staring at the rude boys one moment, glimpsing nothing the next. Later when the lights were turned on once more, James had felt himself in the spotlight, his skull now completed with a titanium patch. Cranioplasty, craniotomy, these were the terms, and the procedure, elaborate names for plugging a hole, filling the space. Scarring, though small, left a distinct siglum, over which hair refused to grow, and looking like a light bulb was a choice preferable to looking like a lawn where moss had left the surface pocked. Certain notes, bass vibrations, bowing a cello, blowing the trumpet or saxophone, seemed to make the head resonate with sounds only James could hear. Explaining the head as a means of introduction, his face smiling brightly, tombstone teeth drawing the eye almost as much as the skull, everything about him illuminated. James glowed, as he unfolded with celerity the whys and whats. Had I noticed him, or his head, that previous week in joining the choir for a first practice before the school year, a new school, a new year, a new home, as I began to settle into patterns? I no longer remember. James was always a beacon, a lighthouse in the stormiest weather, in the most turbulent moments. Rock solid, his voice made up for his physical presence, his immobility. He spoke so quickly, always spoke with a speed, though never an urgency, which relieved the pressure, revealed so much.

Around us the endless motion of others, a swarm in the sticky, too close, thunder bearing air. Older, younger, all uniformed, though not uniformly tidy, even on a first day. Too much energy, febrile and restless, not yet having settled to the routine of school, the mundane sameness, the rote proceedings not yet having institutionalized boredom, not yet having sapped defiance, invention, verve. All playgrounds are the same, all Monday lunchtimes similar, where so many small engines rev in futile resistance to the larger machine's intent to make all its parts idle. Here was the play, that point of accommodation, licensed freefall. The asphalt led away to playing fields, these barely hedged, leading onto open ground, a slowly rising hillock, and the last dwellings: irregularly arranged larger houses that always appeared on the boundaries of a town, signalling wealth, chosen separation. Look one way, the house owners see that fable they have chosen to purchase, the countryside; look the other, they confirm for themselves, from their elevation, their superiority. The unnatural order of things. James lived over there on the hill, he explained, asking in the same breath if I did anything other than sing. Anything other meant something musical. I played guitar, some straightforward piano. I played the piano, I explained apologetically, but was not a pianist. He nodded, understanding the difference. I also, I began to say, adding this perhaps unhelpfully, resistant, defensively (it seems to me), as if wanting to measure James's loquacious exuberance, his too bright energy with a contrapuntal taciturnity and reserve, underplaying all the while—I always underplayed, simplicity a virtue I had learned early, and which only a few years later I was taught how to relinquish—; I also played cricket; had played for my previous school team.

— Bat or bowl?

The question of a fellow player, that of someone who knew the game at least with a more than engaged interest, affection even, perhaps a passion. Perhaps here was the quietness within the noise, rhythm within the rhythm.

— Bowl. I knew the next question, cut it off before it had a chance to be formed.

— Spin. Left-hand. Finger.

— I'm Vice-Captain, school team, bat no. 3. Want a try out for next season? Want to bring the guitar round one evening soon?

Spending more and more time with James in the next few months, I found his life existed as an irregular but inexhaustible pulse of energy in contrast to the ordered, and regular life of his parents, his father a QC, his mother, built to command, an organizer and lover of systems and institutions by inclination if not nature: WI, WRVS, JP. Good works, good instincts, good taste. She had given up the cello early, but had decided, equally early, long before there was a child, that her son—he was always going to be a son—would play an instrument, more than one if the child showed any aptitude. Application would be seen to, talent would find itself. It was always about hard work and application. James had gone along with this before he had known not to. There had never been a choice. Indeed, in the rear view mirror of self-conscious recollection he never saw the absence of choice as anything other than the path to freedom. Not for nothing though did he express an interest in the double bass and saxophone. Still instruments, more or less legitimate, they were, nevertheless, neither cello nor trumpet. They spoke for James in lieu of the words for that spirit, not of rebellion—this would have been too obvious for him—but of some other searching, longing, call it what you will, I still have yet to find the word for what I find at once so laudable, for which I have such affection, and yet that of which, nonetheless, I was always, and remain to this day, jealous. The electric bass came the year I met James. This, he told me he reasoned with his mother, would help him develop. He had argued in the politest possible way with her—his father was always happy to let James pursue the interest, with an indulgent disinterest, a permanent distance—using all the rhetorical skill he had learned from his father, that ability to employ language in ways that bring the presiding judge around to see one's own point of view as if they had always held that perspective. Angela Wroath was won over; she could see the logic. It was, after all, about talent, even if, as she had said repeatedly, she did not understand the need for electrification. This word always hung in meathook quotation marks for her, all the sharper for being invisible, pointed in their very assumption. James could imitate her tone, her delivery, her resigned manner of wearied acquiescence presented *de haut en bas*, with a condescension believed to be equanimity, tolerance, liberal allowance for that which one does not quite see oneself.

James's restless talk, his ceaseless energy, was a carefully calculated conservatism. He kept everything in himself, giving little away. His playing was often furious, but always essential, necessary, economical. It was not in the number of notes he played but the violence, if that could be the right word, implicit in the delivery. There was a menace in reserve. His experiments, his adventurousness, were not of the dissipating or enervating kind. He would often laugh at the restlessness of others, the need for 'change' or something new. Yet for all that he would ground everyone else, he played I believe with an inner vision, keeping time in himself, marking his own tempi. A radical traditionalist, James believed all forms were good, if all were played with equal verity, finding a balance between the needs of repetition leading to technical perfection and the ability to become free to improvise as a result of the tedium of practice. Thinking of James now, I get the impression of a glow that secrets from within itself the traces of an austere passion, that of a controlled demon kept in chains, seldom given to outbursts, moments of rare but spectacular self-destructiveness. Creativity was a given. Emotion had to be given form for him, in him, or it was no use. All his outward Day-Glo ebullience was carapace, persona, shell of a personality learned, adapted.

That first day, the storm that had promised never transpired. Coming to the end of the afternoon, I was walking towards my bike, pausing at the tennis courts to watch the practice, when James appeared once more, bustling, busy.

— Where are you headed?

— Home.

— Where's that?

— Seaview, well, just outside.

— I'm heading into town. Tea?

I felt, I don't know why, unreasonably hopeful. Here seemed to be an encounter I could not have imagined, and with that something in which to invest against the resentment I still held for having being relocated from London to, as I saw it, a small, largely rural, and decidedly mundane rock off the south coast of England. Not yet thinking of a future, I felt nevertheless the possibility of a now.

Though no rain had arrived, no thunder broken, the afternoon had settled early into a gloom, typical autumnal warmth and humidity. At some points along the walk, through the streets of late Victorian terraced houses, bow windows distended like the stomachs of their original occupants, complacent in their professional success, street lights had been tricked into softly glowing life by the premature disappearance of the day. Turning out of Pell Lane, the branches of horse chestnut trees, moved by the soughing autumn air, attempting to make themselves heard above the chicken coop cacophony of a school released on the first day of term, we walked with a purpose and timing set by James. He crossed the street without warning, with that surprise occasioned by a great mass moving suddenly and sharply. I followed belatedly, as we headed for the wrought-iron gates of a local cemetery, which, I was told, made a handy shortcut to the top of the town. This regimented, walled space calmed him, I could see. There was a balance to be found in the organization of the mostly Victorian dead, those who had departed this life, fallen asleep, Grey against grey, shades of indifference, moss spotted and weather etched. They provided passing interest from their potted biographies, as truncated in information as were those Victorian columns, sliced through, broken, all obvious visual hulking metaphor, no stone unturned, as it were, in that nineteenth-century quest, relentless, for the absolute physical image, material trope, figure of speech made oppressively real. Yet somehow, in the open space of the graveyard, the sky had appeared to lift, as weightless above as this caravan park of the dead seemed overly heavy. The light, diffused through a beigegrey porridge canopy that hurt the eyes, made one squint. Quiet and voluble, slow and fast, Tweedle-dee and Tweedle-dum, twin obsessives navigating between the tombstones, the quick and the dead, we moved. A rhythm was already developing not easily described, but felt, accommodated, a possibility borne of chance becoming an inevitability; because of course anything can always happen, if we allow it to, if we let ourselves be swallowed in the moment, finding as quickly as we can, the internal motion, going with the pull of the tide. High in the air, invisible but felt, thunder resounded elsewhere, calling into life autumnal crows, a sound I have since always loved, expected, needed.

~~~

In the months that were to come, there was much wandering, much tea, talk, trivia of all kinds, involving frustrated, belated dissections of the summer's Test series, accommodations of each other's musical tastes, half-hearted defences of one's own. For someone who appeared so removed from others, James, I realise now, was in fact merely in tune with himself. Out of time with everyone and everything else around him, he had no need to belong. Apart he was, and prided himself quietly on being disconnected, but also belonging to a whole that did not as yet exist, save in his own private vision, which, in truth, he barely saw. He connected as he chose, made connections, drew into him, with that often indescribable energy, all the trivia of the everyday and made it mean, or else left it to its own inconsequence. With James, I found that the world did not come into focus, its focus changed. While he was unconcerned with seeing the world, he made anyone who would pause see, and perceive differently. Musically, he had no map for a future, no grand vision of how he saw music or what he wanted to do. Not liking what was already beginning to take place in so many ways, already finding many more 'serious' recordings—by 'serious' he meant the music made by bands for albums, not singles—expressions of talent being wasted, dribbled away, rather he had this dimly viewed idea that the past had sounds, images in tone, which kept returning, ever more diluted, but which were demanding to be saved. This was how he put it: *saved. If we could only put together music from different times, different places, which are impossible to bring together, then the past might be saved.*

This word was first uttered in a somewhat too loud voice, eagerness misjudged and forcing itself out of a body already a mass of energy not to be countered easily…

— Do you have a problem, matey? I've got a plate in my head, I'd be careful if I were you

…one November afternoon, in a café towards the bottom of Union Street. Everything about the place was cheap. Cheap and homely, grease smell steam cosy, with chequered linoleum flooring, everything with chips, plastic laminate table surfaces and melamine crockery. Plastic, invented, artificial, a blueprint for a stereotype, modelling as a cliché in waiting, and captured in a vignette, it was so awful as to be indestructible. Even the windows had the obliging layer of greasy spoon condensation, transforming the winter world beyond of aimless shoppers and the even more aimless unemployed (they at least moved with a rapidity if not a goal) into a silkscreen ghostshow. Inside the steam, inside this stage-set coffee shop, we were, at least, ghostwarm.

— Saved.

The word was out there, congealed, captured in the steamed time of the café. It had floated beyond the two of us, slowing as it rose, attracting the three other customers' attention, catching even Peter, the owner's ear. Would it be too much to say time slowed? Would I be fantasizing the moment too much? Is memory attempting to capture a kinetic blur as a freeze frame or, imagine this, a pop art still life, the very tawdriness of place its own aesthetic? Do I want to give this, rather than any other instant, significance? Or am I remembering a brief upsurge of danger, where a vacuum ruptures, a bell jar implodes and explodes simultaneously, there is a rush of noise, and, in my recollection of a perception, lagging behind the immediacy of an experience, everything dawdled, idling into a silent space, before

returning, reversing, rewinding, speeding up, into the sealed
bubble of everyday indifference? We were turning a corner,
in which an altogether different present slips into the shape
of the one that had, just a few seconds before, existed, but
which existed no longer. There had been almost no time to
change gears, shift down, before cornering, then regaining
control. The non-announced had crept upon us. Waiting
around the bend, an apparition had made itself felt, the ghost
of a promise as yet undefined, undetermined, stripped of
everything.

— Have you been sniffing the chemicals in the darkroom
again? Pete, two more frothy coffees.

I felt we had opened a door, taken a step we couldn't
recover, but to which I was not yet ready to commit
wholeheartedly, without condition. If there was to be
no going back, there should at least be a pause before
precipitation. I felt the need for the ordinary, to diffuse the
situation, if only to allow it time, allow oneself time, to be
wary of a wrong beginning or false step. The world glistened
in this moment, the air limpid. James's eyes lost none of
their brightness, his gaze held, expecting the photographer's
command. Even though faintly embarrassed by the volume,
I loved the way James could affect the temperature in a
room by his mere demeanour. We remained paused in a
small world where, usually, we were invisible. Yellowed strip
lighting, dripping glass, uncomfortable wall paper, puckering
like a too small shirt on a too large irregular torso, and those
bluegrey table tops made of a material that shared its name
with ants set the scene, while David Essex, Donny Osmond
and Gilbert O'Sullivan *why oh why* provided our afternoon
soundtrack, from the transistor next to the register. Saved.
Something, someone, needed saving somewhere.

Letting the silence settle, the small world resumed its
normal rhythms. Halted, slowly stepping, halted again,
Tenpenny paused toothless the other side of the glass,
distorted by steam, made watery, cadaverous through
condensation, walking dead washed up by the tide. James

had been talking like this for a week; no, he always talked like
this but now the subject was becoming more purposeful,
refined, as if he had been rehearsing the phrasing, practising
the shapes again and again inside himself. The direction, the
destination, the departure point all were about to arrive, even
if he couldn't quite recognise them or know he'd reached
a conclusion that was also a beginning. I looked from him,
to Tenpenny, and back again. So much takes place inside,
in solitude, which then presents itself as tones. For all that
we see in the world, we hear more, even if we are not aware
of this. We feel the oscillation of the emotional voice, the
other one inside the figure before us, if we stop looking. I
felt there was a sympathetic resonance between this bald
musician before me and the benignly crazed homeless figure
the other side of the smeared windows. Indeed, it was
popularly believed and recounted that Tenpenny had been a
concert pianist but had lived too near the sun, his emotional
life always breaking cover, breaking the surface, breaking
through the daily straightjackets. As a result, after what was
written on his face as much wayward and weary wildness, he
was now one of the Island's refugees, living in a makeshift
shack in the grounds of St Cecilia's Abbey. Benedictine nuns
fed Tenpenny, the place where your glory abides, his family,
wealthy it was said, sending money periodically.

— Tenpenny...

It was now raining. Hard, the water rushed in the gutters,
gushing from spouts.

— Tenpenny, please.

— Close the door.

James and I both moved, almost at the same time, placing
coins in Tenpenny's hopeful hand, this supplicating scarecrow
granting benediction on anyone who responded. The
thickness of decaying animal odour was more than usually
pungent today, doubtless the effect of the three days' rain.
Tenpenny's cheeks shined, their hollows grimy, the bones
somewhat fevered. Eyes overbright, the face burning from
within, outward signs of something beyond the silence: the

performance rituals only he heard taking place, so many evocative, locked-in incantations *Gaudete in Domino Te laudamus Domine Alleluia Pascha nostrum* and the grace of fleeting harmonious phrasing blindplayed that his fingers would never allow him. Tenpenny, James said, would join the nuns at Compline, becoming peaceful, finding a halt to the demons that played him as if his soul was a series of organ stops, arranged and rearranged, pulled pushed, left half withdrawn. I had heard him once, touching, you couldn't call it playing, the organ. It gave him a voice he never found for himself.

Returning to our table, I thought once more of James, feeling guilty for the comparison. Though kept to myself, I was troubled nonetheless for seeing the one as the future of the other. James's control was far too complete though, or just fractured enough, to allow for torque, to give egress to the pressures. In this was my reassurance.

— We should play. Together. Publicly.

— Yes, yes, what I was thinking.

— Playing simple pieces, but finding ways to renew the sound every time it's expressed, so it's like its never been played before. It has to have structure, but feel improvised…

— a conversation with sound…

— in sound…

— between the sounds.

Our conversation continued, trading phrases, unfinished shapes in call and answer, with no one leading the way, the two of us moving in and out of one another's rhythms. Much later, I finally understood, what at the time I had only intuited. Memory does that to us. At a point when it's too late, no longer relevant, the memory surfaces like a drowned child to break a parent's heart. What is exciting in music is that we experience its performance every time as if it were new. But inside that there is a memory that surfaces, not just previous performances, but the memory of all music, all tone, all sound. The present moment no longer matters, it cannot hold sway. Music lets all the ghosts in, giving them a place to play, even in the most tightly organised framework. What haunts the moment means that every time a piece is played, each time is, or can be, different, even in the most programmed moment. Repetition is memory improvised, memory improvises the moment it repeats and changes it in its return. In moments of happiness remembered, we witness from afar the grace of spontaneity, the sinuous harmonious constellation of fold, duration and, with these, a mysterious sweetness of a pure now. Every performance, every friendship, every love is this: looking at an instrument, any instrument, we only see wood, wire, gut, hammers, keys, metal. We know that there are only so many notes, repeatable lower and higher, but all in all a few. Yet, there are sounds, expressions, emotions, relations separated only by the slightest membrane from one another, and from our waking sleepwalked lives. Much later, too late, belatedly, I knew this. More than that, I felt it. I feel it still, along the spine, behind the eyes, in the pit of the stomach, at my heart's core, when my soul despairs.

After everything was done, much later than any of the trivial events I need to record, I read by chance a passage in Proust, which expressed exactly this. It shocked and silenced me, moved me to tears, because I knew he was right. It was as if he had written this passage on the reality of music just for me. I felt as though a postcard, long lost, presumed missing, had arrived; it was as if I were the only intended recipient. Or if not the only, say this: it had been coming all along, for all of us, the five of us, all of whom felt the truth inside, knew the ghost that touched us within and moved us, between us, together. But of course it was, if not malapropos, too late in its arrival. Had it been on time, what then? I would have missed it in the reading. It would never have been read at all. Could we have been saved, to use James' word? Was there such a thing, being on time? We all understood one could be in time, but being on time, this was impossible, especially in matters of understanding. In that instant of reading Proust however, I felt as if this had been written expressly with the intention of addressing me, being sent to me, calling to me, and demanding that I take responsibility for what James, on that November afternoon, began to strive after, involving me in a planned and orchestrated improvisation. At the time it was about doing, making, not speaking. Words only come afterwards, when there is no other expression. Tenpenny understood this already, his words reduced to a need, a request, a demand, three syllables that hoped for an exchange, made into another transferable medium. One thing translated into another.

~~~

Thirteen months passed before James and I played before an audience. No, let me revise that, fidelity being everything. We played together several times during the Easter and summer of 1974: there were several birthday parties and a school concert, which took us beyond our usual choral duties. A winter, spring, summer, autumn, and another winter. But our first performance for an audience who neither knew us nor cared about anything beyond whether we made an inoffensive sound to which they could lift a pint arrived in January 1975.

A riot for Led Zeppelin tickets in Boston had made the news, but our first appearance caused far less uproar. What stays of that time? What sticks? Where was it? Is there still a set list? What sort of music did we play? These and other questions arrive, sooner or later. They have nothing to do with music or the real memory, the felt souvenir of all that came to pass. There is no soundtrack, neither flashback nor filter to engender the patina of authenticity. Are there those who want to know about choosing songs, rehearsing in one another's bedroom, garage, or, after school hours, in a classroom, before the caretaker threw us out? Are there those want to know about classmates, mostly girls it seemed at the time, who hung around, in order to half listen, ignore or make asinine requests? Do these prying, trivia hungry inquisitors want to hear the sarcastic remarks from some of the teachers, encouragement from a smaller number, and the one or two—Jenny Skipper, John Haddon, Robin Fitch— who provided encouragement by staying around, lending James and I records without the parental label of 'real music' affixed, or who began to invite us to their houses? I could tell the fact addicts this—I find, after a fashion I already have in my diffident and protective way. But would it be about the music? Scene after scene: each trails past. The scenes buoy all that cannot be put into words on the surface, invisible and silent, leading towards what will become the story I have to tell. I am getting there, I promise. A few short rehearsals. Certain characters begin to enter onto the stage in this time, well appointed figures in a burlesque or, if this is not too fanciful but just fanciful enough, a vague approximation of the *Commedia dell'arte*: Duncan, Pete, Morphy, but their roles are not, as yet, defined. It is not time for them to play their parts, and I will not betray my friends by diluting what we share with what is now all too tritely described as backstory. Those of you who would want the facts, if what you want is facts, you have enough, let that suffice.

But of that first, though not first show—I still have this problem with the idea of what a beginning is. I am troubled by beginnings because I know, how I know, that once we admit to a beginning, any kind of start, we have to let ourselves confess to an ending, for which, as yet, we are still not ready. No one is ever ready for the way things end. I am not, at least. So, in lieu of a beginning: I ask myself periodically what remains of this, if anything. Sometimes I fool myself into thinking I remember, knowing all the while that I have found myself involved in making a fiction of the irrecoverable. Seeking for something solid, an image with which to anchor the inconsequential weightless inexistent night, I realise that I am face to face with nothing. Today, James confirms this, he recalls nothing either. He believes that beyond the bare facts of the evening being in Ryde (irrelevant), the place being the Castle (unimportant), and that this was, must have been, a Tuesday—The Castle Folk and Blues Club, all welcome, says the sign, hidden as it is now in a trunk at the back of the loft—he knows he took only the double bass and saxophone. There is neither visual nor auditory memento to accompany this inauspicious event. I could give details of the room, a basement, its smell—stale beer and cigarettes, the carpet damp and springy in places, too many hands, too many unsteady walks back from the bar—but, in truth, these are all pale outlines, a conglomerate of phenomena acquired from years of spending too much time in too, too similar locations. All 'venues'—what a grand word for something so fundamentally tawdry—are more or less the same. Wine bar or beer cellar, upstairs room or basement: events in waiting, unrealised architectures of promised entertainment, belied by indifference and the melancholy of expectation turned pointless in afterthought. Size irrelevant, décor repetitive or variable, a range of choices from a limited imagination, more down-market, more up, less lighting, more, table cloths and candles in small red jars, or standing room only, painted in a dark drab, tending to black from a spectrum of greys, as though the navy had exercised a purchase option based on the optimism of an impending war, and then found battleship paint surplus to requirements.

So it started, everything set in motion, getting into tune, the opening just right after all of what come to seem as rehearsals, practices, false starts. All change, more augmentations, further shifts, masquerading as first days, points of light in the memory where one has to attune oneself to different perspectives, accommodating a kaleidoscopic play of perceptions until the illusion of inception settles into place. A levels and Kate, both, in their own way, came on James and I, neither as a surprise, but both with an insistence we could not ignore. But there I go, speeding up. The readiness is not all—holding back the voice before the throw of pitch. This is everything.

Pause. Silence. A bar's rest. Lift the fingers away from the strings, the keys, the frets, the neck. Remove the reed from

the mouth. Place the hand over the mouthpiece. Become
still. Every time I add something to the account, I am forced,
at least privately, to reflect on the nature of change, the
question of significance. Could I offer other detail? Why this,
rather than another choice? Do I resist the inclination to give
too much away by giving too little? If I record everything,
everything I remember that is—for there is so much more,
I have this feeling, I know I have forgotten—then what do
I owe to the others, or especially to you? With each new
scene, every new figure, I know I have to strive to make
you see, Anna, but only up to a point. I need to tell you
this tale, Annagreth, if only that you might see how I came
to find you by accident. This is not about seeing though, it
will never be about what is or was in plain sight; do you see
that? I know you, of all people, would, that you do. It is a
question of what is beyond vision, what remains in the dark
but felt with the intensity of a star's blazon. Here. It is this,
this, as I recall someone in a film having said, this is what it
is. If I name every song, describe every performance—were
this possible—would the experience of others be mine?
No. Would they, could they feel each and every instant, all
the beats or rhythms, as if those pulses inhabited them,
took them over? No. Chords, major or minor, harmonics,
vibrations, consonance in performance, the part within the
whole, a soloist standing apart, emerging from the ensemble
momentarily: all of this resists words, a facile or prosaic
realism by which such narrative accounts remain earthbound.
Sound escapes the mechanical means of making it, this is its
joy, its power to make us feel, to hit us viscerally, to break our
hearts—if we are willing to allow it in. Nothing I can say can
turn that key for others, or tune them in to the right key.

The imagination falters in prosy inadequacy. It comes
down to a question of finding the right tempo, marking the
time, coming in with my own contribution as I find it to have
been scored. Scored invisibly, though I had believed all along
I was improvising. Music, like memory, displays, when it finds

its groove what Schleiermacher described as a feeling and
taste for the infinite. Prose can only limp along behind, foot
dragging pedant, hoping all the while that, though behind the
beat, always behind the beat, the time it keeps is in sympathy
with the ghostly grace, in the wake of which it follows
belatedly.

Kate was there, but not here, not in the now of which
I am speaking. This is not her time, not quite yet—wait
for the cue. I have to listen with greater care to the space
where the count is missing. This is still James's part in the
story, his rhythm that drives us along. Imagine—I recollect
this image, doubtless pushed in that direction by countless
photographs—that shining head, returning whatever light
there was, a daemonic focus, the eyes invisible, suspended
in angelic transport. There are two faces, one downwards,
turned inward, or, as a variation on a theme, turned away
into some private space; the other, when brass replaced
cello or bass, double or electric, vertical or transverse,
turned outward, over an audience, above the heads toward
a place where, it might just conceivably be, the notes were
being sent. Gleaming beads of sweat roll from the head,
each droplet a translucent miniature of its progenitor;
James felt each note, but, like a chess player, knew ahead
of the game every gambit, each phrase and all the possible
permutations, inversions, variations from a web of possible
lines of flight, currents of energy. His forehead became
a heat sink, radiating the energy that occurs when electric
current flows through a resistance; a human embodiment,
a corporeal, emotional, and intellectual expression of the
Joule effect. James flowed through the lines he played, each
of these moving through him in turn, moved in him, moving
him, a pure expression of his being, the sweat, the heat,
the energy produced, engendered in a relationship between
what was being generated and the flow of sound, rhythm,
oscillation, vibration. As a result, he appeared, whenever
playing, contained within himself but expanding in every
direction, shapeshifting, contracting, poised in a tension of

contradictory forces.

Lately, in the dark, when the night is a purer dark than any light can illuminate, I see one image of James, a vision of perfect stillness, a dense centre at the heart of the world. Flocculent mass, he sits, head down. To my right, stage left, he is poised, enfolding his electric cello, like a female gorilla cradling, protecting its young, on a makeshift dais, beer crates possibly draped in a blanket of the kind today called 'ethnic', 'fair-trade'. The lighting dramatic, his head glows silverblue, a baby spot above him, while other spots, turquoise, teal filtered, cast limpid pools. Patterning the floor, chrysoprase, nickel, emerald and butter yellow chroma, coins of illumination appearing suspended in mid-dance, as if so many visible substitutes for an unheard chromatic form. Tone colour timbre made momentarily available to the eye, a perception of resonance is here, if anywhere, in this studied, but unconscious pose: portrait of the cellist as a study of sound perception. Left hand wraps the neck, double-stopping, the right, a bow balanced like an oversized chopstick, as fingers pluck, pizzicato punctuation. Dressed in black, pinched, twitched inside himself, he disappears into his nightworld, into the dark energies, the almost black areas of the stage. To his left, an amplifier, small red lights, atop a rack of effects, more LEDs, glowing Christmas lights. James remains there, absolved in shadow, crepuscular, retreated. He looks, perhaps this is just my fancy, as if he hears a music all his own, apart from whatever he is playing, a secret tune embraced, occluded, reserved within the more obvious sonic patterns.

James was always following in the wake of a sound only he could hear. Though his playing was brilliant, dependable, his idea of what he called 'audible' sound was restless, febrile. He made a distinction between audible and inaudible sound. With the former he was fascinated. Obsessed with processing the signal, modulating tone, and moving between performance techniques, there was a period where he mounted a piezo pickup, a transducer, behind the bridge of his electric bass, routing this through a separate amplifier, and processing the signal through various modulation and time effects, while leaving the direct signal of the bass from its pickups 'clean'. He would do the same with the cello, two transducers feeding into different racks. Can anyone hear the difference here? No, of course not, and that might be the point, it is this that distinguishes itself in the place between the inadequate words 'audible' and 'inaudible', which, for James, had nothing to do with subsonics, harmonics, the sounds that only dogs or drummers hear, allegedly. The 'inaudible' was neither measurable nor knowable for James. I come back to these points, the need to repeat and emphasize inseparable. It is impossible to escape the very things that remain out of reach. It was always a matter of small differences, frequencies in the imagination, oscillations felt, only noticed in their absence. This was James himself. He assumed a place where, increasingly, his not being there was felt keenly by me.

That time for example, to risk everything on the illustration of contrarieties, when the urge for shutting out all the calls, sounds, the impossible demands of everything he felt and heard was on him, riding his torment. That time when James worked his way with formidable devotion through a bottle of gin. This was later, 1978, another summer, this time in the grounds of Osborne House, following a week in Spain, standing in for friends, needing a break in their interminable summer season of 'hitsnoldies', a word we coined to summarize how ridiculous such moments were. Was this the real reason, though? I don't know. For James, there didn't have to be.

— What you do that for, you silly sod?

Graeme had asked, more a provocation than requiring, or even expecting an answer.

— I was depressed about the heat wave two years ago; I've never got over that.

This was all the answer that was given. The subject was let drop. What I do know is it was also the summer when a

TV set made its way onto stage with us, James and Graeme
in unison—rhythm section solidarity—insisting on the
significance of the World Cup in Argentina. Perhaps it was
the overwhelming emotion of Ian Botham having made
history by scoring a century and taking eight wickets in
one innings of a Test. ELO and the Stones both touring,
the Dead Kennedys' first appearance, *Night Fever* going to
Number One: pick whichever reason one might care to, the
one that makes the most sense for ending up in hospital,
having roundly abused untold numbers of tourists in the
grounds of Victoria's holiday home...
— This island was just fine till she made it bloody well
popular.

 ...and having, as a result, his stomach pumped, as if
that would expel whatever drove him to such rare, but
always spectacular solo performances. All I know was that
I recall with the immediacy that memory can wield, most
often unexpectedly between two and three in the morning,
when guilt and anxiety insist on detailing my failures, my
inconsequentiality, the sense of a loss for which I never
would or could have been ready. This had little to do with
the immediate anticipation at the time of what to do in the
absence of a bass player; rethink the set, more bass parts for
the organ, all possible permutations, hurriedly discussed, until
Kate, who insists on appearing before her time again, said
calmly
— Well, I can do it. Just need a box of plasters.

 A silence filled the space between us, a silence I knew was
always that which only James could project; knowing when
to leave, when to play, stepping back, hands off. There was
the silence as real as any touch, any sea wall holding back
unthinking erosion. Silence was, in so many ways, James. It
was James on that summer's afternoon, the very thing to
which he gave birth, a silence and the promise of an absence
falling in the wake, reverberating on the soft air in the sudden
observation
— never enough

I could hear the silence that was left in lieu of this tall, relentlessly driven, focused, smiling figure. To speak of the music is to miss the point. Already done to death, I must insist on this, it is the heart of the matter. On this subject I can offer no enlightenment. Talking about 'slap and pop'—James's mouth would shape itself in various apertures silently singing—picking, palm-muting, two hands moving independently but in a harmony of motion, the fretting hand shifting between muting for a more focused sound to double stopping, fretting harmonically related notes, or two-handed tapping, striking the string against the fret or fretboard to produce percussive fills, run through quicksilver arpeggios: all the words inhabit a space uneasily. They cover over a silence all the more pronounced for being unfillable. Shuffle, slap, buzz, burst, drive, push, raucous, deft, delicate, brutal: Everything falls short in the gap, and the space remains more pronounced for that.

I am struggling here. James uses up all my words, demanding more, never having enough. He said that once with a disarming clarity on a day when the sky opened up above us, over the sea and sand. His words came, they came back, out of the absence, the silence, the black hole it was assumed was at the heart of everything.

— There's never enough, there's always more, I find when I play.

This, statement of intent, confession and manifesto, had come, an unanticipated mute, in the middle of an unrelated verbal flurry: all joking irrelevance, unguarded quick fire give and take. So many unfinished sentences, brisk, disparate observations, conversational driftwood, an endless dialogue we had learned from one another, with never the need to complete, for ourselves or one the other. All significance was in the pause, the tension, the poise before the detour down another route. Priory Woods gathered behind us, branches contributing irregular creaks in the August breeze. The waters, soft wave white noise crash and decay offering percussive overtones, busy with holiday makers, though we had walked far enough around the bend of the bay to find a place relatively isolated enough that we could make believe the island was ours, alone. The world that day revealed itself briefly in a glimpse of perfection. Away toward Bembridge, where the ruins of the sea wall attested to impermanence, ruin being the natural order of things, little life was there, two horses, their riders, and an elderly woman, dressed more for a village hall meeting than a beach, being of an age, from a time when distinctions between formal and casual clothing were not so markedly defined, with her two boisterous Westies. Wind soft, sand soft, light translucent, foliage dense and dark: we were separate and separated from all pressing needs, all urgencies. Prospero and Ariel perhaps, though as yet the roles were undefined. Sweet airs, sweet sounds. Kelp covered dull buffed rocks, tooth stump breakwaters, leering in the sheen of still wet sand and rock pools. A little place all ours we might have imagined, busy old sun above burnishing our lazy motion, polishing us a dull gloss antique finish, the patina of a long, though never long enough summer.

I knew not to ask what might come to appease that never enough…always more. To do so would be to betray friendship in an admission of incomprehension and, therefore, polite, meaningless tolerance verging on condescension. Instead, I turned toward the sea, seeing in that barely curving horizon to the east, towards Bognor and Brighton, the equivalent of never enough…always more. We see the horizon. We aim for it. We get there, or wherever there is we believe to have been when we were not where we were, just then. In that moment, the horizon still anticipates us. Escaping it is still, always, there, never here. Only a fool pursues it, or an optimist. To know though that I would never reach the horizon, but that I exist always within the limiting circle of the knowable, this was enough. The knowledge that there is never enough…always more: that is enough. James had, as usual, said it for both of us, said what I could only see, and given voice to the other voice inside, his words not the admission of frustration, though people listening carelessly would doubtless take that to be implied. No, there was in what could be said, acceptance.

3. Interlude: Evening (July 1976)

Bach for joy, Schubert for despair. You wrote this on a birthday card, along with other private messages written and overwritten as a babel of tongues, because, you once had told me, there was never enough in one language to express how you felt. German, Swedish, French, English, never enough for what was before and beyond words. We had been sitting that day—*Ja! Heute ist mein Gebürtstag!* I had proclaimed loudly in childish glee on seeing the snow that morning—in a café on Neuer Pferdemarkt: a small *Winterreise* all to ourselves, stopping off in Hamburg for a day before driving later that evening to Lübeck. We had spent the morning walking through Altona, the snowlight calling, even in the warmth of Volker's apartment, to *Planten und Blomen*, leaving behind us failed efforts on my part, successful on yours, to make the perfect *Schneeengel—Schneeengel—, bitte*, you kept repeating, imploring, in your five years' old voice, stretching unreasonably the ridiculous sound of the elongated *eee*, rising higher and higher, causing us to laugh uncontrollably, before a stage pout, then,

— Catch me! *Fang mich doch, du Eierloch!*

And we would run, rime gathering on the edges of scarves, singing a children's song, tripping, laughing, in this too bright white, gold tinged morning of the world, winterbreath visible, angels floating away from our mouths.

By midday the sun had retreated, a too short day exhausted by its efforts, draping the sky for another snowfall. Walking more rapidly, as if in imitation of purpose, we passed through those suburban streets, their brightly coloured eclectic combinations of Historicist and Jugendstil influenced apartments, passageways ablaze with hippy anarchist collective murals, as though somehow here and there the spectre haunting Hamburg was the spectre of alternative cultures lingering from the late sixties, its artist a too large elfchild who had never been told not to open all the paints at once. Sky leaden, it presented the perfect backdrop for those architectural references embodied in the buildings as though undecided whether classic or romantic, but coming together to agree in slicing the air with precisely rendered razor roofs, hard edges, corbels and cornices a reproof to anonymity, reiterated everywhere the eye looked above. Everything poised, on the edge. And so, on this afternoon, to this café where Neuer Pferdemarkt met Schulterblatt: loose formed leather arm chairs, black and white tile floor, white wood, and chrome of lamps, mirrors, clock, and coffee machine. Tables with inlaid chess boards, a place to sit without feeling the need to leave, to eat, drink, play, talk, remain silent, looking knowingly at one another; the complicity of lovers on that December afternoon, snow lately settled; the world below white and black, the heavens over Hamburg cinerous in the distance turning glaucous through slate grey somewhere over the Alster, dark tope and charcoal flecks accenting the denser cloud banks, grace notes for an impending fall, chiaroscuro accompaniment for an unheard tone poem. Coffee, chess, and cake, *Kaffee, Schach* und *Kuchen*: between us, between hands moving pieces, barely a word in that silent world, the space between and all the world there was. Here the afternoon drifted into early evening, as did we through the town, coffeewine high, eyes widened in the evening chill, into the *Weihnachtsmarkt* before the *Rathaus*, gold by green, municipal spire competing, younger sibling ever, for the attention of snowclouds with the cuprous tower of the

St Michaelis Kirche, outstretching limbs across the city sky
imploring festive snow fall; fingers of cold insinuating their
way into clothing, colddrunk laughter, silver illuminations
overwhelming the Christmas tree at the edge of the
Binnenalster
—*O Tannenbaum, O Tannenbaum, wie treu sind deine Blätter*
inevitably, a choir somewhere, with which we joined our voices.

~~~

I had no intention of telling stories. I have never known
how to tell stories. Your stories, the stories I have of you,
however…they insist, they demand, they call. Approaching
that point which in fiction is called a beginning but which
is merely the chance redirection, there appears on closer
inspection the switching of points. I see belatedly a junction
such as this which leads to what seems at first only a spur
line, at best a branch, but which in the end proves to have
been necessary, essential, in revealing the entire network of
connections, communications, and organization. Branch line
tales will always lead me back. They turn me around, getting
me to where I want to go, the longest way round sometimes
being the shortest way home. So, finding the need for stories
I have never known how to tell, I wander. And I talk. Talking
to myself is a habit; I have the impression, which has begun
to assume an increasingly important role. It is as though the
character I would be can no longer be certain of his lines,
cues, or when to come in. It comes down to a question of
faith; I believe that you are listening.
   So, I tell you things that you will already know. To
speak to you though, this is difficult. There is absence of
distinction, between you on the one hand and you on the
other, English as an impoverished tongue. This was a cause,
on occasions, for you to mock, however staged the mockery
might have been, a play at momentary superiority. Once
you had said this, it became a game for the five of us late at

night, as each of us sought to create confusion by refusing to identify which you of the five we were speaking to. Where, you had wanted to know, is the formality or informality, the separation between authority and intimacy that, in German, *Sie* and *du* gave license to? I think sometimes you were playfully scornful of what my tongue missed. And then you would tell me, your tongue playing across those of your mother and father: *Du är vacker; Jag älskar dig också; Ohne dich kann ich nicht leben.* Those last words, the final phrase—in, with, other tongues, you made words music—I recall you telling me with an amused smile, were also the title of a song, performed by the Sunshine Quartett, a song your father had played for your mother, and which appeared, sung by the quartet, in a Heimatfilm. Sentimental romances, homespun and moral, the most clichéd of genres, and it was up to me to decide if you were just having fun, lovingly insincere, or whether those words were real. About those words, you would never say. You did though write for me a piano piece with that title, in the playing of which I felt I could hear the truth. I believe I still can.

Belief is always scant, barely there. When I say you I must believe it is you and not every other you to whom I speak. Desire. Would that be the right word? I desire to know to whom I speak when I am alone, as in moments such as these, with this sense of the confessional all around me. I know—I believe—I am addressing you, the one who will never speak back, will no longer disagree with me, will no longer say my name, in full, with that elongated last syllable, the tone being lowered with the retreat of the chin, the slight pursing of the lower lip, prefaced always with an 'oh', whether indicating some small disappointment, incredulity, pleasant surprise, occasional, disbelieving frustration. So many different intonations for the one phrase, as if in that all that was to be said had been spoken, as if all the rest were silence, and silence contained all the expressions in the world.

That time, let me recall one, another story of another time, when I spoke to you after a mutual silence, or call it,

just to be sure, a refusal to speak on both sides after—was
it an argument? No, I am certain not; a disagreement then.
It had all begun, unimportantly, as a question of yoghurt.
It ended, or rather came to the end of its run that morning
over a breakfast that remained a phantom, never having
happened, when you had looked at me, momentarily, not
deigning to use that all purpose phrase of yours, conjuration,
incantation, communication of everything else, then, turning,
a motion of gold, white and blue, you left. Your eyes had
expressed everything that your many tongues could never
have given vent to, and with the finality of a last chord. The
door was closed purposefully, though without drama. That
was always your way. Like that photograph of your hands
on the piano: fingers a blur, a refusal to be frozen, captured
or defined, while the arms, the wrists, covered in tight fitting
long black sleeves, a muted black to complement its polished
cousin, the wood of the piano, and that heavy golden, coiled
bracelet, these perfectly still, suspended: economy of motion,
purpose of action, and always that attention to small details.
You always loved the small, the miniscule, little things others
overlooked, thought unimportant.

Leaving, I heard the sound of your bicycle wheeled up
the small flight of steps from the front door. Wheel pushing
gravel filled me unreasonably with anxiety. Riding the sea
wall, this is what you did when you needed to retreat inside
yourself, a compact figure, blonde, French braid a thick rope
of ripe corn a crown upon your own—less Rhine maiden
than shieldmaiden, James had once joked, Valkyrie-child, one
of the dísir, after you had with a quite frightening precision
put a too drunk biker three times your size in a place he never
knew was his until then; all that Graeme had said was bugger,
respect and envy merging together; Kate had just laughed,
quietly, knowingly—; but I have lost the path for a moment,
you see how difficult this is? That morning you were wearing
a white tee-shirt, again long sleeves, blue cut-off jeans—blue,
I know I've said this before, but memory is as much refrain,
chorus, as it is the heart's archive, blue your colour, song you

sang, song I sang to you, the sky, the sea, your eyes, playing
the blues—; and again, I stumble. Ever fail. On. Sailing the
thin path between land and water, crimson bike looking as
if it could take to the waves, you moved. It seems to me
now water and sky were always your elements. You rode
that day you were later to tell me, faster than usual, singing
aloud, a song with which to call cows in Swedish. I imagine
unsuspecting tourists caught unexpectedly. Absurdly, I see
them terrified, leaping from the seawall. Though this never
happened, still, it might. You were there, full flight, full sail;
too quickly, felt in the shock, never seen, a bee flew full force,
suicide diving into your mouth, embedding its sting in your
palate.

Later, the surgery on Melville Street called. Nothing to
worry about, but could I come and collect you? Arriving,
the good advice, your annoyance at being spoken of in the
third person tempered by the effects of this unwanted guest's
toxin. Antibiotics, just in case, and ice, keep the patient
propped up, cool; check the swelling does not get worse.
— It's not everyone who has an abdomen in her mouth, is it.

This was said with a cheery, everything will be alright
dear smile, this attempt at humour on the part of the nurse
was met with what those of us who knew you as *that* look,
that cast in the eye, the arching of the eyebrow, your own
venomous glance somewhat diluted by the bee's thrust.
The following day, a Tuesday, when your throat's swelling
had gone down along with the allergic temperature your
small invader had encouraged, symptoms receding enough
to give you back your voice, you told me how, annoyed
beyond all reason, tears welling from sheer frustration at the
needlessness of that Monday's adventure, you made your way
to the doctor's. But not before you had uttered that phrase,
prefaced with its 'oh'. Encircling our world, taking me up,
enfolding me with you, your *O*, a sound to match the shape
of your mouth, expressed everything. I do not have the heart,
much less the ability, to say what was in that *O*, with which
you drew such a circumference, by which we were bound

to one another. That is a story, the story of *O*, but quite different from the book that bears this title, which can never be told, but which I hear nonetheless, each and every time I remember that sound, the purest, most secret of notes.

And there you are.

As always, I find that I am ahead of myself; I wind forward precipitously, having to rewind once more. Why do I hurry to get to an end I would erase? I am talking with you in the dark, once more. Impelled to words, compelled to speak the impossible, I am reminded now, listening to the ghost of you playing, singing, 'Der Leiermann', of Dietrich Fischer-Dieskau's observation that Winterreise was so personal that one should never perform it—and yet he did, repeatedly. We live by such impossible contrarieties. And I see, in this recollection, a Christmas, Swedish, not German; you are playing the piano once more, your sister singing Schubert's most despairing, more than beautiful cycle. The memory stops me. Here is the impossible situation, so I am talking with you, as always now, in the dark. I say with, not to. I know there will never be an answer, nothing direct any more, but I continue to talk with you, sending you messages, long and short. Scribbled notes never found under doors never opened. I'm telling your stories, telling you stories, your stories to you, delaying the beginning, to remain, jealously, with only you, in the memory of you, before all the other ghosts take the stage. Remaining faithful, I betray everything. And all the rest.

~~~

And there you are. Here we were, at that very moment, one of countless first times. Saturday night. Another Saturday Night. Just about to start, the next song, beginning, looking up again. You are at a distance, the far end of the bar, short silk dress, hair loose but for two braids, conjoined twins resting at the nape, just visible through a crowd of cheerful, happy beery, sunkissed lobster faces; faces of that summer: drought faces, holiday faces, familiar and unfamiliar, the large bar crowded, the glass doors to the terrace folded back, full to overflowing, bikers unseasonably leathered, hippies already out of time, flares a refusal to acknowledge the advent of punk, sandaled feet, burned toes, cotton sun dresses, a rugby shirt here and there; sails furled, masts in the sunset across the harbour and bay, a night in which the day's heat shows no sign of relenting.

— The next one's a slower number, 'Little Wing'.

James's voice, Judge, that stage edginess always with a smile. It was a wig evening. James's head covered in a lifeless parody of a hippy mop, The Beatles at Abbey Road, with a red McEnroe sweatband. He could not be serious.

— Yuuuuuuh.

Tool was in especially good voice that evening.

— It's particularly heart rendering…

The same, deliberate misuse, watching to see who got it, who didn't, who thought he was merely wrong.

— …Anyone you want to dedicate this to?

This last throwaway comment, on mic, directed to me. Daylight dying. In that moment I found myself the centre of attention, but not for the usual reasons. Some people appear to be in on a secret. Some people: my closest friends, the band, the ones who make the jokes, give me a hard time from love, as I in turn would give them. Since we arrived to set up, the comments began, courtesy of Graeme. Public, exposed, naked, I feel this unreasonably. After all, why? What has happened exactly? A pleasant afternoon made more so by a chance encounter. So what do I say, or do I say nothing? Ridiculously flustered, my eyes cross the room, playing for time, not playing but tuning, pretending to, finding that, drawn, you, she, Annagreth, Anna, returns my ill-focused gaze, as I look to the very place I least had wanted to, at the heart of the matter, as though her eyes had drawn me. Is that a smile? A smirk? Having to be quick now, I remark

— I didn't know we were doing 'Leila' tonight

— Yuuuuup. A calf in distress wanting milk, a cow giving birth. Tool, ever dependable, beer not required, but capable of fuelling the volume, his voice filled the space.
— Judge won't be at any rate.

This from Graeme, and I begin, aware of laughter from behind, then four simultaneous bells, twelfth fret harmonics Doppler shaped and phase shifting, hanging from gossamer, accompanied by double-stopped viola and the magical anticipation of tubular bells; something floats into the air, sound taking flight, shaping to the image in the mind's eye, anticipating, perhaps desiring, other sympathetic resonances of which, as yet, no one had any idea. Take down the tempo, stretch the introduction, then—wait for it—the drums, I change, knowingly, the word 'cloud' for 'crowd' in the first line. Languorous, lilting, the perfect song uplifted by warmth and the last sealight, flame flickered in the sunset, bearing everyone on wings and waves, as night comes in, the first setting drawing to a close. Someone dreams this moment, I imagine, a floating world simplified, lulled, transcendent, out of any time that matters. Something more. Annagreth's face, across a crowded room, turned towards the dying of the day. Smiling, she directed her gaze, seeing, I imagine the band, impassive, focussed in the heart of improvised melody, marking, it appeared, the changes, not from the sequence of motions, the mechanics of fingers, wood and metal, but in the mind's eye and ear. All attention directed there in her face, I watched in turn knowing that whatever she saw, what her face said she heard; it was nothing physical. I looked momentarily before turning my own eyes across the sea, and with that the octave shift for a final passage, playing out, dancing round the melody, in and out, across the time. Seeing sound as if for a first time, inheriting an unpredictable future, I thought I glimpsed what James had always known by instinct.

Reserve is inexhaustible, reticence doubly so; a gigue in slow motion, different tempi accommodating themselves to brief glimpses of that eternity where nothing is said. This cannot last however. Its instant lasts less than the time it takes for an eye to blink, a shutter motion opening and closing. Then comes the fall, the recovery of the ordinary, all that motion tending to inconsequence. We measure the wrong times, for the time that really counts, where everything of significance resides, quietly inside, is immeasurable, without a space or span capable of apprehension. It comes. It goes. We take note, if at all, in the counterpoint of anachrony.

The set ended. I took time, deliberately and more than usual, placing the guitar on its stand, having first checked and rechecked the tuning needlessly, then checking the tuning of the two other guitars, looking after a dozen details unnecessarily, all the while replaying to myself the conversation that followed as we packed, for leaving the fête, the time of speech shutting out the present, with all its imminent moments.

— Who was that, the blonde girl who you walked over with when we were packing up?

— Who?

Coiling cables, wing nuts released, instruments into cases, after another wipe down, obviously avoiding the obvious.

— Her name's Anna.

— Thanks, Rog, I'd never have remembered. It's actually Anna-Margaretha. Or Annagreth, or Anna, of course.

An off-kilter chorus echoed Graeme's announcement from the others, as I dug myself a hole. Morphy, having returned from the back of the van, asked in a manner suggesting the opposite.

— Have I missed something?

— You told her about trees?

This was Kate, though she already knew; was there irony in that, the suggestion of benevolent tolerance in the face of predictability?

— Yes. I did, as it happens.

— That's serious.

— It never does any good though. It'll be ley lines next.

— Better than a bloody goldfish, even if he is your best, no, your only friend.

And so it continued, throughout the remainder of the afternoon, down to The Harbour Lights in Graeme's Transit, the setting up, and soundcheck, and afterwards on a bench overlooking Cowes harbour, fish and chips defended against gulls, cheese, apples and bread only slightly less tempting. The light was exhausting, unremitting; just like James, never let the dog get a glimpse of the rabbit.

— Ah Na Ma Ga Rey Taaaa…

Judge stretching, weighed each syllable, finding the stresses, getting inside the rhythm.

— She's coming down tonight; said I'd get her a drink in.

— Someone else is in for the tale of George then.

I sought to deflect matters, though holding back the tide might have been more manageable.

— Morphy, we got any spare valves? The Vox sounds like it's got a rattle.

— Not the only one, eh?

The non-conversation continued, tired lines trading across one another, volleys of blanks fired into the air. Kate squeezed my hand in an unseen gesture of solidarity. I smiled briefly.

— Your turn to decide on the set list, Judge, if you've not got it already in mind. Which wig is it tonight? Or are we being treated to an evening of shine?

Graeme insisted he'd like to know, so as to keep his sunglasses handy to cut down on the glare. A klaxon sounded away out on the Solent. It was that in-between time in coastal towns during the tourist season. Families had mostly gone back to B&Bs, hotels, holiday camps, or were to be found in cafés and restaurants. The air was tinged with the oil of too many fried meals, mingled with sour top notes of diesel and grease. The heat caused all odours to hang, humid weight, dead fruit of summer resorts, without the promise or hope of a breeze to blow all away. I wanted the evening to begin, though as yet the first of two sets was still more than an hour away. Waiting, paused, waiting for what? James, to my right, had been scribbling in a large round hand shortened names in marker pen. 'Oh Well,' inevitably. As always the order was known, worked out, with an inevitable logic that understood timing, pacing, nuance, atmosphere, emotion, drama. I knew this to be the case, but wanted to shift topics. Why this time? It always came down to such pointless conversations; they were ritual, mantra, inoffensive and playful. Nothing ever became confrontational because, already, we all knew one another so well, each a prism of the others, four facets of the same irregular reflective object, five if counting Morphy. And we did, count him in, count on him. He counted.

— I'm going to take a walk; back in an hour; got an idea for a song.

This said, before encountering or having to counter any further observations, witticisms, badinage, or bon mots, I set off along the Parade, acknowledging with a wave the remark that I should be back half an hour before we started. Taken by the symmetry of a bridge connecting the jetty to the land, its white metal frame given a yellowish glow in the early evening sun, I walked out towards the water, to lose the town. Looking back briefly, I considered the incongruity of late Victorian buildings, jostling to own the place with dilapidated art deco frontages and fifties utilitarian design. The decades had signalled a shift away from reflections of empire to ugly anonymity, architectural apologia masquerading as public conveniences. The pointless past rendered the present anachronistic, historical oneupmanship embraced by a squirming embarrassment over previous generations' hubris. Even the public houses' names suggested that time had run out, and that all anyone was waiting for was the wrecking ball and asset strippers to make it modern, again. The Crown, the Globe, The Castle: so many examples of late empire Albion, gibecrake detail amassed to front and give bluster, to which the names were witness. It's a wonder there was not also, somewhere at hand, an Albion pub. So much late, belated commercialized Victoriana, onto which had been added extra spaces courtesy of discount modular expansion. Even the bridge to the jetty had a spurious arch, dependent from which was a pseudo-gas lamp, glass grimy, light bulb blackened.

Because of the drought, the ban on hosepipes, and the, by now, weeks of burning light, everywhere I looked were signs of distress. There was all around a kind of heat haze déjà vu. Flower tubs, fake timber barrels and boxes intended to adorn the Promenade, giving just that touch of civic pride, looked murderously parched. Somewhere a dog barked, agreeing with me. Small red sail drifting past, tacking toward the jetty. If I saw her now? What then? Look into your eyes, liquid laughter ready to overflow, knowing, anticipating, the slower response. Your eyes, blue, is there a word for that bluer than blue hue? Your hand, its touch. I recalled the ends of the fingers, the cool of the palm despite the heat. An oasis, a shelter. Continuing onto Castle Hill, the Royal Corinthian Yacht Club aloof, apart, disdaining the town. I wondered what I might say, if I met you, her coming down the hill. The parish church looked down upon the Yacht Club from Queen's Road: Queen's Road, Holy Trinity, private clubs appropriating a Greek port, always this definition of oneself with reference to just enough of a past to warrant constant forgetfulness, selective invention. Church and Empire, everything no longer believed in. Even topography maintains the illusion of hierarchy however, the church on higher ground. Would she see this? Did it matter? I am quiet here, alone; I think this with an arch awareness. No, not my words, another's, that Stephen with a ridiculous Greek surname— absurd his friend calls it. I had, this summer, been reading this comic odyssey, tale of another island, with its mockery of epic adventures. This is what comes of reading, comparing myself to non-existent characters. Hamlet next, as before, during A levels, no doubt, always the introspective ones, sensitivity a pose, inwardness the assumption of a mask. Too reflective, discontented with myself for being so, too tired from heat, I imagined her hand taking the ice cream cone, wondering if she would appear this evening. Hand and eyes.

— Graeme said to tell you, as I was coming over here, that your drink was getting warm. English beer is already warm though; and a brandy. Why Rog? I really want to know.

Brought back from memory's idling to the present, I was taken by sound before sight, voice before face to face, first set over, I still hovering by amplifiers, drums, and instruments. Turning, she was standing there, smiling again, two glasses, one a pint, the other, clear, condensation indicating that ice had already melted, the lemon slice gripping the glass edge. That question again, posed somewhat differently, no longer expecting an explanation of what a Rog might be.

— Is he also Roger? This is another name he prefers?

That smile, the charm of sudden inquisition unexpectedly. I wanted to say, no not a personal pronoun, a verb, not is he, but does he…. Taking the glass…

— Oh, thanks…no, not prefers; that would take a while to explain, and I'm not sure it's worth the effort; just a silly joke, it's a nickname. Like James, we call him Judge, because one night he turned up to play in his father's wig; his father isn't bald, he's a QC; a lawyer.

My comments were taking a turn for the occluded; in an effort to make clear, I was becoming obscure. Change tack.

— Thanks for coming down. I saw you at the bar.

— Is that why you stayed here?

A note of mischief, an undercurrent of amusement in the question.

— No, that is…I just find myself so involved in the music, it takes a while for me to get outside it again.

She nodded understanding, or so it seemed.

— This is very different from this afternoon's show. Do you always play such a variety?

— Yes. Look, it's rather warm in here, there's another twenty minutes or so before the next set, shall we see if we can find a space out on the terrace?

Working through the crowd, I happened to look toward the corner of the bar. Graeme's face burst into a huge grin, as did James's, a mad, sweaty vision, beard by bald. Opposites

attract they say; these were strange attractors indeed, moving
the music along, a dynamic system evolving over time,
unfolding variables of rhythm, remaining close through the
counterpoint of differential drives. As with their playing, so
their personalities, constant and with a constant turbulence
that could not help but be attractive, engaging.

Moving as if with a Brownian flow caused by the
interaction of heat, alcohol and too many people in too small
a space, we made it outside, in what now always appears as
too slow motion. The sky almost completely black, stars
beginning to assume their places, we found a place at the
edge of the terrace, leaning on the wall, directly below which
was the water. Coloured light bulbs hung in loops from
the canopy frame. Small lights across the harbour, some
houses visible in East Cowes, while mostly the pub lights,
now turned up full, cast their illumination across the terrace.
Leant against the wall, balancing my glass on the triangular
copingstones, I sought for, and failed to find an original
conversational gambit, opting instead for
— are you enjoying the set so far?

Don't be over eager
— I heard just the last three tunes, I think.

Not answering the question.
— still, thanks for coming along.

Already said, now said again. Avoid looking too long, or
not looking long enough.
— Graeme, he thought he might get a date, no?

Annagreth asked, but in a way that indicated she already
knew my response, mild incredulity mixed with amusement.
— He's that obvious is he? Yes, I suppose he is. His playing is the only subtle thing about him. I won't ask you if he's
mentioned his goldfish, it's a bad pun, which, if he hasn't
doesn't bear repeating, and, if has, you won't want reminding
of. How do you like the island so far?

Anna, Annagreth, I was still not sure which name, had
not seen that much. She had brought her car so wanted to
explore; perhaps she could find someone willing to a guide?

There were still several weeks before the school year started, and her sister, Heike, would not be returning for another two. Her father had insisted on a car

— You will want to see things, make the most of the year. Get about.

— Would you have time to show me the island? If you have time?

This in all seriousness took me by surprise, not least because I had already been thinking about, and rejecting, the idea of offering. Such disarming directness I was used to from the others, each playing their own variation. Anna looked at me calmly, as the night around us slowed further, human voices in my memory seeming to have been dialled down, while still there, perception remembered prompting sound, glasses put down, gathered up, accidentally or deliberately kissing in short sharp percussive cadences. Waves lapped and slapped lazily against hulls, hollow or more solidly. Her face, three quarter lit, expressively deadpan, less indifferent than serene, unruffled, eyes searching, a golden hair astray here and there, draping carelessly bronze forehead.

— Yes, I'd be very happy, I'd love to.

A smile in answer, then

— Time, bugger, second set. Hello there; he's not been telling you about trees again, has he?

Glowing, hirsute silhouette, backlit, intruding. Portrait of the yokel mechanic as a young bear. Graeme all body, overlarge, too much there, it seemed, the bumblebee stripes of his tee shirt making him into an overbearing insect I longed for the instant to swat away. Beer dried tongue, mouth yeast sour, two now three, the larger public world returning. Annagreth, the slightest eyebrow raised, her face changing, transforming in awareness of change. Looking right, then back again, motions too quick except to tell after the fact. Twice falling behind in one day, failing, exchanging rhythms, shifting pitch, pulse and tempo out of kilter. The musical cadence of her voice, rhythm of features prompting another cadenza—your cadenza, Anna would later say, when we

talked about this summer, tell me how you felt; it was our
shared pun for a double precipitation—complex beat, cross
and counter metre; I noticed at an angle, Kate and Judge,
already picking up instruments, people moving inside
— I'll be right there.

Go away. Now. Then, to Annagreth
— Tomorrow's good? Or the day after? Can you stay till the
end tonight?

She could. She did. Walking away, ahead of me, into the
audience, the sunflowers of Anna's sleeveless dress remained
in my eyes, bright heliotropes adrift on a sea of blue, as the
lesser artificial glow of houselights dimmed, small stars on a
summer's night, trompe l'oeil eyes returning my look in the
full realization of a silent illumination. The world vibrated,
outline and colour no longer distinct, senses opening to
another reality, no words could adequately interpret the
transformation from vision to perception. Visible music,
silent sound.

We began. Grateful not to be playing the first tune, I
stood back in shadow, looking around the room. Kate began
the second set with Judge, a fiddle and guitar tune, 'Dropping
the Bottle,' then a switch to melodeon and bass, with
percussion and guitar, another instrumental, picking up the
tempo, 'Up on the Downs.'
— here's one we wrote after Graeme had an encounter
with a sheep. The case comes up next month.

No longer wigged, shining James. Judge. Joker. Judging
the joke, the delivery, the order of the music, always with
a sense of what was appropriate. Getting it just right. Get
people to sway, to begin to move again, not too much, too
quickly on such a warm evening, at least not for a while. The
heat had suggested instrumentals to him. Matters turned
more electric, the absence of words allowing everyone to
shine, stepping forward, their instruments their voices for the
first wordless twenty minutes. A tune not our own followed,
somewhat new for us, only heard for the first time on its
release two months before. That double stopped, arpeggiated

run, glissando mixed with precision, on the bass, waveforms moving in and out of phase, Graeme busy pulling, pushing, holding back, riding cymbals, short and long spill of the introduction, before a first verse, the rhythm retarded, syncopation behind the beat, as the melody and harmony played between guitar and violin, the bass sometimes adding to the chorus, sometimes filling the spaces between the top line, before the straight ahead drive of improvised soloing, first violin, then guitar, before returning, repeating the complex cross-timed riff. Filled with sound the darkened space contracted, third chorus, then accordion, taking on, and winning, the clavinet motifs from the original. In such moments, we were no more, neither individuals or collective; we disappeared into the sound, pure experience, shaping the senses into an ideal, invisible form. With the immediacy of sudden waking, I realized what I had seen without seeing it, shortly before. And there were the sunflowers before me, not dancing but in motion nonetheless, Annagreth, Anna, her eyes closed, glowing from within, taken up by the tune, the body's ceaseless gesture, so many small arabesques of movement intimating the invisible, inexpressible, ineffable that we sought in music. The visible, like words, dresses poorly, because it veils, covering even as it gives us access to the truth of another vision, beyond the mundane. Anna knew this intimately. I understood.

All concluded, the second set done, the last of the public having left, save for two or three friends of Angie and Dave Farnham, the publicans, the van had been packed, so we lingered.

— Ave another before you go, girls; and one for your friend. Don't mind this lot darling, I employ 'em to stop 'em frightening old ladies on their way back from Bingo.

Dave's sitcom London bonhomie, always ready with affectionate disrespect, acknowledged Annagreth's presence, as he pulled pints for Morphy, Kate and Graeme, brandy for me, vodka for Judge. Just after midnight we could finally pause for breath. Anna asked for, and was given, a gin and tonic.

— Sorry about the door, Dave.

This was Morphy; walking out behind Graeme, amplifiers in each hand, he had turned to answer a somewhat slurred query from one of the last of the punters, not noticing that, as he continued forwards, Graeme, hands and arms full, had let the glass door swing, its lower panel meeting full force with an amp.

— No worries, the brewery expects breakages.

We sat in a circle, introductions all round, along with the information that Annagreth played organ and piano.

— If you're any good and not too insane, or just crazy enough, you should come play with us sometime.

Graeme's face shifted gears, revving for the blindingly obvious but immediately thought better of it, knowing Kate's tone to be genuine. Anna picked up on this also, knowing the invitation not a matter of mere politeness, replying

— Sometime, I should like that.

— Phil can always lend us something, Judge proffered, to which came a chorus from the rest of us,

— And don't forget to bring it back in the morning!

Amidst the tired laughs drawn by the already familiar nag, I explained briefly our relationship—usually one of indebtedness, fiscal and metaphorical—to Rob Thompson, the owner of a musical instrument shop in Ryde. Kate said she already had a Fender Rhodes, and her father, Harry, kept an electric organ...

— Hammond. B3. The real thing,

Judge interrupted, a tone of admiration, reverence even.

— ...In the converted barn where we rehearse.

More questions were asked, and answered. The night, still close, slowed. Insects, little more than noise and wing, came in search of lights from the terrace. Somewhere, off on the water, a horn, the bell of a navigation buoy adding its accompaniment half-heartedly, moved feebly by a disappointed crest of water too enervated to be a wave. Anna thought she should be going, especially, she said, quite out of the blue, if we—she looked at me—were going to begin our navigation of the island tomorrow. Quiet, atomic weighted, settled into place, heads turning, so many automated shop window dummies, towards me.

— Rog, I meant to say, can I stay at yours tonight? It'll save me a trip in the morning. Anna, let me walk you home. Perhaps I'll explain why 'Roger'.

Not this time, another. For now, time unglued itself, like a bluebottle escaping flypaper. Graeme assented with a nod, his typically predictable comments stunned to mute reaction, though rousing himself enough to offer to stick around outside The Harbour Lights till I returned. Kate, Judge, Morphy: looks were exchanged. So used were they to the routines, so familiar were we all with one another's patterns, defences, postures around strangers or outsiders that, for this once, they failed to read any small, slight changes in the pressure of the bubble in which we habitually existed. Time for a change. Changing gears. All change, if only, in the end, to become more ourselves than we had been before or thought possible. There were nearly two weeks without shows, a decision jointly reached, before a month long onrush, little respite throughout August. No meeting arranged till Wednesday, then, through the Saturday, successive rehearsals, learning new material, some writing perhaps, five days' rest, though a meeting, an evening of eating, talking, before ten nights, one double night, and three lunchtime wine bar gigs, two days off, ten days on, once more. Rehearsals would prove to be interesting, the moreso as Kate, having invited Annagreth once more to come along, Anna had accepted for the following Thursday.

~~~

There are two of you, at least. Looking at the photographs, and an old videocassette Pete has copied to DVD and given me, I'm struck by this. There is that serious pianist, quiet, intense, earnest and thoughtful without being pensive, the

one who, in private, at home, on rare occasions at rehearsal,
soundchecking, setting up, or in the studio, played Schubert,
Bach, Satie, Coltrane. Yes, you would, for the sheer joy,
transcribe Coltrane for piano. Then there you are, at the
Hammond, fingers flashing, hair a mass of motion, golden
light, or dancing in an abandoned trance of ecstatic pleasure.
Pete's camera saw more, still or motion, than the naked eye
could capture. He also gave me, I had forgotten, I confess
it, what shall I call them, 'interviews'? Exercises for college
work, for his portfolio. He is filming, you talk in that easy,
slightly hesitant way of yours, hesitant only because you
wanted to be sure your words told, their weight counted.
You look, one winter's afternoon in Hamburg, sitting by the
harbour, directly into the camera: smiling all, or nearly all, the
time. Then the edit of you at the piano looking across the
stage; you have just looked up from the keys, your focus in
your fingers. As your head is raised, the smallest smile pulls
your mouth upward. In blue light, Pete's edit is touching,
for as you smile, your fingers tracing a pattern, the cut is to
my hands, picking and fingering the frets, the two of us, our
four hands, in conversation, unison, as one. It is a fiction, of
course, one born of the heart, but my memory recalls with a
testamentary authenticity that indivisible closeness that Pete's
editing has conjured, as if it were all taking place for the first
time. I am taken aback at another scene, again, a close up
of you at the piano, head and shoulders, gold and black, all
stage light the gold of medieval illumination, as though yours
was an image awaiting exegesis: your head tilts the smallest
fraction toward your right shoulder, toward the camera's eye,
and your face appears to tighten, a wince? Would that be the
right word for what I see? Was there something amiss, out
of tune? Cut to your hands, another performance, this time
across the B3, then back to golden you, your head effecting
a small shake as if chasing away a thought, your nether lip
pulled up, brow raised, eyes closing, as if…as if what?

What do I see, what had you felt in that instant?

Were you just feeling the sadness of a song, a moment of tristesse, melancholy, Sehnsucht, a word your mouth could shape, which in afterthought can make me weep, longing for you achingly? Or is this a sadness, a disappointment your own? Am I giving to you an interpretation because I can no longer ask, and cannot abide this undecidable vision. Less than a second, it passes, and your face changes again, this time a look, how shall I describe it, of puzzlement mixed with the smallest disapproval. Perhaps the matter is merely technical, a misfingered note, a small dissonance, a foldback speaker whistling its electrical shades disfiguring that instantaneous return of ourselves to our ears, or a disconcerting, insistent insectlike buzzing along the wires. I freeze the frame, rewind, replay, in afterglow, in frustration, two, three, more times. Give it up, let it play. The rest of our small world returns: Graeme's pursed lips, his absurdly cheesy moustache, those aviator sunglasses, his hands seeming to wave in all directions at once. Kate, marching purposefully, four beat square bashing in riding boots, a low-waisted thick belt of jewels and bells, stamping on the spot to the thirty-seconds her fingers perform; James, a rare moment of release attempting to take flight, crazy looking flightless bird giving the ground to us all, the fretwork foundations of subterranean heartbeat; and I—I dance in circles, dervish joyful, as you run dance behind the drum riser, barefoot, a kaleidoscope of miniscule lights and reflections from the sequins of that robe you had found in a tie-dye and cigarette paper emporium—what else could such shops be called— in—where else?—Brighton. In this small film, everything is there, everything that is so close, still, and also lost, never to return.

Here you are.

Ne me quitte pas.

4. Second Act: Kate (Autumn 1974)

— What's this song called?
— Your dad would know.
— Well, I'm not going to wake him up, am I. If you want to, go ahead.
— It's called 'The Weight'.

Names were often the subject of our conversations. They are weights. The right name gives a weight and often a shape to whatever, or whoever, it is attached. Names: elusive, decisive, all handles, sigils hiding in plain sight that are more or less authentic. Anyone having owned a cat will know that experience of trying to name it. It appears indifferent to our random yet concerted, provisional efforts, until that day when it chooses its own name, or a name puts itself forward, irresistibly. Names, not just a name for a collective enterprise conveniently called a 'band', but all manner and form of names, nouns, pronouns, personal pronouns. These were the topic of so many small conversations, alcohol laced, late night, in the barn, a place become a shared home, which presented itself decisively, much as names do, attached to Kate. Without the barn, I cannot speak of Kate. To do so would be unimaginable. Visiting the barn recently, the first thing to strike me was the memory, with the force of experience, of those endless open-ended discussions of names, often after rehearsals, always late at night. The next thing I realised, with that poignant immediacy of a familiar but long forgotten scent on a snow-driven night, was the pull of home, the longing for that safe haven coupled with the overwhelming sorrow of guilt in having abandoned the idea.

A constant, the barn remains the same, though it was no longer a barn in function, even when Kate introduced James and I to it. Already at that time, the building had become what we came to know it as, a place for music, for laughter, friendship, parties, gatherings of various sorts, though its name remained the same: the barn. The generic belied, occluding the singular magic of place. Three years before, we were told, Harry, Kate's father, had decided to convert it into something other than what it was. An open form became two storeys. Its appearance changed and, with that, its nationality. From having been an unremarkable English barn, it was transformed by Harry into a building belonging more to a New England landscape, as if transplanted and grown, a slightly exotic species, familiar in the main, but exotic in detail. Two storeys took on different identities. The cathedral ceiling loft-like upper floor had become an open plan living area, with separate bathroom and bedroom, somewhere to stow visiting family without filling the house, Harry had said. Her father knew what he wanted, and how to achieve it. He had installed windows on the upper storey, bought from the US, those unforgettable Gothic Revival arched frames, leading Judge to name the building Church of the Cow. The apartment, in which Kate lived increasingly during Sixth Form, going over to the main house to, to cook on her own or with her stepmother, Rosemary, was reached by an external, or internal staircase. This was the principle, at least. The internal staircase, an old wrought-iron spiral, painted in crimson enamel, given exorbitant golden highlights, apocalyptic flames, a Blake vision, ascending to heaven, offered difficult access through an inconvenient, and so hardly used hatch. Impractical, an architectural joke, an ornate relic from a salvaged vicarage, not a stairway to heaven, but to a trap door. Its corkscrew presence in a cowshed presented embellishment for its own sake, a one-stop visual aesthetic with no other purpose than to amuse, bemuse, delight. And it did, standing in the lower rectangle. Of the ground floor, the walls were panelled, hung with dhurries and skins, souvenirs of Harry's previous life, along with photographs of people, often with musical instruments, whose faces James or I were sure we should have known, or on occasion did. A floor had been introduced, with some basic insulation, to keep the space dry; if never exactly cosy on the coldest nights, sea wind, fret haar and wraith rolling up the north-facing hill, over the top of twisted dwarf trees, this large area, waiting for a dance so that it could be, once more, and properly, a barn in some degree, was at least liveable, a place to work or play, with the help initially of paraffin space heaters, which encouraged the memory of straw.

Here Harry kept a strange assortment of bric-a-brac, memorabilia of what he always called, with the simplest, most unadorned of clichés, 'the business', and what for him were other more practical and creative items that, by association in our minds, conjured an era already showing signs of spiralling into terminal decline, and to which we were all too young to have belonged, except through a kind of phantom nostalgia for something, a time, a place, that had never been ours: a Chamberlin stood against one wall, presumably embarrassed to find itself here, but taking comfort from the fact that it was kept company by an antacid coloured Mellotron. Birmingham's greatest contribution to popular culture, I now hear someone like Timothy Spall saying in his Brummie, Auf Wiedersehen Pet, guise. There were also a brace of Theremin, which, like fish and sheep were indifferent when being named to the subtleties of the singular and the plural. A harmonium, an upright piano with no innards, and an electric piano presented an esoteric gnomon in one corner. A rack of tubular bells, some gongs, several reel-to-reels undergoing cannibalization: all as if in preparation for an Eastern European stop frame animation, completed this wayward collection of hardware. Surreality was the order of things, the order of the day. So many limbs awaiting a body; a puppet expectant of strings.

On first walking into the barn, the impression was that a rather strange German musical collective, definitely classically trained, and certainly all capable of being charged at any time with Class A drugs offences, had just taken a break, and were due to return shortly. Always supposing of course that they had not seen the sun melt into acid drop rainbows and waterfalls, heralding the newest Aquarian age. Pride of place however went to two organs, a small pipe organ, rescued perhaps from the home of the spiral staircase, and the instrument whose sound, the voices of which James and I could have identified without hesitation, a Hammond B3. More than an instrument, its noises, particularly the harmonic percussion, those non-sustaining second or third harmonic overtones, were its voice, defining it. Nothing else came close, 'Space Truckin',' with its nod to Holst, had proved this irrefutably. The audience heard them without knowing, but knew what they'd heard. Drawbars, presets, bass pedals, all played through a vertical coffin with on-board amplifier rotating speakers, the Leslie. Les and Wally, Wally and Les; together they became as indispensible to who we were as their cricketing counterparts, Judge and I christening the inseparable pair, in homage to Ames and Hammond, adding in the process to our various familiars, those inanimate extra 'members' who took names: Cecil, Roland, Clara; anthropomorphic magic bestowing on them personae, euphonious characters bringing a life unseen to metal, wood, bow, pick and magnet. Music: flesh and bone conjuring spirit from technological ingenuity. Bodyline rhythm, cover drive precision, top lines sailing over the boundaries of the heart, or turning sharply, unbelievably, to leave those who really listened emotionally stumped, impossible flight and guile, that unexpected turn out of the rough, to hit whoever really could listen where they lived, rearranging the furniture.

Does anyone hear the voice? Does the name mean anything? Is there anything in description or representation that brings closer the acoustic, the sonic, the aural world?

Music as cricket as feng shui? Despite my misgivings, I describe all this, forcing the most absurd of analogies, try to and fail, knowing beforehand I will miss the mark. I will have fallen short of affirming the possibilities, the effect, the touch of note, tone, resonance, reverberation. I fail in the full knowledge that if there are those who do not know what I am striving to show them, to tell them, to make them feel, if they are not already intimately familiar with the mysterious power of sound beyond any capability of verbal description, then no amount of technical information, no flight of metaphor, can take them across the boundary to the other side. They will not hear the voice, they will not get the name. They will not have been moved. If there is someone, just one, who does though, everything I have said, everything without words for which there are no names will have made itself known to that one person already. Names do so much, but only so much. For everything else, there has to be a communication for which there is no name.

Trying to find a name that expressed who we were, what we did, what defined for us, if no one else, the way of doing things we had already acquired, amounted to a manifesto in contradiction to fashion. Had we been able to have no name, without calling ourselves The Band with No Name, I like to fancy we would. Our definitive name did not present itself until 1977, returning from an evening at the cinema. By the time Graeme pitched up at the barn, we had taken a name, which remained a working title for some little time, a work in progress. What that was, and what our name came to be is, for now, of little relevance, save that, in the end, Paul Newman was our unlikely inspiration, muse out of left field. What stays though, beyond any name, remembered, tried, forgotten, and another constant for me today, long after much else has been forgotten, is barn talk. The building was home, a place of nameless names, of days and nights being ourselves, for ourselves and not for others. In particular, in that place, there is more than any other, one voice, emerging from a chorus. Kate.

Kate and the barn are interchangeable. No, take that back. It would be more accurate to say that I cannot think of one without the other. Today though, if I want to find my way back to Kate, I have to reach her through the barn. Kate then appears. She arrives, always coming back to me as a voice, speaking or singing, glass bell round with that faint accented intonation underneath, resonating, first heard in the school choir, and often after, to herself, traditional songs while carding, spinning, dyeing, knitting wool, always a Jacob fleece from a nearby farm.

— my son John was tall and thin; it's a rosebud in June; the maid replied, kind sir, she cried, I've lost my spotted cow; when I first came to town they called me roving jewel, now they've changed their tune, they call me Katie Cruel; black, black is the colour of my true love's hair...

Her own voice then, or the voices of her many instruments, all of which became her voice, channelling a sound that told those who could hear who she was. Judge, it's the head, Graeme, a single word, a beard. Kate, though— voices more than one, though all her own: violin, viola, mandolin, lute, accordion, melodeon, concertina; piano, guitar less so, bass, alien but once from necessity, then on occasion for the sheer giddy fun, relentless, running through the body. In all of these, the voice came through. A voice, late at night in the Church of the Cow, borne occasionally in solution, fruit, spice and whisky; red liquor for dark red hair, dyed once the colour of jet, or henna'd; robin redbreast red, dark golden to deep teak and walnut tones in the sun, a colour shading, antiqued, sunburst darkening, complementing, counterpointing the voice, the body of the violin, hair thrown in the sun—even the name, a name no one else could have borne or worn, to which no one else so perfectly was born: Cervenka, a middle European robin:

— from *cerveny*, 'red', it's Czech.

Through three generations of American detour, first Ellis Island, then California, to this easternmost village on the

Isle of Wight, courtesy of Harry, a father washed up on the
Island at the end of an era, a daughter in tow, and seeking
escape from that time's more furious forces; here he came
to a halt, in a farm, which like its barn, no longer served its
original purpose. A farmhouse, with barn and other buildings
no longer fit for purpose, on a low, slow-curving graceful
hill, overlooking the cello curve of the bay, slightly apart,
but belonging to the village of Bembridge, a self-contained
community cupped in the curve of shore, hidden by trees,
lulled by the sound of sea, and when the wind obliged,
adding to its own voice the slap and occasional crack of sail,
the ring of rivet at clew or tack, metallic knell on cathole: a
world of breezes and irregular rhythms.

— That's what we should call ourselves, The Weight.
— I thought The Cheese Collective was good.
— No. The Gentry's just fine, for now.

Dennis Hopper and Peter Fonda, riding through the
desert, California dreaming, endless highway, stone love,
endless land, a vast world. Sun going down, a world of
uninhabited mesas and bluffs; a dry heat, crimson sky to
pink, to purple, blackened silhouettes, outlined land mass,
and there through it all, three men, two bikes, a song. Ancient
vistas, older than that, and modern machinery gathered by a
human impulse, all there on the screen. It was all about doing
something because we wanted to, because it was who we
were, no other reason needed. Kate, her voice, her purpose,
her demeanour embodied and sang such conviction. In
its certainty, the precision of tone fully voiced, round and
pointed, it was impossible to disagree. She took any objection,
any indecision out of the game, her delivery precisely footed,
a rhetorical slap shot. Kate was. She was always right, just
right. Everyone knew this, conceding points, understanding
why an arrangement rather than another, seeing the logic of
choice implicit in tone, sure and fully realized. Kate always
spoke directly. Deciding quickly, she spoke what she thought,
what she felt, what she knew. Equally, she knew right away

if she liked someone or not. There was no time to waste. Or perhaps it is truer to say that, with Kate, never a Katherine, never ever Kathy, the former dead queens, the latter minor administrators, time was not to be wasted because being who she was, doing what she wanted just because meant not being sloppy, lazy, indecisive. That was, for Kate, freedom's price, the responsibility attendant on not having to justify, refusing to compromise. None of this should be taken as a sign of sharpness, a hard edge. Instead, all was with purpose, purposeful, practicality being everything. There was, for people she loved—and she always loved or disliked, Kate was never indifferent—an emotional largesse. Rarely were those who knew themselves to be close met with anything other than an open smile radiance of welcome, unconditional hospitality. Everything was done in the heart, and in my heart I know I have to find my way to the small things. Finding my way to Kate through the barn, I know in trying to remember, and finding the hardest words for the most impossible memories Kate directs me, acts as my guide in this.

By the time we sat watching Easy Rider, Kate had been with Judge and I for several months. Already, her presence was inevitable, something without which we could not imagine ourselves as having. What do we imagine genius to be? Quite some time ago the word had referred to one's own personal spirit, becoming over time someone's disposition, the essential quality of her character. Only more recently, relatively speaking, has genius come to mean exceptional ability. Brilliance, the thesaurus proposes. Yes, Kate shone, part Joyce Grenfell, part Margaret Rutherford on first acquaintance, but like the barn, with just that exotic aspect emerging on occasions from inside herself, brighter than any sunlight, brighter than any reflection from James's head. But there was also a formidable flair, artistry, not simply with her many instruments into which her spirit insinuated itself, calling out the voices of strings, wood, keys, horsehair, stops, hammers, pulleys, levers, bellows, buttons, the bellows-driven free-reed aerophone as she would laughingly, sparklingly describe her accordions. There was also that gift with flour, butter, eggs, sugar, or the capacity to reduce all matters, all questions of debate, indecision, or personality to the essential. Cutting away deadwood before it had even abandoned its sapling state, Kate was given, and gave to everything genius, the spirit that caused music to shine from within us, as if we all shared her gift, a gift she gave so freely, knowing us all so well, as I still believe, having insight into that which we neither knew nor could see about ourselves. Having a talent for producing that for which no rule could be given, Kate's decisive genius not only hit its target when everyone else missed by a mile; it also served her in seeing a target all her own, invisible to the rest. That simple. The heart of the matter. I remember this now with a clarity that many other memories lack. Cold, a Wednesday evening, late, pubs about to turn out, incredulous stars watching our return to Kate's parents' house, then into the upper storey of the barn, spring rolls for everyone, wine, beer and spirits waiting, we arrived back, to find the film about to start.

— What's this song called?

— Your dad would know.

— Well, I'm not going to wake him up, am I. If you want to, go ahead.

Names. The barn has led me to Kate. Kate has led me here.

~~~

— You need a violinist. And an accordionist. You need me.

September 1974, a warm, wet month. A frame is required, establish the shape to be filled. Kate comes into focus. It is always a question of imagining a space needing completion, filling. Kate arrives and the space becomes a place, a time, memory of her presence anchoring me, drifting away kite on a November day, the thread of remembrance connecting me to a ground. The first Wednesday of a new term, Judge and I now in the Upper Sixth, I, as yet, still to be called Dr

Who by the First Years in reference to my hair, the knitted scarves and, from the end of this year Tom Baker, the fourth Doctor, James already being called Kojak, with a startling lack of originality. I had spent most of the summer, when not playing, reading Dostoyevsky and Thomas Mann, complaining about the absence of any decent new novels, Le Carré's latest being the exception, and wearing out copies of Closing Time, I Want to See the Bright Lights Tonight and Selling England by the Pound. James had found temporary salvation for his habitually sporadic dyspepsia in Sartre, and was coming around to my view that Late for the Sky was one of the most devastatingly beautiful records ever made, though he still retained a preference for English miserabilism musically, over its California counterpart, I having retorted that melancholy under an endless sun, clear blue skies, was the more profound because all the more apparently inexplicable. Thomas Mann proved the point. Born in Lübeck, an uncanny and unlikely harbinger for us all, Mann had escaped, first to New Jersey and then, in 1942, to Southern California, Pacific Pallisades. There, with all the other ex-pat artists, actors, musicians, writers, he bemoaned the lack of culture. Irony under the sun. Though many of his works had been written in Germany, it was California that made possible, I had said, his greatest work, and the only book that come close to expressing what music was: Doctor Faustus. Mann had been a revelation and a gift at the end of the previous school year. John Haddon, our form master and English teacher, eager, sardonic, and severe in equal measure, an extravagant beard, pointed, consciously shaped in imitation of those worn by Elizabethan poets, fresh from teacher training college and Cambridge, in homemade jackets, pockets large enough to accommodate pairs of Penguins in each, saw me reading Hesse.

— That's not real German literature.

This was all that was said. A week later, before morning register, I was handed a copy of Death in Venice, one penny at a church jumble sale.

— That's real.

The certainty with which this was said convinced me
I should treat this seriously. Did we not, after all, already
agree about the merits of I Want to See the Bright Lights
Tonight, and had he not introduced me to the unspeakable
beauty of the Köln Concerts? The Magic Mountain, Lotte in
Weimar, Buddenbrooks, Felix Krull, all followed, culminating
in Faustus shortly before Kate, talking herself into our
presence, prying open the door to the club house with a
direct, disarming assault. The second year of A Levels had
begun, Hamlet and Henry James. The French Revolution
(toyed with as a name), Napoleon, screen printing, German,
and Art History, James and I seeking to outdo one another
by taking more than the usual three subjects, French having
been completed in a year by us both on a bet—new strings or
beer for two months. Outside our bubble, there came briefly
into disinterested, and faintly scornful focus Helmut Schmidt
and 'Tiger Feet', Richard Nixon and Watergate, Abba and
'Waterloo': strange synchronicities from some perspectives,
in hindsight. That first Wednesday though: the end of the
day, choir, and Kate. After practice, Kate, new to the Lower
Sixth, known to us from gigs in the summer, presented her
statement as if a fait accompli.

— You need a violinist. And an accordionist. You *need* me.

— Do you know any others, then?

Many people might have said this with a touch of
sarcasm. James's question, though odd, was genuine,
sympathetic resonance in the recognition of different tuning.

— Me. I just said. And lute…

— Who plays lute?

— …Mandolin; other things too.

— Everything…

— …and all the rest.

The certainty of her oval, bright, broadly beaming face,
announcements made with all the calm assurance of the
cheery Jehovah's Witness to whom one has mistakenly
opened the front door, caught us unawares. Smiling egg,

cheeks roseate, Kate presented everything of herself in that encounter, words and face together. That face, framed by long, unadorned hair, mostly chestnut tending to blacks, three-quarter lit from early autumn light, flaming into damask, vermeil tongues of flame, or here and there stray fulvous strands, darkness rubescent, her colours were those of her violin, her viola, her lute, her mandolin, each stringed instrument an index to the player, a supplementary voice, but also, a miniature in its curves, arcs, and flowing lines, of Kate. When I say this, I am aware that this might imply physical resemblance, corporeal metaphors already too familiar. This is not the intention, not the desire. Instead, there was to Kate a sense of curve and flow, of the unstraight line or motion, with their promise of endlessness. The instruments embodied who she was, not how she appeared. There was, in the perceived transference of colour—hair and lacquered wood, skin and piano keys—the key to her way of being. One sensed how she moved through the world, presented herself to others, and, from there to the invisible, the shape and tenor of sound that came from her fingers, her mouth. Her singing voice, we came to know, could traverse the space from angelic to demonic, from the purest round tone, to a sound suggestive of dark, sticky heat, too swampy close, throatily suggestive, emotionally brutal, raw with an immediacy of experience channelled but which could never possibly have been hers.

All this was realised in the experience of the next few months, along with our introduction to the barn. Until then, James and I had, increasingly, rehearsed in a deconsecrated church, slowly in the process of becoming the Dominguez family home, courtesy of Judy or, more accurately, her father, reasoned into this by his eldest daughter, with not a little help from her two sisters. Though James and I had at first pushed parental tolerance to the limit, or cajoled empty classrooms after school, we had come to realize the need for a neutral space, a place that had about it a seriousness to suit our efforts, and an acoustic that would support them. In return for the use of the church, which served throughout the summer before Kate, we would help with such renovations as were within our capabilities, and for which time could be found. Kate's arrival, with the barn, signalled though, a shift. A different sound, to this point only imagined barely, heard in the briefest of moments on the recordings of others, or on the odd occasion, after playing when James had observed,

— Did you notice how something was missing? Not sure what, but there's a gap there needs filling

which then shaped itself. With that, with Kate, James's insistent, restless energy, his writhing wraith vision of music, found a seedbed, a shelter, a common ground and dwelling place. The opposite of James's drop forge articulation, Kate underplayed, addressed the world with clarity; where he hammered, she wove, while he pulled making the feel taut, Kate gave to us not a lightness, but the sense of patterning within the form, making the music assume significance. She moves through the fair. Kate skimmed the clouds, atop she flowed, gathering, surrounding, buoyancy and cradle. Though many voices, it is always the violin that presents itself in my thought, stepping out from clouded, crowded recollections, top line tightrope walking over the abyss. Violin, Kate answered, and complemented James's cello or bass, but also answered, and called to the guitar, creating a hinge between James's aural vision and mine.

The unexpected conversation that Wednesday afternoon continued, as so many impromptu discussions did, with a slow walk townward, tea and cake the promise and the goal. This afternoon, we headed for Fowlers, a department store, which welcomed its customers to 1970s' suburbia, all too delicate china incongruous in the presence of geometric orange and mudbrown cube pattern curtains. Accents and artefacts, utilitarian twee aesthetic mingling with uneasy and belated modernist abstraction made easy insisting that, no, the world was not drab, not dull, even in the most sluggish backwaters, the most brackish tidal pools of polite manners.

Fowlers had appeared in the nineteenth century, a scaled-down provincial imitation of its greater capital counterparts. With that time lag that accompanies everything from clothing and soft furnishings to hairstyles and food fads, Fowlers had been, typical of all parochial pastiche enterprises, behind the beat, on the back foot, ever since. On this particular day, it wore its somewhat dusty air of reluctant and disinterested encounter with the contemporary with a more than usual comicality. Walking in that afternoon, through the displays of silver service and Wedgewood, side by side with porcelain statuettes of sad clowns, gypsy girls and puppies, then moving further into the interior, past sofas and chairs towards the overpainted, overworked late Victorian staircase, the walls of the stairwell a domestic hall of mirrors, interspersed with odd, very odd imitation oil paintings, 'reproductions' of works that had never existed—the eyes follow you all around the room—we were Tom and Barbara, and Tom's lunatic day release cousin, in the land of Margot and Jerry, Surreyevo, before The Good Life had so precisely, with such forensic perception, lanced the world of Pinter-lite Ayckbourniana. James broke out his chiselled bare dome bright eyed grin on such occasions, these forays into the heart of blandness, as he led the way to the floors above and the café; I followed on, a mass of unruly hair atop an RAF flyboy's leather jacket, sheepskin collared, worn even on a warm day or depending from a shoulder, indication, if you knew, of my fascination, no call it what it is, obsession, with If…, and Malcolm McDowell's Mick Travis in particular, the archetypal image of futile counter-culture rage in the face of an implacable class system. Oh to be in England… Kate, loud laughing, bell-voiced, sing-song Kate, aged denim jacket, maroon and saffron tie-dye floor-length skirt and sandals, between us, telling us all the songs she already knew, what she could play, why we should play them, and why she was, therefore, indispensible. Too loud, too careless of our surroundings, we cleared a space around us. We existed, and were bearing ourselves along in our own bubble world, neither caring nor knowing whether we created an effect, but causing people to look nonetheless.

Heading toward the café, Kate remarked on a sound like parrots, parakeets, budgerigars, which grew in volume and frenzy, as we got closer to teatime.

— The old dears, their time of day, they flock, blocking the aisles and infringing your personal freedom.

James citing Python explained, adapting as he always did the riffs of others to his own purposes. I gave him a line, mixing, matching, misquoting deliberately, with deliberation, my very best Eric Idle, later John Major voice.

— Funny thing, freedom. Mrs Essence flushed hers down the loo. This is the whole crux of Sartre.

At which point, with a spontaneity that was all too well rehearsed, we began, a capella, 'The Girl from Ipanema', James's voice imitating bass line and percussion, I singing falsetto, to the discomfort of shoppers. And now for something completely different, premise and conclusion, existential vamping, jazz hands of the soul. In the middle of the lingerie department, Kate joined in the melody, finding effortlessly a harmony, a descant, counter-melody, in more than just tune, singing the Portuguese, a sparkling green eye signalling her awareness that she had outdone us, surprising and taking by stealth the fortifications of our boys' club confidence, and taking away our voices in the process.

— Bloody hell.

All eyes now turned towards us, arrived we turned our attention to the tables of the café. Shortly after four-thirty, it was still quite full, the source of parroting being those predicted clusters of elderly ladies, always properly, tidily dressed, I could just imagine the Boccherini kicking into wind-up life, tiddle-iddle-om-pom-pom, and the odd late summer tourist family, hoping not to be observed for the impropriety of belatedness. A table to the rear of the room was available however, towards which we took separate routes through the other customers, as if weaving invisible patterns known only to us, or marking escape routes. Slightly stuffy, the temperature and atmosphere, we presented a Polaroid affront in a monochrome, perhaps barely beige world. Something had become dislodged, an existence comfortable in its unthinking acceptance pushed off-kilter briefly, for no other reason than the appearance of foreign bodies. There was a pitch shift in the conversational tenor, as if a too large amorphous blob had, unreasonably, demanded to be noticed. I am not a number, I am a Hunan bean. A communal self had been prodded, found itself silently bruised, albeit inadvertently. Nothing had changed, no one had dropped a cup, a plate had not been smashed, falling to the floor in exaggerated slow motion; and yet, and yet, clearly, for others the tearoom had changed, its skin pierced, an allergen introduced. We were aware that we were producing a reaction, even though our actions had been at best unselfconsciously ebullient, not seeking attention but drawing it nonetheless. Feeling ourselves watched, looks were exchanged in the complicity of realisation, before eyes turned down, and quiet amusement at our collective effect sounded our mild embarrassment.

— It's your head; again.

— Your hair more likely.

— Well, you've got enough for both of you, so why not give some to James?

Tea for three, scones and jam for two, and Victoria sponge for one ordered, we wandered for a long time in words that touched on everything but the essential, Kate's introductory statement, her declaration of intent embedded in an apparently neutral observation about what she clearly took to be lack on our part. In Kate's eyes, James and I were obviously an impaired, impoverished, disappointed trio, not a duo, a kingdom of two, contrapuntal bookends. We were, she said, a pier, and she could build us into a bridge. For Kate, the matter was simple, no, mine's the sponge, it was never a matter of being considered, or asking for an audition. James and I simply had to see the logic. How could we not, and

with that, accept the inevitable? We were the ones who, in previous weeks, had been auditioned, had been tried out and, if not found wanting, were at the least in need of a few small repairs. Later, I was to realise how all this was already, quietly, effectively decided on, once Kate had chosen to approach us on a common ground, choir, after school, and having made herself known through her attendance at various gigs in the summer. Kate had laid siege to us, and, having undermined our defences, underlabouring, had won, so that when I said,
— When can you come to a rehearsal at Judy's dad's place?

The reply, any time you like, announced that this was a done deal. I advanced the question in full, if tacit knowledge that James was already waiting for me to put it. A string player himself, musician of the less obvious instruments and having not only more than one proverbial string but also several reeds and mouthpieces, he found in Kate a strangely interesting mirror image. He was taken, I could sense. I was on the outside of this chance conspiracy as much as was the extravagance of my Victoria sponge when seen in the light of their more prudent scones. Tinkle of teaspoons completed the musical box, dolls' house eccentricity of what was now our three-way affair, as we continued, in our delighted irrelevance, our imitation of an over-coloured tea party. Hatter, Hare, and Alice. Our tea talk continued, a complex interplay of exposure and hiding, organization and chaos, quietly maintained, as around us polite banalities and the idiom of the unremarkable, a kind of living as hanging on, a perpetual teatime of the spirit, which if not in desperation then for lack of any other conceivable option, were maintained. Our momentary interruption forgotten, we were folded back into the invisible. While others wasted time, we knew already that you couldn't beat it, and were resolved to go with the flow, while going against the grain, all of us loving the voice no one else heard. Cadence in the prelude is all.

Ordering more tea, we close in twenty minutes, James finally put a direct question to Kate, a question he always reserved when wanting to deliver some unexpected turn out of the rough.

— What do you hear when you play?

— If you're going to test me, you might have done better than that. If you want me to realize in words what is there when I play, you would have, first, to distinguish between the sound of the instrument, and whether you expected me to talk about technicalities, which I could but I won't as you already know all of that guff, I mean, 'cello, what's that but a violin with a thyroid problem, or you would have to be stupid enough, which I don't think you are, to expect me to tell you how the sound translates in my head, which I can't because if I could I wouldn't play, and there would be no point, now would there, in playing in the first place. I've seen the faces you pull when you're playing. Everyone else might think it's a gurning competition, but I have an idea of what it is you hear, and more importantly, what it is you *see*, don't you see? But of course you do. That doesn't mean to say I can put that into words, or that I would want to. If I were to try, which I'm not going to, then I'd be as stupid as you think some people are, and you'd be right, or at least as stupid as I would have to think you are for actually imagining that there is an answer to the question. We both know we know, though what we know between the three of us is different for each of us, and so it's the same and not the same, and we also know it's got nothing to do with mechanics. I could say… what's that book you have in your bag, the one that's about to fall out?

This to me

— It's Thomas Mann, *Doctor Faustus*

— I could say all sorts of things about Benedict

— Ben

James interjected, as if giving Kate a secret access code

— if I knew something about the book and about him, but I would still be wide of the mark, wouldn't I? Or would you like me to talk about the dots? They're no more to do with the music in the music either. It's like that really funny bit in *Howards End*…

A Level English set texts become jokes from the more
brain dead such as people doing maths and science subjects,
asking Duncan, *have you seen Howards End lying around, Dunc?*
Have you dipped into Howards End? First year, one may as well
begin, with…with what, where, exactly, all beginnings being
arbitrary? Forster knew, felt the arbitrary nature of things; as
did we.

— …Where everyone's thinking the Beethoven actually *means*
something, or they need to make it mean something because
they can't accept music doesn't have to mean anything, not
in that way, it's not a painting or a photograph; it's not even a
piece of writing about a daffodil or an urn; and if I try to tell
you what I *feel*, that sounds ridiculous; we all know what we
hear when we play, don't we, and if we play with one another
we just have to trust each other that whatever it is we believe
we feel has something about it that is not completely dissimilar to what anyone else might be feeling at the same time.
And I'm not even talking about the audience.

— Exactly, as long as we all start together and end together, it
doesn't much matter what we do in between.

I had felt the need to add this, so much did I agree
with Kate's view. But then so did James, I knew this, and
clearly Kate knew it too, intuited it with a sharpness to
match James's own. Lacking this acuity, I saw it in others
nevertheless. Music did not have an object, it was formal
abstraction in the most severe, no austere sense, even if
lyrics were 'about' something, even when they expressed an
emotion, told a story. Through music, not the dots, not the
instruments, but music, there was the possibility that purely
sensual apprehension might let itself be known or that
you might resonate in response attuned already to its call,
although only in the most indirect manner. This doubtless
sounds like an interpretation. It is as far as I'm prepared
to go. Personal for everyone, everyone who hears, and not
everyone can hear, but those who might be touched by this
piece or that performance, music just is, and it is better not
to talk. Only people who are indifferent to music and fail to

feel want to name. They blather about talent and reduce the oceanic to a shallow, muddy rain puddle, mixing in the dog piss of their own tawdry emotions. Kate confirmed my own prejudice, as she continued.

— Do you know about Schoenberg and Stravinsky? Schoenberg thought people had a childish preoccupation with pleasure, that style is sound devoid of idea. Stravinsky thought form was just sound stripped of meaning. Schoenberg didn't want music to be beautiful or to be thought of in terms of beauty, he thought instead it should be true, authentic. If music communicates anything at all that's because it chimes authentically for us, in us, as it is and because the chime causes a reflection that we don't otherwise have words for. There's that song you both do, not one of yours, I've heard you play it three times now, and each time it's different but it does the same thing.

— Which?

— Really obvious chords, sentimental, and you've played it once with double bass, another time with cello, and a third with trumpet.

A pause, then, looking at one another, James and I said, together

— The Tom Waits number

— 'I hope that I don't fall in love with you'.

— That's the one. It doesn't matter that I think it's got a syrupy lyric, or that the progressions have been used so many times before. It's just very touching, and there's something there that cuts through its packaging. It would work better though with a melodeon in there, or just cello and violin, with the voice, maybe one verse pizzicato. The authentic is right there, though; not in the instrumentation, but something else somewhere else.

We saw it undeniably. This was Kate: strip away the fake, the spurious, the inauthentic, anything that gets in the way of what she always called everything that's not words. If music touched, it wasn't to be debased, rendered, sullied, but left uncut, in its unalloyed condition. Where composers, 'serious' composers were wrong, she continued, was in the assumption that what they dismissed as popular music in any form was not as pure, could not work, touch, in the way serious music could. The store is closing in five minutes. Looking around we were, we realised, the last customers, ours the only untidied table. Around us, without our noticing, Fowler's Café had emptied, becoming a stage set. Terence Rattigan waited in the wings. We had stayed beyond our time, had failed to notice the final curtain, we were oblivious to any hint that might have signalled a desire for us to leave, go elsewhere, anywhere, but just to go. Kate had for this time held time hostage, closed us off from the everyday, the mundane. She had effected this with a quiet magic, a subtle seduction of understated siren song, not wild, but softly impassioned, precise, all the more effective in being delivered in a measured way, andante but varying a piacere, con tempo giusto, not a strict tempo, but just the 'right' speed. She was right. We needed a violinist, an accordionist; we required a lute and mandolin player, someone who could sing, who played the piano, someone indeed who could play most anything if she chose to, or necessity demanded it. That she would name, had named, each instrument in turn told us that she saw each as equally important, each having a separate role to play, a voice to contribute. We needed Kate, and Kate knew this.

Having paid, leaving, we turned our talk to the trivial, to deciding on a rehearsal, when we three should meet again. Descending the stairs, late afternoon sunlight reflected on the large mirrors illuminating the falling momently golden, old dust falling through light, through time; walking through the material of the world, surrounded by the near silence of the store, under the gaze only of the occasional floor walker or the indifferent mannequins, we gradually fell silent, as if taking on the realisation of change, transformation. This day at an end, outside the store, James said merely

— Tomorrow

indicating not school, but our next rehearsal, to which Kate should come. Leaving me with the details, he turned back up the hill, not another word, following the slow curve, already somewhere else having nothing to do with place. Walking toward sea and bus station, I to bike home, Kate to take a bus to Bembridge, Kate asked me why we had included the Waits song. It was difficult to say. The question, not exactly loaded, was nevertheless expecting from me a response I was not exactly certain how to frame, even if I felt the answer was familiar. Stalling for time, repeating myself to the point of stuttering, on the verge of generalisations about romantic quirkiness, the idiosyncrasy of a drunk's take on the world, the boozy delivery saving the song from the schmaltz in which it seemed wrapped should anyone else perform it, I gave up, turned myself in, admitting to loving the idea of how the song's character hopes against hope throughout until it turns out to be too late. Kate said nothing, smiled, with a smile signalling another acknowledgement of complicity, this time one in which James had no part. Again, she had found a place between us, and so once more acted in a way that made us all more fully connected, more completely who we were.

~~~

Am I embellishing too much, or just enough? You would know; you always did even when I, too willingly it now seems, filled myself with doubts and indecisions. All that talent, no self-belief, James later told me. How you would have laughed. Still there, still here, I believe, you already know these stories, variations on a theme. You are familiar with the various *leitmotif*. What I do know is that, while with James, I struggle with words, for Kate, there are always more than enough. James was never in those days enough in the everyday. Being at its edges he felt most comfortable. Kate, in comparison was solid, of the earth, but capable of taking flight in the tunes she could create anew with every performance. As for me? Inside the perfect storm we created it was quiet. I was happiest at the eye, feeling all move around me, happy too to share in what the others could

make happen, what we all made happen together. No me,
save for the others. I remember how, in those first days of
introduction, exploration, casual accommodation, you had
asked about the others, how we met, how things had come
together. I told you, these and other stories, perhaps less
adorned, in a different tone, changing the tempi as the time
or moment suited. Talking. Travelling. You were there. You
are here. Listening. Driving. Talking in return. Overture, a
word, words, you favoured, found for what we did; *ouverture,
Vorspiel*: an opening, openings more than one, prefatory to
everything else…and all the rest. Doors opened onto avenues
of possibility, pathways touching, intersecting, divergences
coming back around again to meet at the heart, each time a
different perspective. Each of us plays a part, independent
self-existing, but coming together. No beginnings then, just
the overture, opening upon opening, play on play, *Spiegel im
Spiegel*. This was where you and Kate met in music opening
in the process other doors already swinging freely on their
hinges. Of course, you had met Kate before this, two years
before; you had known one another, become intimate, closest
of friends during that two years. I know you would correct
me, *opening* you would have told me, as I just realise, not
beginning; *ouverture*, you would say, preferring the French to
the English, and I preferring this also, for the shape it gave
your mouth. So, not *met*, I am happy for you to correct me.
Not *met*, but *found*. Finding Pärt's tintinnabular composition,
your four hands, fingers together and apart, dancing on string
and key in 6/4 time, you *found*, reflecting one another, *finding*
us all, producing prisms wherein we all could see ourselves,
mirrors in mirrors, an infinity of images and sound. Moved,
Moving on, we moved on. We're moving on.

5. Interlude: A First Day—
The Island (July 1976)

Why, I want to ask you, when it is easier to understand is
it often harder to bear? Rationally, everything makes sense,
but this knowledge only sharpens the memory of a feeling,
the first response to every experience. There is a sequence,
a series of events, a recountable tale. But taken together or
worked over one moment at a time, these do not measure
against or bear the same weight as how they cause one to feel.
The feeling is in me but not me. It is other than the person
I believe myself to be. Properly speaking therefore, I cannot
lay claim to this feeling. I cannot call it mine, exactly. It arrives
before understanding, and when it returns, little ghost of an
unexpected gift for which I could never have been prepared,
it is no more available to apprehension than that first time.
So, you know, don't you? I wait. Again. Waiting for that
irreversible step. Which, of course, I will have to take, and
find it impossible to move beyond, each and every time there
comes the memory. Here we are.

How therefore—and I rehearse the question, replaying it
like a riff or motif from that all too familiar anxiety which
has always been mine, after you my closest companion—
to open onto this, one of many first days, first mornings?
Standing here on the edge, on the brink, at the threshold,
the door, waiting to cross, to step over, step through, already
beginning to open myself to the idea of change, finding
something disclosing itself, having the sense, the first hint

or indication of a revelation. Something is being revealed, exposed. A door is being opened. Did you feel this? I am taking slow steps, one after another, as if barefoot across a beach, turning stones with my toes, wondering what might emerge. Here then, waiting for an opening, a cue, for whatever might emerge. Every step we take leaves in its wake a trace, but each footstep finds its echo, future and past, in what had seemed random, unplanned, as if the everything had been plotted. Thus I hesitate, waiting for you to open the door, as I did that morning, another hot, dry day, already contracted. The sky appears close, nearer and yet an infinite canopy, vaulting. Black door, three bells, press the third, wait for the door to open. The sea is indifferent to anxiety informed with hope. Gulls laugh.

Overture: opening, an aperture, the action of opening; a negotiation, an approach or proposal; open or exposed places; a revelation, a disclosure or declaration; a first indication or hint of something; overturning, overthrowing, sudden change. Later, when you had told me how ouverture was one of your words, your special words, those you collected, wrote down, in different languages in those small notebooks, carnet, you valued beyond price, I looked in the dictionary, finding to my surprise how many ways overture, ouverture, Vorspiel, opened itself. The word was its own opening; it was, I told you, a window or lens, a hole through which one looked, through which everything came into focus, it approached matters relating to it, it disclosed its own meanings, hinting at them; it declared itself, disclosing itself, open, opening, assuming its own actions. I realised, only later, much later, too late, how all those different meanings were... were what? Appropriate? A propos? Were they good words, the right meanings, bon mots? For all of us? Between all of us? Between, and for you and I? How many openings are there in a hall of mirrors?

I had forgotten until recently the significance of overture, ouverture for you, to us, you and I, and all of us. In Berlin a short while ago, Arschkalt und allein, everything white, so many spaces everywhere reminders of the absence of history, so much modernity and pan-European institutional architecture all the more evocative for its nondescript anonymity, Kaufhaus des Westens, the past more forcefully at hand in being so vengefully absent save for precisely presented museums and ghostly traces of proper names written on the map—Anna Louisa Karsch Straße, Karl-Liebnecht Straße, Dorotheenstraße, Charlottenstraße, Hegelplatz, always Hegel, too much Hegel—, I found myself attending a festival dedicated to, of all things, ghosts and spectres. How all occasions do inform. Looking through the programme as I walked, coming to the point where Unter den Linden ends, midway between the competing extravagance, the ostentatiously roofed exclamations of the Deutsches Historisches Museum and the Berliner Dom, winter sun casting severe Februarschatten across the silverwhite carpet of Am Lustgarten, making harsh the brightly coloured glossy pages, over which my eyes strained, narrowed to read, the word Vorspiel presented itself with that force of a slap to the face, a Tristan chord resounding; those swelling notes, wave upon wave, surge and tug, of the prelude, the ouverture, the Vorspiel of Tristan und Isolde, Vorspiel as untimely Liebestod, with only the desire to drown, to founder, unconscious, höchste Lust!

Unanticipated, though programmed long before, submerged, the door closed, there it was, there you were, the programme before the programme: exhibition openings, performances, artist talks, special events, installations, light shows, ghosts off the shelf, out of the cupboards, closets burst open. Your words returned in a rush, as a prelude to all else: play the chord as the world falls apart. Vorspiel: overture of course, but also preliminary, prologue, prelude, foreplay. All at once, the dance, dizzying, of too much light in too many mirrors came from the revelation of that word, spielen in Spiegeln, spela i speglar you would say, switching as was your habit, when being playful, from father to mother tongue. Suddenly, that word, Vorspiel, on the tip of my tongue, from

yours to mine, as if the ghost of your tongue had placed
itself in my mouth, I opened my mouth to speak the word
aloud, my consciousness having all its apertures unstopped,
opened opening, equal temperament left ruined, a decisive
irreversible onrush, harmonic suspension causing to open
such anticipation, expectation, onto so many prolonged,
seemingly unending, unfinished cadences, dying falls
without resolution, merely the dissonant bustle of memory
on memory crowded crowding, upsurge swell, unstopped,
unstoppable, the genie out of the bottle, no pressing things
down, no putting them away, no locking up memories, placing
the souvenirs in the prison we call an archive, the taste of
your word, your tongue on mine, speaking that word, saying
it again, say it again as if for a first time, wanting always a first
time without loss of the saltsharpness, acid drop bright, never
to be dulled once more by routine familiarity, everything now
coming to the surface, returning, brought up from below,
continuing to come without reserve, tongue on tongue,
everything touching on everything else, impalpable, immense,
without end this opening…

~~~

Come into the garden, Maud. The island, described to someone
unfamiliar, is no easy task. A precious stone set in the silver
sea? It is, roughly, diamond or lozenge shaped though
perhaps more agate than emerald. Only an island when
seen from the water? Not once I'd lived there for a while; I
realised that an island, the Island, the South Island, was not
just a geological fact. It was a state of mind, a way of seeing,
doing, living. Being different was not rebellion, a statement
of intent, it was, in the Island, just how to live. Time ran
differently, if at all, operating on BST, British Surreal Time—
Kate's definition; clocks on the island were put neither
forward nor back, but sideways—or British Sidereal Time—
James's, not wholly serious allusion to the idea that nothing
seemed to happen here unless all the stars were in alignment.

The largest English island? True enough, but then, being the largest island belonging to a larger island, or group of islands, this statement wilfully missed the point. The place that ruined Tennyson's poetry? There was no proof of this, merely the prejudice of dyspeptic A Level English teachers, though I had some sympathy with the view. Victoria's Poet Laureate had at least given us the title of an instrumental, 'Black Bat Night', the very idea of which had been a joke. I had said that, leaving out Tennyson's comma, it sounded like a bad metal track, a miserable B-side from an ill-advised single, released in a last ditch effort at commercialism before four miserable Brummies refused to play with one another, ever again. One evening, another soundcheck, Morphy had asked me to sing something; I improvised a tune around a line or two of Tennyson's

— All night have the roses heard the flute, violin, bassoon
— Roses don't have ears, bugger; I bet the silly sod who wrote that talks to flowers. It's not one of yours, is it?

Criticism's loss was percussion's gain. The island, it seemed, defied good literature. Virginia Woolf's Freshwater, a play about Tennyson and his neighbour, the photographer Juliet Margaret Cameron, brings the point home. True, Dickens did insist on reading drafts of Sikes's murder of Nancy to his heavily pregnant wife, while on holiday in Ryde, but this, as James would say in deadly imitation of his father, was hardly prima facie evidence of anything, m'lud. Home to the largest rock festival ever held, Hendrix's final gig (Woodstock, please, that was a garden party…). Play the island and die. Having had its afterlife extended through galvanism, the summer of love finally gave up the ghost on the Island, leaving behind it a strange assortment of half-life figures. Thomas Hardy in his map of Wessex calls it just 'the Island', as if what it was self-evidently were enough. If one didn't know, no amount of information would help explain it. Fanny Price understood this, thinking of nothing other than the Isle of Wight, and calling it the Island, as if

She had thought about a doctorate, but wanted to take a year
or so out from study.

— What about your playing, while you're here?

Later that day, light on light, heat on heat, by the
Longstone, our picnic taking its time, lazily stretched burnt
grass itching, I asked, suddenly concerned.

— *Papi* insisted I had an instrument; so, when we arrived,
Mutti, Heike, my sister, we all went shopping. We found a
shop in Southsea, and I could not decide. So, I have two...

Satisfied air of a child, pleased beyond expression on
Christmas morning

— ...electric pianos. A Fender, and a Wurlitzer, the same
colour as Waltraud. This way I don't annoy the neighbours,
I can use headphones. Not as good as the real thing but,
ja, ja. Papi also knows a family here, who have a, what is it,
Stützflügel, a *Bösendorfer*, and that I can play whenever I want to
go to their house.

— I don't know *Stützflügel*, but that's great, you must be
pleased.

An orange electric piano: like minor deities, I had heard
of its existence but had never seen one. Harry would be
in awe. The very idea seemed outlandish and yet wholly in
keeping, having a certain consonance. Annagreth told her
stories without fuss, with little elaboration, her matter-of-
factness underplaying all the while, having its own charm,
dispelling any possible thought of boastfulness. There was in
her trusting, artless manner of recounting a modesty, neither
bashful nor meek, but which, it seemed to me, became the
effect, the expression of her smile. Where its effect was
instantaneous, her words disarmed, perhaps as a matter of
speaking a language almost her own but not quite. Should I
describe her as being, should I say she gave the impression
through her words of being, in that overused, debased
phrase, all sweetness and light that day? Would that be gilding
the lily? Would this be dishonest nostalgia, disingenuous
screen memory? Would cliché and stereotype ruin the fragile

memory sun fired, finished, a patina to accompany the terracotta earth on which we sat? How then, I ask myself, can I begin to tell you? Or how can I speak to you now? Risking everything in the obvious, I realise that behind, inside, that wellworn phrase there remains, like the touch of sound on spirit, sun on skin, wind on water, something else, something inaudible, invisible. Will anyone think first of Swift or Arnold on hearing these words? Too few, though there will be enough to notice their moth-eaten quality. There is though always a limit, always the impossible, from which, in the face of which, despite which, I find I cannot evade responsibility. Like that orange Wurlitzer, this is both extravagant and yet also just, inevitably, right.

— I say! To the lighthouse! The day is fine after all!

Declaiming in what Kate called my stuffed shirt voice, and which, when uttered in the presence of James could continue in strange dialogue for indefinite periods, I say, cheese it you chaps, I clearly took Anna by surprise. Laughing, she inquired, a quizzical expression mixed with the suspicion that sunstroke had got the better of me.

— *Was machst du?*

— Sorry, it's Woolf, Virginia, *To the Lighthouse*. We're not far from St Catherine's Lighthouse, over by Niton, and there's a good pub down there, The Buddle, we play there sometimes, their gardens will be open; they have real ale.

— Warm, flat beer?

— That's what I said.

Happy to go along, at least for now, with the sudden outbursts of inspiration from someone who seemed like a lunatic to be tolerated at all costs, Annagreth agreed readily. The picnic finished, the afternoon beginning to advance reluctantly, sleep becoming by the minute all too likely, we hurried ourselves, tidying, packing, tumbling back into the car, we headed back to the coast road.

Strangely crenelated, octagonal, but with an additional multisided structure appended barnacle-like, midway architecturally between folly and pastiche Norman

fortification, and reaching out on the southernmost point of
the Island awaiting its own Eric Ravillious or Stanley Spencer,
stood St Catherine's Lighthouse. Wight of the shipping
forecast, this early Victorian digit atop St Catherine's Point
oversaw Watershoot Bay to its west, Reeth Bay to the east,
and the more populated parts of Shanklin, Lake, Sandown.
It shone white blindingly in the sun though no lamp was
lighted. White standing out against blue and green was
enough waymark during a day such as this, looking as if it
had been fashioned in imitation of those vials of coloured
sand, but given a purity in deference to the chalkface
of the cliffs, a nineteenth-century technological marvel
acknowledging its natural cousins, the Needles several miles
along the coast. Having parked at the Buddle, we dropped
down a steep footpath onto a single lane, leading the mile to
the beacon. Taking the tour, climbing the 94 steps, we and
the other visitors, a couple, clearly serious hikers from their
dress, and a family with three children in various stages of
disinterest, verging on the edge in the case of the youngest
of an overheated, dehydrated sugar fuelled fit, were told how
there had been a light here since 1323, how the mirror had
been chipped during a bombing raid in the last war, that last
sounding as if the guide were expecting another to kick off
at any moment, and how the Union Flag that had survived
the bombing raid while the three keepers had not was still
displayed as a sign of respect. Don't panic, Mr Mainwaring,
don't panic. They don't like it up 'em. I could hear James's
voice, Cpl Jones perfect, which, had he been here would
have been an unstoppable train wreck of an inevitability.
Trying to avoid feeling embarrassed in that very English way
over mention of the war, I cast our hikers in my mind in
the roles of Keith and Candice Marie, Mike Leigh's absurd
middle-class, suburban, sunburbian, subunburbian, camping
couple, or archetypal ramblers so disliked by Mary Butts.
Anna appeared indifferent to such remarks, and it was not
something I would bring up unless she did.

— What is it with your nation and the war? I mean the light-house is much older, but still, a chipped piece of glass and an old flag.

Walking back to the Buddle.

— We don't win things that often. Take cricket. The only reason we exported the game around the world was so everyone we taught could beat us.

— No, be serious Ben...

How many ways to answer this question, of all the possible answers that might present themselves, and which tone to take?

— I think, seriously, we, or lots of us, are obsessed with the past, or a version of it. We became irrelevant, as a nation, in the 1950s and the sixties, no more Empire, the US becoming everyone's hero. So we keep imagined resentments going. Being sullen is what we're good at. Do you know *Dark Side of the Moon?*

— of course, who doesn't? But it's somewhat obvious musically.

— Well, as James would say, 'the Prosecution rests, m'lud'. His father is a lawyer.

I explained by way of reference, realising in the middle of the statement that this information had already been provided, feeling awkward at the repetition.

— But you have so much culture, art, interesting things, good things.

— Yes, but then you'd have to take an active inter-est. Everyone thinks Napoleon called us a nation of shopkeepers...

Cpl Jones, Jones the Butcher, stupid boy, black market stockings, chocolate and don't sit under the apple tree, with anyone else but me, how to explain one of the BBC's most popular shows, a strange double take which, on the one hand, laughed at the enfeebled efforts of national domestic defence, while on the other, making a point that even old men, incontinent, feckless, and bleary eyed, with no ammunition, a Boer War bayonet, and a couple of broom handles, could withstand, as documentaries always liked to say, the Might of the German War Machine.

— …but it was Adam Smith, who wanted to make the point that ours was a government influenced by shopkeepers. It's not the basis for cultural pride, really, now is it? Perhaps it's being an island, and thinking you're the centre of the world.
— It would be as if we wanted in Germany always to stay with Beethoven, or Haydn, nothing else must happen, no changes, keep everything the same. Or saying Frederick of Prussia was the model for all rulers. Just because I played Schumann when I was nine doesn't mean I want to play just the same pieces over and over. The past is important but not the only thing. Here, it seems to me, you either forget all, or hold on to everything, too much and in the wrong way. Loving your tradition makes you nervous; not you, perhaps, but others. You hold too tight and break.

I could not, did not want to disagree. Giving a form to what I had not previously had words for, and which had always so discontented me the more I had felt at odds with all but a few, Annagreth was right, critical without being judgemental. All the while she spoke, with spirit and feeling, but in a way that suggested she felt as though such thoughts could be shared, delivered in a measured, even temperament. We continued along the path, having slowed as the conversation became more focused. Shortly before four in the afternoon, the air was at its closest, no sign of a breeze, the sound of insects accompanying the, by now, extreme, turbid warmth. Arriving at the garden of the public house, Anna turned to look back towards the lighthouse, the sea. Blue white and gold, her skirt, her blouse, her hair; blue and white and gold, the sky, St Catherine's, the sun. Her head was turned away. I could see nothing of her face. Instead, there was the long, loosely braided hair, its weight creating an incline of the head, or so it seemed; the plait wrapping around the column of her neck, disappearing over her shoulder; hands on hips, elbows back, left foot facing

straight forward, right foot pointing at right angles to the
west. Forming a single line, flight and flex suspended, her
figure gave the lie to the upright too stiff, faintly comical
tower. She appeared as giving as the tower resisting. A slight,
though stolid impression become reproof to the nineteenth-
century solidity desiring to oversee and control nature, Anna
stood taking in the edge of the world, as though she were
undecided as to whether to depart. The air not yet freshening,
the water showed no signs of motion on its surface, calm
and unreflective nether sky. All that was real was here, now,
whatever else there was for that time insignificant. Turning
her head, just, her figure remaining outward facing toward the
ocean, her eyes wrinkled, a smile, that smile, began to form,
and tilting her forehead just a little she said
— We could sail away forever, on a day like this. No?
    What did I hear in this? What did I imagine at the time?
What do I imagine now? Was it just the beauty of the day or
something more? I smiled in return, saying nothing, looking
briefly to the ground, then back again to meet her eyes, her
gaze held steady, steadily on me. How long? Today it seems
either forever or over too quickly. The smile grew larger, her
body turned, and moving toward, past me, in a skip into the
terrace garden with its round metal tables, she said
— We need beer. Warm and flat. You can tell me why it's
good. I'll believe you, but just for today.

~~~

There was that autumn, five years later, a chill, a dark day.
Another photograph. One out of so many I keep in boxes,
ordered by year. Some day, I tell myself from time to time,
I'll do it all differently. By season, by mood, by colour, alone
or with others. This photograph though, taken in woodland.
Almost winter, the cold of the day impatient for the season
it anticipated, leaves drifted into piles. Two weeks without
performing, retreating from everything and everyone simply
because. Not forever, but we had sailed away, greedy for

each other. Ljusterö, an island, to the north of Stockholm, a small wood red white trimmed family house belonging to your mother's family, passed to her. The back of the photograph tells me that this was late October, the light, watery pale, corpse light pallid, confirming this. We had spent the afternoon rowing from one of the outlets to a small islet, then around the shoreline. So quiet the day, so still. Securing the small boat, we walked up into the trees, not speaking, happy to be. *Take my photograph. Buried in the leaves.* You began to gather them in to several piles, I following suit. When you thought there were enough, you lay on the ground. *Cover me. My hair too. Leave just my face.* Working in a counterclockwise movement, *widdershins*, I said, you laughed, foot to waist, to shoulder, around the head, then down the other side, I began to make you disappear into the yellowing, red spotted, dry curling crackling foliage. You had unfurled the neck of your sweater, a large cowl you had pulled over your nose. When I had done, all that was to be seen of you, *make it complete* came the now muffled voice from somewhere out of the ground it seemed, were your eyes, the bridge of your nose, your forehead, the upper part of your cheeks, overly reddened from the bite of the wind. You hold your eyes wide, bright, at once wholly credulous and at the same time knowing all; your eyes are stretched not with surprise, there are no lines on your forehead, but from the most intense of pleasures, taking in the wonder of the world of which you have become a part. It is as if you have just heard the most splendid secret, and are about to share it.

~ ~ ~

We had sat at the Buddle, two hours with the feel of forever, till nearly six, no realisation of time passing. Through Rookley Green by Blackwater Hollow, to Newport, *tea tomorrow*, and northwards, we bisected the Island. Past Parkhurst, it seemed as if neither of us knew quite how to end the evening, so I had asked Annagreth if she had wanted to find supper somewhere.

— We could go to my flat? I'm a little tired, and we could make a salad, perhaps take a walk to the sea after.

— You know, we've seen only half the place, not even that. If you're not doing anything tomorrow how about more sightseeing, getting to know the place?

— I would like that, yes, thank you. And you can tell me how to get to Kate's place for Thursday.

— I could show you.

Extending into evening, minute slipping into hour, the day had moved on unnoticeably to where we were. No awkward pauses, absence of conversation become noticeable in its strain for something to fill the space, we adapted readily to one another's rhythms, accepting, accommodating, as if friendship were long familiar, well worked. Silences, when they came, were part of the arrangement, the orchestration of the day. Heat from gravel greeted us as we emptied the car. The hallway cool, dark after the day, we took the turning staircase, once, twice, around and along. Anna's apartment, first floor corner, one side bow windowed facing toward the sea, a converted family home high ceilinged giving the impression of different ages, the signs all around of domestic ghosts having just departed, or about to return home. Another ghost, that of the day had followed us into the flat. Victorian masonry and plaster, late sixties furnishings, a couch covered with a large Ottoman patterned cotton throw, another throw, cousin to the other, yellows and greens where the sofa covering was browns to darker reds, chairs tweedily defiant, peered teak armed from beneath shawls, scarves draped over lamps to soften light, and hide G-Plan ugliness, and contemporary pastel paintwork, all colluding to intimate an effect that was anachronistically whimsical. At odds with itself and yet Gemütlich.

Signs there were, the sensation received, of a touch, an invisible hand changing space to place. Most impertinent was the orange Wurlitzer, a reproof to Tennyson, to Maud,

in or out of the garden, and everything stuffy. A distended, unround pumpkin, ostentatiously brilliant in what would soon be the last of the sun, it stood there, an exotic musical gourd, promising bursts of sound, runs of notes the juice of an overripe fruit. Cornice, ceiling rose, pediments and overdoors, corbels and panel mouldings, so much busy detail for just three rooms was held at bay, hovering above, by a personal magic, indefinable except in the consequences of execution. Entering, I paused, taking in the detail, first the smaller then the larger, as Anna moved across the main room toward the kitchen. Here and there some photographs in frames, family, a friend or two. Wherever one looked, there was the impression of a quiet, gently urged overthrow, soft insurrection, simple but irresistible occupation. The impersonal and anonymous, standard issue, had been by sleight of hand enchanted, with the merest of touches. Pinkish green light watered to an imperceptible tremor, the ceiling, white cast down reflected light from the still bright but softening evening sun. To the right, windows, the Solent, to the left of the kitchenette, another door, closed; on the left, large folding doors, closed, suggestive of a bed beyond, and the possibility that this had once been a single, large formal room or perhaps a cavernous bedroom. Stepping out of suspended animation, I followed with the basket to the kitchen.

Tidying, washing up, preparing vegetables, then seating ourselves on the floor before open windows, curtains moving slightly, we talked about the following day. The sky turned chalky, anticipating shadings, subtle shifts unnoticed, until the light would be gone. Caught in the between time of days, we spoke of what, of where, of who and when, of why music mattered. Shortly after nine, I asked if Annagreth wanted to take that walk. Assenting, we headed down towards Princes Esplanade.

— What made you choose here, the Island I mean?
— I like islands, in the summer we go north, to Sweden for

holiday. I wanted to live in a small world.

— It's certainly that.

— That sounds as if you want not to be here.

— No, I would never have met James, Kate, Graeme. It just took a while to find what there was to like after growing up in London. It's one thing to have a choice, another to have no say. It's all right; I don't mean anything by that. Anyway. I wouldn't have had today. Wouldn't have met you.

This almost as an aside, an afterthought, regretted for its precipitous display, but made easier in the dark of the night. Again, a buoy, the soft crest of wave, a sound in the distance. Annagreth said nothing; had I overstepped the mark, misread the open friendliness, the relaxed generosity of the day, creating a false confidence? Night came in pressing close, seconds unfolding their reserve of time into a timeless, taut filament. Walking a wire, I found myself no longer certain whether to step forward, back, turn around. I was certain I was about to overbalance. The quiet of the shoreline evening closed and opened insistently, a tell-tale heart. Invisibly, a hand took mine, squeezed, and then, there you were, there was Anna, a voice, your voice, her voice, that voice to which I was already drawn, speaking with a new tone, a softness, somewhere above a whisper, said

— I heard some music back at that hotel; shall we go see? Perhaps they have some German wine.

~~~

Travelling: in clean, well-lighted rooms. I am spending much of this year travelling. You had pointed out to me once the similarity between *travel* and *travail*. Motion involves much work, the burden of movement, of transport, of memory. Moving around, from hotel to hotel, from place to place, the anonymity of one the anticipation of the next, I find myself involved in, enfolded by memory. I am never so much with you as when I am alone. Then, especially when the light is northern, you come to me.

A stranger in another town, and another. At night I read, unable to sleep. Long into the night I read. Stranger still. Or I write to you, sending letters. I place the words, mixing my own with those I steal from a page before me, placing them in an envelope, which, unaddressed, unadorned, secret and silent, I slip into a mailbox. I know. I know. I know you will know where I steal from, just for you, to make you smile, plundering the words of others just for you, making them yours in sending them to you. Sending. To you, for you; always a balance in this. I am always sending. I say I write to you, but, truth be told, I prefer the American idiom: I write you. I'll write you friends say, as if, in writing, someone could be caused to appear, as if writing were a spell, some form of conjuration. So, I write you to bring you here, bring you back. It was always this for us. A secret world of stolen words, gathered up stored against winter storms of separations, distance, being on our own for periods shorter, longer, all interminable. So words: we would take them over, make them into our stories, stories just for us, addressed to us, stories that had been written with us in mind, and printed, published just so that they might one day find us. I write so that this may find you, so that others do not understand. I write you believing that you may be reading this already, listening. Just now. As I listen to your voice, those voices.

At night, in the dark, when the voices won't come, I sometimes believe I feel your hand, as on that night of the day, a first day not a first, but seeming as if. So many days felt like first days, first times, but as if I had always known, that this, you, were where everything began and ended. That first time, for me, not for you, though you said it was a first time for you because it was the first time with me, of seeing those bright yellow mailboxes, in Germany, banana box I called them. Like their Swedish counterparts, bright, brighter, brightest, both illustrated with the silhouette of a post horn, the Swedish box, its horn accented, seeming superior with its crown. Not so in Denmark, Norway, where bolder, more alarmed, more alert, radiant rather than friendly,

post boxes boast a brightness that is red, both with golden post horns. For a while, whenever we chanced to travel you photographed post boxes, mail boxes. Then you started painting them, drawing, sketching, an incessant passion, impatient to find another, repeating, varying, decorating, embellishing. Red alongside yellow, one trip, I found your boxes, surprise presents.

That night, lights in the darkness, Oslo, bitter winter, snow drowning deep, anguish of weeping winds tearing forlorn, abandoned, distressed through doorways opened, or past corners to abuse the eye. I, eyebright, fevered, had wandered off, delirious, made intemperate and reckless by the grip of a temperature, my own personal furnace to keep out the ice hard air. Lost, alone, I walked, you had told me, across Slottsparken. With Judge, you found me near the National Theatre, asking, no, frightening passers-by, with a question why were the mailboxes not yellow? I had demanded. Looking at me, blonde on black, your collar pulled up around your ears, your eyes tear bright, ice crystal droplets lash by lid, your hand stretched forward, your voice a whisper, softer, breaking, then louder, a sniff, a sob, cracked laughter, *you fool.*

6. Third Act: Graeme (Winter 1975)

— I had a goldfish when I was a nipper. I won it at a fair, called him George cause he looked like my dad. He was never a happy fish. He had a chip on his shoulder.

Trite but true, drummers are not the same as other people. Take that opening sally as evidence for the prosecution. Hearing this for the first time, I was struck by the thought that such a line, intended to advance communication between the sexes, would fall dead the moment it tried to stand up on its own. It was only on having heard it for what must have been well over the hundredth time that I realised I was wrong. I knew just two women for whom this opening gambit would give up the ghost before it ever took a breath. But then, with drummers, everything is different: between two worlds they exist, appearing to be at home in neither, quite. In the presence of someone whose stock in trade is making continuous rhythmic noise, as the dictionary has it, the compass goes awry, spins madly looking for its lodestone. Drummers, percussionists, people for whom sticks and skins are vital expressions of the soul, do not come to fruition after careful ripening, long dry summers causing them to swell, grow, ready for harvesting. They grow in dark places when no one is ever fully alert, when winterlight is sharpest, the days shortest, the hydroptic earth gathered into itself, when children and old people are sleeping. Not yet midwinter spring, the world sempiternal then, this is the time for those who beat time, keep time, a time for those who make others move in time with them. Theirs is an internal clock, the springs of which have long ago been sold, or bartered for the essentials of their trade. Of all musicians the only tribe to take their name from some word originally onomatapaeic, drummers belong to, occasionally emerging from out of a place of folklore, where mothers tell their children not to look the strange creatures in the eye, where the touch of a drummer's brush is said to cause earthquakes, tidal waves, the birth of hunchbacks. Every time a drummer is encountered, it is the experience of first contact, all over again.

With a drummer one is in the world of Faerie, confronted with someone the goblins left behind in the dark in exchange for food. Take those instances in a tune where, all other parts locked into a whole, drumming assumes cross rhythms, polyrhythms. Two or more rhythms appear simultaneously. The call of the tide, the pull of the moon, and with this vertical or horizontal hemiola, different cycles three beats over two, and one is lost, taken up, following not the piper but this beating, hitting thing. A pipe merely calls, and one follows. The drum man gets inside the listener, into the blood virally. Cross beats, the magic inside, consumes the listener, infiltrates her, cutting across and raising her pulse. Everyone has to follow. Still grounded in the four, the three, the six, the eight, a drummer will tug at the very fabric of everyone's life, their emotions. To feel the drumming is to feel existence itself, its many threads, weft and warp. Without the drummer, there is no relationship, and this is the vassalage by which rhythm keeps us all in thrall. I'd heard it said that many sub-Saharan languages have no word for rhythm, music. I would not be surprised to find this to be true. While we have forgotten, lost sight of, tuned out to this, and while no words will do for giving voice to what music is, what it does, how it touches, drummers come from their other worlds to get inside us, causing us to remember. I told Graeme once about there not being words for rhythm. Bugger came the reply; I think, just this once, I really knew what he meant.

Every beat bang brush blow strike tap rap slap thud thrum
parataraflamdragdiddle tattoo was a shard of otherworldly
laughter smithereened, sent scattering, piercing the heart its
interrupted pattern echoed, holding in the moment all the
parts together.

Once, upon another time, another winter, holly and ivy
hung and sung, the village, its foetal curve hugging hard the
dark shore in the grip of night, asleep, aslant the bay, all the
little folk dreaming of crackling paper, silken ribbon, silver
green gold and red, the colours of the season, one more
late night, though not one of those that inevitably follow a
show, we, you and I, had made up a fire. Do you recall? You
must. Ashen faggot alight, Yule log, God Jul, candle wreaths
for St Lucia flickering, goats in the tree, the windows bolted
and barred, doors locked against misfortune or visit by the
Hooden Horse, wreaths hung propitiating pagan deities. Cold
from walking the village, going the rounds and wassailing
with friends, we were much in need of warmth. Sitting before
the fire, its only light illuminating a gradual succession of
wine bottles, sharing the seasonal rice pudding, you had, you
told me, put in two almonds, so that we each might find one,
I sung a few traditional songs in-keeping with the time of
the year, concluding not with a seasonal tune, but with two
songs recently acquired, 'Hog-Eye Man' and 'Poor Horse'.
A pause, another glass poured, a seasonal, a loving cup, you
began one of those unravelling reflections on words, the
names for things, their many meanings and the opportunity
for play this occasioned. Wine warmed, your voice softened
tipsy-terpsichorial, the ghosts of your mother father tongues
announcing themselves a little more roundedly, your accent
a little more pronounced, enunciated, you said, holding up a
forefinger to bring me to attention, requesting that everything
be put on hold
— *Schlagzeug*: drums, but also hitting things, really, you know,
Schlag, to hit, *Zeug*, no not *Zug*, not train, not draught or puff,
not trait, not traction, not strain, strain train, *not* train, not *Zug*
Zug, *Zugzugzug*, no, *nein*; *Zeug*, Ztsssoiiiiiiggg,

your voice rising higher, that child's delight in discovering
a new sound, new word, nose wrinkling, eyes screwed
tight, not wanting to see the surprise anticipated. Laughing
uncontrollably, I spill my wine, red on white, the stain turning
purple darkly pink; moving unsteadily to the kitchen, bringing
back salt, our laughter mingling, as settling myself down,
reclining cushion on cushion, I start salt sprinkling over the
stain, asking you to rub the salt to stop the stain from setting;
then wide bright awake, lids, lashes parted, blue reflecting
flicker of flame, very serious, you continue
— *zeug*: thing, things, stuff to hit. But *Schlag* is also whipped
cream, Austrian German you know, no you don't; now you
do. Let's hit the whipped cream. He plays on the whipped
cream thing, watch him really whip that cream. *Klasse*.

Yes, yes. Klasse. Judge went to town with this, had a field
day, roving far and wide. He milked it for all it was worth. Of
his many puns, jokes, windups, witticisms, quips, innuendos,
James, you, Anna, said, er schöpft den Rahm. And so it was,
with Graeme: Rahmtrommler, the stick man, Jultomten, you
had called him, always seen as much through others' lenses,
as he revealed himself, presenting himself, a gift to us all,
appearing anew before I, you, Annagreth, Kate, saw him.
Graeme was always more than himself, you needed to see him
through the eyes of everyone at once, if this could have been
possible.

Another winter's evening: St Dwynwen's Day, two weeks
past Twelfth Night. Pitching up, veering into view in winter
when, early in the year, hoarfrost across the hedges, hill, the
fences and creeping even up the windows, forming paper
doily patterns etching onto glass. The traceries of death's
playful finger, a sigil for those who cared to read. No animals
were moving that night. The world was sunk; all inanimate,
the throb, the pulse submerged, withdrawn and barely
marking the waiting hours. James first introduced Kate and I
to the subject, the idea, the gargantuan enormity of spirit that
was Graeme, the introduction coming with the information,
the door fast shut behind him, breathlessly from the rapid

climb, adjusting from cold to warm in Kate's loft above the
barn, that this drummer was actually good, and appeared
mostly house trained. Mostly.
— You should see his collection of mallets; he enjoys hitting
things.
— What about people?
— Kettle's on.
Kate, interrupting, handed round a plate of her father's
special muffins.
— I don't think so. He did tell me though that he once had
to stop a cow from attempting to kick his dad, with only his
bare hands.
I thought it best to let this conversational road sign
continue to point without following it. A winter already
wearied from a fruitless search for the right percussionist,
there was little point to risk moving beyond a place of no
return. Kate, returning with a tray, said decisively
— Well then, get him over. If you haven't…
— I have, I did. This Monday.
Stunned livestock and stupefied guitar players aside,
Graeme, it turned out, was, for a drummer, just normal
enough. Normal for Newport, we all used to say. Lock the
car doors, it's getting dark. Though Kate, James and I had
met several in the past few weeks, drummers that is, not the
inhabitants of Newport, on cold nights, about which more
than one of us thought hypothermia a more appropriate
alternative to some of the candidates, to say that we had
felt we couldn't work with any of them would be to gild
a euphemistic lily, in a polite sidestep away from deciding
outright that drummers were, collectively and individually,
barking, usually up a tree they had just marked decisively as
their own—and in which, as Kate was quick to point out,
they probably lived, coming down on occasion to forage,
gather more sticks, and frighten the rest of us. One particular
night in the barn, shortly before James's return from some
drink driven percussive twilight zone, shortly before the
revelation of Graeme, we had the feeling that this might

never work when, faced with a really quite special example of day-release culture, Judge said quietly

— Your turn to tell this one. Put him out of our misery. I am just going outside and may be gone some time.

It was just four nights after that the silent unseen magic working beneath the topsoil of our lives made sure of its first tentative grasp of us, pulling us into a different course for which the co-ordinates had seemed impossibly hidden. James had met Graeme on that winter's evening, when deciding that a single-handed navigation of the pubs from Ryde to Cowes was important research. The psychogeography of the inebriated swerve was a speciality of James'. That the day was St Wulfstan's, both old and new Twelfth Nights now passed, but not yet St Agnes' Eve, may have been obscurely significant. How could anyone have known? Perhaps the fact that Led Zeppelin were often finishing shows on their US tour that winter with 'Black Dog' may have been an occult catalyst, the runes being cast, the order decided, destiny arranged. James was reading The Winged Bull at this time, suggesting as a result that we call ourselves The Golden Dawn. All that can be said is that, with James, there were what might best be called points of crisis, and this may well have been one such, into which he had found himself precipitately upended, by one too many barking skin beaters. Reaching Cowes, James, we were later to learn, settled blearily to watching, as through a whisky glass somewhat darkly, a dog with a beard—as he described it—in a horizontally striped rugby shirt, performing in a country and bluegrass band, comprising chiefly what appeared to be refugees from a care home for weekend cowboys, complete with fringed jackets and Stetsons. Single malt notwithstanding, James could appreciate the skill, the dexterity, the technical ability, the finesse this bearded dog was displaying.

Doghead: James's word to Kate and I; this was not a metaphor, insult, poetic figure. Neither was it a vision from a bottle, whisky eyes attuned to some parallel universe, where the true essence of a person would be unveiled, depending on the proof. Nor was Graeme a rare example of cynocephalus. Neither Egyptian Anubis nor Eastern Orthodox St Christopher. No, the night James first saw Graeme, the drummer as cynomorphic manifestation was only the result of Graeme wearing a rubber dog mask. The one photograph that survives attests to its being a boxer. What really sold James on the dog-head drummer though was the xylophone. The rest of the band took a break, at which point the dog—with the beard—played a xylophone version of a Willie Nelson song. Clearly, we were, once more, being sucked back, in through the out door, through a looking glass, the other side of the mirror, to the land of BST, on which the Island ran out of kilter with its larger sister, the North Island, visible from its northern shore. There were, it was said, times when the island moved, and no one saw fit to tell anyone not there. Like a drunk after a particularly strenuous and committed evening perfecting his art, it would wake up the following morning a little blurred but knowing where it was. This was something on which we relied, and James's eyewitness account not to be doubted, alcohol giving him a sharper, if more absurd focus, Graeme was clearly both the quintessence of place, a rural genius loci, neither the Green Man nor John Barleycorn, but the spirit of Rough Music constrained; he was also just the person to give us what James called an engine room, a figure of speech Kate was later to augment, calling Judge for a while Stoker Wroath.

That Monday then, just two days following the twilight tale, Graeme turned up at the barn. He had, he explained, just brought with him a basic kit. Helping him inside, collecting things from the back of a Morris Traveller
— Mind the paintwork, my Mum's car; she loves it, calls it Hugo cause it's the same shape as my uncle's head, she says.
— Hugo?
— Yes. Why?

— Oh, no reason.

James' reaction, a look of recognition accompanying the passing question, was unexpected, the one belying the other, but I let it pass at the time, only to find out later that this was the name of a character in The Winged Bull. The stars were lining up, the mystical forces at work. Kate must have sensed something however, for, in a broad Mummerset accent, one eye squinting, the other overwide, she observed, with a heavy melodramatic emphasis, and dragging a foot.

— 'Tis them island spirits still a-following us.

— Aye, a black tailed godwit.

I replied, with equal ham, cut from nearest the bone, acknowledging a line frequently used by her from a favourite children's book. Getting kit, bags and all else inside the barn as rapidly as possible, it being an eager, and a biting air, a time when spirits walked abroad, we went about our usual rituals as Graeme unpacked. Heaters turned on, as were amplifiers, a general purposeful motion was underway, preparatory to the main event of the evening. Set up, in place, tea brewed, and having got tolerably warm, we began, a song cross-rhythmed I had wanted to play since first buying the single from W. H. Smith's at the age of eleven. A tune, a blues, which featured silences as taut as a garrotte or piano wire, which shifted in its two parts from barely containable electric frenetic collective interplay, to acoustic guitar, recorder, cello and piano, had everything, did everything I, and as I found out, Kate and James thought music should do, should be, and was the musical crucible for any drummer. Guitar first. Alone. Repeat with violin, then again bass, the vocal introduction a capella, then back to a helter-skelter onslaught, barely containable.

— Just a minute. Bugger. Sorry about this.

A stool adjustment, a snare tightened. Again, we started. And again. One more time. Once more. Yet before we had managed even a basic run through, Graeme made himself indispensible. He had found his stall, his berth. We knew this, when, in response to James, asking somewhat impatiently, after a fourth false start to the tune, why he kept worrying at

his drum stool and if he was ever going to be ready, the reply came
— Don't you worry bugger, as long as you got a face, I'll always have a place to sit.

He was in. Graeme had passed the test. Kate had started snorting. James's look of surprise collapsed into laughter. Forearm on the amp, my forehead resting on it, I too could barely keep it together. We had a new toy and batteries were not required.

How to describe Graeme, though? There are so many tales that offer a view, a facet, all admittedly either vaguely comic or scurrilous, or suggestive of something irrational. As the other half of the rhythm section, seen from this perspective in our more conventional moments, the rear end to a pantomime horse for which Judge was the bare naked front and head, Graeme was not so much a percussive, explosive Scylla to James's whirlpool bass beat, subsonic Charybdis pulling into his whirling eddying pulses everything around him. No, Graeme was more Cilla Black: bright, loud, brash, brazenly unashamedly irrepressible, always there, an eye with a gleam, the jester's sense of the inappropriate, a wild child, force of nature, lord of misrule, farmboy, car mechanic, and impossibly attractive it seemed, against all logic. Girls can't resist my charms, nipper. Kate, on hearing the fishing line for the first time, glass to mouth, sprayed beer head inadvertently, unstoppably, foam mushrooming from her nose. Asked that night of wine and salt, Anna claimed her grasp of English jokes was not good and so, had Graeme deployed the one weapon in his amorous armoury, that full on, full frontal, full court press armourious engagement, tongue in cheek, cheek by jowl, dog eager, it would have missed her. I doubted this. Her sense of the English tongue was as nuanced as the flight of her fingers, fleeting over keys. But on reflection, it must have been that Graeme either had not had the opportunity or had, uncharacteristically for him, refrained, held back, for once his approach was as subtle as his percussive abilities. All Annagreth had ever said, in conversation one evening with Kate, referring to Graeme's charms was he is sweet; but no, no.

Single phrases, definitions, these do not work in trying to sum up Graeme. He escapes definition, even as I see him, a figure of excesses, barely under control, always seeming to escape some part of his clothing, part jolly green giant, green man, and another, regardless of actual size, an incredible, bearded hulk. His was always a mercurial motion, even from the still point of a drum stool, motion within stasis, mutability visible. Photographs cause Graeme to appear a strange, pagan deity, many armed, mostly a blur, adrenalin fuelled St Bernard, a birds' nest beard mostly, as though he had inherited a Victorian chin we had only once viewed Graeme jaw naked, denuded for charity. Somewhere a novelist is missing his whiskers. To talk about Graeme would be, then, to act as the prompt for an endless parade of music hall performances, recovered footage from an archive secreted in a half-life archive, every image a prompt, every recollection a punch line: Oi tell 'ee wot, nipper, 'ee alus 'ad a pistol in the car; and a axe for personal protection— sounds a bit over the top, most folk just use deodorant. The incredible line of tales for the incredulous serve best in making Graeme step forward in the mind. To offer a typical, well typical for Graeme, example: he decided, having after a period committed to finding all the reasons for and against, to become a vegetarian. Due to a dislike of most vegetables that were not potatoes however,

— Some of his best friends, rhizomes and root vegetables; I think he has a shrine somewhere.

...he spent six months eating baked beans; and sleeping in the back of his transit whenever we had a trip requiring that we stayed away from home. Wary of complex cuisine, especially whatever he failed to be able to pronounce at a single take,

— What my mum'd call foreign muck

...though gratefully surprised by Annagreth's cooking, Graeme had a sense of the world, his world largely

unchangeable, immovable, but always to be relied on.
There were his certainties. Then there was everything else.
Everything of adventure, the unknown, strange encounters
was either to be found through all things percussive or
women, whose chief attractions were usually that they were
at a gig, not far from the bar, and, preferably, on vacation. A
girlfriend is for life, not just for Christmas, Kate had once
told Graeme, to which Graeme responded by saying that his
dad's favourite song was by Elvis, 'Why Can't Everyday be
Like Christmas', a sentiment he had taken to heart. If our
drumming dervish could be summed up, it would require
an approach reliant for the force of its truth on comparison
with human beings, Graeme always for me coming to
mind as belonging to us, indelibly an extension, admittedly
perplexingly distorted, of who we thought we were, and who
we believed ourselves to be. James could scare you, his smile a
clown's rictus presaging mayhem; Kate could make you cross
your legs anxiously, if a man, her feelings having been made
known to your detriment; Graeme, well Graeme just made
you laugh, raise an eyebrow, or simply throw your hands up in
surrender.

~~~

— Rog, pass us that roll of Gaffer tape.
   Morphy, packing, tidying, checking leads, a few repairs,
mostly small, a pause between tunes.
— *Why* Roger, Rog? *Who* is Roger?
   What is she came back from Judge and Kate, as Anna asked
once more, one long Sunday afternoon, during a rehearsal,
the second or third after Anna had joined us. I had spent,
now several weeks displaying footwork that impressed even
me. My defences were beginning to weaken, however.
— Let's just say…well, he's an overeager and none too subtle
philogynist. Bit like Damian's Sheltie, but less discerning.
— Phil *what?* This makes no sense.

I swerved, playing outside the line, when I should have gone for the leave. I could hear the bails coming off.

— My name's not Phil; and stop calling me Roger. And I'm nothing like that mad midget Lassie. With your hair I'd be careful what you say.

Not usually sensitive, there was in Graeme's voice, a more than usual hint of embarrassment before Anna, when normally, the response, if any came, was habitually bugger off, bugger, rapidly followed by a grin. A grin, gurning that would make you groan. While everyone else smiled, Graeme grinned, beamed, smirked, a deliberate imitation of Animal, which, wonders of physiognomy, also resulted on occasion, lips pursed, pushed out and up towards a nose, moustache an untrimmed hedge separating hollow from hillock, into a rubbery demented approximation of Ringo Starr, especially when Graeme had on sunglasses. No one was to mention Ringo,

— Bugger can't drum; and I don't look like him

…but within our circle this was at least grudgingly tolerated, most of the time, don't make a bloody habit of it having become reluctant acceptance once it had submerged below the general consciousness to become a reflex reaction. Beyond our circle, any reference of the kind served as the line over which none should pass. One night however, Ringo, had come, hysterically loud, drunk, beer laughter eruptions, from the front of a crowd, a Mohicaned scarecrow looking as if the local cemetery had recently given up its dead, out for the evening and in this particular club only out of a lack of imagination as to where else to go, egged on by friends who unmistakenly had left the one communal brain cell at home, in safe keeping with someone's pet ferret. Faster than Tyrone Power in Jesse James, more accurate than Alan Ladd in The Iron Mistress, Graeme drew a mallet from his stick pouch, sending it spinning to find, impressive in the precision and force of its delivery, its target on the moronic forehead. Laughter, applause, Tosser, then retreat, as Graeme stood, took a bow, collected sticks and proceeded with the count-in.

— My name's not Phil; and stop calling me Roger.
— No, but you're always ready with a fill, aren't you matey.
— C'mere, let me shine your head.
— Time for tea, said Zebedee.

Kate, indicating a break was needed, was met, much surprise to us all, with the theme to The Magic Roundabout from Anna, at the Hammond. I picked up the melody, then Judge a bass line, Kate accordion oom-pah offbeats, Bob Marley meeting the Polka, and Graeme, with a bizarre overbusy shuffle syncopation. From that day, this was to become something of a feature, either to begin an encore, or introducing a second set as, one by one, we would all return to the stage. Anna first, after cheering, clapping and the usual shouts and cries had subsided, a quiet settling on the audience, like school children on a rainy afternoon, anticipating story time, are you sitting comfortably? Then I'll begin, to be followed by something serious, earnest, let us pray, perhaps Bach, or a hymn, The Day Thou Gavest, Lord, Hath Ended, before that dissolved, resolving itself into that theme,

— No, we're not calling ourselves either *The Magic Roundabout*, or *Le Manège enchanté*.
— *Das Zauberkarussell.*

...and from there into whatever took everyone over the top.

— *Oh, Benedict*, why Roger?

The voice had deepened, inexorably. A harder resonance, jaw coming forward to emphasise the inescapability of the demand. No escape, no way out, no exit.

— Tea...

The kettle's on, the sun...Kate began to sing, angelic falsetto, a song I loved. From James,

— Roger, wilco and out; whatever you do, Ben, don't forget the sources.
— Roger, milady's muff.
— Bugger off. Bugger.

~~~

Driving back from a show the first of a two night residency, a spring night of poise, finesse, subtlety, not force and battery, sounds to sooth, not to inflame, a rarer night, of cello, trumpet, viola, percussion rather than drums, turned down, acoustic, a stupid word for a false distinction, all music being essentially acoustic; driving then, through country lanes, pitch black, lacking signs of municipal civilisation, overspreading hedges, shades of grey not much lighter than the tarmac in the headlights, closed around us as we moved curving, riding the camber towards Kate's home. Dropping away to our right, across the gentle decline, the sea, moonglow refracting, a clear night sky, star heavy, albedo tinted. Orange before dark blue, Variant and Transit, faces over the dash of the van could be seen in the rear view mirror greenly illuminated. Silent night nearly enough, Annagreth driving, no radio, Kate in the back seat, stretched across. Anna checked behind, eyes to mirror then once more eyes front.

— What are they doing?

Anna checking the mirror, once more, slowing slightly. And again the look, brow wrinkling. I turned to see Kate already looking over her shoulder, the van slowing, not stopping, but dropping behind. Left to right, Graeme, driving, looking in the radioactive dusk of dashboard lights for all the world like a phosphorous gnome grown large in the fallout of the glow; Morphy, no more than the underside of chin, neck exposed, stretched, nostrils twin black holes just visible, his head just having gone back; and James, Judge, just then leaning forward, nothing but the crown of his head, spectral green, ectoplasm green, skull skin tight, a rounded drum, bald drum.

— It's nothing.

We continued, accelerating, settling back once more, returning to our shared quiet. Another half an hour to the barn. Up a gradient, the road ahead curving once more,

more sharply this time. Little on the road, this time of night, perhaps another car, one in the opposite direction, then little else. Always the odd pedestrian, walking from, walking to, walking the long miles home, leaving wherever, for wherever, too late for public transport. Watch for them in the lights, walkers or, this time of year, rabbits, particularly the young, kits, a fox now and again, skittish halt, reversal and then darting, rarely a hare, a leveret. After an evening, I preferred the peace of Waltraud to the always feverish atmosphere in the van. A retreat, not a playpen, the possibility of finding seclusion even when there was conversation, the Variant allowing for realisation, reflection, shade after the evening's glare. Waltraud offered a passage back to a carefully tended sense of order, an unimposing place, a means of becoming more oneself apart, by becoming invisible. The minutes rolled on, with the road. Taking the bend at its sharpest point, I noticed across a field, less than a quarter of a mile probably, the outline of a house, drawing attention to itself for a light in an upstairs window, gleaming, earthbound lantern, in contrast to more distant pinheads of illumination punctuating the placid sky. Caught up in my thoughts of nothing much, I began to notice the car slowing, much more emphatically. Pulling to the side of the road as soon as it had straightened some, Anna's voice broke the silence, as that house light had interrupted the dark.

— They're not back there.

Waiting a few minutes, the engine idling, filling the night dully with its pulse, we sat. Nothing appeared.

— Someone must have needed to pee. Judge is always drinking too much.

Kate's unconcern sought to rationalize the inexplicable, holding at bay any more dramatic imagination. Engine off, windows down, cool air a gentle inrush, water filling slowly a tank. Ten minutes passing with no headlights, no signs of life other than an owl heard ahead, away, from a dimly discernible copse, stage omen right on time, on cue. A third cry, and

Anna restarted the engine, turning the car, and heading back to look for the others.

A mile and a half back, the Transit sat on the side of the road, off kilter, raked somewhat comically, one wheel, driver's side rear down in the small ditch, hardly a ditch at all, off the edge of the road. Finding a place to pull over, we noticed first Judge's legs, extending from the passenger door, pushed back. Getting out of the car, approaching we saw then his right hand rubbing vigorously his forehead, hooting, bursting with laughter, cracking up, sounds alternatively, uncontrollably bass and treble, falsetto, large exhalations of air, a donkey in distress. Graeme invisible, but also laughing, wheezing, birth giving bellows, Morphy also.

— What happened?

— My head. Hit. Dashboard.

A red bruise stripe was developing across the forehead. The white deposit around the nose, cliff face crumbling, hinted at the sequence of events. Powder. Dashboard. Nose. Thus far, but what then had taken place was as yet unclear. Around the driver's side, a drummer was hanging out of the door, diagonally inclined. A sound engineer was, by turns, hauling, pulling, falling over, laughing, on hands and knees then upright again, trying, unsuccessfully because also off his head, high, hovering. Graeme appeared to our view, the centre of attention, a ritual hog, upended for slaughter, a feast in the making, stomach exposed as if for the knife, appeasing the heavens above by offering itself up for some strange ritual appropriate to the season. Bizarrely, his feet were tangled in the steering wheel. No one in the history of mantraps had ever conceived so surreal an ambush for the unsuspecting. Snared the drummer, stupefied the cellist, stoned the soundman. All three unsound, in states and stages of disarray, they presented a symbol of nocturnal disorder and misrule, the endgame of a pagan tradition, the origins long forgotten, but practiced with a vigour nonetheless. Somehow the night had grown larger, unfolding itself more primitive, a past unheard of seeming ready to consume the present, swallow it whole.

— What the bloody hell happened?

— Boys, boys. Graeme, *Du bist mir ja Einer, Du bist schon was!*

Kate, impatient, her question delivered with no expectation of a response just then; Anna, maternally tolerant, mocking, ironically indulgent. Both, expecting no less, getting exactly what they could anticipate, though the precise manner of the delivery was always a surprise, looked at each other, then to me, and back toward the bucolic bacchanal. Knowing no answer could come just yet, we disentangled Graeme, folded Morphy and Judge back into the van, Kate assuming the driver's seat. As the night began to turn to early morning grey, we finally heard the entire sequence of events, just one more of Graeme's tales from the Transit. Driving behind us, Graeme had realised that he had left his watch behind. A conversation, quick-witted if obvious repartee, then laughter, not so much kick-started as ignited, Graeme finding everything impossibly funny. His laugh was infectious, disabling, virulent in its insinuating ability to get through your defences. Weakened, unable to resist, you succumbed to terminal hilarity. Morphy thought more stimulants were necessary, demanding that James pass him the tea tray. This returned, Judge could not wait, and began to use the Transit's console, with some success. The collective body oddly uncontrolled, all mirth, merriment, impossibly gleeful, euphoric, as the van began to be transformed into a bell jar, all oxygen being sucked out of it. At which point, hands inexplicably off the wheel, a pothole was found. The van, veering vehicle wildly wheeling, then back under control, pulling to a stop, Graeme no longer able to drive, such was his hilarity having been entertained by the sight, and more impressively the sound, of James's forehead coming into sharp, percussive contact with the dashboard. Halted, engine off, the jocularity continued, as James, then Graeme opened their doors. Overbalancing, how exactly was a mystery, Graeme then fell sideways, toward, into and out the door well, his feet heavenward, and trapped by the wheel, as rapidly as his head and torso fell to earth, like Faustus head over heels, tripping towards Hell, aided by the invisible angels and devils that drove him. But what, Kate insisted, did you say? You haven't told us. James found the energy, the dawn chorus providing a backing, to repeat the conversation.

— I left it on my traps. On the snare.

— So? It's not going anywhere.

— It's new. I'm going back.

— Don't be daft, it'll be fine. It'll probably get a gig, anyway.

— Eh?

— Well, it keeps better time than you do.

~~~

Forward, back, always a question of time, of keeping time, marking time, speeding and slowing, timing being everything. Once more from the top, in order to find the chorus, take it to the bridge. State the themes, emphasize the motifs, this time with a different accent, a further variation, intonation. There you were. And there we are. Another Saturday night, poised, balanced, between pasts and futures, variations. Summer. Late July. Night. Eighteen months after meeting Graeme, after Roger, as we came to call him, as he came to be called, but never Ringo, no not that, after Graeme had been born, untimely, out of season, stepping fully formed, larger than life into the little world, expanding to accommodate him. Eighteen months, give or take; and there you, we, were, are, here, there.

At a distance, the far end of the bar, not that far, seen between heads and shoulders, short silk dress, hair lose but for two braids, conjoined twins resting at the nape, just visible through a crowd of cheerful, beery, sunkissed faces. Full to overflowing the bar, leather by cotton, the air viscous, beer scented; sails furled, masts across the harbour, glass on glass, small chimes, within, bottle and tankard, table clearing in imitation of chance arrhythmic sounds drifting in from the bay.

— The next one's a slower number, 'Little Wing'. Smoochy time…

— Yuuuuuuh.

— it's particularly heart-rendering…anyone you want to dedicate this to?

— I didn't know we were doing 'Leila' tonight.

— Yuuuuup.

— Judge won't be at any rate.

Graeme. So I begin, bearded laughter from behind.

But this is Graeme's time, I have to keep in step with him. With Graeme, events could always take such a turn, that to understand them fully, to see everything as completely as possible, you had to be there. If you couldn't be, it was important to find the most reliable witness, in order to hear the whole truth, so seeing for yourself as clearly as you could, using what you knew of Graeme as co-ordinates for an otherwise inexplicable detour, footpath, route map. Back on that Christmas evening, the night of wine, cream and rice pudding, Annagreth told me how things had unfolded after the first set.

The set over, I taking evasive action by doing nothing, Graeme had, with Judge, made his way through appreciative faces, words of approval, hands slapping on sweating backs, to where Anna had found a bar stool. I owe you a drink, I'd promised if you came down, and I never go back on my word, if I can help it. This was not the story of George. If George had not been introduced in the first sentence or two, and there could be variations, then the fish would not make his cameo appearance as the opening act to his owner's solo performance. Why, in talking to Anna that evening, he had omitted the tale of George, is beyond understanding. Graeme was at once absolutely transparent and yet a tightly tied knot, impervious to loosening, without a chink through which light might shine. Whatever he was inside, everything about Graeme was there, on the surface. You had to be there. It was, I think, that Graeme had an innate ability to grasp situations in which he would appear absurd. Though his was a world of alternative imaginings, a place in which he existed according to laws that none could fathom, when viewed from the outside, his sense of his own absurdity and when to play the clown was as finely tuned as any well tempered keyboard, as delicately constructed as the most delicate, ornately finished chronometer. If characters like Graeme step out on occasion through the looking glass to our side of reality from the Land of Faerie, it is to charm and entertain, to give us all often much needed comic relief, so that happiness might be found as a brief point of light in our otherwise unremittingly dull, muddied dramas weighed down by the rhythm of minor tragedies. On their side, from which perspective we can never see, disallowed any view or vantage, having no conception of what in truth lies beyond, people like Graeme might easily be heroes, the stuff of myth or legend. Graeme was, unquestionably, non-reflective, beyond the fixed point of any mirror image in which you thought you saw yourself or your world. Graeme was integral to the perception of reality that Kate, Judge and I had. He had the knack of seeing to it that we fully understood our relationships to, our dependencies on one another. So when, Anna, you told me of that conversation, and in particular its opening, I knew, by the time of our winter's tale telling by the fire, of all that, which in retrospect, was implied, implicated in your talk with Graeme.

Buying Annagreth a gin and tonic,

— Angie, can you put it on my tab; I'll settle after the gig.

…Graeme continued, polite and deferential. Where I would have been evasive, either saying too much or not enough, anxious over saying the wrong thing, and so coming across as diffident, having as a tendency, a little too much liking for my own carefully considered posture, Graeme simply, brilliantly, didn't care. He could set things in motion, make their onward movement irreversible. We're not bad are we? I've been with this lot for over a year, and it's the first time I've got to use all my kit. Did you like us more this afternoon or this evening? We do lots of different music, always get a good crowd. I bet he didn't know what to say, gesturing toward me, when he met you. It's a wonder he talked to you, thanks Ang, here's your drink. Cheers. Graeme had directed traffic, leading in the direction of the stage area. He doesn't always talk about trees, you know, he does that when he doesn't know what to say. Silly bugger, sorry. Judge, mate, can I get you a drink in, this is Annagreth, she was talking with Ben this afternoon at the school, Leila, the usual for Slappy, and get us a half of Sand Rock and a brandy and all; one for yourself, lover. Can I ask you a favour? This was said, Anna remembered, with a look and a wink at James; realising he was caught in the act, Graeme tried to cover it by wiping his eye, explaining that, what with the heat he was more than usually sweaty. Look at that, he gestured towards James's head, the wig now removed, looks like someone polished an anaemic bowling ball. Anna reminded Graeme that he'd asked for a favour. Yes, look, you wouldn't mind taking his drinks over, you can manage those and yours, can't you? the beer'll be getting warm, and he'll be faffing over there till we start again otherwise; I've got to pop out to the bus; bugger, come give us a hand. Very nice to see you again, see you again soon, you're always welcome.

~~~

Graeme. Roger. Graeme. *Rahmtrommler*, the stick man, *Jultomten*. That Christmas night, as I slipped in and out of sleep, you told me the German folktale of *Knecht Ruprecht*, Farmhand Rupert, a strange figure, wild foundling and companion of St Nicholas, who, accompanied by fairies, walked abroad bearing a long stick, sometimes several bound together, whose clothing had bells stitched to it, so that he was said to make rhythmic noises. Though some thought him the Devil, he was first written down as part of Christmas processions, and was often thought a benevolent house sprite. All the things most people think about drummers, think they know that is, are really just a collection of urban myths, easy, obvious, clichéd. The truth about those who hit things is stranger than any mere gossip grown through idle groundswell. Graeme. Santa's helper, the last of the feral men.

7. Interlude: A Second Day, the Barn (July 1976)

Being here, this is everything you once said to me, *it is all there is. We are all needed for a time, in a certain place, by others, and we are needed all the more because, even as we are here, we are fading away, diminishing, we disappear a little each day. We don't often think of this. We couldn't bear it, our ending, the end of everything. When, if we do, why it is a bright lamp one moment, and shattering into darkness the next; we live without the thought. So we pretend immortality. We play at it, in what we do. We find flowers beautiful, the landscape overwhelming, not because these are in full bloom but because we realise that bloom does not last. We see, how would it be, we know, without seeing this, that the end is in what is most wonderful and alive.* Pausing, seeking consolation in the thought you could not hold back, as if to give voice to what I knew to be true, but could not speak, you continued. *We only have one response to our anguish that we barely acknowledge. In love. But we look for things that are like this. In music, in art. Love is where we are most in life but closest to the end, closest but also on the outside looking in. We have to keep getting close to the window. We press our faces against it, looking hungry inside for a sign of something that is nothing at all. Love keeps us all at the other edge. Words don't do for this. It's like when you look into my eyes or when I look into yours. Sometimes it is unbearable and we look away. Not for what we feel but because we see too much. There is the end at the heart of feeling. Love is what we do when we are, what did you call it, ghost ridden, yes, when we find we are haunted by this nothing that is all the time there. Every one of us,* you insisted, *everyone, only here the one*

*time, just once, no more. We will never have a better time to be here, we
will never find a better time. This, this,* einmal, *this once, is the time;
we are here, and we cannot not be here, we cannot take this* once *back.*
I had not understood this last remark until you explained to
me that, *we cannot have more than the* once, *we cannot exchange it for
another once, this is all, and we have to make everything of it.*

~~~

Climbing, rising, descending, not falling, both directions at
once. Small resolutions. Then, off once more, patterns tightly
precise, ordered, organized within their self-contained shapes
and having an inevitability of completion in their openings,
from the start, and in every phrase. Yet tending towards,
opening out onto, promising the infinite. The infinite finite,
Kate called it: one within the other, a Moebius loop of
rhythm and harmony. *Listen!* Your face excitedly, you had
stopped to play the phrase again. *Listen. Marbles tumbling in
space, water cascading on the keys, light on water.* That so familiar
tune from the *Praeludium*, followed by the German tune,
called *Allemande*, once dance after another, *Courante, Sarabande,*
a *Menuet*, no, two, and the final *Gigue*. Names impossible for
such beauty, such *galanteries*, such…there is no word, no way
to say, so names will have to do. Here is shorthand for what
we feel and cannot speak. Here are the words when we speak
in the place of a feeling at once overwhelming, sublime, and
yet having no translation from sound to word.

Now? This moment as I sit here. Listening to the ghost of
your fingers playing over the keys, hammers, strings. Just so
much wood, ivory, metal, pedals, or what you produced from
these? Haunted, the inevitable frisson. Is that you or Bach,
Bach through you, you in that Bach? Recording of sound,
the material invisible. It returns. Or then? Is the recording
demanding I think of that moment, a new home—a
piano!—A first, together, and the surprise on your face. The
door wide open, you sat down immediately, all else forgotten,
beginning, returning to the Bach. Partita. Or was it the ghost

of a memory that had impelled me? Was it you telling me,
play this? Remember that new opening, Praeludium, Vorspiel.
Opening the door, stepping through, opening the piano,
lifting the lid. Begin. Beginning all over once more. Now or
then? A partita, a division, one divided off, that is what it
means you know, partita, divided off, the one from the other.
Now and then. You and I, we join. Then We, no more: a
partita. Divided off from you, I look for a way back.

The recording recalls me. Always to have this, this
playback, replay, the near endless possibility. Torture and
refuge, safety and torment. Play it again. Imagine the
fingers. What do I see when I hear? After Bach, Cage: Satie
haunting the American, music for dance, Merce Cunningham
choreographed. French rhythms, single melodic lines,
occasional doublings. Little ghosts you had once joked,
Kleine Gespenster. Cage's indeterminacy, music left to
chance, so different from Papa Bach, all control, everything
in its place and in relation to everything else. Here was
the contrast you so liked. Indeterminacy you explained, in
composition or performance, allowed for the fixed properties
to disappear, to seem to vanish into a fluidity. But then,
you would play the Bach once more, and in doing so, show,
make me feel, what could only inadequately be hinted at by
words such as fluid, that it was not a choice, such technical or
historical questions
— Such silliness
did not matter, finally; the partita became undivided,
the one in the other, there, now and then all along. How
you loved silences, the spaces in between. Speed, delicacy,
precision. Your hands. If it is not your voice, your eyes, your
smile, your hair, it is your hands to which I turn, which come
to me in dreams, asleep or awake. Their absence touches
me. Your hands at play. Your hands, talking, describing,
explaining: in photographs suspended above the keys, about
to descend or having just retreated, twin birds in flight, each
finger assuming in readiness a position for the next landing,
the run, that kinetic foray. After suspension, a swoop, then

the drive, so fast the lie is given to what is captured in the image. Blur, confusion, indistinct and out of focus. But that is wrong. This is not what is there at all, is it? The music escapes, fingers shaping what the heart hears, to which it responds belatedly, directing the play of hands. And when you would talk, becoming thoughtful. Bach, then Cage, your hands, your face, your voice. You are coming back to me. You return once more. You reassemble yourself in my thoughts. You resemble her, again. Everything comes together. Once more, all the pieces begin to fit, they want to fit even if I do not know how to make that happen.

And, once again, there you are. Here.

~~~

There you were.

Then Annagreth was gone, end of the day. There I was, that Sunday night, having left you at your door. It was only then in walking down the slowly sloping hill out of Gurnard that I realised that I had not arranged with Graeme to stay the night. Too late for a bus, the idea of hitching back to Seaview did not appeal. James would not be concerned, would not have thought to reflect on my absence. Assumptions would be made though. I knew, realising this as I walked, anticipating the questions, the looks, the comments, the laughter. Verdict decided, no mitigating circumstances, guilty until proven innocent, all evidence to the contrary circumstantial at best. The absence of an alibi is proof of complicity. Walking back towards, then into Cowes, I considered my lack of options. Under a tree in Northwood Park, sharing with the red squirrels; Graeme and a line from Benny Hill to do with guarding nuts. Mike might have been in the studio, a late session and it would have been easy enough, calling him, to cross to East Cowes on the floating bridge, then a walk, up the hill, out of town.

— Don't you have a home to go to?

How many other thoughts were running without order, everywhere, that I failed at first to hear, much less recognise the voice of a friend? Calling my name, intonation lilting lifted as if a question partially formed, a rise in the last note, at which, were you to hear you might imagine a question mark shaping from out the air. Not broad, a rhotic accent nonetheless, the register mellifluous, warm, like tablet on the tongue.

— Shona. Sorry, miles away.

— Clearly. Where are you away to?

— That's a good question. What are you doing here?

— I work here, remember?

Looking up, I realised I was in front of The Fountain, an old, a modest hotel, overlooking the quay and boasting long since forgotten residency by a French Charles. Everything about The Fountain Inn was quiet, aging, neat and tidy, a place to which I often escaped alone, or sometimes with Kate following a sound check, before the evening had properly got underway. Having been to several of our shows, Shona, the hotel's assistant manager, had one night invited us back for a drink, friendship developing from that point at a time shortly after Graeme had become a permanent fixture in the band. Over the intervening months, she and I had become good friends, this having developed partly from a knowledge on one side, and enjoyment on the other of Single Malts, and partly from a mutual interest in the combination of condensed milk, sugar and butter, she in making it, I in eating it. Hard to describe, all too easy to eat with its grainy texture, it was, Shona had told me, a small taste of heaven in an otherwise dreich country, and her grandmother's recipe, so not to be taken lightly. How, or rather why she had arrived here from Garelochhead stopping off in Glasgow for a couple of years, had puzzled me but Shona had once explained that, having trained in large hotel chains, she wanted to work in an independent establishment, and this had been the first opportunity.

Though now nearly midnight, the closeness of the streets, and lack of any appreciable breeze, left whatever air may have been around with a cloying staleness, the cramped town needing a strong westerly gale to clean out this cul de sac of the world. Invited in for a midnight malt, on the house, and there's some tablet in the office, I happily accepted, if only to delay the inevitable. Sitting in the now empty bar, barely lighted save for the reflected bulb illumination behind the optics, I took the whisky, ran my hand across my face, and deadpanned into the mirror,

— Of all the bars…

— Well, where else would you get a drink on a Sunday night in Cowes, you numpty?

A quiet chuckle between the two of us, I explained how I came to be roving the streets of Cowes, seemingly without purpose.

— You'll not be looking for any local virgins, then.

Shona wanted to know more, and I was pleased to be able to talk with someone who would neither judge, nor ask the obvious. Someone beyond the magic circle, outside the circus. Though Kate would have avoided such approaches, I knew her well enough to know she would, most likely, wait until I said something. Shona was, right now, neutral, an older sister without the baggage, at a time when too much sun and the absence of sleep were beginning to be felt, euphoria having, if not drained then at least made way for the start of enervation, leading to ennui. We talked the day. It had been a small, perfect place; remembered, the retelling doubled the feeling. I hardly knew what to think. Shona understood, keeping questions mostly to the general, the vague. Avoiding asking the impossible, with an obvious tact, the extent of any personal interrogation, what's she like, then, recognising that whatever feelings I might have had, they were not as yet known to me, except as nebulous shapes seen from the corner of the mind's eye. Those images that appear, brightly lighted through frosted glass, or the moment of unfocused perception as eyes adjust, opening after sleep, night glue stuck, watering weakly. Across the harbour, barely heard, slow motion homeward bound, a yacht, masts reclining, made its way to its berth. Shona knew, or could only imagine, she said, what Graeme's reaction would be.

— Tomorrow, eh? Sounds committed. Well, whatever it is, you're going to have to put up with some heckling from the back. And elsewhere. Still, for now, you'll not be too worried about that. Take it as it comes, water off a duck's and all that. Give me ten minutes and we'll be away. You're stopping at mine, no argument. The sofa's plenty comfortable. I'll even give you the loan of a tee-shirt, you'll not want to turn up without a change. It's not like you're a drummer or anything, now is it? Oh, and I'll give you the alarm. You'll not want to be late.

~~~

Whatever prologue to the act, prelude to a semi-improvised performance that Sunday may have been, or which it later came to resemble, Monday gave no indication of the way everything was to change in the following few weeks. August, the cruellest month: Elizabeth Taylor divorced. Again. Six times. Clearly, strange forces had been set in motion. It was a month of earthquakes in the Pacific and China, George Harrison was found guilty of plagiarism, the Drought Act was passed, *I'll just have to drink more beer then*, Clive Lloyd scored a double century in two hours against Glamorgan, and Michael Anthony Holding went 14-149 at the Oval, the month ending with the Notting Hill Carnival Riots. Whispering Death, grim reaper rigged for silent running, bearing in his hand not a scythe but a small highly polished cherry, replied in the deadly action without words to Anthony William Greig, possibly the least popular Scotsman to lead the England team since Douglas Jardine, silencing, no burying the publicly stated desire to *make them grovel*. One

Anthony dancing to the tune of another. It was as if there were, running the length of the Kennington Park Road all the way to Peckham and the Elephant and Castle, a ley line, determining any relation between cricketers of Scottish descent and the environs of SE11 the harbinger of baleful consequences, to which the riots on that Bank Holiday served as a somewhat forceful, if overstated Caribbean coda. Though James was to become increasingly curmudgeonly over the month, his observations on particular victims in the audience assuming an ever more acerbic tenor, this was always traceable to the descent into madness that was English cricket, and not at all the result of more than twenty shows tightly packed together. Severe drought, continued industrial kitchen swelter, forest fires and, eventually, torrential thunderstorms, all of which served only to indicate to us all that nature was providing the accompaniment to various social disasters.

Before the gathering storm had collected itself though, the last Monday in July promised a lingering glimpse of an eternity to which one would want to belong. A very oasis of calm, gentle, continued acquaintance, growing friendship, it held August's precipitant fates at bay. Subtropical, or so it seemed, sultry once more, the day took us south, driving through Godshill,
— speed up, it's fifty points if you get a tourist, close your eyes if possible, the horror, the horror! They say the church, when it was built, was at the bottom of the hill, but moved to the top, *they say*, by strange powers, mystical forces
…through Victorian Ventnor, under St Boniface, to stop for lunch; and to walk along the beach at Bonchurch on the Undercliff, two churches, a fresh water spring, and a battle against the French in the sixteenth century, Swinburne, the poet, grew up here, Dickens used to rent a villa; then in an anti-clockwise motion, Shanklin, Sandown, briefly touched, blurred in passage, too tourist ridden, commercial, a baked bland purgatory of desperate, obvious pleasures. Taking smaller roads, staying near shore, bay and coast at first,

then inland past Bembridge Airport through Steyne Wood,
a windmill appearing away to our left midway between the
wood and the harbour, separating Bembridge and St Helen's
to the North. Deciding after very little deliberation to forego
all mention of estuarine deposits, the middle Pleistocene age
or, indeed, anything geological, I followed Annagreth's lead
as she asked questions, talking of family and home. Passing
pubs, here and there along the improvised route, a game had
developed, from my offering irrelevant information.
— You play here?
— We've played here.
— Here?
— Not here.

Having little to offer of lasting interest beyond all the
useless information I had acquired about the island in that,
self-confessed obsessive love of trivia,
— I don't know that there's that much left to show you after
we've been through Ryde; it is a small island, as islands go
— where do you live?
— Seaview, I share a place with James
— Is it in our way? I should like to see it
our conversation veering to the subject of living on the
island, our talk turned once more to music, to the others
in the band; then, of Morphy, not his real name, but his
surname is Richards, like the appliances, which itself required
further explanation, and so to those adjunct figures Anna had
yet to meet, or, in some instances, encounter: Menna, Pete,
Rob Thompson, you mentioned him the other evening, other
musicians of this and various parishes. And Damian.

If there are circles of Hell, there are, it is not
unreasonable to suppose, circuses of the insane. James, Kate,
Graeme and I, I explained to Anna, knew, clung on to, and
maintained our particular circus. Damian not only occupied,
but had had an active hand, along with various of his other
members, in constructing his own bizarrarie, a cabinet of
curiosities not to be entered into lightly, on your own, under
the influence of any substance, or without a guide in the dark.

The Minotaur's labyrinth was child's play when considered beside Damian's personality.

— It's just as well Damian wasn't around on Saturday. You'd have been driving straight back to Germany by now if he had been your first impression of us. Don't get me wrong, he's great. Mad as a hatter though and, well, you'll find out. He's of Austrian descent, he says, says two of his middle names are Wolfgang and Amadeus, no, really, and that his father is a Habsburg, an Esterhazy, something minor from the remnants of the Austro-Hungarian Empire. Seriously.

Annagreth had reacted, it seemed to me, almost visibly, as if the fact that he was Austrian was explanation enough in itself. Saying nothing, she clearly wanted at least something approximating a reason for Damian. Many of us had had that desire in the past, but had long since abandoned it. It was in an instant when, in packing up the equipment one night, Damian had pitched up intending as ever to help, but in reality only to hinder, and had seized suddenly Graeme's drum stool. Sniffing the seat, an oxen bellow proclamation stated Odour of Attar! Those not well acquainted with Damian's foibles and turns began to take a mental, metaphorical and in one or two cases, quite literal step backwards, cowardice clearly being the better part of valour. Or perhaps, I said, it was the cassock, the riding boots, or simply the entire package.

Morphy though, could manage, tolerate, restrain Damian for the most part. The relationship between them was almost touching, like the smarter of two animals keeping the more highly strung, ultimately dim companion believing that it, the thoroughbred was the smarter of the two, while everyone else around knew the goat was the brains of the outfit. So, vouched for by James and I, kept usually on a leash by Morphy, Damian was permitted to act as a particularly inept roadie when he came out, or at least to believe that his position was what he liked to call with an aggrandizing flourish a general factotum. Safest Damian was then, when given the gaffer tape, and told to fix things to the floor, but not the bloody pedals, Dunc, a phrase assuming over time a choric purpose, witness to the imminent fall of the House of Atreus! Judge had once intoned, all sepulchral camp and entirely appropriate to the figure in question. Morphy, when not studying electronics, kept an eye on the animals and the clowns, making sure the troughs were filled, the grease-paint at hand, and all the safety ropes in good order. Not just our engineer, for which we paid him nothing other than the occasional beer, or a meal at Kate's, Morphy was our wizard, someone for whom soldering was a fine art, the mysteries of last minute solutions to impossible problems, nothing more complicated than were a change of fuse required. Morphy, magus of the circuit board, the valve, magnet coil and mixing desk, assumed something of a priestly air, one whose hieratic credentials were without doubt, as we had never seen him not dressed all in black, with thick, long straight black hair suggestive of the more intense members of an orthodox religion, the mysteries of which were known only to one such as Morphy. Superficially, there was a resemblance to James, though the obvious feature of baldness aside, there was a noticeable distinction to be made; James, his baldness emphasizing this, had eyebrows that could only be called heavy set, an overhanging near monobrow, Babylonian, the space between each eye canopy implied rather than stated. It was this particular feature that had caused Graeme to notice a particular resemblance. He had, one day at the barn, noted in the pocket of my jacket a somewhat severely abused Penguin…

You said a Penguin. This is a joke. Or is it a toy? I saw the goat the other day at the High School.

Explaining the three-legged goat in passing, three friends made it as a present, they thought it would look good on the stage, with us, I also explained that this particular Penguin was a book. The book was the battered Penguin. Anna nodded acknowledgement, an impatient motorist hitting his horn, overtaking us, somewhat dangerously.

— Leck mich am Arsch!

Annagreth must have noticed my surprise, for, laughing, she told me that her father had said it was ok to swear as long as you had a cultural precedent of some sort, something to give the vulgarity gravitas. This phrase, she continued, the patient teacher once more, a tone that often came to be used at rehearsals when either one or the rest of us were failing to grasp a new arrangement,

— The phrase is the title of Mozart, a canon, K.231.

— And the key?

— Bb. Major.

Of course, naturally, natürlich. I ventured the opinion that it was a tune that we could incorporate in a set some time. By now, we had reached Bembridge, and parking at Fisherman's Walk, removed our shoes, to walk down and onto the beach, the tide having retreated to its furthest extent. Large patches of kelp, brown, green, darkly vibrant or sombre, sinister of hue, were gathered across the still moist flats or broad tan rock crops, lifeless, awaiting the turn of the tide, in order that they might, once more float, just beneath the surface of the calmly stirring water. To the north the mainland, strange name for what was, after all, just another island, however much larger than the one on which we found ourselves; and away to our right, all blue light meeting at the horizon, two planes of blue bisected by a single line, the open sea.

— We are at the easternmost point of the Island now. Bembridge used to be an island all its own, you know. Well, no, of course, you don't. Away to our left is Bembridge harbour and the Duver.

— What is this, Duver?

— A beach; but the name comes from Anglo-Saxon, meaning sand dunes. Not that there are any now.

— So typisch.

— Isn't it? But this Duver, and the one at Seaview, no it doesn't have any sand dunes either, these are the only two in all England with the name still.

Silence returned, soft wave on wave. No tankers were

in view, no ships, no sails, no sign of human life upon the
glassy sheet, too calm to distinguish by the use of words
like breaker. Framed by the intersection of land and sea,
it seemed as though our being here together had been an
inevitability. Gathered by chance today on this headland,
I felt, without knowing there might be a word for such an
experience, as if something were beginning to reveal itself,
the canopy of sky above the sea, its mirror reflecting its
dome, extending to the point at which we stood, and into
which we were gathered, closing around us. Something
summoned me, us, here, together.

— This Penguin, not a bird…

— Oh, yes. Sorry. Not a chocolate biscuit either

— Again, you are making no sense, is this always the way?
You are…

   That smile, indulgent, approving, I felt encouraged.

— …either mad or a philosopher

— Are the two exclusive?

   Apologising, explaining, again briefly, that a biscuit and
a book could assume the name of a largely flightless aquatic
bird without being the same, I returned to why the book had
encouraged Graeme's comment concerning Judge. The book,
Thus Spoke Zarathustra, the mention of which I thought
produced the merest arching of the eyebrow, had on its cover
a drawing, close up, all eyes, brows and moustache, black on
terracotta monochrome, unmistakable in its terrier intensity,
as though the philosopher were about to pounce and savage
a passing provincial or, worse yet, some burgher well wadded
in stupidity. Bugger, Judge, must be your granddad, nipper.
I mean, look, it's the same eyebrows. He's got an extra one
though, on his lip.

   Two small children had come running into view, excitedly,
as if from nowhere, buckets, spades, flippers all extended
from waving arms. The beach, become suddenly a benign, if
overheated playground, Anna with an impulsive desire to join
in the revels, grabbed my hand, as starting into a run, pulling
me behind, as if I were no more than a recalcitrant kite to be

encouraged into flight, headed for the distant water's edge. It was a fine day made to show us what things might mean, and so to feel the world's imagination at work. Sweeping skies unfurled above showing those of us who saw that day what it was like to feel heaven's playfulness, the memory of the world in a single grain of timeless time. Slow sequenced light, sonority at the edge of the visible, washes of colour verging on colourlessness, an absence of the spectral in the immediacy of illumination's touch. Touching, touched by heat, by light, by sight, by sound side by side with silence, wave after wave, within wave: a fine day, a perfect day. It was, and it remains, don't you feel that too? I feel still its echo tugging, pushing, calling within me, just below the surface of ordinary time. With a gasp of surprise, I realised then that Annagreth did not only have my hand as we hit the water. In talking of the others, in being encouraged in my subject, I had failed to notice how by a stealth more complete than any direct approach she had come to hold my heart also. Hold fast and plunge.

~~~

...the lightest of breezes, the lightness of those lightest hairs, white gold on your forearm, blonde on brown, lying in the sun, asleep, vagabond strands refugee floating free to settle softly across your soft breathing mouth; my finger pushing gently away those fugitive filaments, to see your slow opening eyes, an aperture flutter, narrowing against light, to focus, dispelling sleep's damp stickiness.
— There you are...
    ...said sleepily smiling...
— Yes, and there you are...
    ...smiled broadly back...

~~~

Leaving the beach, we headed back through the village,

toward the windmill until we turned just before it onto a
private road. Having got back into the car after closing the
gate, and taken the half mile track up the hill, Waltraud came
to a halt a little way from a farmhouse.
— That's the barn; where we practice.
— And, oh look. A *copse*. Somewhere to keep the police.

Amused sarcasm, playful and arch, hung as heavy as the
thickness of the afternoon air. I said nothing, merely widened
my eyes in amused recognition and response. The door to
the loft opened, Kate having heard the engine gunned before
dying. Her face at first unrecognizing, then in the full light of
afternoon, a smile widening rapidly, in recognition, and, was
there something else? We were a little too far away for me to
be able to judge properly. Anna waved, then turned, taking
everything in, looking around, moving in a circle as we moved
up the hill, feet still bare from the beach, sand still clinging, a
little, here and there. O this is so, so, beautiful, the barn!
— Kate, hello.

Anna called, as she descended the stairs.

This is not like English barns. It is…the windows, they are
wonderful; it looks like a church; the colour, red
— Yes, my Dad wanted it to be more like barns in New
England than old England. It's a terrible joke, but just laugh
if he tells you.
— It's ok to stop by? I'm looking forward to Thursday but
wanted to find out where you lived and say hello.
— I've got cake, just made this morning, and I'll make some
tea if you like; do you want a tour of the place while I get the
tea made?

The barn, a baked brick semi-solid colour, had in its tint
the suggestion of rust, of oxides wearing away a ferrous
surface, eating it; a rich stain, blood ripe in its intensity, the
colour caused the barn to stand against the low hillside with
a vibrant acid bleed disorientation that was usurped only
by the orange of the Variant. Put too close to the barn, the
car would complete the hallucination, all in readiness for a
psychedelic album sleeve, a Technicolor trip.

— I could sit here forever, watching the world change and me at its centre, quietly; I would eat too much, become a Buddha, plant myself in the ground, it all feels so perfect right now, everything. We could not have arrived at a more perfect time. Here and now it is everything, you feel that? The grass is warm, feel the heat coming off the wood—and look! The sea, it is smiling in the sunlight for us, like so many brilliants, jewels floating. It is like a necklace and the string just broke onto the surface, *O Benedict, es ist so wunderschön, so unglaublich. Es ist alles zu viel…überwältigend….*

Across the field, to the bay, its wide crescent rising away slow North, the entrance to the harbour to the left, St Helens on the northern shore. Annagreth was entranced, left hand upon her hip, almost at her back, right hand cupping over her eyes, forgetting sunglasses pushed high on head, a black winged bird nesting on a golden thatch, tilting head slightly seaward her gaze lining up, unknowing through Bembridge point toward a church spire, the church on the hill. Away to the right on the coast, I pointed out, follow the line of my arm, a barely discernible plaster stump, the tower of Old St Helens Church, at the Duver. Anna had not heard me come up behind her, turning her head a little, to see me there, our faces close enough to feel momentarily each other's breath; shy smile, then, where my finger's pointing. The church tower, its masonry eroded, its upright all that remained, peered, a single tooth between an otherwise unbroken barrier of trees, tracing the curve of the shore line, away, around, becoming wholly invisible to continue through Priory Bay on toward Seaview.

— This is so much prettier than the west, it is not so open, it is more comfortable, closed around, and such a nice harbour, no, what did you call it, don't tell me, I remember, yes, *esplanade*. A big word for ugly.

Rhymed with lemonade, not roulade, I having said earlier that this word for commercial ugliness could sound like either. Annagreth had chosen the stickier, cheap alternative, all fizz and no sophistication, somehow the right decision,

the rhyme suggestive of the qualities of such places. Said
this way, esplanade lemonade, the English word, the same
yet not the same as the French, oozed vulgarity, all candy
floss and kiss me quick hats, tawdry colours and crude post
cards, unlike its more sophisticated European counterpart,
promenade. Anna had said that Strandpromenade sounded
more, what, more proper, more old-fashioned, very Bismarck,
sehr Weimar. Looking closely at each other, we paused, not
quite sure what was to happen next.
— Tea, children!
    Broken into, our private bubble dissolved; turning, I saw
Harry and Rosemary following Kate. Exchanging nods of
welcome, and recognition, I colouring a little…
— Warm one, today, hi there, who's your friend, Ben?
    A caterpillar eyebrow arching its back on the rockface of
Harry's forehead, face wrinkling full beam welcome with that
slight suggesting of a wink, Anna and I made our way toward
Kate, managing a folding table, on which were balanced,
as in an uneasy truce with gravity, various plates, cups,
and other teatime paraphernalia, her parents following on,
teatime paraphernalia supplemented with hastily assembled
edibles, late lunch, high tea, each confusing the other happily,
rubbing shoulders side by sideways. The Larkins transposed
to California: perfick. Cheese, beer, wine, bread, cakes, both
home made, half a chicken pie, apples, muffins, cold meat
and anything not nailed down that could be scrounged,
rustled, liberated from the kitchen. Kate's parents introduced,
you play organ? Anytime, you want, the B3's yours to use,
Harry became the perpetual tie-dye counterculture nineteen-
year-old he always seemed when animated, his usual, very
American largesse irresistible, so much more hospitable than
the calm, the reserve, the sang froid of the English middle
classes. Talking music, any residual parental patina fell quickly
away, enthusiasm a bubbling stew overflowing. Rosemary, her
eyes rolling, all am-dram here we go again, indulgence, placed
a loving hand, much used to the gesture, habitual by now, on
her husband's back, talking to him much as she would Fred,

their, no, Kate's Jack Russell, who was noticeable chiefly by his absence. Rosemary told Harry, in a tone all posh prep school polish that carried command as easily as a dog fleas, to stop frightening the guests; the poor girl had only just met them, she'd never come back again, and anyway he knew what happened if he got too loud; we didn't want a scene kicking orff like the one earlier in the summer when painting the barn had culminated in several blazing rows, overheated pow-wows by the natives, elders of the tribe, and a visit from the local plod. Kate explained how painting the barn baked brick red had caused all manner of ructions at the parish council and beyond, matters of planning permission, blot on the landscape, eyesore, bloody Yank, the typical responses from the tweed and twinset brigade, all pony club, regatta, snotty yachty, ex-India army types and their memsahibs, the kind who insisted on wearing a tie (the men, mostly), cavalry twill and polished brogues, even when gardening. The story became a family entertainment, a slightly lunatic at-home for the guests, everyone doing all the voices, including the police, when, no, Harry, really, said Rosemary, you did go too far that time Harry had promised to go for a gun he did not possess. It's good to make the locals crazy once in a while; keeps 'em alert, gives 'em a reason to live, was the response. Helps their goddam circulation.

Having been shown the house and barn, Annagreth's face alive to its wonder and weirdness, we left, Kate and I acknowledging Wednesday's rehearsal. Harry had urged Anna to play, which she declined, promising soon enough. Next week, he volunteered as he walked back to the house, waving goodbye, the collection was to be augmented, a calliope would have a new home. Kate reminding Anna about Thursday, Anna promised she had not forgotten, she should arrive when? Around eleven would be good. Thursday then. Here we are again, happy as can be, all good friends and…

~~~

To Seaview we drove that late afternoon, the four miles
around, *I love the walk around the coast, past the old church ruin, and
up to Kate's, we should do it together some time*, across the harbour,
climbing the hill. After six already, there was cricket practice
on St Helens Green. Seaview bustled even at that time of
day, last children taken, tanned and lingering, home, leaving
the beach, some tired, some tearful, *we'll be back tomorrow, I'll
buy you another*, more with ice cream fuelled giggles, chortling,
reliving the seconds. The Old Fort was already kicking
into life for evening trade, tables occupied, the takeaway
line nearly to the door, *two cod, one plaice, add an extra saveloy.*
Parked on Fairy Road, walking back, we circuited the small
village centre, up and down short but steep hills, nodding
acquaintance, the occasional hello with familiar shopkeepers,
shutting later than usual, making the most of seasonal trade,
*I'll be in tomorrow, Dobbie, thanks for keeping it, haven't had a minute
since last Thursday*; answered, a look towards Anna, *no, James
come in today, said you'd been absent without leave since Sat'dy night.*
Village Newsagent and Post Mistress, I offered, knowing
everything that went on and everyone to ask. Chips, with
vinegar, of course, *you don't really eat them with Mayonnaise in
Germany?* Sitting on the sea wall, watching again, as if always,
the changing light. We, James and I lived, responding to
Annagreth's question, on Salterns Road, five minutes away,
a small fisherman's cottage we were lucky enough to have
got for a peppercorn rent, something resulting from a legal
matter James's father had been involved in, in a professional
capacity; not as one of the litigants though, I added. James's
father, John, knew of just two rents where peppercorns were
actually used as payment, one being paid by a cricket club
in Sevenoaks, Kent, for use of the ground and pavilion, to
its owner, the local Baron. From nowhere, Annagreth said,
wistful it seemed, a hint of melancholy perhaps, or maybe
just imagined on my part, sensing the same, the sense of
an ending to the day fast approaching, known to be ahead
though as yet unseen, approaching.

— *so leben wir und nehmen immer Abschied.*

— I'm sorry?

Rilke, she countered, a favourite poet, especially for moments like these, brief revelations starting up, unfolding, dark flowers, purple poppies to stain the otherwise unalloyed joy. We were always living this way, there was always a goodbye, an end, forever the farewells. When things were perfect, they were too perfect; did I not feel that too? What was perfect never lasted, she continued, a quietness, a purposiveness of expression that was new to me, another note, dying cadence in the voice heard. We only knew something was perfect when it was too late, after the bloom was off the petals. We always missed perfection. She had been reflecting on the last two days, how completely, was sagst du? Meine Güte, I do not know even what I want to say in German. I let the silence stand.

— Like this afternoon, like now. Look. I would like for this to stay. And for me, for us, sitting here looking out over the sea, that little sailboat, the odd looking stone thing out there in the water, the clouds so thin, so high. But it cannot, so we have one moment, and another and another, *und so weiter.* I like photographs for this, I take lots of photographs, all the time, too many my parents say, but I want to keep a souvenir. I will be an old lady archive keeper one day, very grumpy, *don't touch!* I have no photographs of today or yesterday; it makes me sad, but my camera, it's being repaired, Heike will bring it with her when she comes back. But right now, I cannot get these moments. So they will go from me. The clouds, look what a beautiful sky, but already it changes as we watch. In German, we call those clouds *Schäfchenwolken*, sheep clouds. You see, you are not the only one to know silly things.

Mackerel sky. Buttermilk sky. Soft cream luminescence, lambent, a lesser light, deferential before the refulgence of Annagreth's eyes, in which there appeared illuminated her apprehension of the world, and which, in its turn found transport in her words, making visible the sensuous quality of how she saw the world, how that world touched her. She took time for the moment, letting her imagination surrender itself to a here and now she was all too aware would soon slip in silence from view, whatever was special about it lost except in the fragile skein, the clews of memory.

~~~

Special. That evening stays with me. I want to let you know, it remains. I hesitate over using this word as I have always hesitated so often about so many things, special. You would have liked to have known, I am sure, that this unremarkable word, *special*, one we use far too frequently, comes via *species* from the Latin, meaning *appearance, form, beauty*, and these in turn, again from *specere:* to look. A snaking and a pedantic route, worming its way across, to hide in plain sight, just below the surface of every overly easy, thoughtless use, whatever resides in this *special*. That evening, as you looked at the beauty of the sky, the form of the scene before you, its appearance, I looked also, wanting equally not to leave the moment. Though shortly after that, whisper of a greater sadness having departed, what remains with me is the memory of looking, with you, at the early evening. Unknown to you, though perhaps I think you always knew, I looked at you, realising that you were revealing yourself, without the least consciousness of how you appeared, the form you took that evening, as *special*. I want to let you know.

I want to tell you, how much I want to say. Searching for the words, two, not my own, yours, two special words come back. With them, a vision of you: I see, as if rewinding and replaying a found reel of footage, home movies, super-8, videocassette, you sitting there, at the piano. You seem to be telling someone about why you wrote this, that. Always those questions, the why, the interminably repetitive desire for autobiography, which you always handled so courteously; no, I have never been to Louisiana with a shotgun to kill

the man who cuckolded me, James had once said somewhat
impatiently; but he could always make an exception in your
case, Kate had added, with a smile to the stranger, unnerving
in its sweetness, the tenor or intent of the remark impossible
to judge.

But you never grew impatient with the question, did you?
Or never showed that, at least. You allowed your hands to
protect, you, to make whoever might have asked feel as if
they deserved an answer, which only they would receive.
Your hands would talk when you sought to retreat. Having
been asked, you start the song again, the song starts in you
once more, the silent music before the tune everyone hears,
your hair tied back, though loosely, eyes down concentrating
on your hands. What do you see, what did you see, when
you saw your hands, playing? Serious, your face, or perhaps
merely lost in the sound, no you there, just your other self
inside the melody, the other side of sound where silences
caress. As you play, a slight sideways sway, at first tentative,
upright again, then once more, moving toward your left
hand, bass part, rhythm underlying the top line, a wooden
footstep, above that Chopin skipping, but playful, Parisian,
not consumptive, agonized. There, on your face is a smile.
Somewhere inside, recognition, or memory. Slightest smile,
less pleasure than a delight in locating a source, finding the
lost moment inside the song, eyes closing, merest gesture of
the head, visible counterpoint to the unseen souvenir, as if
to say, yes, this is why. Ending the phrase, you turn towards
that question still hanging expectantly in the air on the lips
of someone unknown, but who, you know, just has to be
told. They cannot leave with the memory of the music alone.
And as you turn, your smile wider, as if you have realised
in that instant a story, not the story but a version of the
tale, to safeguard your secret, in full view, while offering the
authorized account. In that turn outwards, shielding the inner
vision, Geheimnis, the homely hidden truth, for the home
alone, in secret always, so your finger, first finger of your
left hand, upreaching, pointing, raised, as if to beat time,

but coming to rest on your lips briefly. Here it is, your finger
seems to say, just this once, but no, it is hidden, unheard, not
to be spoken, I am sealing my lips while telling you. Looking
away, upwards into the unseen, head arching slightly towards
your right shoulder, a motion I knew would open your fable,
compelling your testimony but with a gesture of benevolent
grace, as if to say so süß.

That phrase of yours; it sits the divide, traces the line
where the partita comes, between us, between us and all the
rest dividing off the private and the public worlds. A phrase
used in both, for each; but only in knowing the intonation will
the person to whom you speak hear and receive it. Or not.
So süß. There, the slightest of leitmotifs, by which you either
gave yourself away or kept yourself inviolably your own.
There was that use reserved for affection unreserved. Du
bist so süß. And I hear you, catching your voice unguarded,
opening to some imperceptible or unnoticed touch, causing
your heart to thrill, your eyes to grow blue ocean wide. You
would, sometimes, say a second time so süß, emphatically the
first word, eyes closing, head forward, encouraging intimate
recognition. But there were also those times when these two,
almost inconsequential words, were not given; and there
were times, ironically, when they issued forth as a shield, in
acceptance of formal, polite praise, or answering the familiar
words what made you write that song, making the hearer feel
as if they really knew why they wanted to know. So it came
quickly to the gesture of the eyes, the head.

Then you would begin, this tale, fable, legend for the
song, an easy, an acceptable explanation. And as she spoke,
as you speak, reciting those words of hers, your invisible
lines, your head turned away from your hands, her arms, I see
them there over the keys catching the question first nearer
your face, her arms upraised, then lowered as you settle into
her performance; she is still sitting, patiently, sitting still at
the piano. You play out the part, so well rehearsed that it
has assumed a grace, a natural and inevitable semblance of
authenticity. No longer speaking, you are living the words to

which you give birth.

Your hands would shape, I see them now, they mould the story. So slightly cupped, your fingers, the palms imagining a ball of something malleable, a dough from which to shape your phrases, forming, accommodating, balancing. Wrists turning, pivot motions, fingers never touching around that spherical place, a dance around an emptiness, giving to the nothing, a perceived weight; there, there a pause, one hand over the other, measuring the moment, before your hands resume, the lower hand describing a small arc, the upper hand its mirror image, though curving down, not up, as if no longer giving form but tipping, from one receptacle to the other, a liquid solidifying, taking shape.

As the movement draws to its conclusion, this brief animation, so the oscillations become less pronounced, the palms uncurled, fingers straightened, hands coming together to embrace one another. Finally, you would, with your left hand again, piano on your left, start to draw an imagined line between you and your audience, until, as if to say we're coming to a close, you would swing gracefully around to face the piano, your right hand and head in comic duet mime the ba-dum, ba-dum, ba-dum, of successive descending patterns along the keyboard, to give a visual clue to the music's play. This is this, you seem to be suggesting, what it is and nothing else. Neck thrust forward, lips slightly pursed, head moving in a backward forward motion, wading bird walk, wagtail swagger, you are showing a child something for which there are no words, when what was asked for was something altogether more mundane. So süß.

8. Fourth Act: Tout Ensemble or all together, now (August 1976)

What is there of the dream? What stays, can you tell me? At the time I thought you were waking me, but awake, I find that to be untrue. Yet, there you were, you are here I tell myself, before consciousness robs me of the already lost illusion. April is a cruel month; every morning for the last three weeks, anniversary of another last month, I have woken just after two. With a precision and numerical iteration too odd to be an invention or my own imagination, the small, glowing numbers tell me the same: 2.22. Do I want this to be significant? Is it? From an ocean in which the current draws me to you, I find myself washed up on the shore, salt water burning my eyes, each night, no landmark, nothing by which to orient myself. Eye rims smart, sting, salt crust enflamed, throat dry. Tongue, lip touching in the dark on tear, causes the flood to come, memory's tidal wave; the deep in a grain of salt, the smallest pebble. A tremble. I tremble, as if at a touch, your phantom touch. To have drowned in your ocean love, you opening yourself to engulf me, take me in, taking me down, the pull of a tidal eddy closing over me, would have been the better alternative than being beached, unable to slake this thirst. Better salt than sweet water. Better to be with you, there, than to admit that you are not there. I want to say *don't go without me* but you already are far ahead, out of sight, plumbing the estranging waters.

~~~

August had been stalled, July coming to a halt before it
was all over with three last days in a row, all out of time,
ahead, independently of, any calendric logic. Last days,
first days, days which, by their unexpected, stranger eddies,
idling motions and recirculations were both first and last
simultaneously, and yet neither. Becalmed and adrift, all at
sea, rudderless, waiting for a fresh wind, a last day, a Tuesday
without the charms of the previous two days arrived. While
an ocean away, on another continent, Operation Glowing
Speed was to be set in motion in order that the US could
achieve world record speed and altitude flights, on a small
island off the south coast of England, no escape velocity
was possible. In France, the Guillotine made a return, while
the United Kingdom was about to break diplomatic relations
with Uganda. History was, yet again, an intrusive irrelevance,
a pestering sibling looking to force its actions on everyone,
column inches or a story for the six o'clock news of no
lasting personal significance; except of course for Christian
Ranucci, who by the time I woke, had already been executed.
Little Big narratives to interrupt, divert, distract, inform, and
perhaps entertain. The Tangshan earthquake was still a day
away, and no one had, as yet, heard of the 'Son of Sam'.

While the Gregorian calendar told me it was the twenty-
seventh day, of the seventh month, in what was doubtless the
year of someone's Seigneur, one thousand nine hundred and
seventy six, the Julian calendar lagged behind by thirteen days,
limp foot dragging, lame. Had it been not the morning of
the 27th, but July 14, the Summer Olympics would not have
begun; I would not yet have met Annagreth, and so would
not feel as if Wednesday evening would never arrive. On
the previous evening, I had no real sense that the following
day would open onto the malaise of tedious introspection,
mixed personal expectation or anticipation. Knowing that
the German word for this was Weltschmerz hardly added

any false grandeur or provided compensation. There was
self-conscious surprise, and not a little general irritability,
particularly when faced as I was with the prospect of being
patient with children of various sizes through music lessons
of more than usual atonal, arythmic iniquity. Guilty as
charged, incapable while in charge of a musical instrument,
depraved indifference in the face of the Muses' Art. Off
with their heads. I realized in anticipating the drag of the day
ahead the extent of my own foolishness from the previous
evening.

Having walked with Anna back to the cottage, James,
happily for me, nowhere around, selfishness mixed with a
desire to hold off the inevitable in me quietly celebrating
a little victory, I made us tea while Annagreth explored
bookshelves and record collections. I have this, this is sweet,
oh, I hope this is James's, not yours, and other expressions
of discovery, interpretation, critique, wafted into the kitchen
on warm evening air. The tea made, the tray set, we sat in the
garden in the rear, the Elizabethans used to refer to them
as backsides, so komisch, always children's jokes, the air
giving the merest illusion of cooling, we talked once more
of trivial matters, of personal interests and aversions, small
conversational non sequitur, the cottage was built in a leap
year, in the seventeenth century; later Bram Stoker's widow,
he wrote Dracula, bought the place, that allow people to map
one another without seeming to try. In the evening air there
drifted at the edge of sense, and all the more sensuous for
that very evanescence, the memory of the garden's flowers.
Recalling the carefully tended plot, I see it twice, with visions
each the palimpsest of the other, both riotous catalogues,
contained only by the order of their learning and their telling,
the one for me, the other for you.

It was, and remains for me distinct. Image, visualized
ghost of itself, and spun out, overwrought preponderance
of words, poor substituted dried flowers, husks of the
real thing; an overblown catalogue, archive of name and
description, memory tricks to register everything beyond

words, everything of the little plot that in its efflorescence
I recollected even as I began to speak, heading down an
indexer's road of no return, a style John Haddon had once
described, dismissively, as Lawrentian excess: Balloonflower,
velvet blue five-pointed star; Coral Bells, also Alumroot,
starry night, ground hugging, palmately lobed and purple
leaved; Daylillies, three types: Tawny, orange cinnamon,
Golden Needles, and Hush Little Baby, peach red to golden
at the heart, folded frill petal sensuous, soft skin to the touch,
darker red veins in translucent skinfolds unfolding, folding
back, intimately revealing, a floral picadillo; Phlox, pale blue
and violet, erect and fragrant, dehiscent fruits separating
explosively, then early blooming Autumn Joy, Herbstfreude,
pink to red, deeper dusty reds, succulent, dark green below;
and above all a top note of lavender. Old Lady plants,
Annagreth said. Butterfly Bush, Bethlehem Sage and Blue
False Indigo filled in the spaces. But you sound like you've
memorized all this, you are like a page from a book, it is very
funny, no it's lovely really, but this is not a lesson. She was
right, I had given in, retreated into my world of indexing,
registering, inventorying, as a way of hiding embarrassment,
shyness. Memory never let me down when other personal
attributes might. Sorry, I can be something of a train spotter,
I explained, or so I thought; was? What…? Making clear the
meaning of a phrase, I alluded to Graeme's comment on
my having volunteered information about trees. Annagreth,
seeing I was digging myself a hole in the middle of this
gardener's paradise, asked if James and I kept the flowers.
No, we did not tend the garden, this would be a waste
land otherwise, the legal agreement allowing us use of the
cottage for £1 a year also saw to it that a gardener was to be
provided.

This awkwardness over, between Annagreth and I
conversation had become exceptionally easy, unremarkable
in its familiarity so that, when Anna made to leave, asking
directions to Gurnard, there was a pronounced awkwardness

made all the more so by the fact that neither of us expected it. Half finished phrases, speaking one over another, then stopping, start, then stop once more, an embarrassed laugh, standing a little too close, looking away, down, up briefly into eyes, blue guardian vision, flowers faced, then once more towards something unseen, ghost thought drifting past the seen. As the light began slowly to suggest the possibility of its fading, I noticed that Anna's eyes had darkened in shade, appearing violet in the half light, pellucid. Iris mirroring, echoing Indigo, true not false; a look; a, a what? Recognition? Understanding? Reading a sign in a foreign language when, just after you had looked, you realized it was as if you had read this in your own tongue? Touched by that sudden gaze, I asked her to wait just one second, to gather a small nosegay from the garden, Black Eyed Susans and Irises. Returning, the awkward dance of half words resumed, string cut marionette twisting on the tongue. How could it be so difficult for two people to come to an agreement that, not disliking one another, seeing one another once more could be arranged? However it turned out, overhasty yet not wishing to seem so, and responding to Annagreth's commenting on the fact that she had an orientation meeting on the Tuesday at the High School during the following day, I excused myself from Tuesday evening, claiming I'd already agreed to some kind of half commitment, both of us saying, as if there had been an unheard count in, two, three, four,

— Wednesday?
— Wednesday.
    And a laugh.
    Reminding Annagreth, Anna, still getting used to which name to use, needlessly that we, I, the others, we were rehearsing Wednesday, I suggested she come out to the Wishing Well, a pub not far from here, you play there sometimes too? Yes, half laughingly, half smilingly said; to the pub that evening, around eight; I could, I offered, show her where that was when she left, and put her on the right

road back, towards home,

— and don't forget, take the turn off for East Cowes, it'll save you going through Newport, and, even taking the chain bridge, you'll be home earlier, should only take about 45 minutes and I'll walk back from the Wishing Well; it's not too far, I could do with stretching my legs.

— Okay, why don't I just pick you up here, Wednesday?

~~~

Tuesday then, which sat there, undigested, indigestible, lumpen, undercooked suet pudding, sticky, cloying to the palette, heavy on the stomach, swelling. As immovable as an oil slick promising to smother a hitherto pristine bay, offering to pull down anything mired in its viscous grasp. My mood was not helped by the state of play at Headingly. Though that morning, the final day's play, England needed 114 runs with five wickets in hand, we would require more than just *Johns of their day*. James had still not returned on Monday night after I had walked back, which was not unusual for him at this time. He was, I had little doubt, in Cowes, currently a twice-weekly excursion at least, in an effort to convince one of the Harbour Lights' barmaids, Leila, that, really, no seriously, going out with him was an option. Had he had a bonnet, instead of a couple of US Army issue caps and a small wig collection, Leila would have been most decidedly the bee in it. Signs of James were noticeable that Tuesday morning, so I left early for Ryde that day cycling the sea wall. There would always be something, I reasoned with myself, with which to help Rob Thompson at the unimaginatively named but marvelously overstocked Aladdin's Cave, the Guitar Centre. Always something new, *you just wait till you try this*. Even though he would not yet be there, having the use of a back room for lessons, I had my own keys.

The day was not without incident, either in the Test Match or in my own small corner of summer. As with the second session of any cricket match, the afternoon hours from two onwards at the shop were marked by a slowing of tempo, and with that a gradual, inevitable gathering of at least three or four musicians, who having finally crawled from theirs or others' beds, had made their way to free tea and gossip as a substitute for late breakfast. Greasy bags and pastry flakes clinging to bag, to shirt, to mouth, acknowledged already consumed sausage rolls. Between lessons, I brewed up for six: two Phils, Oswald and Truckel, kept only separate in conversation using the former's nickname appropriated from a Gibson guitar, ironically a model, which, though aesthetically pleasing, lacked balance; the other was, well, Phil, cricketer and bass player, the yin balancing the yang; then Keith, stoned perpetually, Geoff, Ron, garden gnome percussionist of this parish, and Jon Liddell, another bass player. Three bass players in one location: so much moodiness in such proximity. Pathetic fallacy or not, the world was shaping itself to my present disposition. A small transistor tuned to Test Match Special was reporting on the final day's play, it's all happening out there in the middle, Johnners, Benaud and Arlott in fine form. Holding had taken three wickets, Whispering Death in the air, on the airwaves, the sound of nothing but the aftershock of collective despair. One could taste it. No one had ever seen the like of Holding. No one would ever forget him after that parched summer. Richards had already swaggered his violent best in the previous innings. It would all be over, well before tea. Settling down, playing ourselves in for a session of pointless talk, Geoff all feathered hair, as ever noodling funk on a semi-hollowbody 335, sunburst, built the year I was born, Keith, always, doing something he should not have been, do that somewhere else, I don't want to get arrested, we were interrupted by shouting, heavy objects being thrown, possibly bricks and the breaking of glass. Jon, with Ron, that's it, send out the rhythm section, there'll be another along in a minute, went to discover the cause. Tea drinking resumed, a few minutes later Ron's spikey nose, bastard child of an old world arboreal monkey and Carlo Collodi's much loved puppet,

preceding his equally spikey hair, more Small Faces than
Sex Pistols, appeared, the rest of him following on shortly
behind. His Artful Dodger, macaw squawk voice, pitched
higher, raspier by excitement, demanded with an urgency it
was impossible to dismiss,
— call the Bill, it's a nutter with a knife!
    …Geoff hurried to the office, the rest of us taking up
positions in the window to watch the afternoon's unexpected
sideshow. Drained of all vibrancy, colours leached and
bleached in the sun of another blistering day, no signs of life
on Monkton Street, the buildings seemed as if made by an
ingenious, if unhinged set designer from uncooked pastry,
waiting for an egg wash, masonry the colour of the outfield
at any county ground that year. High Noon or an Avengers
scene, awaiting Gary Cooper, an ageing Bentley, or a woman
in a one-piece leather catsuit; everything played out, as if
scripted and surreal. Gunslinger or fast bowler though, the
fast draw or the yorker, the inevitable outcome of the face
off or throw down. All poised on the edge, in the moment.
Nothing. No sound, no movement, except for what is taking
place in the middle. As anyone who has ever followed intently
a Test Match knows, there are games within games, times
moving alongside and differently to other times, several
clocks ticking over at once, time counterpoised within, against
itself, the sound of one, the countersignature of the other,
while at least one not having been wound for what feels like
a decade. There is that slowing suspension shimmering down
to an almost complete cessation. The actions watched by
the crowd repeat themselves: collecting the ball, the walk,
the turn, the run up, the release, and then…the defensive
shot, the block, the leave, the nurdle to third man, again, and
again. And Again. Et cetera. And so on. And so not forth,
und so weiter, you would have said, but staying in the same
place. And then…and then…a suspended chord in a minor
key, a tritone adds to the tension, and… the bowler, eyed
by several thousand barely breathing spectators, in search
of lost time, wheels in once more, the stumps exploding so

that the clock can be wound, normal service resumed. The
bell jar is refilled with oxygen. St Michael's Lane, Leeds, or
Monkton Street, Ryde, someone had yet to press the play
button, release the ball; and then…and then…and then,
suddenly, Ron, supporting Jon, almost taking the door out of
its frame, followed by incoherent shouts mingled with crazed
obscenities, and Jon's voice, wobble warped, an overstretched
recording tape, steeped and stoned, frantic but strangely calm,
unworldly in its own disbelief. Like watching a film in reverse,
where following the sudden bomb burst, and the after shock
of emotion's collective eruption, time starts to move. With
the slam of the shop door, its forceful thrusting open, the
world rushed back in, deranged life resumed, Jon's voice
announcing,

— I've been stabbed, man! I've been stabbed.

~~~

The wound, far from serious as it turned out, merely a
scratch, *don't bleed on the amplifiers!* a tetanus shot would be
required nevertheless. The afternoon began slowly to resume
its usual course, siren song interruptions now passed, the
unknown assailant returned to his hospital ward, statements
taken by the police, and Jon taken to casualty. Hanging
around till closing time, I cycled slowly home, taking this
time the main road, the long steep hill around Priory Woods
beckoning, a means to burn some nervous energy, to make
tired muscles twitching with too much adrenaline, in thrall to
an already restless mind. Home, James still nowhere around,
I grabbed some fruit, a notebook, heading for the beach,
thoughts of a new lyric rattling around, intercut with replay
highlights from the day's play, over and over, the mind's eye
distracted, unfocused. I thought back over the afternoon's
diversions, its grim entertainments. They were comic in a
manner that only the Island could make happen, they erupted
from the heat of summer in a fashion wholly typical of

Island time. The Island, I and James had always thought, made things happen when it was bored with the ordinary, or when it felt us becoming bored, when it wished to distract us from our own distractions, those moments where tension settled along the bone, in the nerve, the sinew, making us conduits for its stranger conjurations. The Island had brought Annagreth here, had brought me to James, Kate to us both; it had put a percussionist in our path, first seen wearing a rubber dog's head. It had gripped us in the summer, the hottest anyone could remember, and slowed time's passage, causing its flow to cease, becoming instead, the slow, barely creeping ooze of crystallizing honey, visibly grained, clouding, as if onward motion required some more violent coaxing. Sometimes, I thought that evening, heading through the village, and hearing in my head another's words, Roy Harper's, words about villages and prisoners, television shows a metaphor for our stranger existences; sometimes, the Island caused ruptures in the fabric of its own pleasantly mundane realities; surreal surges, they sought to push us on, make us act. Everything had tended towards a bursting point in time, bringing back the onward flow. Compelled by this thought, I had to tell someone.

~~~

— Haven't seen you in a few days; thought you might have run off to join the circus. I was going to tell Kate she'd have to take all the vocal duties; or else we'd have to unleash Graeme.

James had been the first to arrive that Wednesday at the barn. I had been there since the previous evening, Kate letting me sleep in the loft, after I had called on a whim from a phone box on the sea wall. I had needed to cycle some more, the words of a song, ideas for the melody, and chords already formed; and I had needed also to talk, replaying in my head the stabbing, its strange slow motion moment too

cinematically incidental to make it any more bizarre in the
retelling. Though not exactly neutral like Shona, Kate would
be, I reasoned, and indeed was, on my side, whatever side it
was I believed myself to be on. So, calling from a call box on
the way, having met at the Vine shortly after eight, we talked
and talked, of everything and nothing, of the day, and of
Annagreth, Anna. Three hours later, together we cycled back
around the harbour and through Bembridge, to sit, talking
till late or early, accompanied by John Peel and, silently, the
highlights from Headingly.

But what of that conversation stays with me? What comes
to me from the evening, as we sat, airless, a breathless hush,
isn't that what the poem says, yes, a breathless hush in the
close that night, and everywhere else also. What stays? Island
time had resumed its stalled, idling nature, waking itself
just enough that day to make me act, to add to the scales a
small weight, enough to unbalance, causing the fulcrum of
my indolence to sway, precipitating, however slightly, small
actions. Talking through the afternoon, the stabbing with
Kate, I explained in the wholly unself-conscious way I had
with only those who were close to me, my theory about
Island magic. Sitting that evening, in the trellised, vine-
encumbered garden to the back of the Vine, martens rising
on the warmer currents, unknown to us below, slicing with
the blade of their outstretched wings through the yellowing
air, Kate paused before speaking. Thinking to roll a cigarette,
she hesitated, clearly thought better of this, as something
getting in the way of what she would say. This was, I thought,
unlike her. Kate was either silence or all for playing an array
of expansive verbal shots, cover drives and cuts. No playing
in for her. Finally,
— I think there is something here, this place, but it doesn't
do to talk about it. There are already too many words, do you
know? Look around you, no, not literally man, I mean, listen.
Background chatter, information that's useless. We eavesdrop,
overhear, and the result is what exactly? It's all useless. We're

not like that, because we play, we sing. We don't need the everyday words; this is why you tell people about trees, flowers, ley lines for God's sake, because you think these things matter—and they do, they're part of the world, much more so than all the big world bollocks, politics, so-called historical so-called events, which only have any importance to the extent that they generate more chatter, and more and more. Words are overused and they never express, most of the time, what they're meant to. The Island gives us all a nudge sometimes when those of us who are in tune with it need pushing off the edge, into the sea, back into some meaningful flux; other than that, it's happy for us to circle, waiting for the next feeding. You needed today to take you out of yourself, don't you get that, you needed the shove, the shock, to get you to act on your own; the German girl,

— Anna, Annagreth, she said to call her Anna.

— Yes, whatever, her, you see how words get in the way? Annagreth, she turned up the other day because she was meant to; why here rather than somewhere else doesn't matter a toss, the why is unimportant, it always is; no, that's not right, what I mean is that the why is everything but there aren't words for the why; you did *Howards End* didn't you, with Haddon? Yes, so did my year. *Only Connect*…. Oooh, what's that meant to be? Portentous? Mystical? Wistful? Longing? And then he ends with a crop of hay!

— "such a crop of hay as never!"

I quoted, providing the punch line I knew Kate expected me to offer.

— Writing it down, he's right and he's wrong; right for the feeling, wrong for even trying to express it. The *why*, the *only connect*, well yes, and no, they're the directions, not the goal, and working them out, which is worse than expressing them, misses the point, but they're there for others so that we can get on with the important things, like music, like feelings, man. Get me another pint.

I returned, hands wet from the condensation already

gathered, cellar cold liquid against warm air, separated only by glass.

— So, and here's a thing, she liked the music, you say. That's the obvious bit. She spoke to you though, not to me, not to Graeme, not to James.

— Well, you were already engaged, don't you recall, Graeme was in the ducking stool, I don't recall exactly what James was doing but I know I saw him, off somewhere

— You're missing the point again, looking for the *why*. You might as well say, why did she wait till then to talk, why not find any of us, why, why, why? You can keep asking till this pint refills itself, but it doesn't answer, does it? No. She spoke to you. You liked her. Clearly you did or you wouldn't have come here this evening. You never talk to the others when it comes to something you're not sure about, or you are sure about but you're not sure you want to be sure about, or you're sure you're sure, and don't want to be unsure, but you need me to give you the shove that you don't realise the Island gives you anyway. So you come here, you tell me about the afternoon, you don't tell me about Annagreth, you avoid that, and it's so obvious you're avoiding that. You really are obtuse at times, I think you do it deliberately; my dad said, just the other day, *that boy*

Kate dropped into a perfect imitation of her father's east coast, surf softened intonation, bringing with it the ghost of her own younger self.

— That boy is just a mass of feelings he's not even aware of, and he knows he's smarter than most but isn't comfortable with that so he hides it all, even from himself; someone needs to tell him; well I'm telling you, and if you don't just let this be what it is right now with her, you'll make an arse out of a pig's ear; you're not like James, you don't blow your brain cells out with alcohol; you don't go down the pub like normal idiots, get ratarsed and then return to normal stupidity the next day; you're your own kind of idiot, aren't you; I bet you've written a song already, you see, I knew it, and you're going to have to put it away or get used to the other two making comments; or, you'll get it all arse about face, and we'll spend the next couple of months as you mope. So don't worry about the why, you know what's happened. Annagreth likes you, she spoke to you; you like her, otherwise, otherwise, everything else that's happened wouldn't have happened, or it would but not in the way you're seeing it.

— *Time, gentlemen—and Ladies—please, last orders, time.*

— Oh good, time's winged bloody chariot, the only time when it actually gets a move on around here, when publicans want it to; get another round in, then we'll head back to the barn; you can play me that song.

The next day, Wednesday, was to be got through, I had thought, endured. When Graeme finally arrived, inevitably behind hand, late, just like your fills, less joke than meaningless already well-worn greeting, I, with various additions from Kate, had recounted, for the benefit of the Prosecution, all the salient facts that were the case. Whether his thoughts were more on the rehearsal and new material, or whether he was finally making in-roads through Leila's defenses, James surprised both Kate and I, with the serious, considered, and considerate attention he appeared to give. Seems you like one another, was almost all that was said, other than asking Kate whether she'd already heard Annagreth's playing the day before, no, she was looking forward to surprising us all, tomorrow, I think; I'm not like you, I don't push people. James already had a vision of a five-piece, what we could do extended further, another new beginning, a fresh departure, landscape broadening before our collective eyes, with someone who played keyboards, and might also be able to sing. Graeme would, I thought, be the one with the questions, the comments, the jokes, all innuendo and wind-up; on the drums, I had once introduced him, Captain Clockwork, a deliberately chosen alliterative allusion, which on the surface could easily have referred to his metronomic precision, but which was also a tacit acknowledgement, unless you knew, of his ability to egg people on, get them going, set them off. Just having a laugh,

bugger, was always the excuse, the explanation as he saw
it, as if, to some, it seemed he had no idea that it was even
plausible to go too far. Just far enough. So it was with some
relief then, that when asked, how was Sunday then, where'd
you get to, what'd you get up to? I gave a cursory outline of
the day's journey, knowing there had been a previous, secret
pact between those of us who still resided on a planet that
was round, not flat, to omit all mention of Monday. The
devil's bargain had been sealed, by my promising James a
bottle of malt, and Kate such help as was needed with her
newly acquired fleece, collected earlier that day. No love
without bribery.

~~~

One of those many conversations I hold dear. Whenever
we talk, we know, don't we, that in choosing to speak of
this rather than that, we conceal. Of course, we don't always
do that deliberately, most of the time we are not aware that
this is what is passing. We cannot help but choose. That
Wednesday evening though, through the radiance of your
smile, the good gracious humour of all, in everything you
didn't say, of all I felt I wanted to say if I could only frame
the words, much, so much was being said, without us saying
anything directly. Or at least, we said everything other than
the very thing our silences revealed, beneath the covering, the
hide our words prepared. But then, within the conversation
and the silence, a music, pure sound. After, I remember: not
the words but, once more, always as if for a first time, every
time a first time, *overture, prelude, opening*, your voice, her voices.
     Arriving at the cottage promptly, *have a nice time, kids, don't
play rough*, James's voice booming from somewhere unseen *in
loco parentis, at least one parent is insane* had always been his very
loose translation, Annagreth, Anna was wearing again the
silk sunflower dress. Deciding to walk, with advance warning
that there would be a stile, we followed Pondwell Hill to the
pub, its dusty dry winding motion curving right to reach the

apex of a triangle formed by the path, Oakhill Road, and the Duver, the triangle's base separating land from sea. Grass on every side no longer golden brown, but burnt to washed out paste grey white, brittle to the touch, hard enough to trace small white lines on the skin. Already busy when we arrived, the pub buzzed insistently but low, without energy. There was a table outside, near the ornamental well, toward the darker corner near an even darker oak canopied lane. With the exception of strings of light bulbs edging the roof's guttering, only the lights from inside the building illuminated the patio, which, dusk touched, offered the promise of solitude in the middle of the crowd. Far enough from the road, the occasional car or bike caused little interruption to conversation. Shadow on shadow, deep dark wells gathered into black from overhanging horse chestnut trees, from in and out of which small children ran, circling rapidly, then halting, only to head off again, around the well. The sound of two pennies hitting the water, the odd burst of laughter, and away up the hill a barking, possibly a fox, penetrated the busy wash of subdued conversation. Dark enough to be obscured, light enough to trace in the face of the other person hints of thought, secrets unexpressed, there beneath a sky indifferent to emotional turbulence, any sudden human activity. Last, diluted pastel strokes of weak colour washed out the heavens. Meticulously textured, the coming night anticipated in its dusk, eventide the more perfect word in a place where sky and sea were sympathetic sisters, by the friendly presences of strangers all around, half ghostly, crepuscular in shape, your voice, Annagreth, Calliope's voice unfurled. Silken wrapped, greyness darkening downy. As Anna spoke, we were submerged under the weight, air kissed, of the end of the day's disorganized tenderness. Outlines merging many folded, the fond enormity of night touched us spellbinding. Her voice, the voices in her voice that night touched, a call to the heart, a kiss on the eyelid causing sleep.

What was said? I hear that question forming, impossibly. What was said, I cannot tell. Not because I cannot remember,

but because I will not say. That would be to betray, to break
a spell. Certain words remain a secret; confidences trivial
or otherwise stay so, even though the stranger knows the
secret to be one, not to be given away carelessly, wasted,
spent without thought. I would sooner sell myself. Even
though, just imagine, the very idea, even if I were to spell
out every word; even had I the heart, the heartlessness, to
attempt the nuances of tone, the ways in which the sounds
of Annagreth's voice insinuated themselves like a breeze
from a half open window on a warm night into the deepest
slumber to call through dreams, I know they would not reach
anyone as, that night, they traced themselves in me, leaving
in their wake a thread to follow, as if a night scent; fragrance
of a voice, imagine if you can, fugue interwoven throughout
the lighter words, entwining, wreathing, spiraling, curling,
looping, interlacing, weaving, through the distances of sleep,
as intricately as that night Annagreth's hair was braided.
Threading through me, Anna's voice. Can anyone hear this?
Were I to repeat the words verbatim, would anyone hear in
the way, that night, I heard, underneath, below the words,
the silences, the pauses and the gaps, a stranger resonance
unplumbed? No. There, where she was. Just that, where
whatever is seen is not, whatever not seen, is. There you are.
What I hold dear.

~~~

No hesitation that Wednesday night in conversation, no
awkward parting volleys, miscued, mistimed, wide of the
mark. Thursday already planned, Anna and I agreed dinner
on Sunday. Rehearsals might extend late into the evening over
the next few days, as was usually the habit, concluding with a
quick drink over in St Helens, at the Vine, *yes, we play there,* and
some Chinese takeaway, settling down in the barn, upstairs,
for a late night film, if there was one. There was, I had
suggested a small place in Ryde, Alice's, virtually unique on
the Island in that it served food of Mediterranean and North

African origin. And, then, I added, leaving the door open, four days' of doing nothing.

Thursday came. When James and I got to the barn that morning, Anna was already there, with Kate, the two of them, with Harry's help, having pulled the Hammond into place, the Rhodes at right angles to it, all cables arranged. James and I organized the PA, and the first pot of tea of the day making its appearance as we waited for Graeme. Always this way, we knew, inevitable for so many reasons, but there would be at least forty-five minutes' wait before we could hope for a sighting.

— Does anyone mind if I play, while we wait?

Settling to the stool, a brief adjustment, looking around her, then toward somewhere none of us could go with her, Annagreth composed herself. Perfectly straight she sat, yet relaxed, hair again in a complex weave of braids gathered into a heavy, thickly gathered tail, conforming to her back, a soft off-white, eggshell muslin blouse, older than any of us, finely embroidered with flower sprigs. Elbow-length poets' sleeves left the forearms and hands free. What came next none of us could have expected.

Fierce, ominous chords, ferociously intense, steely scale runs played fortissimo, intended for pianoforte, but now transformed by the hammer on tine arrangement of the Fender, producing a shimmering fire, ethereal, a blazing world of tonal sublimity. Is it possible to imagine Schubert played on a celesta? How to describe that sound, the thundering runs, intimating harmonic tintinnabulation, bell on bell, small undertones, echoic oscillations, resonances, the sonic palette pushing towards the slightest distortion momently, here and there? A mood shift took us into the lengthy, strangely calm, yet uneasy transition, all anxious top lines, squirrelling above ripples of watery sound, the electronic amplification from within the keyboard adding to the gauzy harmonic wash, small instances of dissonance, before a decisive and irrevocable movement into the Adagio:

contemplation vied with bruising triplets, unorthodox, a
departure from the classical forms of the opening movement,
a chromatic harmonic structure, the pulse driving on, the
rhythm tattooed from the bass as ghostly chromatic scales
swept across that Amen, that plagal cadence leading to the
haunted sonority, modulation, terrifying sforzando, before
a semitone ascension. Then that sombre acoustic world
of the Menuetto, moving to those interruptions, silent
bars every fourth one. Finally, Allegro, 6/8, a tarantella:
incessant onrush, the discursive three-key exposition so
often employed by Schubert, then modulation, modulation,
another, a new theme, growing, unknown, unseen, to
be followed by a recapitulation and that long expectant
passage. No story, no narrative, just the ineffable sublimity
of pure music, the impossible made actual, another world,
outlandish, inexplicable, glimpsed, but for which there was
no representation. Smooth melodic lines over staccato left-
hand work moving the piece, moving us, moving inside, the
small but spellbound audience taken up, into the coda and
conclusion. Hear what can be heard, if that is possible. Hear
not in the words but everything else not in the words, that
which lies the other side of silence greater than any sound.

Her hands lifted, hovering, kites eyeing invisible prey,
Anna swiveled away, not looking at us, to assume a rhythmic
repeating twelve-bar bass line on the Hammond, a walking,
no a sashaying line, at once recognizable, syncopation
seductive. Lifting herself from the stool, her head beginning
a nodding punctuation, Annagreth began to smile knowingly,
eyes sparkling as she looked towards us, a sense of mischief,
coquettishness, the vamping bass line accompanying the
provocative smirk. No melody as yet, her right hand reached
behind for the piano stool, bringing it before the organ
keyboard, as she seated herself once more, to take up the
melody, the tune's chromatic minors and ominous triplets,
riffing repeatedly, shifting keys strangely consonant in the
mind with the D.958. Then it was we realized that Annagreth
was also playing the bass part on the pedals; looking at James,

I mouthed smilingly there goes your job, as Kate picked up
the viola to begin laying improvised and understated lines
over the B3. Then a drum, a tabla. Graeme had arrived
towards the end of the Schubert, but had not wanted to
distract or take attention away; with the shift from Schubert
to Stax, he had decided to join in. James and I looked at one
another, once more. We could only join in.

~~~

That day the question was asked. Nearly seven, tiredness
creeping everywhere, in everyone, looks exchanged on several
occasions, *this was right*, we began to unwind, slow down,
moving to a slower pace. Harry, never one to intrude, had
kept dropping in, *just dropping by*, standing silent in a corner,
eyes alight with something akin to religious fervour or his
first trip, foot tap-tapping, electric signals sinewing their way
along the cortex, through the muscles, alive and independent
of thought, called by the music. The first three hours, we
played through material we had played at the Harbour Lights,
the School, deciding what we would leave in, leave out,
for the coming shows, choosing also other less frequently
played pieces for gigs less typical, a wine bar, a barn dance,
and a birthday party, with specific requests. This was not
an audition, no one had expected to see what Annagreth
might do, how she would situate herself inside the existing
arrangements; Kate's invitation had been open ended, *just
come along, sit in, have a play*, that encouraging warmth she
would exhibit infrequently with strangers, outsiders as she
thought them, and which feeling she had, more than once,
made plain. So, Anna came, just to sit in, to play. All she
asked of any tune was the key, occasionally the principal
chord progressions, and so would sit, still and listening,
to opening bars, a verse, a phrase, before adding, with the
lightest of touches, the most sensitive of responses, call
and answer, into gaps, spaces, across and between melodies,

punctuating, counterpointing, adding colour, accenting. As
the barn warmed throughout the morning, so the sound
of organ and piano involved, insinuating itself ever more
irresistibly, infectiously. Collectively and individually, we began
to notice how at times we were following, not being followed,
melodies, harmonies, rhythmic transformations, working
themselves out, opening up playfully; drawn in, enthralled,
spellbound, feeling the fever tow of an ineluctable, at times
hallucinatory, high, willingly addicted. Soundscapes opened,
hue, shade, tint, tone, colouration, wash, broadened, warping,
taking on novel piquancy, every piece, each riff or phrase a
new vitality. Even the most familiar of tunes reinvented itself
in inexpressibly small ways, the most delicate of caresses.
The heat, enclosed, mutated as though we were together
dissolving into one another, a prodigious synaesthetic trip.
Euphoria had found us all.

Taking a lunch break, stretching, walking outside, nothing
was said. Perhaps it would be truer to say that everything else
had already been said, anything but that which was to the
point. Annagreth seemed, simply, as though she belonged.
This was so obvious, like sun rising that it was not a matter
for a question. What could be asked, or stated? Day after
day that summer would be followed by yet more of the
same, summer become eternity: reservoirs emptying if not
already emptied, riverbeds cracking, forest fires flaming into
dangerous life, standpipes policed; signal boxes burning out;
roadsigns appeared stating the obvious, you are entering a
drought area; Graeme had asked if such a sign had been
placed at Customs in every airport. No one any longer
expected changes in the weather. So it was. Neither Kate,
James, Graeme, nor I thought that what we had heard, what
had taken place, whatever it was, was anything other than
what should be, and what would be, the song, in changing,
remaining the same.

Viking digs a trench in first stage of hunt for life on Mars,
a headline read in 'The Times', which James had thrown
folded. Looking at this, wondering at its statement, I realized

that it was making no sense. Had a longship lost its way several hundred years ago? Did I have heatstroke? Was I dehydrated, or was this just one more sign of our sideways drift, Island tempo folding, tectonic confusion, slices of time plate on plate colliding?
— Bugger wants to dig for signs of water. My dad's at his wits' end.

Graeme weighed in, restoring if not normal service, then, a percipient common sense in the face of otherwise unfathomable, but patently inescapable evidence of predestination. Elsewhere in the newspaper there were other signs of incipient strangeness, with 'The Times' accused of confusing Australia.
— Well, I'm confused, so it must be widespread.

James offered this. Germans were leading in the dressage, gags were called for on MPs, there were no Test prospects from the ranks of Yorkshire and Worcestershire, while Middlesex shone with bat and ball, and Graham Gooch was described as an improbable agent of destruction, taking a fivefor, Essex playing the West Indies. Graham Gooch. Bowling. Medium-paced, right-arm seamers. Our need for a pianist exposed, when we had been quite happy to get on with things believing ourselves to be doing quite nicely thank you. No, the world gone mad, the world turned upside down.

Resuming, we began work on new songs, instrumentals, pieces with words, mostly our own, a traditional dance tune, and a shared favourite to which we all felt we could do justice. At first playing along, Annagreth remained silent, largely, watching, listening, finding her own place in the forms. Back and forth, a tug, some tension, then working the material, dough and clay showing their true shapes from within, as we found how to breathe life in each piece. One song though, 'It's Not Safe', remained recalcitrant, unsympathetic to all our efforts. We had spent more time on this, the afternoon grinding ever slower, more frustrating, than on all the other new pieces together. Though outside the sky was that, by now, contemptuously boring crystalline blue, in the barn Kate, who was to sing this, looked thunder. We had stopped making suggestions, offering insights, all the maybes, what ifs, perhaps, how abouts, and why don't we's abandoned. Every so often something doesn't work. A sentence, a rhyme, a recipe, a relationship. The substance does not cohere, mismatched elements, qualities, ingredients, personalities, all expressions of form resolved are an impossibility, and the failure we feel, closely, agonizingly, to be our own, recrimination, annoyance and guilt making brash proclamations, often, too often, in equal measure, an equality you realise was never to be found in what became failure. Silk purses, sow's ears offered greater hope.

— Can I, do you mind? I have a thought.

Annagreth talked us through an arrangement, orchestrating, emphasizing, harmonizing parts she had heard, which as yet we had not. Playing a phrase with her left hand, slowing down a great deal the tempo we had thought might have worked, Anna suggested I play this, developing it into a repeating arpeggiated form, adding a note to resolve itself back to its beginning, in order that it became a hypnotic arabesque, as she sustained beneath that a single, minor chord; telling Graeme to refrain from playing underneath the opening two lines, then only to add the lightest, briefest of fills, some bells, vielleicht ein bißchen, sorry, perhaps a little, or shimmer the cymbals, do not bring in a regular beat until the third verse, no high-hat then, just bass and tom-toms, while for James, not bass, no, I do that, a trumpet line, single long notes, sehr langsame, high, like Miles. The song began to show itself. Ending, everyone stood there not knowing what had happened, quite. Graeme was all twitchiness, his face alive, replaying, rethinking, as he tightened the snare. Kate, remaining still, had been looking at her feet. Looking from underneath her brow, not raising her head completely, a wink to me, a smile acknowledging certainty. I looked from Kate, to Anna. That gesture, that motion that said, there you are, acknowledging that everything had been just as it should be, eyes slightly widening, the forward movement of her head, a hand tidying a wayward strand of hair. James dripped, bowling ball, slick bright dome, a fountain, the only water readily available this summer of drought; rubbing my face, stretching my eyes wide, as a question and a punctuation for what had just happened, passing him a towel, as he removed the trumpet's mouthpiece, tapping out the moisture.

— Here, stop yourself from drowning.

Let's do that again.

A bright, earnest focus consumed the room, a nearly visible frequency taking all available space, condensing air, restraining us through its close packed immediacy. Somewhere between us a palpable but unheard broadcast was released, murmuring and luminous. Does this make sense, I ask myself again, insistently. Is it possible to give the impression a manifestation self-evident in its every evasion, failure of assault and swerve, all expression failing? I cannot tell. The lines converged, the threads of sound, of note giving way to note, others sustained, above, below, bass keyboard chord sustained and bearing in it onward the high, fragile sounding trumpet, bright filaments of light dissolving, twins closely twined, inseparable grasp, as metal wings darted and dodged, sheering off, bearing aloft the drones, the whirling dervish half-time motif of bell-like strings, all coruscation scintillating, kaleidoscopic. And over this all, Kate's voice, but also, higher yet, pure coming from a place where there is no oxygen, Annagreth, a harmony, taking a note, sustaining, then glissando or melisma. The verses ended, we had moved into an instrumental series of variations around the chorus, Kate having taken up the violin once more. Then slowly, one by one, everyone playing slightly less, one after the other, diminishing in volume, withdrawing, until, we found, as if waking from a dream or a children's tale of magic and other lands, we had returned to end where we had started.

Then the question came, from Kate.

— Do you want to join us?

~~~

No answer to Kate's question came for another two weeks,
did it? A Friday. The Harbour Lights once more, Friday 13th
August, the eighth night of fourteen shows crammed in ten
days. Superstition was to be more than tested that evening.
You were not being evasive, I know, I believe we all did. You
had not expected this however, so asked Kate, asking us
all, whether we would mind being patient. You told me this
quite spontaneously, later that same year. You had not meant
to leave the answer hanging, but had found it impossible
to respond immediately, you said, not knowing the source
of your own recalcitrance. It just happened. Was anyone
surprised by your not accepting immediately, so impossibly
right had everything appeared? Was there a destiny? Had your
arrival here now, when we had all become denizens of light,
always been coming? Talismanic alignment having before
always been the unquestioned lodestone in our collective
belief in who we were, how was it possible that the inevitable
was not the same as the immediate? As someone anxiously
cautious, I had not been surprised, expecting nothing, at least
with regard to musical direction, reformation, transformation.
Graeme, enthusiastic, blithe to a degree of bovine fatalism,
was unworried. He knew, he had always known, he said, two
weeks on what the answer would be.
— Bugger, I knew it, I told you, you daft tosser, you.
    This to James, grabbing his shoulders from behind as the
words boomed through cow catchers arranged in a grin; to
James who, though having said nothing directly, at least to
me, had become distracted by the wait, Graeme was to tell
me later. James had been visiting Cowes more often than was
either usual or ascribable to Leila. This came as a surprise to
me, one more, one of many that summer, when all I cared for
was to play; all I cared for, that is, until a Saturday afternoon
when you stepped from the light, a voice, a silhouette, a
hand. As for Kate, Kate showed no signs of being troubled
by your, Annagreth's answer. I believe, I told you that day

you expressed your concern over having not been more forthcoming, that had Kate been troubled, had she not taken your eventual signing on to our band of refugees as the inevitability it afterwards appeared, written in the stars, bugger, that's what they say, then she would have said so at the time, pressed matters.

Thursday into Friday, then Saturday. James more than typically enervated after the experience of a high. Dies caniculares, Latin for bad luck, evil times. Dog days were upon us, sluggish time, idling, malign influences, heliacal ascension, Sirius rising. Wheatley might have been on to something, Crowley, it seemed, was not the least to blame. Nothing doing and too much canned chatter, the absence of any willpower in those days as evidenced by James's withdrawal into his, mercifully infrequent, taciturn, saturnine other self, whilst waiting for August to get under way, giving us insight into the worthlessness of talent at such a time. There would, I knew, be a day for James soon, to go missing in action, one of those periodic, if sporadic right brain sabbaticals, which would come, it was to be hoped, with a fervour tending towards prayer and the offering of sacrifices, to arrive sooner rather than later, and certainly not the day before we started playing again. Annagreth had stayed on into Thursday evening, but Friday held commitments. Saturday then, we said, as I walked to her car with her.

~~~

Stairway to…where did that doorway, deep magenta, off Union Street, up the staircase lead you and I that Saturday? To Alice's, *go ask Alice, living not next door, but upstairs with Alice,* an indoor souk, exotic wonderland, Araby on the Solent. A small, secluded restaurant above Oz, heavy draped, scented with patchouli and, from the kitchen, nightscent of spices never seen, or smelled in most English homes. And, of course, just that little hint of very English whimsy, Carollian folly. Dark heavy drapes depended from the ceiling,

rich purple, red, damask brocades; large cushions, golden
tasseled, deep rich blues, into which one folded rather than
sat, their generous substance as dense as their coverings were
elaborate and rich. Small, ornately inlaid tables, were placed
around the room in its several alcoves, their tops displaying
marquetry detailed peacocks, flecks of ivory white material
accenting wood and marble, agate shards, abstract geometric
patterns, repetition tending to the promise of infinity.
Hookah pipes, Persian pattern vases, adorned shelves, inset
into walls painted a light consuming porphyry, edges stenciled
in curling whisps of exotic, suggestive floral shapes, picked
out a darker blue purple, hinted at around circumference
curve in golds and silvers. Transported, taken up, we found
ourselves fallen upwards into a little afterworld, antechamber
to an eighteenth-century traveller's illustration of Paradise,
pairidaeza, pardis, a tiny oasis where, through its magical
doorway, the Isle of Wight became one of the Fortunate
Isles, all rose aroma frippery and indulgence. Though we had
not as yet walked the streets of paradise, we had, we found,
entered one of its many houses, this amongst the most
delightful.

Colin, small, ginger, balding, spritely, co-owner, with his
partner Jon, of Oz, and Alice's spritely, fey guiding light, its
genius loci, greeted us, with his usual mix of archness and
camp dismissiveness, kindly condescending to anyone not
gay, as if from pity, leading us to one of the deeper alcoves.

— Just the two of you, nice. Hello I'm Colin; trying to civi-
lize him, are we? Did you wash your hair? Good luck dear,
nice to meet you by the way, lovely dress, beautiful. Saved
you the best table, not that you deserve it, ungrateful child,
especially on a Saturday. Still, you've left the others at home
for a change; did you remember to change the straw in the
big one's cage? You are, by the way? He'll never remember to
introduce us.

Annagreth's eyes sparkled in the reflected lights of the
room, subdued but pointedly brilliant here and there, as she

smiled responses at Colin, amused, wholly involved in his performance.

— This is a lovely place, *entzückend, sehr reizvoll*, charming, enchanting, no? Excuse me, I have to get used to speaking English all the time, almost all the time.

— I knew you were cultured, I could tell. Barbaric lot we are, the English, most of us anyway. He's not as bad as some, I suppose. I'll get you menus.

Colin whisked away, all stage business, pausing briefly to enquire of other diners if they were enjoying themselves, having a nice evening. We had hardly settled ourselves, when, a genie out of his bottle and determined never to go back in, there was Colin, menus in one hand, an ice bucket, ostentatiously presenting a dark green bottle, orange labelled.

— On the house, my lovely, we're graced. I'll get some water for you both.

Smiling conspiratorially at us both, Colin was gone, once more.

~~~

Nearly midnight,

— The witching hour, my lovelies, your bed, *sorry!* Your *beds* are calling to you! And so is mine, I'm not a young man you know.

We found ourselves the last diners.

— Thank you, this has been lovely, special, thank you. You are a lovely man. I look forward to coming back.

Hugging Colin, his face over Annagreth's shoulder all knowing smirk, collusive Cupid that he was, she turned, took my hand, and we went down, beyond the closing door, cast out of Paradise, fallen back into the world. Union Street's Victorian fronts slumbered stonily, lampposts strung light to light with festive bulbs, interspersed with Jubilee bunting. No breeze at all, no breath, no life in wind upon the moribund air, and yet there was, somehow, the perceptible lifting of a weight, the felt removal of something that had been overshadowing the summer these past several weeks. Time

was beginning, if not to move, then to be wound up, ready
for its intricate motions to resume. We knew ourselves inside
the mechanism, making little adjustments.

— Well…

— Well!

Suction of the dance, irresistible the steps, measuring the
tempo, before stepping in together, complementary shapes,
gestures, lines imitating, mirroring. Already, we had agreed
to spend the following day at the beach, a day already here
in essence, both of us agreeing that, well, things would be
getting busy, it's important to be organized, to plan, yes, this
agreed with embarrassed laughter, so, well, then, allowing
for commitments, Monday out, lessons for me, you were
spending the afternoon and evening with your parents'
friends, you couldn't wait to play a real piano again, did I
want to come over Tuesday for supper, yes, and we could
meet beforehand at the Fountain for a drink, you could
meet Shona, could I, would I mind, no not at all, perhaps
Wednesday Osborne House or Carisbrooke Castle, why
not both? A good idea, then you've really seen everything,
Thursday you would probably want to spend some time at
the piano, we had a meeting before Friday night began the
next round of shows, but you would be welcome to come for
a drink, no, you didn't want to intrude, of course not, I quite
understood. So. Well, then. Tomorrow. The cottage, then
Priory Bay, it was agreed.

Who had been there, how many, what they had looked
like, what we ate, I find it impossible now to remember,
Anna. When I go back to that place, I come to you, you are
that place, you are all, she is all he sees, sunflower golden
cotton sundress, a loose scarf of silver threads; everything
that night was you, was her, Anna, Annagreth, nothing else
mattered. Lost at sea, though safe, we two, sailing away in our
own imagined pea-green boat. I find, in seeking to recollect,
I disappear into you, into the thought of her, the idea of
a feeling, ghost of a touch upon skin, long remembered,
afterglow of caress, though on that night no lasting touch

as yet, nothing more than brief hand on hand, the brush of lips on cheek, the momentary collaboration of eye touching eye, impossibly close, falling into the other, one in the eye of the other, an endless refraction. There you were. There you are. Here. Yesterday is once again now, though not today. Never the present, the now returns, remaining to return, surreptitious souvenir, always to come when I least expect it.

~~~

Dreamlike those days: recently, I was recalled to this belief when, visiting a gallery, Houseman and Hardy cheek by jowl in my satchel, I read in the catalogue of the exhibition the assertion that, in English visionary art, the landscape and countryside were metaphors for our more complex emotional landscapes. I knew this, had felt it often, even before I had words to express it at a distance. Around me, paintings of box hedges, high skies, undulating pasture dotted here and there with clumps and copses of thickly impenetrable almost blackgreen trees, badminton or cricket games frozen in time, or sun descending at the edge of a frame, blazing one last glory golden late afternoon, everywhere around surreal Wessex world, manicured yet dangerously priapic, pagan in its very Englishness. Everywhere the physical world, the material landscape, conduits, channeling feeling, sensuously wrought experience and perception, engendering memory's overflow, from eye to heart to head and back once more, a Moebius strip, figure of Mneme's dance, moving in the wake of Calliope's voice. Never and always, those days. I turned, feeling you behind me, looking silently over my shoulder. How I wanted to tell you. In such a place, at such a time we lived. You made the place for me what it was, what it became and how it has always remained. This vision. But like all visionary work, it shows me something impossibly close, impossibly far, somewhere once or yet to come, but no longer now. Green remembered hills a foreign country. Excluded, I am shut out and weeping for a loss made plenitude in memory. How I want to say. *Sehnsucht. Saudade.*

Words for which there are no words; words that make do
when no words can, or ought to, describe. Write to me your
wordless words, speak those silences, sing your silent music
that in dreams enters through my ears to call me back to then,
to when, to you, to her. Oh my love, how much…

~~~

The beach that Sunday, the woods, rambling, swimming,
exploring rock pools, the first day of August. Tumbled into
the week we went, together, apart, together once more,
coming and going, assuming the rhythms of separation and
closeness, all too quickly but seeming at the time as if it was
out of time, for all time, never and always. Keeping safe the
memories, guarding them jealously, as if behind a *jalousie*,
a word you loved, one more which you collected, and on
which you played, in order that not everything be seen, only
what appears through the gaps of the blind, now wider, now
narrower. Tuesday evening, you were exuberant, the piano
had, the previous day, been wonderful, to play again, even
after so short a time, how much you said you had missed that,
as if seeing someone dear who had been absent. The length
of absence did not matter, you said, a week, two, or just a
day, there was something you continued in the nature, the
experience of absence that made it unendurable. Dogs know
this, you had reflected, why not more humans?

Then Wednesday, I having stayed once more with Graeme,
this time more organized, to Osborne, it is impossible to
imagine a prettier spot. At least for this time, Victoria was, it
is to be imagined, for once, amused; and on to Carisbrooke,
the castle, prison to Charles I, but, more impressive to you,
the castle donkeys, Donkeys, Janet! I proclaimed falsetto, all
Edith Evans, without the handbag, frightening the grockles,
what, gekkos? no, an island word, tourists; haemorrhoids,
Kate and James call them, the same in German, you replied,
hemorrhoid, but why? Because, you see, it's Kate's joke really,
but James will insist on shouting it at them when he's had a

drink or three, because tourists are red and blotchy, they hang around in groups for a long time, and are a pain in the…
in the back garden, you said. Touché! At this, the absurdity of association, I began to laugh uncontrollably, the sound ratcheting up through decibels, your allergic response egging me on, until all air spent, I started to bray and snort, to which, much to the amusement of the collection of beetroot, leathery tanned and peeling impromptu audience, two of the donkeys began to reply.

Sitting outside the castle walls that afternoon, the nearest convenient grass verge, ice creams eaten in haste against their own meltdown, we talked about the upcoming gigs. Without raising the question of joining us, I touched on the subject of seeing one another despite the band's being busy. Yes, there would be the possibility of a lunch here and there, but,
— You know, if you'd like to get a full idea of what we do, if you care to waste your time that is, hearing the same things over and over, why not come along to a few? You'd be doing me a favour, saving me from having to make small talk with strangers.
— Yes, you could make small talk with me.
Wrinkling nose, head forward slightly, bright smiling broadly catching me in the tease.
— You know what I mean; I mean, I'd really like to see you, if you wanted to, that is.
Always the word dance, yes, and the delight in this, playing at playing, play within play. The carefully contoured spontaneity, as days slipped by, lives entwined, unwritten lines unfurling with that perfection of an improvisation haunted by its ghost partner, the well-crafted phrase learned by heart. But it is the heart which writes our lines, isn't it? The delivery comes, as it should, from the autocue of the other, the beloved, whose touching prompt encourages the ad lib, not off the cuff so much as from the open hand, blown, an imaginary butterfly in your direction, your hand reaching up, before your face or just above your head, clasping lovingly. And always, with a smile, the invisible. Arriving.

~~~

— Here, take this.

Ten days. Fourteen shows. Always the exhaustion
competing with the elation, adrenaline the tensile binding
between the two, another one up, one more down.
Enumerate the styles, name venues, give the playlists. Back
once more to the too predictable, in the face of just doing
what we did. Why? To what end? Compiling archives for the
imaginary trainspotter, the want-to, got-to, have-to know,
a task in futility, result: pointlessness. How many covers,
how many originals, how much new material? Today, some
hobbyist would have launched a webpage, with photographs,
soundclips, audio and video files, press cuttings scanned,
virtual memorabilia, the cabinet of curiosities become an
afterlife horrorshow. And with each song: isn't that one
of, oh, what's his name's? *No, it's not, it's the other bloke you're
thinking of.* Once more, the always factual account desired
by those who could never begin to understand, but sought,
and still today seek, a short cut to whatever deadening
authenticity, determinable truth, butterfly pinned in the
collector's cabinet, they believe to be of necessity, to make
their lives easier. I say this, knowing I have said it, perhaps
all too often before. But like the poor, the obsessive, the
archivist, completest, bibliographer, ghoul, all such creatures
are always with us. If the reader recognizes himself, and
it is usually, almost invariably, a *him*, this self that lives
through feeding off the energy, the serious fun of others,
then that glimpse in the mirror I have afforded through
repeated polishing has been worthwhile. If I appear to have
scratched the surface, causing the image the other side of
the looking glass to have become distorted, consider the
scratches sympathetic outlines. Then there is the desire for
biography, pinning down the context to a single detail. The
biographical fact: is there a clue in the lyric? What made you
want to cover this rather than that? Every night the inevitable
why don't you play, more irritating than the solitary Johnny no

mates, standing at the back, nursing as if a bruise or grudge, the cheapest pint, the most tasteless swill, carbonated, cooled, metallic in its mass-produced back of the tongue sour shriveling, bile enhancing ethanol based stimulant. When everyone, the members of the band included, end their evening tired but elated, lifted for a moment out of themselves, this withered specimen approaches, *fuckwitling brain-dead bore* was James' assessment, sidling, insinuating, to tell the players, the minstrels on display for a penny in the gallery, how he thought, wisdom of the ages, walking Pandora's box of spleen, how everyone seemed a little...*off tonight.*

— Here, take this.

— What is...a lyric?

> *Not for all, these words have found you*
> *Not for all, the bell sounds true*
> *Not for all, you feel far stronger*
> *Not for everyone I say, just for you.*

Mostly though, gigs were a joy, even though it is the exceptions that tend to stay in the memory, as well as the exceptional. Making music, making people dance, nod in or out of time, feet tapping bodies sweating swaying, working the balls of the feet so as not to spill the pint. Working for the collective trance. Ritual groove. Or music to be ignored: paying well, well enough not to refuse playing, in order to stay doing this rather than something else. The more the fee, the more aural wallpaper got hung. Particularly, lunchtime duos or trios, wine bar jazz, bottled good taste, polite, inoffensive, innocuous, something to accompany the décor. All plastic sincerity, *nice to see you, come back again soon,* the last consonant rising with its rictus set platitude. Duckbilled platitudes, Kate would say, or conclude with a parting shot, *of all the places we've played, this has certainly been one.* One afternoon, in a place of more than usually tasteless good taste, ambience by the numbers, polite and petty, *break out the fondue, soup in a basket time,* we played a trio, Hot Club arrangement, bass, violin, guitar, of Brel's heartbreaking sublime plea of desperation

and repulsed, thrown away desire, *ne me quitte pas,* introduced
by James as *not my kitten's paws.* Each of us played our parts
in different keys, three whole tones apart; no one seemed to
notice. If we were playing the Devil's music there were times
when we behaved as if possessed, facing all the lost souls,
lunchtimes of the damned.

— Here, take this.

— What is…a lyric?

— Yes, obviously!

— You want me to write music for it?

> *There's a seat for us still,*
> *There's a sound in the dark,*
> *Follow me, don't look back,*
> *We won't miss the last bus.*

Friday 13th August. For those who remained at home
that evening, their cultural high point would have been *Going
for a Song,* featuring that night the somewhat bizarre pairing
of Frank Bough and Felicity Kendal: everyone's nightmare,
the porn purveyors' dream. This would have been followed
by a heat of *Jeux sans Frontieres,* though only in England,
Scotland and Northern Ireland, Wales, by some odd matter
of quantum physics, having to wait two days till Sunday.
Welsh clocks obviously ran, Kate had thought, thirty-six
hours behind the rest of the British Isles. Graeme had asked
if we would have to set our watches differently, if we ever
played over the border. James's response was that we would
probably be best off leaving watches behind, as almost
certainly they would never function properly again. James had
brought on this evening the TV set, which, like the cuboid
goat, *something else to leave behind if we go to Wales, might make the
natives restless,* a gift from friends, life size, all chicken wire and
papier maché ingenuity, was an integral, if only occasional
stage prop, too fragile to be brought out in public regularly.
*No point in having to make people choose whether to come see us, or stay
at home.* Despite the traditions surrounding the conjunction
of day and date, I felt somehow lucky, in good humour,

the day having been announced as the first observation of International Lefthanders Day. I proposed to everyone else as we were setting up, once more back at the Harbour Lights, that we celebrate somehow the sinister alignment. *That's not a good name for a band, no one even think of suggesting it.* The day was also made the more auspicious by the Bahamas' succession to the treaty on the non-proliferation of nuclear weapons. We all felt much safer. Cables sorted, gaffer tape deployed, all last minute repairs made, drinks in, we sat out on the Terrace, watching the yachts. No air left, the drought at its worst, Angie and Dave having doubled the barrel order, preparing for thirsty punters.

— Here, take this.

— What is…a lyric?

— Yes, obviously!

— You want me to write music for it?

— Yes, please. And I want you to play it. Tonight.

> *It's eclipse, all the curses they're rigging*
> *Trip the words, from the senses that shift*
> *Take the wheel, drive with blindfold tied tightly*
> *Let me guide you, a smile on my face, your hand it won't slip.*

Annagreth had been to see us the previous seven evenings, always half an hour before we were to start, always happy to leave after we had packed, her appearance as yet untainted by any sign of Damian, who was, Morphy reminded everyone, on holiday, probably half way up a mountain with his parents. *The hills are alive…still, the goats can run, if they have to; bugger; exactly, Roger, the goat! Bugger off, bugger.* Though I had said I'd invited her, no one, least of all I had expected Anna to attend every evening, as well as one of the lunch shows. *Above and beyond the call,* Kate offered, returning with her second vodka. *Serious stuff,* said James. I said nothing. In those previous days, Annagreth and I had caught a couple of afternoons together, but still everyone thought an eighth night unlikely; not even the most dedicated of our followers had such stamina. Well, there was Garry, but that was another story entirely.

8. Fourth Act: Tout Ensemble or all together, now (August 1976)

A curious calm surrounded us, as we sat, overlooking
the picture perfect still life of the harbor that early Friday
evening. Not even a gull. No cry, no squawk, not even in the
distance any motor sounds, or the piercing treble of a child's
fractious cry. The heat had smothered everything. As pieces
in a puzzle, the picture was almost complete, each piece
nestled tightly, fitting correctly, but a gap perceived, near the
edge, those final fill-ins of blue sky. Familiar voices drifted
in, first Pete, back from Portsmouth, then Shona, an evening
off. A clan gathering, we occupied more and more space,
appropriating a table, more chairs, everyone in the pre-game
huddle, an already soporific scrum. Group portrait, a Kodak
moment: Family Portrait, a holiday snap, the Group, and
Associates. Pete, already busy with lenses, clothes, checking
film stock, *Russ, get us another,* first pint already gone, *make mine
a double, make your own,* the reply to a chanced interjection.
Just gone seven, less than an hour to wait, another in the
inevitable pauses, no doing, only anticipating or trying to hard
to avoid thinking about the anticipation of the doing.
— Here, take this.
— What is…a lyric?
— Yes, obviously!
— You want me to write music for it?
— Yes, please. And I want you to play it, Tonight.
— You don't ask for much
— If you can do it, write the song, play it…if…*Dann bin ich
auf ewig dein, immer. För evigt, alltid.*
— Tu solum, in aeternum.

> *There's driver, he hasn't a road map,*
> *A direction, with no sense of where,*
> *Though the bus has no wheels*
> *Yet we keep moving*
> *Travel hopefully, though we'll never get there.*

The inevitable question, deciding the set, shifts in order,
a few changes, what in, what out, what didn't work, keeping
it fresh, something not played for a while, something new,

at least here: *Oh Well*, always start with this, for this kind of night. Then? My decision this time, no democracy, rotation of decision, everyone dictator for an evening, benign oligarchy sustained through mutual accord, overseeing the collective circus: *we'll do the new one*, Make You Mine, *Bold Choice* [James], *wooooo* [collectively], *sod off* [me], said not this time with irritation but a smile; then next, *Bach to Bach*, not unreasonable; *slow number?* Of course, with the temperature as it is, how could it not be? *I think* Walking, *and pick it up towards the end, follow me*, Up on the Downs, *extend solos here and there, that'll get us to the end of the first set nicely*. Pausing to think, writing boldhand, looking up briefly to notice, on Kate and Shona's faces, smiles of recognition. Slight shadow from behind, and my right, a hand passed briefly, shyly over my head, to rest on my shoulder.

— Hey; this is Heike, my sister. She's just got here this afternoon. And Volker.

There she was, *there you are*. I had failed to mention the arrival of family to the others. Knowing looks came from all round, as I craning, looking up, over my shoulder,

— Volker, drinks.

This, Anna's sister. Anna, looking down, a smile with the suggestion of inquiry, wanting to talk with me for a moment, alone, can I see you? I should… Well he's sitting there uglier than sin; Rog, haven't you got a goat to see to? Sure. Excusing myself, Kate, can you finish set lists, thanks. Anna took my hand. The bar area already too full to move through easily, we went across the patio where I was handed a piece of paper. Unfolding it I saw a poem, no, words for a song, one I didn't know. Looking up, those blue eyes, confident, mischief and certainty, a gambit, a play to trip up the opponent, calling my bluff, raising the stakes in a game the rules of which I was barely, as yet aware.

— I have been listening to The Doors a great deal, *The End*, when I'm not listening to Dylan or Schulhoff, and I liked the line about the blue bus. It got glued, yes, glued in my head. Here was an opening move intended to gain advantage, set the board, determine the end game, all in one, breathless, bold gesture. On the back foot, confronted with this overwhelming ultimatum, *what if I play too far across, mistake the ball as it comes out of the back of the hand?* and left with only a parrying reply, disarmed already. Utterly.

~~~

> *On my tongue is a name, it's a secret,*
> *On the bus is a box with a heart;*
> *If the key is the one that's forsaken*
> *Play the chord while the world falls apart.*

— Here's a new song, haven't even got a title for it, yet.

A pause. Everyone the other side of the stage, those not in the goldfish bowl, imagines I am joking. Annagreth standing right in front of me. She never stood there; back towards the bar, or at the back of the crowd, a little forward perhaps, not much though: those were the spaces I was used to her occupying. Heike, then Volker, slightly behind, the room sardine crammed, the ceiling, once again, showing signs of beginning to drip condensation; no promise of relief. Pools of water, clinging clothes, the moisture of close night, room overflowing, pulses, temperatures raised. Everything, every second, each passing day, slow, fast, timeless, out of time: all coming down to this one instant
— *Bus.* That'll work, eh chaps?

> *Though the bus may not finish the journey*
> *You and I have to climb while we may*
> *There's a peak and we never may reach it*
> *Still, we hold to each other for today*

Stop. Back up just a little.

At the end of the first set barely a word and passing through the crowd acknowledging them not at all hardly seeing as I make my way to the back of the van, having been reading over and again the verses, no chorus whenever not singing imagining the shape of a sound to step out from behind the lines surrendering itself hostage to fortune. How to do this? How, in thinking about this song, a new song, to give it a life in twenty minutes, less, parts written copied out, explained? What did the words say? Simply told, a voice, a monologue, but having so much to say, confessing in full view, privately, intimacy on display storing a secret nevertheless. No one would know; and in there, an unstinting, joyous surrender, voicing desire, admitting defeat and victory, whispering need and hunger, having come from a solitary winter, endless night into the light of day, everything said here so far unsaid. Hearing everything in those words I could wish, not daring to hope, and wanting, needing to find for this, a simplicity and directness of response, pared down, humbly, an anthem…? No, a paean then…, an alleluia…, encomium.…

Does this all sound too much, over the top? I have no doubt that it does, finding myself trapped once more between the mundane and the inexpressible, between the blindness of moles, burrowing, feeling the way, and the sad, soaring freedom of Angels. Time regained only to be preserved in amber; caught between a now like every other, searching, seeking, striving to find, and a *then*, conveying the impossible. What would anyone have me say? What ought I to say myself? I feel the urgency of a restatement, a recapitulation of themes, all the motifs, the tunes in one place, given a new, more insistent orchestration, to focus the mind. In any extended composition, wholly scored or having places, giving place to the play of improvisation or variations on a theme.

Take the classical form of the sonata, for example: first, the exposition; next the development, then the recapitulation; at its simplest, here is admitted from the beginning the need, the inescapability of some manner of repetition. Perhaps this is why beginnings are so impossible, so much to be dreaded, and why, as we work towards a climax, the peak of the development, we have to hold off, introduce the pause, the break, return to what can and cannot be stated. Extending the form, introduction before exposition, then development, followed by the recapitulation, and the coda. With the recapitulation one alters a repeated form of the exposition, completing the musical argument; if there is to be a coda, which, in itself, repeats material from the recapitulation, repetition of a repetition. But the coda may move its audience on, may get its audience beyond the point, the purpose of repetition, to lead somewhere else. I am giving everything away here. The whole secret in its entirety for whoever who receives this, whoever may wish to apprehend: this is here. Not in so many words. And there are so many words. But in the manner of what is said and written. In its *how*. As if words were music, as if this were a sonata. Everything is there. Only connect, avoiding the temptation toward the obvious.

So, I repeat. Once more from the top. Annagreth would insist on proper form if only so as to break with it, taking a new direction. Whatever was, is, the music, in the music, is eternal and evanescent, never and always. My words pile up, car crash on the highway, twisting and distorted, ruined, because though memory will hit with the sharpest, most poignant of terrible, beautiful powers, nothing other than that experience can convey the feeling, eyes welling, a tremble on the lip, in the throat, the hand unsteady, the stomach upended, legs no longer able to move us. Or that glimpse, that precious insight, as overwhelming as it is fleeting, when in the tiniest of temporal displacements, we are blessed with the touch of air from an angel's wing, we see as the poets see, feeling the beloved's breath on our neck, just below the surface of our sleep. This all though remains the other side of words. Words never do justice; they can never serve. They can only, at best, intimate, gesture in indirection towards the something other that was already there, souvenir, coming from underneath, underlabouring us the while, in which promise we trust, invest our fragile, delicate, all too easily broken faith. Say it again. I am looking to create a shape for something that is beyond and before description, a gossamer sugar strand tracery, threads drawn out to their finest, and woven into sympathetic, *endlessly* touching patterns, lighter than air; but I am working in a loam, clay heavy, imperfectly balanced, drenched in a season of rain, using a filigree christening spoon to shape it.

Telling the chords would be of no use. I have already said this repeatedly with variations, but I have to say it again; recapitulation and restatement to insist on this point, to make felt, and not seen simply with any simple false equivalent of a trompe l'oeil illusion, *trompe l'oreille*, what memory insists remains as the ghost of the time. To write Em, G, Asus4, then to say G, D, Am7; to suggest the finger shape of Dsus2, as an F chord, fifth fret, with a bass D and open top E, before a descending bass line: D-B-A, then a shift to G bass and a Bb chord: this tells us nothing; that these are an annotated analogy serves only to veil, obscuring what is already invisible. There is nothing here, any more than in those more obviously overwrought turns of phrase.

As for the words? Everyone sees them, a series of postcards scattered without stamp, without address, without name. Without the music they fail, impoverished skeleton at best, at least or at most, awaiting flesh, dressing, animation, spirit, even though, if they can be heard, if what is to be heard within, the other side of black ink on blue traced lines making its way through, to reach inside you, holding your heart in its grasp, a child cradled in the arms of the eternal. On the page, these precious few words, simple images, not, never and always not, the whatever it is they mask and trace at the same time, revealing to protect; these apparently uncomplicated phrases do not, cannot, must not bear the weight of ink, staining their innocent trust.

To hear what I hear, to hear what I have heard; to hear what Annagreth's face that night, before me, told me, unspoken, but with an eloquence unbearable in its naked display; to hear any of this, no it is as impossible as bringing you back. Only two people know even though it was always an act of absolute faith in the other that what was known was in some way perceived however indirectly. Only one can say now, but say only in confessing the impossibility of saying. I can only bear witness to my inability to say. For all that they came to love the song, neither James, nor Kate, nor Graeme, heard, as Anna and I heard, as I hear still. for all that they had some idea some understanding from a distance the special pull this uncomplicated, unadorned tune held, they also knew it was not for all.

Only we two, You and I. In that song. There you are.

The bus is still waiting to take us
Room for just two more inside
All our preludes lead us to one road
Take the bus into winter
We'll hide

II Entr'acte:
After the Rains Came

A lost breath blows the wood awake

Remembering griefs it used to know

Are you there? I woke, just now, the song in my head.
Dreaming a lost breath, I wake, remembering. Do you hear,
do you remember this, those words, the plangent tune? As if
to step out of winter, from the year's midnight, from death
itself. To wake from winter would be a delivery of sorts, even
in the depths of cold, of the dead everywhere, everywhere
dead, nothing but loss, and grief. Why, tell me, do you think
that grief remembered is so much more powerfully felt than
the first experience of that grief, that sorrow? What would
you answer? And why winter, when so many winters were
times, not of the dying but feeling in that brilliant shining
cold alive in, with, one another? I would like to hear you,
just one more time; just once more, a one time forever,
without end, an endless winter, without grief, where there
is no more loss. Is that possible? Imaginable? Is the loss felt
more keenly, like a north wind promising the brutality of
a bite that ruptures blood vessels just below the surface of
the skin because winter is here all the time now, even in the
very depths of summer, in, what was the phrase at which
you laughed, your eyes alive as ever, yes, *seasons of mellow
fruitfulness?* And then, we would read together, melancholy and
longing mixed in with the brighter feelings: Houseman, Clare,
and Hardy, the poets of the land, of memory, of loss, of the
memory of loss, as they map their ghostworld landscapes ripe
with the memory written in the soil, on the land, memory
held by the land when humans no longer remember. I would
like to hear you once more. Not tonight though, not tonight.
Turning not to photographs, I can take no more of those
right now, I look out diaries, old letters. In one diary, your
last, I find a sheet of paper torn hastily, its edge attesting to
force. Here, you write, a poem of winter.

> *Horn worn*
> *Gnaw food*
> *Land drawn*

Deep dumb
Quick the weave
Loose the gloom hoarde
Wordhoarddead
Save for the livid scald
On a dead dove

Shear, the plough
Unfast, the land
Awake, the dead
Alive, the quick
Astride the ridge
Atop the hill
Undecided: halt

Past or future
Last or first
Secret, whisper
Hunger, thirst

Your fountain pen had moved in haste. I know the signs, though the words are unfamiliar. To tell the motion, the urgency, without understanding: standing the other side of a mirror, behind the tain. Which of us?

You would hoard your scraps of paper, guarding fiercely, a protective mother. I feel ashamed now to read, but cannot help myself. Cannot stop. Though undated, I believe I can imagine the when. A winter when women formed a human chain, 30,000 links together; bridges built, steelworks closed, the launch of a Welsh language television station. As if this had been a prompt, you had been reading, I recall, the names shuttling back into focus with a frightful celerity, Edward Thomas, Dylan Thomas, David Jones, that rat-eared copy of the *Mabinogion*. Something otherworldly, harsh in its beauty, stripped and austere called to you, *in my blood* you had said. *The Red Book of Hergest*—*like the album*, you said, wanting to visit the hill on an impulse—was a particular favourite.

Finding a postcard, I read
Here, is winter.

As if to say, pointing to the ground, the concrete beneath
my feet, this place is winter, in winter. But also, as Benedict
knew at the time, as I know now from the other side, winter
is here, now, you are not. Without you is always winter, but
never Christmas. *Here* you were telling me. *I am here, and here
is winter, without you.* You wrote this for me, to me on a post
card, once the one, the only time we spent apart, one January.
The frank over the stamp tells me it was 1980. Say it twice, as
you wrote it, doubling every word, small modified Sütterlin
hand, old worldly, English, then German: *Here is Winter /
Hier ist der Winter. Hier,* which, when voiced, sounding not
unlike its English counterpart, the smallest of emphases, the
difference in the voice, nothing to give the tongue away on
the single word, merely the ghost we call accent, intonation
or stress. Timbre, less an ictus. Then a third tongue returns.
Hier-hiver. I joked over the phone with you that third week
of the year, just two after your birthday, slipping tongues,
transposing tones, touching telephonically. You asked me to
sing to you down the line, *and the living rub their eyes, and wake
from bleary winter.* Here is winter; yesterday, winter. Yesterday,
this is winter; winter and today. Across two languages: *Hier,
hier.* Write it down I said; through the wires I imagined I
could hear, hear there, not here, the soft scratch of a pen.
Here yesterday, yesterday here. Nothing to be seen, only
heard. In the absence of the voice, who knows which comes
first? Yesterday, or winter? Where is the place, *while the living
rub their eyes,* I carry in my heart?

Hanging up that day, *break our hearts,* waiting for the cradle
to nestle the receiver as I could not you, *cleave us apart,* could
not receive you that day in my arms, that winter's yesterday, I
turned, as I do today, in all seasons, to photographs of you.
At that time, you were always close captured far away, or so it
seems. Happy, sad, pensive, abandoned, always looking to a
nowhere. So many photographs, looking where I cannot see,
where no one sees, not in this world at least; you are seeing a

place where I can only imagine but cannot go. I imagine you there now, and cannot wait till I join you. Although the time has not yet arrived, already it is too late to say what I would have, urging you not to go without me. I hope that, one day, I will join you, never and always a yesterday remaining to come, yet to arrive. When finally I leave, will you be there?

There is that photograph of you, hunched over the console in the studio, listening to the playback. No one else around, the lighting warmly brown, wood tones. Cream the console, black the sliders, umbers and earth, even the patch cords and cable fuzzily unfocused, though multi-coloured, are obligingly muted accents, complementary with ochre yellows, brick reds, hung loosely from a racked panel display. The monitor lights, small windows, screens for the VU metres, emit a warm yellowbrown glow. Only track lights at the head of the desk are pinpointedly at odds, small yellowgreens. And you, far away but right there, are smiling. Shadowed, cradled in penumbral light, crepuscular illumination so that even your hair has assumed brownish hues, a sweater chestnut or mahogany, a scarf wrapped closely, encircling your neck, terracotta coloured. Dusk descends, darkness shining, as if burnished and, yes, yes, as you listen you smile, your hands, one balled, cupped inside the other, elbows on the desk, held against your mouth, keeping yourself quite quiet. Perfect attention to the inaudible, plainly to be seen. The visibility of silence.

In the other photograph, you are sitting in a field, legs pulled up under your chin, brown boots to the knee, red buttons down the side, the boots otherwise unadorned. Your coat, Red Riding Hood flame red, crimson scarlet coat, the one with the hood, do you remember how attached you were to it? A cold day, sky grey to biscuit, unbaked, undifferentiated. One hand, your right, rests on your knee, no, you are holding your knee, not resting your hand; almost seeming to hold tight, as a child might having fallen but not broken the skin, hugging though the tender place, pressing to deny the throb, paused before any greater expression of discomfort. Your other hand pulls back your hair, gathering it to you at the nape, holding it tight to the curve of the neck, while, your elbow resting on your other knee, the left, you have just tucked your left foot beneath your right leg. Legs, uncovered, are white as the sky, more pale than the broken, unfocused wisps of dried hay, straw or grass that; cast down, your eyes, looking away, into this hidden, obscured place of yours, and yours alone, gazing not at your knee, the ground or anything discernible. Here, yesterday. The yesterdays are here every time I reach for the photographs, here and not here, never and always I think once more, inescapable the haunting thought that where you are, this *here*, is always there, always taunting, haunting the present, every present whenever I take these images, these *looks of you*, the look of the camera, but your look also, in the camera's eye, the direction of your eyes revealed, by the impartial mechanical lens, which captures your look with a perfection, a precision that is never memory's province. The provenance of the uncaring image reproduced is no one's. It steps out from itself, presenting itself, a radix all its own, jealously guarding its subject, shutting the viewer out even as it appears, even as it causes to appear the one desired, the beloved. Shining silver gold, in winter light, angelic. What, where, the provenance? What comes forth? Dissymmetry: longing. I turn my regard, examining, waiting for you to peer back, look at me, just the once, once more, waiting for that turn of the head, the glimpse that closes the circle. Here, is winter, in the waste land, the ice floe of an unsuturable space. Where is this, where the place, when the look once more I carry, seeing unseen? A lost breath blows the wood awake, remembering griefs it used to know

> *Only the child beneath the weeds*
> *Weeps for the lack of love and air:*
> *Build me a little house of skin*
> *And bone and woven hair*

For the living rub their eyes
And wake from bleary winter

There you are.

~~~

January. First day of a new year. Time to move, boxes in
the Transit belonging to yet another Phil, always Phil, this
Phil, that Phil, another and another, the ubiquitous name
though everyone as unlike as the name conspires to deny;
and the Morris, lovingly preserved. More cars, more friends,
everyone enlisted; a time for moving; the time for parties.
Snow was to fall in Miami that month, but on a small island
as unlike Cuba as it was possible to be, the world had been
cold, wet, changeable, storm ruined. Obligingly, remained dry,
impossible to conceive in the previous week. Frosts had come
unpredictably, waking otherwise sound sleepers who, pulled
at nose and toes, felt some stranger call. Getting out of the
car, daylight already gone, having pulled into the drive, I told
Annagreth to stand still and wait a moment.
— We can't go straight in. Wait.
— Why? It is cold. *Es ist arschkalt.*
    That child's voice, rising, play petulance; this stage whine
could always produce a smile from me, indulgently amused,
Anna's face crumpling into a mask of wrinkled impatience,
pretending not to understand, and wanting now, now, now.
— Patience child, I have to blindfold you.
— No!
— Yes.
— Pfffghh!
    Blindfold on, the victim was steered carefully along the
gravel, *careful, three steps down*, then to the porch, the door
being opened, a welcoming glow beyond, by a tall dark figure,
shaved head shining in the solitary light, backlit silhouette, a
rounded shape standing in relief. A smile was just discernible,
one of being in on the surprise, aimed not at Anna, but at

me. Smiling back, winking at James, I steered Annagreth inside.

~~~

Just a month before that strange restive exhalation was being heard off Fairy Road, a sunken area entered, a door opened, exactly one month prior to this the season with a pugnacious will, well settled in its querulous habits building by the end of the month to a violent tantrum of a storm, days dawned dark, the grey of stolen slate, the sky assuming the guise of a church roof, upended, there was a party. A Wednesday. First day of December. All organization had been assumed by James, all transport and lifting arranged by Graeme and Morphy, all food prepared and cooked by Kate and her mother, *baking, its the new rock 'n roll*, and all alcohol donated freely by various adjuncts and associates, Harry leading the way, Rob Thompson feeling generous, bringing up the rear with some notable vintages, Steve Payne and Kevin Wright liberating unnoticed crates from the brewery at which they occasionally worked, and from which they always came home having sampled the product. Pumpkins, homegrown, carved with comic book grotesqueries extended Halloween at Harry's insistence, and were already ghoul glowing, vegetable faces suggestive of eager, deranged expectation. Lovely, dark and deep, the woods away behind the house kept out the larger world, shut out the greater lights, taking us into older times. We inhabited a pagan moment sustained, touched by a cheerful twistedness.

The memory of that evening is marked in a contradictory way. On the one hand…on the other… On the one hand, I began in a distinctly sour frame of mind. The other hand was not to be revealed until later in the evening. As it stood, already by seven I had settled, *Thames, Dover, Wight, Southwest 5 or 6, becoming variable 3 or 4, moderate to rough, squally showers, visibility poor*, into a low depression. Recollection of morose inertia, wilful and perverse, because fuelled that day for no reason other than the evening's celebration, *well then, Mr*

Grumpy, King Grumpy of the grumpy people, let's celebrate Anna's quarter-anniversary of being in the band. Seeing the immediate future that night, watching as four younger men were egged on by an older, this one all boozy investigative journo, on live national television, I recall with a sharpness akin to the taste of bile in the mouth, not the spectacle itself, banal in its obviously contrived journalistic baiting of equally obvious, even then, contrived rebellion, but the dreary mood that settled on me with the anticipation of an immediate musical future, as unstoppable in its onslaught as an avalanche from on overtipped slurry tank.

— Can you believe this?

— Of course, like my dad says, things will always get worse, given the slightest opportunity. Cheer up, you miserable sod, it's your birthday.

Kate continuing past the back of the sofa, having retrieved a bottle opener, left, down the stairs from the loft. The door only briefly opened, winter's chill, skin-tightening, scraped at my neck, anticipation of a small mortality in the wind's bite or perhaps just that experience of someone walking over a grave not my own. Could I have any idea that Freddie King, one of the three kings of blues guitar would be dead before the month was out, perhaps a delayed reaction to what had just passed on the TV screen, blue glow for a blue mood, the death of the blues in the face of boxed and packaged, carefully marketed diatribes and musical drivel? Or, as James was to reason a month later, on the first day of a new year, our surprise on Annagreth sprung successfully, having heard the news on Peel a few days before, King's death was brought on by one too many Bloody Marys, in lieu of lunch. Whatever lay at the bottom of my mood, I was, as was later said of Bill Grundy following that moment of televisual history, tired and emotional.

— Hello, m'dear! Been given orders to come cheer you up or thrash you into happiness. And to come give a hand, no one seeming to trust me with the electrickery.

Atop an outsize Afghan, incongruously juxtaposed by

a hair cut more suited to Jack Hawkins or Kenneth Moore,
navigating a path through enemy waters; coal dark eyes a
blaze, shoe buttons in a puff pastry snowman, overhanging
eyebrows a darker jet, nose and teeth prominent, a younger,
raffish Edward Heath marionette, Damian sailed through the
door, all hearty camp good humour, brandishing a carefully
wrapped, but nonetheless recognizable cricket bat.

— Oh, hello, Biscuit. That's Morphy's coat isn't it?

— Yes, he insisted the SS great coat was going too far. Mr C
looked offended, can't think why.

— He has a point.

— Boy lacks any aesthetic sensibility.

Deciding the conversation would never bear the weight
of logical disquisition, knowing that Damian did not have
that kind of better side to which an appeal might be made,
I moved to go downstairs, having received my marching
orders to make myself useful. The barn was what can only be
described as decked, a stage set for a Christmas Carol and the
coming of some festive spirit. A large tree dressed obscured
the spiral stairs, a small stage set, rigged, adorned, mic stands
twined with winter garlands, holly, ivy, large fake candy
coloured flower displays atop amplifiers, piano and organ,
crates currently full, stacked, trestle tables topped with pies,
cakes, bowls, cups, cutlery, plates and more cakes. Another
area had been cleared for other entertainments to begin the
season properly, ushering in winter with Morris and Mummer,
a Turkish Knight, St Nicholas, all other parts already assigned,
remembered over years of repetition, *the old boys of the village*,
conjured in the fire of wine, homemade, elderflower and
others, autumn, winter-berry seasoned and ale, local brews.
At the sight of so much possible overindulgence, I began
to relax, deciding that no, this was not simply for me, about
me, I would not be the sole centre of attention, the birthday
boy, but could become lost in the ensemble revelry of winter
worship, caught up in the evening's increasingly frenzied
embrace. To be in the barn that night, was, as so often, to
step into timelessness, to step back through time, to step

to a timeless tempo of imagined happenings, benign port where fictions became real for one night at least. All was safe, a collective, joyful insanity that said no, which refused the outside, resisted change for its own sake, denied fashion, celebrated seriously silliness, and placed the dancing boot heel firmly on the neck of all that was common sense, all that the world's monsters told us made sense. Sense, order, the common, none had any dominion here, the lesser motions of the world diffused, dispersed. To step into the barn that evening, and other evenings like it, was to know, to feel, a different, a finer flow of loving madness.

People were due to begin turning up around seven, but there was, as yet, no sign of Annagreth. An engine, the Transit, was heard, Graeme having made the last run, with James, Pete, Linda, Pete's sister, and several mutual friends. Then more cars. At first just one, Mike with Carla, Kevin and Garry in the back, followed not long after by Steve, his old estate overfilled, as was often the case, bodies perched on armrests, astride handbrakes, and even, on Steve's lap, Judy, so full was the car. Mandy's giggle could be heard across the dark, dismissive of winter night and biting cold. Fred, Kate's terrier, was everywhere, in and out, rushing dementedly in that manner so familiar with Jack Russells. Assuming the role of comic sheepdog, he began a circuit of the barn, haring around its inner perimeter, ever faster, the building become his personal velodrome. Accelerating, yapping, barking with a delighted demonic abandon, he circled everyone, as if to suggest simultaneously that as a makeshift master of ceremonies, he was announcing the festivities begun, that no one was to leave in any state of sobriety, and that he would personally ensure everyone would remain, unable to exit the building; Buñuel had missed a trick or several, Mike remarked to Harry, when he cast only a bear and sheep in *El Angel Exterminador*. If that film were a parable, an exposé, a scathing indictment, as the press have it in their very own way, of the thin veneer covering the baser aspects of the

Mexican bourgeoisie, Fred's present performance determined that tonight would become the archetypal statement of forgotten English paganism, part *Wicker Man*, part Thomas Hardy set-piece. It was only to be hoped that this evening would not turn out in quite so dire a fashion, that its ultimate denouement would not be as tragic or apocalyptic as anything inevitably the consequence of such narrative precedents. Magic on magic, surprise on surprise, quantum accelerations within reality took place with every passing moment. With the slightest creak, the door within the larger door opened to reveal otherworldly figures, stepping from the dark to the light, a portal between universes momently gaping, as black face, black on black, blood red ribbons threaded in and out, crimson corseted, in ones and twos, gathering in numbers, the unstoppable flow of Blackstone Border Morris, singly, collectively. Even Fred paused, standing silent before the Winter Fool, acknowledging his darker Overlord, greater demon to a lesser sprite. *For O, for O the Hobbyhorse is forgot!* Came the cry as greetings were exchanged, one of the dancers, just recognizable as Menna, silversmith and flautist of this parish, and occasional player with the band, coming up to James and I,

— You'll never guess what happened.

— Arrested?

— No, but it did involve the police. We were on our way up here from the village, and a police car stopped us, someone must have seen us from a window and phoned. Anyway, there we were, in the middle of the road, the officer gets out of the car, and asks what we're doing walking along a country lane with large wooden sticks in our hands. It didn't help that Guy corrected him, telling him they were *staffs, not sticks, officer.* John explained we were a Morris Team on the way up here. *Oh,* says the constable, *that's all right then.*

Of course. Walking through the night, uncanny gothic vision, black clothed and painted faces, armed collectively with large lumps of wood, decked in ribbons, rags and bells, faces painted, *Día de los Meurtos* visions, their sound on a quiet lane apprehended before anything, if anything at all, could easily be seen. Why would this not be all right on the first day of December, the first night of the last month? How could it be anything but all right? Everywhere else was odd. Everything else made no sense, turned upside down. Here was normal. Here was winter; here we were. As yet though, no sign of, or word from Annagreth, *I'm sure everything's ok, She'll be fine, bugger, don't worry. I'll go call her place, see if anyone answers.* All this had been said variously, but with a shared desire to say something rather than out of any true conviction, tone betraying whatever lay beneath the words. We had not seen Anna since the previous evening, it having been arranged already between Kate, her mother and Anna, that Annagreth would make a birthday cake, everyone having been invited to dinner at the Cervenkas by Rosemary.

An hour passes, Morris dances completed. Food is being consumed, the tables begin to relax, but not yet show any signs of being cleared. Damian is getting louder, generally excited by a shared conviviality, rather than through any stimulant. Always his own high, Damian's irrepressibility, his entirely automatic and always permanently ramped superabundance of self-promoting, yet, largely inoffensive euphoria is in its own element, a fleshy sausage of a man, human counterpart to Fred's canine excesses, and just as ready for the chance encounter with, or blindly amorous assault on anything, anything male that is, and this is what distinguished Damian from Fred, if it stood still long enough. Drinks are passing easily, as everyone, in some measure, to a lesser or greater degree proves that perception, if it is to be shared at all, involves loosening oneself from the anchors and guide rails of reality, in order that something be revealed beyond what is usually seen.

Still, getting on for nine, I was not the only one to be concerned about Annagreth's absence. I was not alone in feeling distanced from the greater enjoyment of our friends. In the past months, since that lucky Friday thirteenth, Annagreth had become for us all, but for me particularly,

indispensible. As a musician, she completed us, took us
in new directions, made us who we had always wanted to
be: making us what James and I had first imagined over
tea; making us make music in a way that Kate understood
passionately could not be given words, Anna giving to us
in the process something beyond, before, other and much
more magnificent, essential, sublime than words. Graeme,
he just knew. He felt the fit, feeling also the impossibility
of imagining how anything could have been, or ever could
be different than the way things were. As for me—simply,
there was nothing to be said, everything was there in a
touch, a look, a smile, the turn of the head, its gesture in
the direction of a shoulder. Everything was carried in the
voice, for which tone, tenor, timbre were poor orphan words,
starveling children for something invisible, born in the sound,
sublime, without depth, because its depth was immeasurable.
Anna carried with her an aura, not a calm exactly but, how
shall I risk describing it, a composure, a serenity all the
more her own because so unconsciously, lightly borne.
Those she touched felt lifted out of what she once called
Herzensfinsternis, the heart's darkness.

Whatever my mood had been at the start of the evening,
that lowering toad of exhausted resentment had been
replaced by such a darkness, the sullenness supplanted by
a tactile anxiety, an electrical discharge pulsing just below
the surface of the skin. Formulating possible plans between
us, Kate, her mother, Pete, Morphy, James, Graeme and I
decided who should do what. I would phone Shona, to see
if someone could go over to Gurnard, Pete and Morphy
would take one car, James and Graeme another, and, taking
whatever possible routes they could, would see if there
had been an accident, a puncture, whatever we could dare
imagine that was not the worst, the absolute worst; Kate and
Rosemary would phone police stations to see if anything had
been reported. It was impossible for others not to notice our
cabal, though some would have thought it merely a matter
of deciding on what we would play this evening. Then time

seemed to stop; thrown suddenly, in full forward motion,
into reverse simultaneously. Everything came to a halt. No
winding down, no slowing, pure freeze frame. Harry was
at the door... Who had noticed him leave? How long had
he been out of the barn? Where could he have gone? ...
Sodden, not so much rained upon as soaked, cold and clear
giving way to a storm more ancient than any legend, thrown
into some deep end, the ship gone down, a last survivor on
a shipwreck night, draggled, dragged from off the beach,
still clinging to some shard of wreckage. It was as if, and still
today it seems as if, everybody had been gathered for a set
piece, group portrait, to be etched into a plate by long, and
necessary exposure, before the magnesium flash blindingly
revivifies the still life, shock of the bright explosion pulling
everyone back into the now.
— It's ok guys, she's fine, Anna's here, our lovely girl is here;
she just fell asleep.

There you were; there was Annagreth, Anna, half
disgusted with herself, somewhat abashed, apparently
embarrassed briefly; then,
— Cake time!

~~~

On the other hand...On the other hand, what had begun
brusque, bruised, and bored, moving through anticipation,
anxiety and expectation of the wrong sort, to end with a
revelation, a request that was also a demand, however politely
put, that would brook no objection had there been any. It
was, in short, a gift of the heart. At the end of the evening,
or the morning's start, Damian lovingly entwined with the
spiral staircase snoring, everyone else away home. Even Fred's
tank was on empty, his juice used up. We sat, Kate, Anna and
I, James, Graeme, and Morphy having vanished for some
little time, away with the fairies into the greying night day:
crepuscule. *What, no, say it again. Crepuscule, crepuscular, crep-us-
cueooooolllll. Again, bitte, bitte, noch einmal.* I spoke, you repeated,

Kate watched, amused. *Küß mich. Say it just once more, Küß mich. Bekomme ich einen Küß von Dir?* Harry had met Annagreth, Anna had explained, at the bottom of the farm road. He had, he had told her, walked part the way to the village, intending to go to the police station, having decided to walk quietly away so as not to raise any suspicions. As he got to the road, Waltraud had turned into the only road leading to the lane. Orange even in the night, its headlights, Cheshire Cat eyes blazing, showing in the beams the by now flood tending rainfall. Gullies forming, bubbling to overflow, running away, sounding the gurgle of excess, Harry had opened the gate, then closed it, Anna waiting long enough for him to get in, *no don't wait, I'll get the car soaking,* to drive up before the barn. That was the end of the story, or not quite.

— O, so stupid, I know, no I know, I insist, it was dumb, I fell asleep. I never do that, *Schlafmütze*! But, you know, it made me have an idea. Driving here, I thought of something. Why don't we find a place to live? Together, yes, of course, let us live together. We look tomorrow. There. It is decided. Isn't it. This last statement, more a desire for confirmation than a question came with the broadening of the smile already there, tiredness and wine encouraged. An oblique, not quite covert, failed furtive glance at Kate, complicity in the sharing or seeking support, I could not tell, before, returning with a sudden focus on what must clearly have been the surprise writing itself across my face. *Well, you know you'd never ask, would you? You'd be the last to suggest it.* Looking from one to the other, between us both, Kate beamed approval, the plan, if executed slightly later than intended, carried off, carrying all before it, carrying the day, with a swift certainty not to be countered.

~~~

The storm that night, you were later to write. A journal, Kate had rescued, in which lately I have become absorbed. Giving flight to words as you would notes, sense not to the point so

much as sound and mood, tone and resonance, image after
image fleeing, huddling together in complex knots, irregular
and tough to the tongue. To read this now, in recollecting
what you once called an interlude, a prelude to a beginning,
old year new year, old homes new home, indicted across the
graph square pages, archaic and idiomatic together, the play
being all you had said, having read and come to understand
the phrases, *hugger-mugger, hucker-mucker, hudder-mudder,* which
afterwards became the sounds of scales you sang, your voice
and fingers in perfect unison, until emptied of all sense and
leaving only the *mood* of a nonsense poetry.

On reading this, a first time, you had, I find, absorbed
yourself. So much taken in, remembered. The weeks since
September you had taken seriously and with a studiousness
intense and fierce in its concentration and devotion, an
interest in folklore, folkways, place, and everything that
you had once called *the memory of place,* explaining to us late
one night in a tone that would accept no contradiction,
how particular locations, landscapes, buildings, even trees,
Ja, Graeme, even trees, especially trees, would record and hold
memory, to be released only for the right person, and then
not at will but solely for a time, a single moment, when the
occasion was right. Borrowing books, talking to people,
pursuing relentlessly but all the time with humour some
arcane field research, you gathered, gathering to you, such
knowledge about the Island, nursing it your *place-child of the
imagination.*

We would rarely speak of this, only as you chose to offer
a seemingly trivial detail, an unremarkable instant borne
orally, beneath the consciousness of history, though later,
this would return in song, in lyrics at once eerie and of the
earth, strange estranging conjugations wholly new and old
beyond the most familiar words. The one time you wrote at
length, I had now found, and which I read ceaselessly on first
discovery throughout a single night, returning to the start as
soon as I finished, as though all were a circle, to which I have
come back and as I now find, in pausing to reflect, returns to

me. *The storm that night*, you write, your invisible hand moving before me,

and rain falls. Persistent now. The world is water this night, the flow a flood in the making. Somewhere not that far away, rivulets gush, dun turbulence, all violence: helter-skelter, pell-mell, headlong hasty, reckless messy disarray. Larger waterways begin to tumble, roil and roll, rivers bursting banks before the morning comes. Across the Island, trees loose their moorings, upended, and suspended by nothing more than the indifferent caress of other branches remaining in the way, impeding the final fall. Roots all exposed, half clinging, holding for one last moment to soil, as more now upface skyward. Steep, narrow roads, barely roads though tarmacked, wide enough, just, for a single vehicle, are awash, every runnel a river, every path the place of torrent, torment, deluge; overspill, the centuries themselves a flood washing away the present, drowning time, denying order: oferflōwan. Foxhole, molehill, warren and sett drift apart, falling in, collapsing and washing away; landslide impedes progress, no way to get through the steeper inclines. Away to the west, the back of the Wight, waves pound with the fury of end days all too precipitately arriving, returning to claim the land, the settlements, village and community, sweeping up the all, the every one. Lawns and parkland give the impression this night of rice fields, paddies where grass floats at the surface of the water, sod drowned, submerged. Density of clouds now rent, here and there, moon appearing brightly through shreds, casting copse and lane in saintly pallid corpse light, livid and dank. A neverwhere's refulgence. In Carisbrooke churchyard the scarp overreaches its stone boundaries, a tented grave, unfilled and waiting for Joseph to come to his long home, no longer maintaining its form, incapable of absorbing the rains, soil turning to clag, while, around the walls of the castle, the counterscarp promising to give way, acknowledging in sympathy the minor catastrophe its spiritual cousin promises to deliver. Giving up the ghost. At Fleet, at Bonchurch, Brighstone and Newchurch, at Bembridge and at Calbourne, land loses footing. At narrower points the Yar and Medina violate propriety, limen no more but mudslides simply, the riverbed ashore, aqueous rapine. The marshland around the Yar appears no longer to the nighttime's eye, merely inner sea, anticipating its gathering into the Solent. Green and blue mixing to sullen umbers, blurred dull, drab, snuff coloured in the waters' vertical and horizontal oncome, untamed, intractable, salt and sweet indistinguishable, irregular and imperious, groaning wreak, wrack, rank, importunate. Russeted landscape barely that, tinged palely green, livid at extremities or on the surface of unnatural tides, framed silhouettes of tree and hedgerow. Copses all unseasonable, huddling hillside nakedly exposed, ripped, overburdened and, ultimately, rent, torn, ripped. Finally, shattered, sundering within themselves, the topsoil shuddering, groaning in the heaviness of grief torn too soon from its season. River within us, sea all about. Too precipitate; night roils in its obscurity. Too much, too quickly, too heavily downwards all, carrying away with the deluge everything that matters, everything of matter, the living with the dead. All too soon everything will be washed away undoubtedly, though imperceptibly at first. There is that slow dribble, meander in miniature. Watch: in the soil a channel forming, as water finds its way between more resistant, all too solid clumps. These too will break apart, inevitably, if the water continues. But for now, here, at this moment, that impossible space, neither day, nor night, nor yet quite evening; series of instants, Polaroid hued, day somehow reliving past moments, each instantaneously replaced by the next, fading into the next appearance, that magical moment of ghostly realization, there, there is, what to call it, twilight in all its transience, crepusculed. Wait here, slow down the inevitable creep, so swift as to be invisibly slow, without noticeable measure until—too late, it's gone, a memory's touch, lightly that lingers fading at the edges. For now though, at first there, it is noticed, that little trickle. It wears away, pushing, finding its course at verge or bank, in furrow and by field. Now imagine: this everywhere, all across the Island. Water surrounded, water bisected, on the verge of becoming water engulfed. Rains come harder, what had been silent now becomes vociferous, a soundscape insistent. Above,

the clouds move left to right, west to east,
those about to disappear a cream and pink,
soft sleeping skin, full fleshed and rounded,
downy, against the last blue of the world;
following, hurrying, pushing there come
greys, more haggard, wind worried, slivered,
sharded and shattering, unkind dead tree
shapes cut free, forcing onwards. Light
diminishes, wind soughs, wood creaks and
guttering, engorged, disburdens itself at the
weakest points and places of egress, every
outlet. Pulled apart from within, overflow
pressing at every gap, crack, join, fissure,
crack, each improperly seated joint, and
every imperfectly settled mortar seal. It is
now almost eight o'clock. Already wracked
to the verge of collapse, the little world
of field and copse, hedgerow, barrow and
down, are overthrown, quite. Trees made
mourners, strewn, prostrate, collapsed upon
the ground, hurled in grief's abandon: Priory
and Steyne Woods, Whitefield too; Kelly's
Copse, Combly Great Wood, the twin
woods of Knighton; the copses of Hoglease
and Ramcroft, Briddlesford, and Combe;
America Wood; Lushington, Woodhouse,
Withybed and Chessell; Clammerkin
Brook, Great Werrar Wood, Berry Shute,
and Brighstone Forest. Shalfleet Lakes
overrun and submerging road and field
alike. Even the private foreshore of a once
great empress and now dead queen shows
signs of a giant's trampling, some petulant
sprite child, invisible and vast, playing at
havoc. Light fails. Saltmarsh, reedbed,
mudflat, and sand dune, estuarially awash,
Curlew and Godwit gone, blackthorn

*winter unseasonably lingering, wiped away
in a single night. On the air, the plangent
chatter of the fern-owl might be imagined,
somewhere within, but even this is an act of
will, of faith.*

~~~

*Near midnight. Though the storm
continues, even in the narrowest lane, the
tightest, leaf smeared path, over folds of
downs, light enough from rent of cloud
cast line against shades of sear and dun.
In the air always, promise of return,
insistent, imminently battering, while cloud
sifts, lower from higher, wisp against flock,
stuffing heaven's mouth, and there, the tear
that gives the moon its chance, barely, before
passage in the lower heavens, seeming more
rapid, appearing to close up, smother finally,
the brief eyelid opening in the sky. Once
Echbriht's Tun, named perhaps for a barely
remembered King of Wessex, Brighstone
home once to Samuel Wilberforce,
William's brother, Rector, and William
Fox, Palaeontologist. See again, through
steady veil, the soil, the grass, the undulation
great and small: these have about them little
enough suggestion of life, of growth, their
animation, where any may be perceived,
the mockery of motion brought on by
another's hand, artificial, mere semblance.
No owl, no fox, no farmyard cat. No living
thing this night abroad. Unimaginable.
Impossible to believe that the vegetable
world, impoverished as it is by night, by*

*lack of light, further travestied by all that
is so much more than simple words such as
rain or wind suggest, could have anywhere a
pulse, an inner energy, so beaten, so battened
as it is. Withybed deserted, Chiffchaff
bereft, Blackcap abandoned, Goldcrest
gone, no trace of Hairstreak, purple or
green, the wing of a speckled wood, torn
tattered wet pressed against the bark of
a fallen white poplar. Willows abused
beyond recognition. Salix acutifolia, bitter
to the taste, Edward Stone's discovery; even
this is broken in the night here and there,
shredded, ripped, acids flavouring the air,
but ineffectual against the fever fret of the
world. As it fell out on a holy day, the drops
of rain did fall, did fall…it was an upling
scorn and a downling scorn…oh the withy,
oh the withy, it perishes at the heart. The
withy man walks, gathering the branches for
the making of a wicker coffin, once more
that all the dead should be housed. Furzy
downs and combe empty of hogs or sheep,
Blackwater Hollow, Clatterford Shute
submerged; trackways and eroded basins,
designated cirque, called corrie by the Scots,
cwm by the Welsh, once eroded into shallow
basin or trackway, named grundle in East
Anglia, millions of years before, at this
low point of the Medina or in that dip
between hills along the road to Bowcombe,
now impassable, nocturnally debauched, the
result of abrupt, steep pasture fields that
drain too swiftly, called steethe in Saxon,
perpendicular banks that give up all. Were
someone so foolish as to be exposed on such
a night they might be witness to the strange*

sight of worms, sickening, expelled from the earth, curling and unwrithing toward their end. Blackthorn hedgerows, wild, fiercely dense, thickly blossomed—even these are ravaged, the last shriveled remnants of Winter Kecksies quite blasted from the storm's harrying. Nothing holds.

And then a separate entry, unknown to me at the time.

Keep the brightest memory, and the best, closest to your heart; and recollect these words at night before you sleep, if I should ever chance to be so heartless as to leave you behind.

~~~

The living rub their eyes.

January, first day of a new year. Moving day. Stepping from the car, daylight already gone, twilight past its time, Annagreth waited Barely. Impatient, having been asked to stand still.

— We can't go straight in. Wait.
— Why? It's cold. *Es ist arschkalt.*
— Patience, I have to blindfold you.
— No!
— Yes.
— Pfffghh!

Blindfolded, I directed the birthday child along the gravel path with care, *careful, three steps down,* her dark red shoes, each feeling out the way, as if blindfolded; then to the porch, door opening with almost no sound, beyond the glow of lights in other rooms; a dark figure, shining shaved, backlit, rounded, in relief. James's smile barely discernible, having helped

prepare a surprise. Winking, I returned the smile, guiding
Annagreth, Anna, Annagreth, over the sill of the door. But
pause, wait right there. I knew Anna, Annagreth, was eager
to remove the blindfold, eager to come home for the first
time, begin a new home that night, but wait. Wait, you have
to wait, while I remember, calling up all the ghosts, shaping
the flow, from the previous month, from what you and Kate
had started between you, in the wake of which I followed,
acquiescent, smilingly so. Wait. Patience *mein Schatz*. I know, I
know too that impatience, *Ich auch, mein Schatz*, but we will get
there, together. You and I. There…

~~~

The day following the night of the party, rousing slowly,
breakfasting barely, coffee, tea, then with greater relish,
homemade breads toasted and honey homemade too, the
morning almost gone, as we made our way from loft to
house, barn to kitchen. Dry though damp, sky lifted, a lighter
grey, grey on grey, cloud by cloud, a blanket of some little
weight. The world that day, not exactly new, but different.
I could feel it in the bone, in the blood, in skin and hair,
waking from *bleary winter*, taking softly underneath my breath
the song carried on the morning breeze, as we walked to the
farmhouse. Black leaded, the crackle hiss and flare of fire
in the hearth, the Aga in full swing, that kitchen, that day,
and Kate there, busy, efficient, brightly bubbling, expectant,
knowing more, saying nothing. Only a song already underway.
Lord Bateman was a noble lord.
— The address is there, you're all set for one, I phoned earlier; can I come with?
    Set off from the road, hidden behind trees, a large,
spreading property, early nineteenth century, the house
stood in its own large ground, impressively aloof from its
neighbours and, it seemed, the rest of Fairy Road. Reaching
greedily for the sea the property extended with a slight curve

of the land across to the next road, Bluett Avenue, the police
station its neighbour, in the mind's eye a gatehouse guarding
the estate. While everything around, three storey family
homes or bungalows dated the neighbourhood as having
grown from the end of the nineteenth century through to
the early sixties, the house into the driveway of which we had
pulled must have stood here for quite some time as the only
property, possibly with an unbroken view of the sea, perhaps
its garden, certainly its ground extending to the beach. Of
a size and design found now mostly, only, in Yarmouth,
the house resisted outwardly all reference to modernity.
Welcomed by the owners, the Colonel and his wife, Sir
Charles and Lady Marjoribanks, *yes, I know it makes no sense, but
really it is pronounced Marshbanks*: a matching pair, old worldly,
colonial and comfortable, all precise military bearing and
charming propriety, vague good humour and grace, cavalry
twills and twinsets, reserved warmth and *noblesse*, appearing
ancient, preserved, *horses, yes, I remember when the first tanks
arrived, a good thing too, too many of the poor beasts slaughtered*, we
were invited, ushered into the drawing room for tea, *do sit
down, a little chat, yes? Before Marjorie shows you the basement flat.
Yes, it's a lovely garden, not looking its best though at this time of year,
I'm afraid, weather's been simply too wretched to get out there and do
much, lovely come spring though, around April, that's the time to see it.*
The tall, simple, elegant room, in the corner of which stood
a piano, elegantly unassuming, high ceilinged, matte walls an
unobtrusive green darker by a few shades than pistachio, on
which were hung, here and there, paintings depending from
dados, undeniably family portraits, while elsewhere, smaller,
some water colours, local landscapes, beachscapes. We looked
out through expansive French windows, across a balcony,
to the extensive lawn, neatly manicured, well tended even
at this time of year. Ghosts of the past could be imagined
there, stock figures but no less real for that: men in flannels,
white-shirted, a blazer here and there, school tie holding
aloft the trousers, cuffs furled having recently retreated from
the beach, young women loosely, elegantly dressed, children

miniatures of the adults, gauze, linen, lawn, and muslin,
delicate white, or bone, ivory, hints of lesser hues; equally
imagined, a game or two, croquet, possibly badminton, soft
tock of shuttlecock in a haze of summer laughter, light,
secluded, shielded, protected, watched over and down upon
by tall trees, priapic or gracefully declining, submitting: Large
Leaved Lime and Maidenhair, Wych Elm and Yew. *Oh Ben,*
that affectionate mockery in the voice, *you will be able to tell me
all about the trees!* Kate stifled a laugh. Sir Charles, willowy and
having the look of a well-trained Airedale, kind solicitous
eyes saddened by age, inquiring, unaware of the tone, our
now familiar joke, if I knew and cared about trees.

Tea over, *we can take care of references, papers, all that gubbins
later, if you like the flat,* we were shown back out the front
door, and, with a sharp turn, down three wellworn steps to
another door, opening into the basement, long ago a kitchen,
scullery and cook's room, we were told, but, well, *it has been
unused for so long, such a shame, that Charles and I decided at the
beginning of the year to have it converted into something more snug; we
are not as young as we used to be, though I dare say you can see that
for yourselves,* this said with an air of collusive humour, *and
thought it might be nice to have the right young couple around the place.*
From the entrance angled diagonally, one room opening to
the left, another, smaller to the right. The apartment would,
it seemed on first appearances, assume the dimensions of
the house, and this we found to be so. Turning right from
its initially angled trajectory, the hallway ran the length of
the building. While the front had been dark, rooms at the
rear were light, airy, spacious. The main room, immediately
beneath the main house drawing room, generous in size, and
imitating that room's French windows, looked out onto a
flagstone patio, generously proportioned, before a wall, the
entire apartment being submerged below ground level, giving
access to the lawn up another small flight of stairs. Ignored,
invisible, and happy to be so, I followed, exchanging the
occasional pleasantry with Lady Marjoribanks, answering her
questions, *oh, a musician, how nice, you're not loud are you? Oh good,*

and Annagreth? A pianist? Lovely, did you see our piano, we don't play at all, I'm afraid, my daughter, you know, but she lives abroad now; we keep it tuned of course, listening as Kate and Anna imagined, planned, considered, reflected, filling the spaces, moving the furniture that was there; out of the living room, turning left, *a bedroom with a fireplace, süß!* Then, at the end of the corridor, two doorways, one opening, to the right onto a small box room, the other, the larger, light, black and white tiled floor. Throughout, the walls were gently softened with colours, more shades, of Nordic light, bone or alabaster, eggshell delicate, blue tending to teal though lighter, more liquid, and a ghost grey suffused with the shade of antimony. Heavy drapes, dark burgundy velvet or, in the main room, a metallic gunmetal shot silk, embroidered with exotic flora, magenta, green and gold, diffused, absorbed, calmed, while darkly polished wooden floors, rich earth in colour, shone upwards. — *Das ist wirklich unglaublich,* unbelievable, truly, so pretty, *so hübsch, echt!.* I love this place, we must, yes, yes, *Ja!* Ben.

Annagreth saw home. In those few minutes, she envisioned everything, knew with an instinct how it would all be, how it would be to live there, together, imagining not only practical possibilities but, I could tell from her look, far away but also there at the same time, seeing herself in that place, seeing and anticipating days, nights, leaving, coming home, through seasons

— Oh, and to go swimming whenever we want, James is just down the street too; please,

...a brief glance at Kate and I, not for approval but to carry us with her

— we would love this, yes, can we take it?

~~~

...Das, was uns am innigsten verfolgt ...

~~~

One, two, three steps down. There we are. Carefully. No, it's okay, the door is open. Mind your step, good; door's closed. Let me get your coat, yes, no not yet, I know, I know, really, trust me, it will be worth the wait. Alright, we're going down the hallway, that's the way, mind the table there, right, okay, and we're going to turn, yes, we're going into the living room. You can see the light's on from under the blindfold, yes. I'd asked James to come by earlier, make sure some lights were on, that it was warm; I know, you wouldn't want to leave Graeme in charge of lighting the fires, would you. Chopping the wood, perhaps…And, to your left, couple of steps more, just to the right, turn, almost there. Yes, of course everyone's here, that's why the blindfold, it's a surprise birthday party, naturally. The key there is 'surprise', right, so pretend you're surprised. No, you can't take it off yet, I'm going to do that; yes, everyone's being very quiet, but you can hear breathing; maybe we've got a ghost. No, I'm trying, the knot's a little stuck, yes, yes, I'm hopeless with them. Got it, and one… two…three…

— No! I…*nein, Benedict*…

That long last, back of the tongue elasticated sound, bafflement, disbelief, incredulity, utter shock, the shock that registers before delight follows in its wake

…*Was hast du gemacht? Wie*…

Shouts of *Happy Birthday! Welcome home! Happy New Year!* And, from somewhere in the background, *let's get stoned!* ran into one another, all the tributaries of celebration pooling into the larger tide of joy in the successful climax of the surprise, people appearing in the doorway, from behind, coming out of hiding in other, darkened rooms. Anna's face reddened, as Kate came forward, a glass of champagne at the ready, before tears filled her eyes, as she turned, around and around, seeing everybody's smiling complicity, back and forth before turning back to the object of such amazement.

— A piano…

~~~

I have a vision of you locked inside my head
It creeps upon my mind and warms me in my bed.
A vision shimmering, shifting, moving in false firelight.
A vision of a vision protecting me from fear at night.
The seasons roll on, and my love stays strong.

— Play 'Vision' for me.

Later that night, the revels ended, when everyone had
left, you, Anna asked this, asking not imploringly, not
beseechingly, not playfully; you simply asked, directly, as
we sat quietly before the fireplace, watching the last of the
embers glow ever less, almost imperceptible the change;
you, Anna, Annagreth, you asked for a song I had sung one
night toward the end of the previous August, that second
stretch of ten nights. Bold, for me, I had dedicated it to you,
to her, no one had expected, that very last time you were in
the audience, not to my right, the other side of Kate, then
James, or, as increasingly became the case, taking centre stage,
sharing that place with Kate; but those are other stories, for
another place, as you know. This, now, is the tale of a first
night, first night of the year, first night together in a place
of our own. Yes, you asked me to play this song, the words
of which still haunt, still conjure you for me, a reason I no
longer play it, can barely hear it on occasions, though no less
loved because of that, because of you, the memory of you,
that vision of you, inside my head, I carry with me, my own
heartbeat, my pulse. You asked. A last birthday present for
the day, the last one, the others were lovely, wonderful, silly,
you knew you had had too much, but still, just one more,
just this, something you couldn't hold, couldn't touch, but
which could make you dream, make you smile, make you
cry, make you melt. Please; *bitte.* I teased, even though your
voice teased me; knowing already I would give in, I never
refused you a song, I taunted, just a little, imposingly if mock
authoritatively, pointing to the clock and telling you how it
was past 2am, yesterday was your birthday. This was so, I
insisted. *No,* you reasoned, *I am still awake. Tired, yes, but still*

awake; and if I am awake it is still the same day. Leaning forward,
stroking your cheek, kissing your forehead, Anna's head, I
admitted to the inexorable force of your, her logic; okay, I
would play that song.

> *I don't know where you end, or where it is that I begin*
> *I simply open my mind, and the memories flood on in.*
> *I remember waking up, with your arms around me.*
> *I remember losing myself, and finding that you'd found me.*
> *The seasons roll on, my love stays strong.*

Outside, wind was whipping at, through, the trees, a night
of strong magic James had predicted earlier. It was magic
that managed the day for us, as well as more than a little
imaginative fiction as the reasons for postponed arrival, a
magic somehow performed between everyone, in concert, all
the players assuming their parts. The day had been planned
over dinner two weeks before, but that particular piece of
well-coordinated organization had hit the skids, caused
unintentionally by a gesture of unexpected, unlooked for
generosity on the part of the Marjoribanks, mentioned to me
in passing one afternoon. Would we, would Annagreth, like
the use of the piano? They had talked about this, after having
heard her play a little Beethoven, their favourite composer
they had said, would she mind, no of course not, as we were
there to sign the final necessary documents, and collect the
keys. The conversation had continued between Sir Charles
and Lady Marjorie, he thinking the young lady might like
to come up and play occasionally, a view the impracticality
of which was immediately pointed out to him, for all sorts
of reasons, *He's such a dear but he never thinks of the practical
side of things*; why not, if the young people could arrange it,
have the piano installed below? After all, it was meant to be
played every day; it was a sin to leave it sitting there, doing
nothing but being a somewhat oversized photograph stand,
to be enlivened at certain times with the addition of a vase
of flowers. Teaching lessons regularly, I had given the Guitar
Centre's phone number as a contact, should it be required.

When the phone call came, the idea of the New Year's birthday surprise appeared immediately to me. Of course it was possible to move a piano, nothing easier. The most difficult aspect of a new plan was to keep Annagreth away from the apartment in the afternoon of the day we were due to move in. Having spent the rest of the afternoon making phone calls, trying to get in touch with various useful people, Mike, the owner of the studios in which we recorded, and Rob, the owner of the guitar shop, would be, most immediately, most practically, the two who could help, knowing about such matters, piano moving, and having ideas as to the practical achievement of the goal, but it would still need a large number of willing hands on a winter's day and scaffolding to pull the whole event off. George, Graeme's father could help with the last matter, Graeme assured me, having friends who were builders, and who would be happy to help out for a drink or several. Always, someone, somewhere, happy at the thought of drink to be obliging, alcohol an alternative currency on the Island, as in many circles was weed, especially during those rare visits by the legendary, some would say mythical Milo. Additionally, alcohol, legal, illegal, home brewed, truck *s'amazin' it never breaks, nipper, way it keeps fallin' off the back of a lorry*, was a medium for inducing the successful inauguration of Island magic. Knowing those on the inside at the brewery would be only too pleased to help, *one of our loads has gone missing*, and having also an acquaintance with a garden plot large enough to provide competition for the GNP of certain Caribbean Islands, I told Graeme to do the necessary.

Leaving him to arrange materials and a certain amount of muscle, I asked James to inveigle, beg, rope in, cajole, or otherwise embarrass enough people to make the plan feasible. Marching orders would be issued, the clock would turn. All that remained was to keep Annagreth away during the afternoon, it having been worked out, a few days later, by George and Graeme, following a visit that it would want around three, say four hours to be on the safe side, to transport the piano safely, get it in place, get in the piano tuner, *and on Bank Holiday, that'll cost*, someone had uttered, Eeyore to everyone else's Tigger, *piss off Jones, you miserable git*. Fortunately it wouldn't as it turned out, Rob and Mike both knowing someone who got all their tuning work, and so would, they assured me, be happy to do this. So, I turned to Kate, for the most important question, that of the ruse. For magic, a conjuror was required. If the stars wouldn't come right on their own, a little *leger de main,* a small but diverting misdirection had to be effected. Everything had to be achieved *pianissimo*.

— Just tell her we're arranging a surprise party, but that you're not meant to say. She'll like the idea you've told her, she'll like knowing it's supposed to be a surprise and will go along with the whole thing, even pretending to be surprised, and I'll make sure everyone knows that she knows that we don't know she knows, if you know what I mean. Once you've told Anna that I'm in charge, she won't ask any questions; tell her you're taking her out in the afternoon, that it's all been arranged for Graeme to take all her things over in the van in the morning from the Gurnard flat, and we'll get everything out of there, and into the flat, Anna can even supervise so we get everything stowed, by about twelve or one at the latest. It's easy.

If Kate said it was all easy, it was bound to be. This was a given. How could it be anything but? The fates would not dare to revolt. That morning therefore, having stayed in Gurnard the previous evening, following nearly five hours of playing, seeing out the old year, welcoming the new, *mad as blind ferrets, the lot on 'em*, Graeme's assessment of the warders at Parkhurst let loose for an evening's entertainment, and with too little sleep, we completed the final packing, Graeme arriving, *Morning Bugger, tea on? hello sweetness*, with the Transit emptied around eight. Away by nine, Graeme following the Variant, we arrived in Seaview shortly before ten, to see James

waiting, a mug of tea and a glass of something stronger
in hand, sitting on the sunken wall. The sun was over the
yard-arm somewhere; or perhaps had yet to go down. Lady
M had noticed him arriving, and without letting him in, *must
have thought I was a tradesman*, brought him *something warm, and a
snifter to see in the new year, she said*.

Breath visible hurrying from mouths to stall, vapour
on the verge of freezing so it seemed, frost whitening tips,
edges, laying along brickwork, crackling glass. Voices behind
us announced the arrival of Morphy, Damian, and Rory,
Seaview's very own not so ancient mariner, whose father, a
member of the merchant navy had taught his son all of the
techniques necessary for, and associated with sailing, but
had handed on none of the luck, agility, or a general ability
to keep a weather eye open. Rory, as a result, though he had
no albatross about his neck, the thing having come back to
life just to escape another voyage, was cursed with about as
much good luck as his Romantic counterpart, a seven times
broken nose, close experience of the spinnaker, to prove
the point. They had all thought it a good idea, bit of fun, to
come pitch in, if we needed any help that was, *don't suppose
there's a drink going?* Any pictures to hang? Damian had asked,
no came Annagreth's reply, a little over-emphatically, *but make
yourself useful…oh, here, we will go and get tea started*, she corrected
herself realising as she was speaking the dreadful scenario
that might unfold were Damian, soul of a ballerina, dexterity
of a Troll on acid, left on his own with cups, teapot, boiling
water, and what in his hands could all too easily turn into
instruments of torture; or otherwise objets d'art, defined thus
by Kate once as *that old rubbish in antiques shops*, you could feel
the hook of the quotation marks digging in, *which have lost
handles, spouts or anything else vaguely useful*.

Morphy, who for the really important part of the day had
been made head magus and stage manager due to his being
the only person to have inside knowledge on the herding
of cats and the irrepressible good humour of someone
terminally parental, had clearly passed on the word, James

and Graeme already in on the plan. The next couple of hours
were spent in unpacking, hanging, tidying, arranging, clearing
up, and flat-packing boxes originally, *he'll be wanting them back
in the morning,* borrowed from Rob. Lady Marjoribanks had
once ventured below stairs with a plate of biscuits, Jammy
Dodgers, Garibaldis, and Digestives, to inquire if we were
all doing well, to the sound of Damian being stifled with a
tea towel, and some quite theatrical coughing, as he began
to impersonate an aged store owner, saying that *you've all done
very well.* Place, move, sort, direct, shift, no, yes, unpack, hang,
give directions, avoid, nearly drop. By midday, everything
was stowed, cardboard boxes flattened, a few framed photos
placed, mostly Anna's brought from Germany originally,
then from across the Island this morning. Put in place, other
items also, feeling their way into occupation, accustoming
themselves to the task of transforming uninhabited space
into a home, as yet undefined but already, even in those first
hours, accommodating, reshaping as it were the vacancy,
a blank sheet lightly sketched, dim outlines of a stronger
definition. All the things one never sees in stop frame
animation had occurred, transformation, space become place,
rooms reoriented through personal perspective. Looking at
my watch, I made the suggestion that we begin the birthday
rounds, *first Kate, Harry and Rosemary, they're expecting us for lunch,
James's parents insisted on seeing you at some point, I think Angela has
made some all purpose House-Warming-cum-Birthday-present*
— You don't want to keep Ma waiting, you know how she is.
James offered this insight, a nicely timed piece of stagecraft,
just believable enough to sound spontaneous, a popping
cherry ripe for the catch at second slip. I continued, pointing
out that we said we'd be there by three, *then just before five, short
stop, at my mother's*

— Have a nice cup of tea, dear.

Anna's voice mimicked what for my mother was
possibly one of the most important phrases in the English
language, having an insistence that carried in it the promise

that resistance was futile, capitulation inevitable. Anna had joked, on first meeting my mother, that it was little wonder Germany failed to win. *The war or the World Cup*, Graeme had asked, unthinking innocently enough at first; then realising in that horror of a too premature release the curse had come upon him, his face reddening, until Anna, almost as quickly took his head in both hands, pulled it towards her, and bestowing the crown with a kiss, not unlike that given by Snow White to one of the Seven Dwarves, remarked archly, *both*. Absolved, he reddened, gurning, a solstice beacon casting winter rays. About to leave, the sails dropped, the wind had disappeared. Becalmed we found ourselves, nearly rudderless, as Annagreth, looking around said,

— I don't want to go; I want to spend the afternoon in my home.

Time froze, the apartment having a spell cast over it, everyone set in place. A game? A double bluff? She knew about the party after all, or did she suspect something else? With Anna, it was often impossible to tell, her ability to wrong-foot people, to be presumed innocent when saying something wicked, and wickedly funny, signs of another form of magic, impervious to comprehension. Looks were exchanged.

— Look child,

I said, an uncustomary moment of thinking on my feet, the defensive play become a boundary through a chance, if risky inside edge.

— It'll be just like seeing the Island again, for the first time, but different…It'll be like your first trip around the Island, but with frost, everything is different in winter; we'll even stop in some of the same places, we can make time.

As we left, James promised to lock up, saying that he would see us both later, with Kate and Graeme, he thinking that Anna had no idea of the larger, if lesser surprise, the greater gathering, let alone the fact that several sets of parents had been conscripted into the afternoon's subterfuge, a large plan underway, its cogs, gears, and wheels set in motion by a violinist, singer, accordionist, baker, player of the *mandoline;* Annagreth, in response, looked away, a brief smile flickering, as slyly, she turned her eyes to me as if to say, silently, in on the secret within the secret, that, *yes, we know, don't we,* even though of course she knew but didn't know, and knew both more and less than James.

As we drove away toward the Duver, Anna noticed a truck and van turn into Fairy Road, the former laden with planks and scaffolding.

— If they are working today, they will be paid well. Why does your mother insist on a *nice* cup of tea? Does she imagine I would like one that is horrid?

~~~

> *Be my child, be my lover, swallow me up in your fireglow.*
> *Take my tongue, take my torment, take my hand and don't let go.*
> *Let me live in your life for you make it all seem to matter.*
> *Let me die in your arms so the vision may never shatter.*
> *The seasons roll on, and my love stays strong.*

The song played, we made, eventually, to move. Two cups would be left, they could be patient till the morning came much later, a morning so late as to be afternoon. The rooms were, that night, alive with as yet dormant memory, pregnant with happy phantoms, their spaces invisibly maintained by a taut skein, bearing all the pressure of what was yet to seep slowly in, over the coming five, no, more than five years. Walls felt the absence of a photograph not yet taken, a painting or a sketch as yet unexecuted. Tables, shelves, the mantelpiece of several fire places, each was empty, vacant lot, but having somewhere on them traced the unseen place marked reserved for this souvenir, that object, a small love token, or fetish suggestive of a trip, a visit, a vacation. Hallway, box room, living room, bed. Everywhere awaited its ghostly imprint, gathering in shape and intensity with every unimagined, yet gradually realised repetition, silent falls, footprints gathered, pressure of back, of head, arm against arm, the lightest touch, unconscious motion of a hand along a chair back, the one accumulating in the place of the other, the line of habit.

Turning off a side lamp, picking up a solitary candle, already guttering, Anna, Annagreth, Anna turned back to me. I see you, her turning, taking my hand, saying, *there you are*, as if I had vanished; then, *here we are*, quoting then from a poem I now recognized, a favourite, one we had read more than once already in near dark, by candlelight: *nur* ein *Mal, Ein mal und nichtmehr, Und wir auch* ein *mal, Nie wieder*, her face delicately underlit so that she appeared, barely a ghost of herself, breath of golden down along the curve of jawbone, captured by candle. Then in Swedish, she spoke; for when you didn't want me to understand, you changed tongues, didn't you, father for mother, saying

— *Kom till sängs med mig. Min ljuvliga man.*

III Four Seasons

9. A Journey North (Winter 77/78)

I miss you.

You had said this to me one morning, winter light the white of ice reflected sun.

Shortly after waking, laying in bed the words arrived, I having come back from the kitchen, coffee, black and strong. Long shadows, deep, pooling, still and deep, boughs seen, either side the drive, seasonally sprinkled white on green. Handing Annagreth a cup, *careful, it's hot; no? really?* You waited, thoughtful, your gaze away past the protecting conifers, biting slightly your top lip, a little dried, the skin a little chapped, last lingering trace of a recent cold, until I had settled back. Then. From the silence of a winter's morning, you said simply, but with the weight of consideration, an age in the reckoning leading to that neutrality of expression.

— I miss you.

Surprised, I ventured the opinion that I had only been in the kitchen fifteen, twenty minutes at most.

— No, silly man. *Sjåpig!* No.

A pause? A silence. The silence of thought arriving.

— In my sleep. When I am asleep. When I wake, I know I have been asleep. Knowing this, then I know you were there but I know in my waking that I did not know. At the time I did not know, though now I know that then, I did not know. That is when I miss you. I realise. When I am asleep.

I knew from your tone, from that slight lowering of the voice, as if you were gathering yourself into a smaller space that you wanted, that you felt the need to be serious, what you, what your family would call your 'winter' you.

Wait, stop! Anna had nearly seemed to shout one night, emphasis a punctuation. *Here is winter Annagreth, everyone pay attention, this is important.* This, I remembered, had come in a moment of gradually building frustration during a rehearsal, when none of us could work out exactly the nature of an arrangement, how best to give life to the formless lump of music everyone had been kneading, pummelling, coaxing, encouraging for several hours on a fog-ridden February evening. Arriving late enough in the day to see the last of light, early enough to see coming from across Culver Down, the Yarborough Monument barely visible, we knew the mist would thicken, to roll, and creep, and climb, down through Whitecliff Bay, then upward, grasping slowly at Knowle Mill to cover Bembridge, shroud swathe vanishing.

— *Here is winter Annagreth, everyone pay attention, this is important.*

James tapped his bow against the 'cello, imitation of a rule rapped on a desk. You had never used that phrase before, and its exclamation took us each by surprise. Perhaps you had laid too stern an emphasis, certainly an emphasis unexpected because never before heard. But as if to make light of this oddly dangerous situation, your eyes widened, eyebrow catback arched with that joking gesture I already knew to say, inside its silent mime, *no, everything is okay.* You, the pantomime villain. The clocks started up, the blood began to flow along the veins once more. Normal service, if not resumed, was waiting at the door to be admitted. Kate, the first to respond, repeated as a question, her voice rising to emphasise this, *winter Annagreth?* To which you replied not at first in words but with a silent film, suspenseful expectation of dire consequences, sequence of chords on the organ, the final notes all crazy tremolo. Then you continued for the benefit of us all, James, obviously nonplussed, Graeme slightly nervous, his eyes moving back and forth between us,

mute appeal of a puppy having realised too late it had had
an accident, and I, wide eyed with incomprehension, feeling
as I so often did in other unexpectedly tense situations,
adrenalin leaking through, pressure applied on the dam wall
of the hitherto unremarkable. A moment was arriving. *I have
a solution for the arrangement,* you told us, reassuring the children
that there was nothing untoward beneath the bed, nothing
lurking in the fog, *but first,* you explained, emotionless, in that
matter of fact manner wherein impatience is masked through
the calm of rational, inevitable logic, how, as a child, no more
than four or five, vexation beyond expression, beyond anger
at your inability to grasp a figure on the piano, *clearly it was
obvious, otherwise how could anyone play it, and if anyone could play
it, why not you,* your small face would lock itself in a frozen
rimy mask, your snow queen persona, James was once to
anoint it on another occasion. Seeing you quietly sitting at
the keyboard, your will, steel and iron in equal measure, your
mother had said you recalled, *Look, it is Winter Annagreth; thaw,
child, you will never play it else.* From then, this had been a family
name for you in such moments.

This morning was such a moment. Everywhere else was
winter beyond the window, beyond the bedroom that day.
You had found your winter self, gathering the will to speak
of those fleeting shadows, small predatory shades, shapes
below the surface of an untroubled calm, noticeable only
in that they caused a slight disturbance. Though not angry,
it was clear you wished to speak about things that troubled
you, matters intangible but which could dog your lighter days,
your brighter steps. I knew, barely a year after we had found
our safe home together, that you would feel the need to tell
me something, speaking in your mother's voice. Swedish
was there for when you felt the need to say what no one else
around could comprehend; which I failed to understand in
any simple or direct manner, not having, being mute in, this
tongue, but forced to listen to what was inside, beneath the
words, that which illuminated them with a darker, a winter

light. To watch your face in those instances, to see your eyes, mouth, eyebrows, cheeks, shaping themselves the outward and visible signs of an inner passion, a torment, a realisation, and to strive to see, and so to hear, and so, finally, to feel— the task you always set me at such times. You paused, to look again toward the window, having been studying the slight circular motions in the coffee, your eyes narrowing as you did so. Your head turning back to me, your hand raising to touch my mouth, you spoke in that private language reserved for us, because you knew I didn't understand, and, because you had also told me once that not understanding was when I loved you best. You spoke the words of a Swedish proverb you had taught me.

— *Älska mig när jag minst förjänar et, för det är då jag verkligen behöver det.*

Silence after speech has about it a quality of remaining touched by what has retreated. Ghosts of words reluctant to retreat finally hang expectant. Saying nothing, but everything that could be said by a touch, I remained compelled by your touch for some time still, watching, your eyes tracing the contours of my face seeming to draw its outlines, sketching the image for posthumous memory. Like the silence when wind rattling the windowpanes falls, or that quiet between the upsurge of waves, the instant after final raindrops of a passing shower cease upon glass or roof, that morning filled the entire world. It was every morning, you were all the mornings then. There you are, I see you. And from that silence, I see your lips begin to shape, begin to form the thought behind the eyes.

— We should write to one another, all the time we should. Not to wait for absence, being separated, apart for any reason. Promise me, please, promise that we will write to one another every week; I will give to you letters, cards, and you must do the same. In that way, we will each have souvenirs of the other, we will still have something there, then we will never have to say again, I miss you, because writing will be there for each of us to read, when we cannot hear each other speak; but we will, won't we? We will hear each other, and I can say to myself, *there you are; there. And so will you.*

~~~

Winter: always a special time, private moments stolen in the middle of what seemed inescapably most hectic, most public. Summers were full but with an endlessness of rhythm, rote and repetitious. Winters came, bringing sharper vision in clearer air, gesturing towards climax, celebration, festive rousing from the depths of darker sleep. Fewer successive nights, greater periods of intensity. Living in the dark created an urgent undertow, flow beneath the feet, in the bones, a more insistent, sometimes fevered, short-day driven pulse. Record snowstorms, colder temperatures gripping the Midwest, promised waves of colder air over the north Atlantic, eventually to settle, consequence, effect, over us. We too would feel the greater storm, lessened, made weak in its travel. Even Florida saw snowfall, the news had reported. Even Florida. Orange trees frosted, killed in the growing, squeezed lifeless. Winter death, cold, quiet, bringing its numbing sleep, cradling, the eyes closing, with a cold that feels like warmth. Slipping, one slips, caressed. Kate had taken to playing Bach on the accordion, transcribed between her and James, cello lines transferred to keys and bellows, squeezebox Bach, a sound more strangely northern in its temperament, more of winter in the notes, more the sound of sitting round the fire, keeping out the night, its impertinent emissary the wind gusting impatience; brief cessation, a lone bird calling, barely hidden, hedgerow battered. Then the greater voice returned. That first winter, together, *we few, we happy few, no, The Happy Few is not a good name, really Judge, get a grip, man*, sounds evolved, experiments in private, changes in order, combination, arrangement, and then before an audience, extended improvisations. Texture,

layer on layer, sound on sound, a freedom arriving with
familiarity, everyone there for everyone else, ready to catch
if a foot slipped from the wire. December that year, our first
year, fourteen months in total, as what Kate had called the
not very famous five brought in the advance party of winter's
war, first flakes of greater flurries, falls of a different kind,
a gift from North America. January drifted deeper into
endless winter, from which there appeared no waking, at
times no escaping. The sand spit crab claws of Bembridge
harbour were dusted, making entrance even more difficult.
The various whites of frost and ice and snow held even into
February, winter's lupine hunger, relentless, showing no signs
of exhaustion, continuing to scent, and so pursue its prey,
invisible to all but felt by everyone. Seventy dead reported
across the Midwestern States.

No one was expecting the severity of that winter, when
two months before, Annagreth had wondered about the
possibility of our visiting home, first Lübeck, then a flight
from Hamburg to Stockholm, and the hour's drive north
to Ljusterö, Christmas an important family time, *and you
should meet my parents, they want very much to meet you.* This said
one night, the question raised, put to the table, our circle,
our circus, the same evening when we had found our name,
finally: Old Time Hockey. An afternoon of rehearsals had
been followed by a suggestion from Graeme, that *there's
a really good movie at the pictures, s'all about Ice Hockey.* Not
sounding that promising, especially when every question
asked about the exact nature of the film was fielded with the
response, *I don't know, bugger*, the film did come recommended
with Graeme's complete, if unfounded enthusiasm, and the
rejoinder that *at least it's not miserable, no one dies, I think, and
it hasn't got subtitles.* Such arguments were as compelling as
the fact that the heavy fog was seeping everywhere, coming
up from the bay, and making practice distinctly less than
anything that could be called pleasurable; unless of course
anyone could claim to enjoy clammy, damp numbness, the
prospect of consumption, the visible air entering, eating up

and smothering the lining of lungs. Raw, wild, leaden, that afternoon, cold, creeping death at the doors, misting the windows, fingering the locks, smearing the land, blinding those outside, a rapacious mugger greedy for nothing more than the breath of the unwary. So it was, we decided. So it became, Paul Newman was responsible for giving us our name, even if it was Kate's exclamation, *that's it, that's the name!* undeniable in its earnest, epiphanic, emphatic certainty, which, exploding in the dark, caused for someone to request the manager silence *those rowdy youths*. Graeme redressed the balance somewhat however. For, as we left, the movie seen out in silence, he sidled to the pensioner who had wished us removed, remarking *sotto voce, see my mate, missis; he's got a plate in his head, been known to turn quite nasty*, at which point, he then walked away, hands deep in pockets, whistling, grinning with *that* expression.

— Back at the barn, the name mulled over, accepted unanimously, drinks all around to celebrate, Annagreth broached the subject of visiting home. While the question was allowed to accommodate itself to the evening, there drifted across the fields faintly, a strange, dissonant tintinnabulation, *ta-te-tah-te-tah, ta-te-tah-te-taah-tah, ta-te-tah-te-tah-te-tah, tiddly-tiddly-tah*, warping, far too quickly, phasing, redshift distortion. Dementia given form in frequency, the mad, racing chimes blaring through Grampian horns,

— We really do have to get some of those.

— Why, are you planning on selling ice creams between sets?

— Morphy, why not build one? It's just a musical box mechanism with a pickup run through an amp.

— you wait, next week, bloody Wagner. With a spoons accompaniment.

vanished with the promise of a certain return another time. The portal closed, we turned back to the question at hand. *Oh Good, I get to sing more*, Kate's immediate, unironic reaction. Like her familiar, Fred, Kate rarely lacked energy, enthusiasm, or a clarity of purpose; James offered to take some other vocal duties; *not too many*, it was felt, otherwise his focus lost, dispersed, all energy dissipated in turning outwards. Graeme demonstrated, surprisingly, a pragmatic turn, *how many nights we talking about, bugger?* Though not one to express concern, Graeme, like all of us, recognised the importance of continuing to earn. Here, was a question, not of time away, but of shows to be rethought, gigs to be rearranged.

— We could leave December 22, drive and be in Hamburg the same evening; on to Lübeck the next day, then after Christmas Day, to Sweden, the New Year there, then home, *therehome*, before back here, *herehome* not *therehome*, by the first days of January.

— So that's…what have we got Kate? I know Christmas and New Year's Eve; It'd be nice for once not to have to trot out Mick, Keith, John, George, Ringo, Chuck and Elvis…

— well for you maybe.

— So am I forgetting anything?

Kate returned with her diary, a large already spine-broken, red covered, wine and grease stained notebook.

— We've got all the weekend, four in a row from the previous Thursday before Christmas Eve, Tuesday a birthday party, Wednesday, yes, that's the 21st, a lunchtime, then two seasonal lunchtimes, all 'God rest ye's' and mince pies, plus the Thursday, Friday and the Saturday, that's New Year's Eve, so, don't worry about afternoons, it's really just four to cover.

— Well, most of the material for then, it's not exactly brain surgery for the guitar parts.

— What about Geoff?

James offered up the possibility. Geoff Daly-Bassett, 'dolly' to some, 'hound' to others, the layered hair and Hawaiian shirts aside, was amongst the most technically accomplished guitarists we knew, his a gift more than an ability, to hear, learn and imitate, note for note, just about any piece from the previous thirty years of popular music. Give Geoff a recording, play him a complex figure, it would be played back as well as, or often better than the original. I had played several times with Geoff in wine bars and bistros,

playing, no, keeping up with, his own arrangements of Pat
Metheny, Joe Pass, or Django Reinhardt, always coming
away happy from the experience, but feeling as though
my wrists could not survive another minute of such work,
long involved chord progressions, chord solos, beautifully
ornate runs, sequences, arpeggios in 12/8, 6/8, or 5/4
time. Several years older than any of us, Geoff's threshold
for being a regular fixture in any band was singularly low,
boredom a quality of his personality that bordered on a trait,
so pronounced as to appear obsessive. Preferring to work
endlessly on his two motorbikes, a Greeves Fleetwing and a
Vincent Black Lightning, or to be Rob Thompson's unofficial
luthier for all aspects of guitar repair, electric or acoustic,
Geoff spent his time as a professional tour guitarist for hire,
through an agency who organized backing bands to play
for various big name soul acts on tours, often for US forces
based in Europe. Currently away for over two months on
such a tour, December would for Geoff be 'down time'. That
he would agree would hardly be an issue, always ready to play
with any line up on a limited basis, with an enthusiasm the
inverse reflection of that disdain for any suggestion that he
might front a regular band of his own. So Geoff, duly asked
on his return to the Island said yes, of course, as we had
expected. The drive to the north, one country after another
to be planned, anticipated. In the interim, our lives together
and separately were steered by autopilot, maintaining a course
without a destination, but always with that shared heading.

From the time of the meeting well before our northward
journey though, leading up to a trip so inexpressibly
happy, there were numerous performances, and with those
the gradual evolution of our various, shifting collective
identities. Making arrangements for the music, our own,
increasingly, and that of others, we also found we could
rearrange ourselves, each of us assuming different roles
from night to night, or within the same night, depending
on venue, audience, type of event. Bread and butter rhythm
and blues, folk dances, private parties, and the odd ticket

only evening for the well-heeled, well-dressed set, wanting
what they thought of as capital J-Jazz, but into which we
could smuggle in plain sight certain wilder, ferral numbers,
inventively rethought, not wholly housetrained and having
a long leash. Graeme was able to come out from behind
the kit on occasions, freed and playing amongst the various
congas, bongos, shakers, gourds, hand drums, ingeniously
devised racks of tuned metal, wooden keys, a skeleton piano,
a dancing bear whose kinetic energy assumed a greater
space than his physical presence. Kate, as ever, always
restless, changing violin for viola, for mandolin, accordion
or other squeeze box, the bass once in a while, and singing
with complete control and abandon, spinning, weaving her
body between each of us, flame-haired, hennaed shine, or
breaking, tambourine in hand, into hard shoe rapid leg and
foot motions, Irish dancing with abandon. Judge, bewigged,
bald, sitting, standing, cello, bass, his prized beast, the hybrid
six string oddity, a cello-bass, or as demanded trumpet or
saxophone, that always inner focus, the eye of any maelstrom
sound and motion; I? Georges Braque to everyone else's
Picasso, happily having the least changes, but altering as was
necessary my voice, ventriloquizing, mimicking intonations,
accents, switching between guitars, electric, acoustic, six- or
twelve-string, harmonica, and on more than one occasion
the recorder, my neck lunatic fulcrum, almost off its hinges,
circling stationary.

And Anna: In that first year, I see her, I remember you,
sitting mostly still, a small point, motionless, Hermione still,
the only indication of life the blur of fingers, the face alive to,
or pushing changes, an eyebrow raised to indicate a laggard
response, or eyes turned out to somewhere in the audience;
Annagreth at piano, organ, occasionally singing, at first only
quieter numbers, in the early months not venturing much,
if at all, beyond the fortress of right-angled keyboards, the
Hammond, the Rhodes, a keyboard bass or bass pedals,
freeing Judge; to this array soon was added a synthesizer, a
Mini-Moog later traded for a DX-7, the tops of instruments

dressed with fake floral displays, which seemed strangely
to grow starting from Annagreth's side of the stage, taking
on lives of their own, finding themselves beginning to
twine around microphone stands; flora became augmented
by fauna, equally unreal, surreal, some evenings the stage
area assuming the look of a bizarre menagerie, various
carved, stuffed; or two owls, depending from cymbal stands,
taxidermied raptors atop amplifiers, the cuboid goat an
irregular feature, all of which was granted a special magic by
the rare appearance of Graeme's doghead, that disturbing
canine mask, the stage become carnival; or, other nights, our
space became a living room, into which the audience was
invited, rugs, standard lamps, the television set, a couple of
arm chairs or even a coffee table, more than once.

Broadening, deepening, honing, redefining: how many
different ways are there to describe who we were, what we
did? Or in the end, is it not the case that all such descriptions
are found once more to be redundant, lacking point or
purpose? That we did what we did, in different ways, in the
year between the party in the barn and the Christmas journey
with different sonic registers; that we could explore so many
musical forms, or could easily move between genres, styles,
reinterpreting as we went so that, from one night to the next
a song, an instrumental might turn chameleon, suiting itself
to its surrounding; or else, reinvention, portraits reimagined,
particular pieces becoming during this period collective
favourites, lodestones, points of common reference to be
conjured in varied ways, to distinct effect, a process that
we were only beginning to discover the possibilities of, and
which, in the next eighteen months we slowly fashioned as
an essential strand, numerous fibres plaited together, giving
added strength, sinuous, animate, organic, harmonious lace
braid of sound at the heart of what we did and who we were
that held us together. As first I had with James, then we two
with Kate, and so, subsequently, with Graeme, and again with
Annagreth, everything came about through a lightning strike
of another kind: the instant appreciation of what was to be

seen in everyone, each in every other, that quiet trust, faith, belief in one another, an understanding, which in its intimate apprehension belied any need for speech, for framing or explication. *The air between us*, Anna had once said, explaining once, without explaining, when Pete, always the camera gathering faces, gestures, bodies in motion or at rest, once asked jokingly of me, *what do you see in him? The air between us.* All she said, but in that was everything, her words attesting also to what passed between the five of us, as Kate's look of appreciation on that occasion revealed. If something failed to work the failure was ours equally; if it worked we all took equal share in the success.

From these months, a year having passed since Annagreth's joining us, we found ourselves having written enough new material, which we believed good enough to take into the studio in November. Anna and I had begun to write together regularly the previous autumn, a process where each would contribute, suggest, talk through both words and music together. James and I had written before, and continued to do so, no less infrequently, Kate with us less so, on her own, or I also, alone. With Annagreth's contributions, we found ourselves able to explore a loose, interchangeable process of composition and arrangement. Only Graeme remained largely silent in this process, happy, he once said, to be in the final execution, completing the musical form, bringing to life the rhythmic coup de foudre, playing how he wanted he thought as important as writing what one played. Where we wrote was also a matter of exchange, impromptu gatherings, whether in the barn, at the basement apartment, or the cottage, now James's alone at the end of Fairy Road, looking directly down towards us from Saltern's Road. Being no more than five minutes apart, there were days when James would rush to us with an idea, Anna and I returning the visit, Kate and Graeme too, if we all happened to be together, which we were so frequently, or some variation thereof, and so it would go, back and forth, often a new piece a collaborative and a peripatetic process. Music as walking as sharing as rhythm. Where did we begin or end? It is hard now to tell, if even possible. Every beginning starts only because of a happy event that precedes and makes it possible, two or more attractors, different in themselves coming together and perceiving in the other a sympathetic resonance. Entities of a single endlessly mutable organism, as ridiculous as that sounds, comes closest to expressing a series of evolving relationships for which the word symbiotic hardly does justice. To say we lived together gives the wrong impression. As I write that, now, I know that we did not so much live together, did not simply share spaces and experiences, as, individually, together, we lived. And individually, together, we found ourselves each in the other. So it was when, over the years, going to the studios, we found a truer, because private validation of ourselves. Recordings were always two: the window dressing, the display, a front. And inside, hidden, in full view, plain sight, each of us, together, separately, touching and being touched.

Solent Studios, owned by Mike Stanger, was, like some gingerbread house of folklore, hidden away in woods outside East Cowes, somewhere almost Whippingham, on a slight hill. Willows, cedars and conifers kept the property and its grounds from sight. It was only on coming to the end of the private road, turning into the drive that the house and studio, all one large, chalet construction, dark stained timber, with outside stairs, a large deck, outhouses, a workshop, and the rehearsal studio. Large and small spaces, comfortable, warm and welcoming, designed to be welcoming and to control sound quality in each of its spaces, the studio was a retreat, the rooms wood panelled, blonde on darker blonde, by polished brown, curved panels serving as deflectors, reducing flutter echoes, every wall treated, while diffusers, irregular of surface, complexly patterned, damping and eliminating echo and ringing. Free standing bass traps across corners deadened sound further. Mike had provided a number of instruments, organ, concert grand piano, electric keyboards, amplifiers and speaker cabinets, of various kinds, *a divers parley of instruments*, had been my own observation when in the midst of reading something seventeenth century, to minimize setting up time, and to control as far as was possible the aural signature, the sonic image of the place. There was also a drum kit, but over this he give way to Graeme, *bugger*, he was told, *I'm not using that. It may be good enough if you don't know, but I do.* This was said, without menace or umbrage, grin wide set, and with that mildness of delivery usually associated with avuncular figures or grandparents making it clear that while all foibles could be indulged to a point, enough was enough. This far and no further. Once inside, we found ourselves in a bunker, the personality of which was its very absence of personality, designer architecture suggesting something for some reason Swiss. Inviting because neutral, comforting because when in the live rooms, the control room, or the very necessary kitchen, *more tea anyone, or is it time for beer? It's always time for beer, but make mine a coffee,* there was no more outside, nothing beyond. Unlike Beckett characters we could not even go to a window to view the absence of life in a waste land. Here, we were, here, everything that was, was all there was. We saw only the task, living in a world of sound.

Blind to the outside world, we were either in the studio or not. If we wanted a break there was the patio, furnished on finer days, opening onto the downward curving lawn, or, topping off the roof of the rehearsal studio, a deck, with a view of the Solent, rippling white blue, sun winking in spring and summer, or petrel darker on those cloud covered afternoons of months on the cusp of seasons, waves the arching break, shading grey through white of diving Fulmars, the waters a dumbshow in the winter's winds, of aerial displays above. Seabird falling, arc describing, visual counterpoints, Annagreth had one afternoon supposed that November responded to string, key, voice glissandi, the visible world slip-sliding around us, in time with the tonal bends, smears, falls, the runs descending or ascending. *When I play this, when Kate plays that, James, you, even Graeme's bells, the glockenspiel,* this pronounced, referring not to the instrument but the play of bells, accented emphasis richly thickening, unwritten *shhhppp* admitting the final gliding vowel, dipthong, falling and rising, *opening and closing, falling, rising runs of notes*, admitting that rounded *l*, her German tongue wrapped around it with a precision, an aural muscular hold lacking in its lazier English counterpart, *when there are these sounds, those out there, the birds, the waves, the movement and the moving caused by wind, this is what I feel, these are the shapes to play; we play sometimes what is here, in the sky, across the water; we sound out what the world shows us. I feel here already…O es ist ein geheimer Ort; Ein heimeliger Ort; heimisch, heimlich, yes? Secret, homely, safe, hidden.* Yes, I knew, I understood, responding with a line remembered, the source forgotten, irrelevant: *Durch gedämmtes Licht und Kerzen wurde das Zimmer heimelig.* Absolutely unseeing, the landscape before us ignored, the words grasped after what was folded in the vision, invisible to the eye. I realised, I saw, I felt the truth of what Anna was saying, as we stood on the roof deck, holding ourselves tightly against the cold, I holding her, standing behind her, looking out to sea, over her shoulder, as Annagreth gripped, ever tighter with each successive phrase and in defiance of the cold, a mug of coffee, steam rising, signalling to the spirits of place and afternoon. Yes, this was the studio. A place that became increasingly a hide, a bolthole, sanctuary dry land anchorage, secure from all buffeting, a second collective home beyond the safety of the barn, somewhere to experiment, explore, test, try out; and every so often to try Mike's patience.

This November, our second visit to the studio, the first with Annagreth, we had come to record a number of new songs, instrumentals and, as it would turn out, several pieces that were either wholly or partly improvised. Though we had intended this should be a single visit, in the end we were not to be finished until February of the following year. James and I had written one study together, another with Anna, who contributed a further three instrumental pieces of her own; I had something that had been knocking around for some time, while Anna and I had also a song, 'Daughter', written shortly

after we moved into Fairy Road, having had its life started
from phrases she recalled from childhood, used by her father.
A winter song, its tale and sounds those of solitude, chill and
soft, broken light illuminating the rebellious soul, hiding in
wait somewhere in a forest older than the word can measure,
it brushed against the heart with a darkening, a shadow
shaped touch, chilling. Viola, cello, two guitars, a bowed bass,
tremulous percussion, coruscating metallic echoes, playing
against the lustre of a high, lone voice, lost somewhere in
the woods, distant in the mix, returning to tell its father that
its vessel would never return, unless as a passing shade, a
revenant spirit. Radiant, alien, hinting at a mordant whimsy,
the voice and percussion were further treated, pulled in
stranger directions by the inclusion of a new toy recently
purchased by Mike, a Theremin, in response to the sound
of which Annagreth insisted on adding a further line on the
studio's ondes Martenot. 'In the Can', that piece composed
between Annagreth, James and I, having been completed in
just three takes on the first day. Then 'Daughter', we decided.
By the fourth day, the twenty-seventh attempt completed,
finally, the first rough mix was being played back through
reference monitors, not in the control booth, but in the
kitchen. The song had seemed simple in design, which, in
essence it was. It was also, however, a question of being
unable to decide on an arrangement, the orchestration
not working, as if liquid matter refused to solidify, the
temperature not at the right point. Putting in an instrument,
taking something out, changing the line being played, little
was working. Breaking for lunch on the fourth day, Anna and
I went up to the deck, to watch the fragile sky, illimitable,
snow laden in its promise, the air cold scented with the tang
of shivering tree. Waiting unexpectant, we talked of little, till
Damian intruded.

— C'mon Chaps and Chapesses, the natives are getting
restless.

Finally, we found our way through the maze of 'Daughter'
coming out the other side, three hours later, just over four

minutes of crystal fragile threads, warp and weft across mute space to form the song. Morphy, who had in previous days been experimenting with the interplay of hand and oscillator that the Theremin offered, had said, when we came down from the roof, that *this is what's wanted, it's like the ghost of your voice, Anna, listen*. And we did. And she did, eyes growing wider, a smile beginning to emerge from its hibernal seclusion of the past days, a few hours only but with the duration of an ice age. One run through, with stops, pauses, repeats; then a take, and another, then, *the ondes, Mike, the ondes Martenot*. Levels reset, acoustic guitar, cello, viola, percussion; then, run-through second guitar and bass added, small finger cymbals also, singing bowls ring ringing, the scrape beneath the tone denying the possibility of purity, the ice and snow growing in the sound, falling, hardening, deepening; another playback, run-through, and the addition of the vocal, all bleak chill hoarfrost in highest registers, beyond the regions of the earth, translucent, yet strangely threatening in their evanescence, each phrase, a tracery of rime, clawing at the window, gripping at the heart. *I want it to ascend into… was ist es, was hat Kafka geschrieben?* …die Regionen der Eisgebirge, *ja, yes, the regions of the ice mountains*, was how Anna had described it to us. Listening back in the kitchen, having listened a first, a second time to the rough mix in the control room already, this was where Annagreth's eyes seemed to strain, as her head turned slightly to the left, her gaze had ascended to the right, and away, towards the corner of the ceiling. Sitting there together, expectant, tensely so, expecting the music to reveal another failure we had not in our desperation noticed before, scarcely a sound to be heard other than 'Daughter'. Only the shutter's impersonal capture intruded, Pete having come straight from college, wanting to capture something of the day, unaware of the weight of nervous expectancy mingled with a ragged languor. One photograph survives of Anna's face, chin up, head back, those so familiar braids embracing her head. Looking at your photograph I see you as I saw her then, impassive, the more beautiful for that solitude of composure, there but hidden in another world, your eyes, her gaze somewhere no one could join her, Anna, you, Annagreth. Without motion that moment, as you are forever in the photograph, framed against a grey door to the left, orange and yellow tiled wall to the right, the way you set yourself expresses everything beyond the power of speech. A flecked vee neck sweater, a size or two too large, moss and furze hued reveals collar bone and neck, slight scooped hollows, delicately shadowed, a pair of miniscule moles vertically adjacent grace the breastbone, a line leading the eye, mine now, as it was that day, feeling what the camera could never feel, up through the column of your neck, Annagreth's neck, back to your face, lips full, mouth closed, nose straight, eyes lifted, all quiet anticipation. There you are. It appears to me now as if there were no longer any time, there is no time in that image, its faded yellows making of the here and now a perpetual yesterday, yesterday always here, always now. The Bee Gees may have released an album that was to become what at the time was the best selling album ever, but for us, 'Daughter' was perfect.

~~~

December: Wednesday evening leaving the Island in order to be in in Dover in time for the first ferry after midnight *let's take the coast road, through Brighton and Hastings, it'll take another hour, but it's better than having to go almost to London then back out; we can stop midway for supper* Waltraud overladen, presents from James, Graeme, Kate, gifts for Annagreth's parents, her sister, for Volker, Heike's boyfriend. Arriving in Antwerp shortly after seven the next morning, aiming for Hamburg, a first halt, stopping with Heike and Volker that night, Lübeck the next day. Breakfast was needed. Leaving by nine, Benedict and Annagreth expecting to reach Dortmund shortly before midday, heading then north, past Münster towards Osnabrück, stopping there for lunch after one. Finally, last leg, to Bremen and so on to Hamburg, through the Elbtunnel, under the river, turning onto Elbchaussee, skirting the river and into the borough of Altona, west of the city centre, to arrive shortly before six at the apartment on Stangestraße daylight already gone.

That first night is vague now as are many of the subsequent busy welcoming family days, though you would remember, no? Too long a day, tiredness, and trying to take in too much. A quiet residential street, the terraced apartment buildings distinguished by their pastel shades, or, occasionally, a brighter hue, a thick red door surround, the ground floor walls the same, on top of which, one storey up the smooth plaster façade a peach tone; *gelb, grün,* or infrequently a masonry offwhite, pink below puce, or cooler blues, shading through an architectural lividity, made warm, welcoming, in the street lamps. Most of Stangestraße presented itself thus, the exception being one larger utilitarian building, possibly municipal, an acknowledgement of fifties slab anonymous brutalism and a reminder that this was no longer Weimar Germany. Altona, all hippy shabby seedy chic, though bearing still the signs of activism and revolutionary hope, already diverted elsewhere, political futures traded in for Green Party compromise. Red for Green. All go. This first brief stay in Hamburg, one of several, left the impression, midway between memory and phantasy, of quiet northern comfort and easy civilization, a small world at ease with itself, a world away from St Pauli, not yet, not quite the bourgeois politesse of Blankenese. Altona hovered in the air, a feeling, a tone given, a state of mind, as much as a place; here was somewhere in which it would be very easy to live, never minding the passage of time, changes beyond. Here was a quietly accommodating district, faded, dilapidated, charming, with the odd, but entrancing air of a conservative bohemian commune, happily out of time, having moved to its own internal pace for hundreds of years, Hanseatic hippydom, content with itself, ignored comparatively when considered alongside its aggressively self-promoting Prussian cousin, Berlin. Here, and Altona was Hamburg in miniature, was the North, once Danish, always Schleswig-Holstein, a less familiar Germany tending in temperament to resemble its Nordic relatives.

Over the days that followed we floated. We drove the next morning, once more north, always going north, to Lübeck, then after Christmas Day coming back to Hamburg, flying from there to Stockholm, driving from there into the north, again, to Ljusterö. Lübeck for Christmas, Ljusterö for the New Year. I find I want to keep those days, that time, secret. Wishing not to make ordinary, so sullying that first Christmas, *erste Weihnachten*, I find myself greedily hugging to me the memory, those memories that appear to me, wanting to protect them, keep them safe; memories in which I see myself not at all, but see through the memory of my eyes, what my vision had recorded of you, traced in me, etched, tattooed into my recollection, and through which, sweet ghost, living in a pure phantasy, as if I were seeing the days, as if I were in those days, as though there were no *I*, only the days, experiencing them once more as if, pure phantasy of time, of place, commingling with the memory of you, your touch, your look. A gaze. One to the other. Between? Everything, the invisible air. In the appearance of memory, there you are, there is the apprehension of my impossible belief that the phantasy is to me as real, more real in fact because it haunts me more nearly, with a more complete and inescapable, a terrible closeness, indelible, ineffaceable, you, your beauty at the very heart of the absence which torments, as if you were there still. As if. As if. As if it were easy enough to say, *there you are* and there you, Anna, Annagreth, there you appear; there, there Annagreth, you would be; as in those moments today, when looking at a screen, from nowhere, there and yet not there, a message, an email arrives, unexpectedly from an old friend. The name. Imagine. Opening the application, launching it, a panel, a screen within a screen, called misleadingly a desktop, comes into being, and, half watching half ignoring, I wait. Then, in the small bar at the bottom, a message tells me that mail is arriving.

Looking at the main panel, I see it arrive: a name, part of an address, more or less cryptic, more or less straightforward. Much more ghostly, I find this, I confess to you Anna, than the ring of the phone. The phone can be ignored. In the time that it rings, I can always choose not to lift the receiver, I can let it go, allow its fall into silence, or otherwise remain silent expecting the other to leave a message. Email though is truly haunting; before opening it, I see that name, I see it in darker letters, its boldness telling me it is there but not yet read. That not yet insists. I cannot escape the name once it is there, whereas the ringing of the phone tells me nothing other than the fact that there is someone wanting to make contact. Memory emails me, today; it has been doing this, calling me, demanding I read what I cannot choose to ignore for a long time, before there was ever email. You send me yourself, I cannot choose but see; no closing my eyes when your ghost appears, no closing my ears to a sound, perhaps a voice, intonation, or, unbidden, Anna, simply you, whispering; as if you had spoken to me, whether in sleep or in those waking moments that you come. As if. As if. It is as if that feeling of seeming to apprehend that it is as if you were there is in the reality of the phantasy, through the phantasy of this trace, which this trace simply is, the trace, the phantasy of a *you* more real than mere memory, comes to me, always unexpectedly, though always desired, longed for, as if I might say, to you, Annagreth, *there you are*, as if this were so, as if I had just turned around, and been taken by surprise; as if you, in turning around had been taken by surprise, by me, by my camera or that of another; as if; to which you would, I know, I believe, how I want to believe, yes, you would say to me, *yes, yes, I am here, and there you are too. Here we are. This is the happy moment to which all others have tended.*

So what would I want to say? What could I say of the first *Weihnachten?* Torn between the selfish wish to keep it secret, to keep safe even the smallest of details, I feel an obligation nevertheless to say something, believing you would wish that. *O Benedict, tell the story, some at least; what we had, what we have,*

*that remains a secret, no one can know, no one can hear our music,
even were you to tell every little detail.* You could always convince
Benedict; she knew, you know what to say, or when to say
nothing, bearing me, turning me, in that silence. So, yes, I will
say what I can, and we shall keep safe our secrets.

To Lübeck, then.

By the time we arrived, with Heike and Volker, snow
had begun to fall steadily, though it was not yet ten as we
entered the Brick Gothic realm of the *Queen of the Hanse and
Christmas Capital of Northern Germany.* Volker, perpetually,
constitutionally ironic, had joked, alluding to common
guidebook phrase. At the house, we were met by Annagreth's
mother, Sofia, and her mother, Ewa. In the drawing room,
the Advent wreath, four candles alight, took pride of place
on the piano, while on a nearby table an old wooden nativity
scene, *the girls loved to play with this as children,* was also on
display. In one corner of the spacious, tastefully grey and
white room stood the Christmas Tree, Sofia letting us know
that Walter had gone out much earlier, *it was the middle of
the night, practically,* to cut it himself, today most his time,
naturally, being taken up with matters at the church, he
would be back, briefly, for lunch, *so, ladies, you know what you
have to do,* the command for dressing the tree being issued
while, *Volker, Benedict, come, you can take your bags up to your
rooms, then some coffee and Stollen in the kitchen.* A tour of the
house followed coffee, chiefly for my benefit, all relevant
historical detail being included, Sofia taking pride in her
official roles; built in the Neogothic style, *designed by Simon
Loschen of Bremen,* in the nineteenth century, using the same
baked red brick that was found in some of the city's oldest
buildings, as well as the *Holstentor,* in the suburb of Lübeck
St Jürgen, just a few minutes from the university, it was
also near enough to the old town to walk there easily; *we'll
go there this afternoon, find Papi, say hello; you can see the Kirche, it
is beautiful, and the Weihnachtsmarkt will be out, of course, as well
as the Fairytale Forest; and we can see also my church!* This last
remark of Annagreth's left me puzzled, but there was not

time to inquire, as necessary rations deposited for the benefit of Heike and Anna, the tour continued out into the snow-laden grounds, a monochrome playground, Narnian stage set, as if I had only just stepped from a wardrobe, and was expecting to find somewhere a lamppost. The cast-iron table and chairs appeared as if weighted by snow billow cushions, perfectly deep, perfectly undisturbed. Trees, skeletons of themselves, presented starkly glorious, a charcoal sketch of the forest world, where it might not be fantastic to see appear creatures of myth and child's cautionary tale, part animal, part human. Withdrawn from roads, apart from neighbours, the house stood in a large, park-like garden, on the banks of the Wakenitz, *Amazonas des Nordens*, Volker, once more, quoting the tourist guides, to the eastern end of the city, which fed in one direction into the Trave, and, to the other, led into the forest. As we walked on, toward the river, hardly more than an oversized stream at points, the house at first receded then vanished from sight entirely, the trees behind us closing ranks.

After lunch, the tree dressed and expressing a cultural entente cordiale between the traditions of Northern Germany and those of Scandinavia, *I think sometimes,* Heike had once said to me, *here in the north, in Schleswig Holstein, particularly, with the history of the Hanseatic League, we think ourselves as much Nordic as Germanic,* inspection approved the children's work, *good, you found the Yule Goats, not enough kringel, though, more chocolates Heike, we're not all on a diet,* allowing Annagreth and I to escape into town.

— You impressed *Mutti*, you know.

— Really?

This came as something of a surprise; while absolutely, unimpeachably polite, welcoming, Sofia, on this our first meeting, seemed not a little formidable, stern even.

— Yes. She said it was a pity about your hair, though some-thing could always be done about that; but no, she said she liked you; it took six months before she said that of Volker, and that was qualified...

and here, pause; I, listening, head slightly bent toward the ground, squinting against the brilliance of the day, realised that we were no longer moving, as I felt Annagreth's hand slip from mine, that last touch of finger tips through gloves, before a separation stepping in between. Turning, I saw she was waiting for my full attention, she was preparing for one of those moments of imitation that she so enjoyed, her loving mockery of others, a small acknowledgement of the gift she had for seeing into people, getting at who they really were, and making playful, unmalicious fun that signalled the pleasure she took in others; but I also saw in a heartbeat, between the beat and pause that makes the beat; I saw, in the blink of an eye, to use all the clichés at once, as if the image, already a stereotype or vignette etched into memory were somehow the more ephemeral, fragile visual presentation of the too, too leaden banality of the words; I saw, *im Augenblick*...no, it is impossible, strictly, to say; see what I see; if possible, imagine from within the brief amused commentary, an unexpected revelation. For in that instant, beyond the humour, the mild irreverence about to be vouchsafed, I witnessed something inexpressibly precious: Annagreth, tucking in her chin, standing perfectly still as if she were the centre of this snowscape, crimson and gold, displaying herself the solstice queen, the regent of winter, blazing out at the heart of her demesne, her monochromic dominion, over which she ruled with a benevolent sovereignty, becoming the brilliant child she had once been and still was on days when all else was busy, public, overlooking the quiet intimacy of detail; the sun seemed to shine more brightly, the gold of Annagreth's hair, laid loose over the flaming colour of her collar, burned that moment with an intensity as great as that on those first summer days, but with a difference. Her face shone with a sheer joy of just being, at this moment, in this place, here. All had stopped. Everything stationary. The world drifted, leaving us alone, as one. And then time resumed, I starting time again, this small, intimate epiphany come and gone in a fraction of the time it takes to tell.

— Well? You have your audience, ma'am; your vassal awaits your pleasure!

Perfectly channelled, Sofia's voice emerged from Anna's mouth, its Swedish intonation colouring the German.

— I have decided I like him; and it will be good, after all, to have a doctor in the family.

The little performance over, muffled clapping, a broad smile and a high pitched distant cry of *brava!* to signal my approval and pleasure for this small impromptu, Annagreth ran up, took my hand and we continued

— But yes, no; she liked you, silly man, because of your silly knowledge, all the things you know for no reason.

I still had not realised what Annagreth was referring to, a look of puzzlement evident

— Why…

— *O Du Dummer, ich liebe dich wirklich, darum hab' ich so lieb, mein Dummerchen! Ach du meine Güte!* Because you knew about the goats.

It came to me immediately. Penguins had once more been my familiars, along with a Scots anthropologist born midway through the nineteenth century. On having commented on the small straw goats decorating the tree, Mormor Ewa had asked if I knew about them, why goats at Christmas. I supposed, I had said that it possibly went back to Norse mythology, and here Snorri Sturluson, *your pronunciation is quite good, young man*, in the *Prose Edda* was useful, as he tells the tale of Thor killing the goats for his guests, only to resurrect them with his hammer on the following day. I had then, helpfully as I thought, without any consciousness of seeking to impress, though imagining, as I spoke, the faces of certain musicians of my acquaintance, to offer information from *The Golden Bough*, about the tradition in Swedish custom of the *Julofret*, in which performance someone dressed as a goat, in mantles of different colours, red, blue, white, and yellow, I thought Frazer had said, and who, so dressed, was led into the room where the entertainment was to take place, was sacrificed while the slaughterers sang a song, and then was resurrected, coming back to life to dance around the room.

The afternoon and evening passed too quickly, the hours, the light drifting with us, as we in turn drifted through the day and into the night. Standing before the arresting façade of the *Marienkirche*, its thirteenth-century Romanesque brick façade with double spires rising somewhat overwhelmingly, the brickwork making it look like a somewhat precarious and oversized lunatic mosaic, which one day had stood up, and was trying to decide not to collapse as a result, Annagreth explained how, on summer afternoons, when she was no more than five, her father would take her walking, or riding on his shoulders, *your sister was never that much interested, but you always liked churches, didn't you,* to show her, telling her the history of Lübeck's churches and cathedral. On first seeing the *Marienkirche* and asking its name, Anna told me, she had clapped her hands delightedly, exclaiming loudly, much to the amusement of passers-by Walter added that evening, on hearing how I had been told the story, *oh my church, my church, Pappi, this is for me!* Why this should have been so, no one knew until it was realised that Anna had been reading a child's story of the Marienkirche's most celebrated organist, Dietrich Buxtehude, whose wife's name was Anna Margarethe.

Entering, disappearing into the thirteenth century, we could hear Anna's father, the organ resonating through a space at once so ornate and yet seemingly infinite in design, the repetition of figures suggestive of an immeasurable space, so incomprehensible as to promise terror and awe in the hearts of believers, who saw and felt beyond architectural magnificence. Having found, and quickly said hello to, Walter, in the midst of preparations for the evening, we continued outside once more. Everywhere in the churchyard of the *Marienkirche*, baked brick red topped with copper green overlooking the stalls of the *Weihnachtsmarkt*, the small world was busy, glittering as the light went, countless small coloured bulbs everywhere. Jugglers, entertainers, musicians mixed with, moving through the crowds, eating, drinking, laughing.

Next to the church the *Märchenwald. Es war einmal…*that afternoon as we watched with all the other children, gleeful, excitable, small squealing voices of delight, mock terror, and equally mock surprise at the familiar tales, all the more entertaining because so well known, of the *Schneewittchen und die sieben Zwerge, König Drosselbart, Dornröschen*, and, best of all, *Der Gestiefelte Kater.* Leaving the church, Annagreth's face filled with a thought: *Let me teach you a verse,* she said quickly, expressing as much excitement as the smaller children gathered around the Fairytale Forest, a children's rhyme, *one of my favourites when I was small*; and as we walked on, swapping pretzels for Wurst, *Glühwein* for mead, so I learned the tale of the *Heinzelmann, Himpelchen*, and *Pimpelchen, ein Zwerg.* In return I told Anna tales of English boggarts, hobgoblins and Scottish brownies, that dark afternoon, precipitate night hiding the pleasure we found in one another.

~~~

So much seen through a haze, that trip, our first journey to the north. So many other stories that might be told. There is a counterbalance at work, I find, a measuring between what I see indistinctly, and what I remember with that fidelity of detail that always threatens to engulf: counterpoint of sketch, outline of an image, against which the endless replay of words, of tone, of moments snatched in private or, there, in full view, unobserved, we thought, the presence of the family. I could, Annagreth, fill a book with our private conversations, had I the will, the energy, or, perhaps, a desire to betray you, me, us. But I don't, you know that. I never could. What of the blur is left me now, and I think I have, in order to protect you, us, erased partly so much from that time away, returns when it returns at all, as a succession of frosted illuminations, a magic lantern show, scene passing scene, phantasmagoria of day and night, festivity and celebration as when looking at the Lübeck skyline, walking back, the family together after

the service that *Heiligabend*, for a simple meal and then the
Bescherung, the time for gifts; turning back, *let's walk over the
river and back, it's such a pretty night*, the city was alight, but
I remember it as if gazing only on the night time wonder
of light blaze in the surface reflection of the Trave, those
smeared colours, vague outlines, illuminated in part by the
reflections of the city's lights, also, I recall, that night, cloud
hidden, full moon glimmer. Winter solstice diaphanous, wisp
insubstantial luminesce, hanging gossamer on the heavens,
guarding the fairy tale marzipan city, the water below less than
water, oily in its smudged stillness.

Coming back though not only images of those days
shadowy in winter sun, or nebulous and nocturnal, but
music from Christmas Day and Night persists, sound in
silence, the silence of perpetual memory, that busy passage
of to and fro, of celebration, ritual excitement, though
keenly experienced for all that it was expected, accustomed,
anticipated. Sound there is that stays, all in the silence, and
sound there was, from every direction, bells heard from every
corner, impression after impression that everywhere a voice,
voices, more than one, so many, impossible to tell, Lübeck
at this time and every year at this time, Queen not of the
Hanse but *musica sacra, heilige Musik*. Church music, choral
voices, lifting Bach, greatest servant of a sterner God, the
Weihnachtsoratorium, to the curving flight of medieval church
roof, *the highest vault ever, when built*. Buxtehude's ghost was
there too, haunting every touch of Walter's on the organ,
while the shades of Buxtehude's seven daughters brushed
laughingly up and down, passing through the aisles, playing
in the ambulatory. But though these chiefly aural scenes
persist, while Buxtehude and Bach side by side are phantoms
supplanted by the more familiar ghosts of my other family,
as you, Annagreth, had once called them, taking me in with
your spoken kindness and unspoken love, your generosity
shared by all your family, it is a more private performance
that Christmas evening that touches me most nearly, *a family
tradition, first I and your mother, eh Anna, when you and Heike*

were children, before you were born; Walter's words explaining, ushering, and for this responsibility assumed more recently by the two daughters, black dress and gold dress, outshining the tree in candle and firelight, scintillating *irrlicht, irrbloss in Swedish,* Sofia whispered to me of one of the song titles, in the antique nutbrown gloss of the fortepiano; *last year was the first I had to play again since you were young,* this spoken by Walter, to you, to us both, a slight wistful smile playing at the corners of his eyes, a loving, lingering look bestowed on you, Anna, Annagreth, acknowledging it seemed to me what I saw, but also admitting the father, giving himself permission to emerge, the private man, the parent, for the first time since we had arrived. Walter told the story lovingly, not with any recrimination at your absence the previous Christmas, but, I believe, with something of a smaller sadness that his younger daughter was to pass out of his life, that she had become more completely herself; or perhaps it was that Walter was remembering, as you explained later that evening, how as a music student he had first accompanied your mother playing the very same song cycle as you and Heike had that Christmas night, by candlelight and moonlight, nearer, further, lesser, greater, but all pale ghostlights. You, seated, golden dress, golden hair, swept simply back, a single clasp, small pearl earrings, an understated string of pearls around your otherwise bare, supple neck, skin no longer summer bronze but winter hued, a pale cream; Heike, jet on raven black, hair loose, flowing over blacker velvet shoulders, as if she would disappear into the night, leaving only her voice and the iridescence of skin the white of moonlit snow; neither seen with clarity, Annagreth, flaxen luminescence, Heike, sable midnight brilliance: together, they played and sang those songs of the lost beloved, the desire for death and the absolute, abject emptiness; and, in the end, all hope foresworn, the winding call, the fateful resignation signalled by the figure of the hurdy-gurdy man. *One hundred and fifty years this year, did you know that? Since* Die Winterreise *was written,* said Walter, *Schubert wrote that he was eager to see how their eeriness would affect others, having affected him more than anything else he had written.* Smiling, as much to himself as to me, Walter took Annagreth's hand, continuing to speak to me while looking at her

— Anna's playing is beyond words, it is very affecting you will find.

An expectation? An injunction? A desire? What was there to hear in these words? Thinking of nothing I could say, looking at them both, appreciating Annagreth's little embarrassment, before me I believe rather than at the words of her father, responding with a slight sideways downward tilt of the head to praise she had clearly heard so many times before, and never given with anything less than the admiration and sincerity I heard in it that evening. Then, taking my hand, while keeping hold of Walter's, she spoke in all seriousness Schubert's own words, to which her father had just alluded, with one little change, so slight as to escape almost unnoticed, not to be caught in fact, unless the composer's original words were known. Though I did not know this at the time, Walter did, showing this with the merest glance between us, as Anna spoke

— Mir gefallen diese Lieder mehr als alle, und sie werden euch auch noch gefallen.

You were right. Schubert had been correct, and that evening Annagreth, Heike, playing, singing, were illuminated by the ghostly irradiation that came from the music within the sound, illuminating their small audience in turn, filling us with a light beyond description, beyond the power of speech to touch, to outline, or coarsen. In, no, through the music, came the perception of all that was to be loved, of love itself, the inexpressibility of love in anything but the most indirect means, to be caught, if at all, only through the agency of a rarer medium, passing between two, in the air between the hands about to touch or having just touched and parted, to know oneself beloved, but realising also how indispensable to the lover is even unrequited love.

It is the barely remembered hovering of lip on neck or cheek, anticipation of the finer touch, or memory of its having already happened, already over. This is what memory means, this is what music makes possible on rare occasions if we know how to listen, if we let ourselves hear. You had told me this some time before that first Christmas, and in telling me this you had echoed the words of our friends, translating them, rephrasing them. This is what I see, what I felt, what I heard and what I hear in the recollection of that Christmas.

Or in that evening at Ljusterö, first of the new year, the last before returning south, first to Lübeck, then England, the ground frozen, hard as death, unforgiving as loss felt in the bowels, tight clenching the cold, death's fingers rising through the packed, snow buried ground at the edge of the water to penetrate our boots, desiring us to join them down below. That evening when we had walked to the water, stealing a moment, as Walter, Sofia, Ewa, Heike, Volker, amidst the illumination of candles only once again, watched, incongruous in the woodland setting, and for a second time, the tape of *Kalle Anka*, not having been able to see this, as was proper, on Christmas Eve, but still everyone saying *Kalle Anka och hans vänner önskar God Jul*, because Walter's church duties had kept him for some years in Lübeck. How things appeared that night, starbright and cloudless, I have little recollection. Your words come back to me though. Your voice, that voice, here now,

— We could take the boat.
— Where?
— Nowhere. Anywhere. We could drift. Out of sight. Out in the dark, on open water. Perhaps we might catch the flow. We might drift until we came aground at Helsinki, Talinn maybe. Yes. Let's drift away, together. No, you don't want to?
— We'd freeze before we got anywhere.
— Always practical Englishman! That would be okay, to freeze, to sleep. That would not be so bad, I think. To freeze with you, on the water. To fall asleep with you there, drifting, drifting away; and we would be together, never to lose one

another, never to lose sight of each other. Yes, it would not
be so terrible. To freeze, next to you, in your arms, with you
in mine. We would slip away. A fisherman might find us. We
would be like some sculpture in ice. He would take us ashore,
to the authorities. Everyone would be baffled. *Where have they
come from?* Someone would say. *Where were they going?* Someone
else would ask. We would have become our own story, a fairy
tale that parents would tell children, inventing all the parts,
the reasons, knowing nothing; and so, knowing nothing, they
would make a story perfect for us, inside which we would
keep our secrets for ever. The story would grow, and grow,
like a fairy child, and none would understand. We would be
forever silent together, not answering their silly questions.
So frozen would we be that they could never separate us.
We would break if they tried. They would see how much we
loved each other. That is all they would know, always. They
would understand that, or nothing. Just that. Nothing more.
Never again.

~~~

That winter morning, agreed in bed, we promised to write;
and we did: notes, verses, songs, poems, letters, in pencil,
in ink, a simple crayon squiggle on a scrap, songs without
words, phrases within tunes. All the time we wrote, for one
another, to each other. I have two notes from you before
me now, a postcard and a letter, both winter deliveries.
Secrets. Confessionals. confidences. Is this why winter
is so important? Winter. Do I associate this season with
you more than another? With the postcard and the letter
there are photographs, two from so many. So many vibrant
images, stark or rich, dramatic in the acuteness, the severity
of their focus pursues me. Is it you in your red coat, or the
longer dark grey, the shade of thunderclouds, heavy hooded,
cloistered, or that other, midnight starless black, your pale
blonde, heavy hair loose inside, outside the turned up cowl?
No, I think not. Every season promised another you, as did

the nights, the days, public, private instances, that secret you, those glances or looks in full view but unobserved. Or else and otherwise in those crepuscular hours, your face sweet-tempered, your golden shock the last, dying light resisting gloom creeping evening. But winter calls me back now. You would know why. You always did hold the answer to those questions that could worry away at me, nagging at what to others seemed my certainties. You appreciated, yes that was the word you once used, which at the time I thought so odd a choice; singular, yes, yes, a singular word: you *appreciated*, you said so tenderly one winter's day, another winter's day, so many overflowing in my memories, too many, I can barely keep them at bay, my words, I cannot find the words, cannot keep up, as, riverbanks bursting, my heart is overwhelmed, the watermeadows immersed, submerged, drowning, drowning, pulling at me, pulling me down, taking me; why will you not take me once again, just once, keep me safe, any more? Why is this impossible? Why can you no longer do this? I want to ask, so much I need to ask you; I need your voice, your smile, your eyes speaking with a language only we could share.

I surface. Exhausted, surrendering, I let myself go with the flow, my anguish no longer gripping me. You appreciated, that day, my unreasonable, my selfish anxiety; you appreciated why. You told me this as, on that day, we sat together, cold, windswept, a northern seaboard, waves violent pounding, hammering the land's edge, struggling to break down, breach the drier world. I wept, no longer able to lift my head this day, day after a night not to be remembered, but all too presently visible to that never closing eye, seeking out the worst amongst the best, the doubt within the faith, a night before where I lost, for the evening, all semblance of ability. *Playing with mud gloves, it happens*, Kate had said. *No worries, we all have them*, James had sought to console. *That lot, they wouldn't know, bugger 'em, bugger*, Graeme wanting to embrace me, small gesture of helpless, bereft solidarity. But, Anna, you said nothing that night. Knowing as you always did the inefficacy of words, you allowed silence to enter, with the closing up of night. And the next day, I unspeaking all morning, you said, *let us go then, you and I*, daring to quote, choosing another's words when more original efforts would have failed, had failed. So, we sat, eventually, tears of exhaustion and incomprehension heralding a flood tide of self-recrimination. *I appreciate*, you told me, a suspended breath rounding off the word, leaving it to hang on the North Sea air, hanging in expectation that a Tern would steal it away violently, *I appreciate this hurt*. Unable to lift my head, the weight too much to bear, too small I felt to bear the way I knew your eyes would look into me, seeing me bare and small, I saw your hands, the left removing the glove from the right, the right repeating this small undressing. So cold that afternoon, so bitter the wind, your merciful, naked hands turning white, imitation of a deathly pallor. First left: your hand around my neck, my head, an intimate, a devoted, a dear and cherished pressure, fingers weaving into hair, hiding themselves. Then right: around my left, coming to rest upon my already bent back. Pulling me to you, you whispered, in different languages, the quality, the tone, a spirit in the voice the same, from one to the other. In that embrace, I felt myself in that instant saved.

What was it that day though? And what, from that day, has called to me? What has called me to you, in search of you on that day, searching without finding? What are you telling me, what do you want? Is it what you later wrote that same afternoon?

After all the storms had passed, a resigned calm restored, we found our way to a deserted sea front café, welcoming in its very desolation. Dilapidated and forlorn, it stood, a dreary bunker of cheap occasion. Smelling stale, tasting of desperation, it offered, nevertheless, a kind of refuge, which in its peeling, chipped demeanour fitted the bill for even the most stringent definition of pathetic fallacy. Having ordered coffees, which surprised with both strength and taste, and two pastries which, while no longer, in truth, definable as fresh were edible notwithstanding, Anna, you got up from the table, walking over to a postcard carousel. Choosing one, paid for quickly, you wrote something at another table, then handed it to me. The picture, faded, slightly creased, flyblown tainted, was of a lighthouse, *because,* you whispered, *weißt du? There is always for us, a lighthouse, you know. You know when you see a lighthouse that my innermost soul whispers always to you.* Turning over, I saw you had written a verse, in Swedish.

> *Jag är en främling i detta land*
> *men detta land är ingen främling i mig!*
> *Jag är inte hemma i detta land*
> *men detta land beter sig som hemma i mig!*

Looking up, I smiled, water eyed in my incomprehension. — This is by Gunnar Ekelöf. *Mutti* has a signed copy. This is how we all feel, at one time or another, *kannst du?* Never feel like a stranger as long as you are with me; I feel at home in you. I am always at home in you, with you.

10. Lines, Lives, Converging (Autumn 77-83)

Thursday. 1 Sept. Autumn.

Last of summer reluctant to depart before the squall of days.

I find this line in an old diary, the year 1977, scrawled, ugly drunken insect stagger, on one of the first pages. *The old men have been saying that there's never been such a harvest.* It is hard to hear you today, so I read, waiting for you to arrive. Some lines, irregular follow, half life poem grasping after coherence, moving toward an image or idea I no longer recall.

> That instant when everything begins to stop,
>
> To cease,
> To crawl,
> Ever slower,
> To a halt.
>
> Where though the motion is barely imperceptible,
> Yet
> It is there,
> It continues,
> Refutation of Xeno's paradox
>
> Instances smaller

Measurements tinier

Human desire mistakes the impossibility of arrival
Wilful refusal leading to erroneous logic

Paradoxes are all very well
As hypotheticals,
Mere games to illustrate:
The inventiveness of the mind at its most aberrantly
creative

We can think the possibility:
Ever-smaller spaces of time
Ever-smaller times in space,
Where conclusion is never reached

What fun
What larks, Pip old chap

A game to make believe
An end never arrived:
Here is the fiction Xeno constructs
Everyone is off the hook from mortality
As long as the end is never reached,
We never have to die,
Simply live
Smaller and smaller,
Significance more desperately grasped,
        Invented,
        Fabricated,
        Woven
Inverse proportion to the smaller span

Yet reality:
It tells us otherwise

There is the realization of that which picks up speed
Headlong in the onrush,
The past a library where disorder reigns,
System and catalogue fall apart
The timbers are rotted
The shelves are decayed
The paper is eaten
It crumbles to touch
Fingers are mildewed

Reverse time,
Cause the film not to stutter,
Bulb burning celluloid
Events turning backwards,
Each gesture,
      Each action
      Each reaction
Moves contrary to its destination:

Crumpled paper unfurls.
The frame lifts itself,
As if (the philosopher had once imagined)
On invisible strings
Eyes open
The glass finds itself broken
Pieces in the sink.
White enamel staining
Vermillion, turning ferrous, ochre,

Rivulet spiralling viscously,
Snaking around the shards,

Your hand, not quite recognized

At what point does everything change?
How is a moment defined?

There is a sudden falling away,
A loss, a loosening
Involuntary and swift,
Yet somehow
Disorganized.
All at once sinews give up the ghost,

Marionette's wires go slack,
Tension lost in
Something not quite a collapse,
Though more than a mere failure of coherence

Another lock turns,
Another door opens
The changing world enters
Time slows: time speeds on
Barrelling out of control.
Words half unheeded echo unnaturally.

Outside: the thunder throws around the sky,
Tormenting anything unweighted
Airborne on the instant

A troublesome bad child,

Who will cost me a world of scolding

Clouded, unconcentrate
Taking everything in,
You see nothing,
Focus not quite in this world

A yellow field, with small blue cornflowers

Everything is gathered,
Gathering again,
Small circles in a pool being carried,
Force of gravity,

Into a sinkhole.

You level in your heart,
Small crimes for which you alone are responsible,
Moments of neglect,
The inability to speak,
The failure to save another from any suffering,

Large or small

Sleep assumes the shape of guilt
The weight of judgement
For seeking daylight
Abandoning the gift of darkness.
Concupiscence shaped the dreams
Of anxiety uncaulked,
Assuming illegal occupation
You tenant the house you make and burn

World grown quiet, inside and out, time measured
Stitching fabric, suturing tears,
Hemming the edges—reassure;
The normal and the necessary weight
To stay demise, ventriloquize distance
In the absence of volume.

There, in the tune,
The impression of arriving, without distraction
Without the obvious, pretending toward
Illusion of place-holders

Lightness is everything
Equilibrium
In the brief interlude, as,
Forehead down, feet on chair, arms to legs
You hold:
A private dance approaching peace
Thrum and drone, half purr, wordless
Unabandoned

Tarnish of light, sun after storm,
Almost tangible, the experience of distraction
I drown from within, I long for that consistency
—A slow amber anticipation

Beneath this I had written

sonorous undertow, a steady current beneath the cascading rills of fast,
delicate high piano notes

Had you been practicing as I wrote? While scribbled and
crabbed the pen made the illusion of forward movement
though in truth going nowhere, had you been playing in the

other room? The absence of memory in the face of apparent
affirmation torments. The persistence of ink attests to your
absence, everywhere. Reading again, I find myself wondering
if I had laid clues, all the time, without knowing, in order
that I might scent you on the wind, and so find my way back
to you. Do I read too much, or not enough, or read in the
wrong way, too quick, too slow, do I read into the forgotten,
and abandoned word a significance that never was to be
borne?

And then, another entry: *must ask A.* What was it I wanted
to ask you? Can you tell me now, what I wanted to know
then? Did I ask you? I no longer remember. I would ask you
but you are not there, you cannot tell me. I know *A.* refers to
you, you were always *A.* in my diaries. What was it I had to
ask? Can't you tell me?

There are periods in the year during which you remain
yourself, silent and unapproachable. Impossible to talk to
you at these times I find still a congruity remains between
us. Though in this case, it is a consonance of loss, as though
there were a sound I knew to be there but which I only
apprehended through not being able to hear it any longer; the
cues for which I search I find written, with care, in haste, in
journals, diaries, on the reverse of photographs, though not
much help beyond the facts, I turn then to our letters, our
notes, in this hunger for you, this desire to have an unending
thirst quenched, a longing for you to pour your sound in at
my ears, or to be drenched in memory's scent of you; and
from these, so many being private, withdrawn, *for your eyes
only*, and, if nothing else, irrelevant to everything that was
not, secretly, secretively, selfishly us during those years, I find
I need memory's prosthesis more than ever. So, climbing,
delving, digging, wading, drowning in paper, I search
notebooks, diaries, paper, card or leather bound, yours, mine,
to search for, select, choose, page to page, those broken-
off narratives of the everyday made momentarily special,
noteworthy. A funny word: noteworthy, a note because
worthy of attention, the worth of a note, worth noting; small

instances, images, captured in and across ruled feint lines, blue ink for me, magenta for you, black repeating wires, narrow drawn, or neatly formed lettering filling tidily, within the lines, or graph paper, charting little eruptions of a life, of two, of five lives, the idea for a lyric, short reflection on the way light dances on water, or plays off the street, the memory of an evening, sunshine or spotlight on your hair, your annotations of behaviours, personal tics, which when written, become the mechanics of our existences; bodily signatures for everyone, in everyone, the writing in the flesh, along the nerve, in the muscle.

And through your note books, day books, diaries, and journals, you kept so many, everything now languishing, dust covered or wrapped, protected from inevitable decay; through all your back pages, drawings, sketches, for paintings you would later, sometimes never, execute. Pencil, ink, charcoal, always the delicate filigree, traceries shading grey to greyer yet, thicker, richer, weaker still, small abstracts, little doodling ambulations, or hastily taken, snatched, buildings, masonry accents, or someone seen, sitting at a café; otherwise, Kate, James, Graeme, Morphy, Mike, Dil, Fred, Pete, Menna, Guy. Marty Swann, Rob Thompson, Phil, Phil, and Phil, Oswald, Jones, and Truckel, Truckel-Oswald-Jones. Pairs of brothers, one forever in and out of jail subsequently, his crimes a chain to bind us all to that older time. Not for you, though. You never knew. Or do you now? Then evenings conjured through names, coming and going around the flats along Belvedere Street, one more gathering after yet another party. Informal dinners out in Wroxall with Neil, inevitably stoned, as were his cats, or nights with Jim and Sue, their small house holding back the wild copses of Ashey, guarding the top of the town it seemed, before the dark arrived. And so on, annotations of proper names: people of slighter acquaintance, even Damian, usually drawn, furious, ingathering of dark knotted twines of ink and lead. Unending, line after line, a spider's intricate weave of thick and thin; using up the space, though leaving

little fractures of untouched paper peering through a nimble
thicket deftly handled.

Then hands; hands fascinated you, didn't they? You told
me that once, I recollect. Thinking Sartre very silly for being
made abject in being wilful at the sight of hands, you loved
their independent life, unseen, acting, we all unconscious
of their motions. Hands touching, themselves, touching
another's, in play, at rest, self clutching, with instruments,
without, hands writing, hands drawing; *I am drawing my own*
hand drawing my hand drawing, you answered, when once I
asked. And hands writing: mine, yours, you drew, I wrote. All
these words, how many words? A landfill of ink, a mountain,
a dustheap of drying vegetable matter. So much to read. So
many. What do I choose? How? Why do I choose? What
do I want to say here? What do I need you to step forward
to observe, and at what moments do I have to act as your
translator, stepping forward in your stead, your counsel, never
your judge, getting in the way as little as possible to speak
on your behalf, to give evidence, bear witness, hopefully not
false, in the place where your silence falls most hard, in me?
Your silence descends through me, small guillotine blade
of the emptiness already there, in which surges the tide of
loss. So, yes, yes, I promise, as I did one afternoon when you
had asked: I will read the diaries, they will help when you are
not forthcoming, when you have wandered elsewhere. And,
hard as it is, I will choose from these, reading, remembering,
transcribing, filling in the details, across the years, over
the autumns of four years, reading again the memories
represented, given their little archive in these books we
collected, from page to page, leaf to falling leaf.

The diaries confirm it. Autumn had always seemed the
start of another year, rather than the beginning of its end.
First school, then tourist season over, shifting back to a more
private life before delving into winter, into long evenings,
longer nights, little light, and what there was remaining for
the most part bleak, grey white, with those short outbursts

of brilliant biting blue radiant clear skies. Autumn had been when James first appeared, when Kate came into the orbit. Autumn meant movement, transformation, journeys, days and nights in car and van, roads, ferries, and, increasingly, new routes mapped. Autumn was always a point of departure in so many ways, our diaries demonstrate this irrefutably, their simple existence, the fact that they start not in January but midway through the year. I remember our mutual surprise in finding that, independently, we kept our year according to the same twelvemonth foible. We each, we found our first autumn, had a fascination in almanacs, keeping our own calendar books with the annotation of traditions, customs, folklore, and always beginning with that anticipation of the fall, the pages waiting poised to begin the downward turn from harvest through the fallow months, awaiting ice, then slowly, slowly up, pushing through the frozen, hardened earth; *there were three men came out of the west, their fortunes for to try.* I see that you have written out in one diary, spread throughout the times of the year, the various verses of 'John Barleycorn', and other songs belonging to the land also, sounds from the soil, felt in the earth, handed on, changed, turning themselves, seasonal wheels rolling, and moving across the land. Your daybooks and journals tracked English song, so fascinated at one stage did you become by the rural world's traditions.

You belong to the tradition, you're part of it, I recall once saying, my own fascination with alternative English rural cultures, myths and legends giving my imagination free rein. This followed a prompt of Kate's, because, as she pointed out you had arrived that late July to complete, fulfil us, a gift of pagan deities. It was a fancy, a conceit to be embellished on long winter nights, *tell me your story, weave me into folklore,* descended from who knew where, all golden glowing, nutbrown tanned, in anticipation of the harvest. You were, I continued, something to be stored for winter, to sustain life amongst the lower orders, to give us all hope through the long winter's nights; to see hoardes of bikers ogle you slyly, it was all too

easy to believe. Turning a page still remaining in this the first
year in which we lived together, I see the origin of this, in
your script. Kate had called you, feigning obeisance, *Ceres,*
pretending to ceremony one afternoon, a late summer, light
flooding the barn, you appearing alight, illuminating the world
before the darkness, the lesser world descended.

After hearing this something began, a game of
impersonated, make-believe cult worship, *the cult of K,* for
of course there were two: Kate, we said, goddess of winter
solstice, you of summer but also harvest time. Graeme
arrived later the week of Kate's new name for you, another
rehearsal, see here, written down, there on the page it must
be true, with a crate of corn dollies made by his mother,
who pursued the various regional practices in plaited straw
work: the Barton Turf, from Norfolk, the Essex Terret, the
Stafford knot and Suffolk horseshoe, the Drop Dolly of
Yorkshire. This had led James on a tireless pursuit through
libraries, in books, Aleister Crowley by now abandoned,
current obsessions being the Inklings and the Apostles,
talking to old men and women of various villages for more
than a week. Somehow, he even managed to find examples
of straw work popular in Germany and Scandinavia, work
tied not plaited. In another box I find his discoveries: the
Swedish Oro, the straw crown, the Tomte or Nisse, and the
first of what became our own collection of Yule Goats. All
of these adorned our stage set on your birthday that January,
the second after you had joined us, when we played that night
in Newport, the Wheat Sheaf, Pyle Street, alternately a name
amongst us suggestive either of Pothead Pixies and Hatfield
and the North or, and this was Graeme's contribution, with
Morphy's encouragement, to wit, haemmorhoids, *got to be
a back passage round here somewhere, bugger; it'll be,* James had
replied, *where you parked the van.* Leafing on through our diaries
for 1977/78, I find in mine a set list, in yours a note that
Shona had brought you as a present that same night two
straw figures, the Gobar bacah from Skye, and the strae bikko

of Orkney. Inside your diary from that year there is folded, in James's obsessively small hand, miniscule letters formed on cartridge paper, illuminated by inks of blue, gold and red, inserted inside a birthday card, a passage from *The Golden Bough* on the Corn Mother and Corn Maiden of Northern Europe. In seeing this, I remember now, this leather-bound volume he had somehow tracked down, probably his father's doing, during stays in London, of Wilhelm Mannhardt's *Letto-Preussische Götterlehre*, exquisite tooling, carefully preserved boards and endpapers, the edges only slightly foxed.

The diaries help, but only so much. You are not there. Or rather: you are, there you are, but I cannot hear you just now, I need to find my way back to you, to swim ashore, pull myself through the undercurrent towards you as you retreat. Hearing you indirectly, through these pages, is it I who am underwater, the undertow dragging at me, as I try to speak, my mouth filling? Or is it that I see your lips moving, without hearing clearly your words? Perhaps, I think, as in a dream when lovers' faces exchange their looks, become someone else, suddenly seen up close, shockingly near, perhaps you are there beneath the water, whispering silently, *dive in,* you seem to say, *swan dive down, I'll wait for you;* I want to say, *don't go, not without me, don't swim away.* Between us, washing through us, waves smoothing, troubling the surface, dissolving us; your words on the page are like shells beneath the waves, tugged by the tide. I reach, grasp, my hands a bucket, teeth closing, grabbing everything, pulling up through the wash. Then I realise, as the water runs away, you remain ungraspable, running away between my fingers, and I am left with the shells, the sand, scratches on the page. There you are, where you are not, the pages of the diary, just one more shoreline at which I have to wait, across which I cannot pass. An open mouth shapes words. I strain to hear. Knowing you will remain silent for now, I have to plunder all the pages, searching through every autumn for you, until, turning away from the beach, lifting my head, admitting defeat, I find that you were there all along, behind me, waiting in the sun, as you

had been that late summer day, the world's illumination your
personal halo.

~~~

*Barely awake, lucent sunrise, drifting footsteps meander, unechoing. Early,
Sunday, St Germain de Près and among the few, barely seen, streets, narrow passages adjacent to broader boulevards, wet, washed down, gleaming
in the sun, unhurried walking, saunter to dawdle. Autumn, just, first
September day, prematurely promising sultry climax. How did we get
here?*

~~~

How did we get here? Barely awake, we drifted, the others still
asleep, the rare luxury of separate rooms rather than the usual
crowded chaos and bonhomie of a shared, low budget space.
The sound of our unechoing footsteps. A Sunday morning,
early in the day, early enough to feel at home, St Germain
de Près. There we were, among the few, the inhabitants of
the morning. The streets wet, washed down, gleaming in the
already warming sun, unhurriedly we walked. Strike of cool
from below, the coolness of bare feet extending beyond
the comfort of sheets, scent of cleaned paving wrapped in
heavy shadow, rising, meeting matutinal heat descending;
brightness reflecting on opened windows over balconies,
side by side, pale honey, milk stone softly worn, apartments
atop bijou store fronts we noticed, from inside which
faint noises of stirring, signalling life elsewhere, unseen.
Antiques, exorbitantly simple, elegant clothing, taste and cost
synonymous, spines outfacing sober, heavy tooled, calf grain
butter soft, or small galleries, obscure artists represented,
unstriking and always in the style of. No hurry, no rush.
Everything has its own pace. Annagreth and I finding our
own speed, in step with one another, deriving pleasure in a
quiet camaraderie, finding in our shared rhythms, recursive

patterns of motion and touch, brief escape from everyone
else. Widening, unfolding streets, to lose direction, then to
double back, we moved. We lingered, together and apart,
touch of finger or lip, barely speaking, *look at this* at most,
or a hand beckoning, something in a window worth noting,
just for the pleasure it gave. Slow movement in already warm
passages, easy, lazily. Losing ourselves in street after street, the
inevitability of our complicity in one another, but steering by
the abbey tower, appearing disappearing through the spaces
in between. No sign of tourists yet, much too early. *My eyelids.*
Kiss them. We embraced the make-believe of belonging having
entered into this empty neighbourhood morning. A tired
morning happily so lazy, not weary, the call of an unmade bed
still felt, earliest day of anticipated autumn, so beforehand
as not to be worth the name. Somehow though, no longer
summer.

Walking the year's division, looping back on ourselves, *no,*
back down here, let's go back, we missed a street, we've already walked
down this one, just, entering the first September days. Keith
Moon's death less than a week away. The Grateful Dead
playing to the Pharaoh, at the foot of the Great Pyramid of
Giza, the night of a lunar eclipse, not yet having happened.
Georgi Markov was still unaware that he would be poisoned
in London, the tip of an umbrella the weapon of choice. Had
the Bulgarian Secret Police been able to engineer not a micro-
pellet but the prevention of 'Boogie Oogie Oogie' going to
Number One the following week, justice and history might
have been better served. *But that's history for you,* James would
say, *the village idiot making decisions about fate.* Today would be a
last, lingering blaze of summer across Paris. Tonight, the last
of three shows before returning home. Already, so quickly
done, so slowly moving, we slowed, turning and returning,
crossing the ghosts of our own footsteps, *I am walking*
through where you were, through you too, I am walking, so as to
halt the onward flow, to linger just those few minutes more,
pretending that, in tracing our own steps, we were walking
ourselves into the fabric of the place, *this timeless town*, that if

we could just find the right pattern, the occult shape mapped
invisibly on the streets, we could exit time and remain forever,
this autumn sunlit morning, in Paris.

Steep raking shafts of tenebrous light transformed small
side streets into geometric shapes, light and dark so harsh,
eyes could not take in everything easily. Locals, already a
few, heading for, returning from the *boulangerie*, paper bags
in hand, butter grease stains already marking the corners,
areas where sweet flaky pastry touches, crescent curved, or
baguettes under arm, extra limbs, part arm, part tree branch
already anticipating the later weeks of the season, bare of all
foliage. Strolling from the small hotel tucked securely away,
secreted unassuming in the one of the labyrinth of narrow
streets just south of Salpêtrière, in search of coffee for me,
chocolat à l'ancienne for Anna, breakfast, *le petit dejeuner*, moving,
as we imagined, in the footsteps of Camus, Sartre, heading
for *Deux Magots*, obvious but calling nonetheless. A short
vacation for all of us, the three nights' booking the perfect
excuse to arrive a little early, stay on after, a day either side
Anna had said. And everyone had agreed; *no more than we
deserve*, Graeme had decided.

— How did we get here?
— That is not a serious question.
— No, I mean, think about everything that's happened since
we got the flat in the last year and a half...
— ...more, twenty months.
— Is it? Yes, suppose it is; you're right.

As we moved unhurriedly I was struck, in Annagreth's
pointing this out with such predictable precision, how much
had taken place, to get us to a small Parisian club, playing to
an audience who knew nothing of what we did, but who, it
turned out, were genuinely appreciative. *And for a change we
didn't end up drowning in our own sweat*, Kate said afterwards.
So much had happened, so many small events, much work,
all tending away from any perceived mainstream, from
any need to stick to one style, one formula, verse, chorus,
verse, chorus, bridge, chorus, repeat till fade. We were our

own backwater untroubled by larger currents. Embracing
our home, we celebrated its irrelevance, steering out of the
current, and searching for a stream untouched by the current
tending wilfully, stupidly, toward a waterfall, the cascade of
which could only presage disaster. We had become our own
direction. We made up the map as we proceeded. We had
found each other, and were not letting go, careening with
little control of any rudder other than that which steered our
own choices through what we still laughingly, and with not
a little disbelief, thought of as unaccountable good fortune.
Happily carried along, with little reflection save for questions
over the music we wanted to play, to make, we were now at a
point where the various entities into which we sought to form
ourselves were, we all thought, fully accomplished. Barely
awake, the memory of your bodily impress still recollected,
I wondered to myself, in the wake of asking, in the wake of
Annagreth, how we got here.

~~~

Following that initial session when 'Daughter' was recorded at
the end of the previous year we had written more and more,
having decided shortly before the trip to Paris to visit Mike's
studio over the coming winter. This included two songs first
played in Paris, one a simple, yet odd, not to say whimsical
version of 'Theme from *New York*', sung by Anna, the other
written by James and Kate from a series of violin, bass, cello
and accordion parts they had begun by improvising together,
with lyrics in French, 'Les Catherinettes'. The sessions would
unfold in a series of visits over nearly four months, the
interruptions dictated by playing and, increasingly, travelling
away from home. With Annagreth a permanent member,
her year's teaching commitment over shortly before that first
recording date, we worked ever closer, with greater insistence
and a sense of shared purpose on writing, arranging and
finding forms we were all content to commit to the finality of

recordings, practices of play and work that would punctuate the coming years. Writing had become increasingly important during this time, as had extended improvisation, some pieces beginning only with the agreement of a key. More and more we explored, tested, pushing each other's abilities, finding various roles we each could play, chameleon colours shading from one to the other, across instruments and voices.

When at home, Anna, Annagreth and I would spend long nights lasting into mornings writing, exchanging ideas, playing together, frustrating and challenging one another to think differently inside familiar frameworks, even as we learned how to anticipate each other's phrases, changes, exploring and prompting the writing of pieces where it became impossible to tell who had contributed what, and where, more importantly to both of us, it didn't matter. Annagreth's compositions with mine flowed unstoppably, excitedly from us, as if in meeting we had released and realised in each other something we could not find within ourselves. James, though writing fewer 'whole' songs, wrote parts insistently, sketching feverishly, as if possessed, line on line. If not committed to paper, or written on the stave, heard only in the head ahead of any performance, he would play the phrase, the line, an entire bass or cello figure, sequence after sequence for a song, an instrumental, which we would clothe. So too would Kate, though her shapes assumed not lines so much as webs, spread as in the imagination spatially, divergent and converging. Though Graeme wrote neither music nor words, his percussive, carefully evolving shapes, forms, and structures were as much a part of composition and arrangement, his an equally articulate utterance essential to the sounding and singing of our music; Graeme's contribution, one voice involving itself intimately, inseparable from our five part fugues, his the most directly fugal, with its struck repetitions, recurrences and variations, within, outside, across.

During this time as their deep receptive friendship developed and grew, Kate began to write with Anna, encouraging her to sing more, and, eventually to get out from behind the keyboards, to explore other vocal styles than her accustomed softer sound. One late afternoon during the summer while Brearley, Botham, Taylor and Edmonds, Miller and Willis, Gooch, Roope, Radley and Old limped toward a total made respectable only by an insouciant contribution from Gower, Kate insisted, with her mix of impetuosity and take no prisoners certainty, on a free improvisation outside the barn. This necessitated the impromptu rigging of everlonger cables, and many nervous looks in the cannibalizing of shorter lengths, soldering, ductaping together length after length, to move the orange Wurlitzer outside but capable of being played through amplifier and speaker cabinet remaining in the barn, creating an acoustic not quite underwater, but boxed; tanked. Yes, placed inside a container, with little appreciable reverberation or echo, sounding flattened on all sides, piano squared, cubed, cupped in a wooden container. Beginning with melodeon, Kate switched after ten minutes or so to violin, then, lute, as hitherto unexplored textures revealed themselves, drifting across the fields. Nearly half an hour later, still playing, Kate saw James's car approaching; *tell him to get the trumpet and the double bass*, and so we continued, Graeme arriving a little later, I content to play various percussion instruments, as Graeme set up a marimba Harry had acquired. So the afternoon moved into evening, as we in turn moved with it, inside its shifting hues, in and out of the softer, then stronger August breezes. We found within the play hooks and riffs, which became in time parts of instrumentals, 'Oh Yes!', '*Windgesänge*', and 'On Ventnor Sands', all recorded the following winter. Rosemary appeared with lemonade, then after a while with two chilled bottles of wine, followed shortly by Pete and Morphy, with Linda. More than three hours in, we began to slow, to wind down, but Anna and Kate then began to pick up a song, 'Black is the colour', Anna gesturing at me towards the piano, signalling I should play simple held chords underneath the floating lines of voice on voice; James retrieved an alto saxophone, laying underneath a third voice, sinuous, raspy, andante, sostenuto, joined then by Linda's soprano, Graeme adding textures and tones, moving across, defining lazy rhythms. The afternoon just over a month before this Sunday morning had been the perfect expression not only of everything we had become; it was also the purest revelation of a friendship.

~~~

But how did we get here? How and here, inseparable twins, were only partly accountable for what we found ourselves playing. The 'how' involved also taking decisions of a more practical nature. Having acquired an agent in the spring of 1978, at Harry's suggestion, then instigation, *let me introduce you to an old friend, just talk, really, you've nothing to lose*, we had become able to pursue a living along with our own commercial irrelevance, *our refusal to do what record companies thought they wanted* had been how Kate had put it, with a cheerful delight, performing the conventional and unconventional with absolute abandon, with equal energy, existing in a parallel time to that of the larger world but having become our own small island. Jill Trefusis, a small, focused incessant chain smoker, flame haired, brazen burnished, madly curled and with an intensity of personality that surfaced on occasion from beneath a genial appearance shaped around controlled chaos, ran a small agency in which she dealt personally, with the help of two assistants, with the various acts she represented. As long as we were happy to travel, we would work, Jill had told us. *I wouldn't normally take a risk this cold, but Harry and me, we've known each other for too long; ten years ago, I could have got you a contract, but now, if you want, I can get you shows.* Travel, on Jill's terms, meant Europe, Germany, Scandinavia countries, the Netherlands, and, once or twice France, while she left us free to maintain our favourite residencies on the Island. Once or twice she got us onto local legs of tours as support to a band keen to promote its first album, arranging also trips throughout England, the southwest mostly. Northern Europe was, it seemed, an island of its own, its musical currents, if not impervious to fashion, the musical novelty du jour, also maintained a broader culture of live entertainment than did the British Isles. The past few months, since signing with Jill, had seen us begin to venture further, both geographically, and musically, experimenting with strange hybrids, labels for which were not forthcoming, but having elements from folk, jazz and chamber music. Traditional songs, 'Katie Cruel' or 'Black is the Colour of my True Love's Hair', *folkabloodydelic*, found their way through different transformations, as within ourselves we were variously a duo, solo, a trio, quartet, or quintet, often all in the same evening, when not working the bread and butter evenings, sets dominated largely by what for want of a better term would be blues inflected rock. How leaden that sounds. How bluntly undescriptive. *Still*, James would offer, *those who know, know, those who don't wouldn't get it.*

And now Paris in the autumn, cue Kate, Cole Porter at the ready, *oh why do I love Paris? Because my love is near*, as we entered the city on a Wednesday afternoon, feeling as if we were starting, once more; time to begin again—here we were. Yes, autumn had always signalled another start, a season of change posing as introduction. A time for reassessing, shifting gears, considering options, getting back to doing more of the same done differently, the how and the here converging. Not quite fully awake, wandering thoughts dogged my steps with quiet persistence, as, with Annagreth, we found our way to *Deux Magots*.

~~~

Sitting here, waiting for a train. Thinking of you. When don't I? Gauzy gleam, dazzling diaphane, water meadows shimmering. Reading Keats, singing to myself a song you love, this brings me closer to you. Do I imagine I hear your voice in the wind that causes the trees to sing? I like to think so. I will be with you soon. We shall return to bed early, we will sleep.

~~~

How did we get here? There is of course no answer to this, unless an answer is in chance acquaintance, collective will, a shared desire, but getting here, wherever the here was, felt inexplicably right. There are never answers to real puzzles. If the answer were ever to appear, it would just as soon vanish, softly and suddenly away, sublime for one moment's revelation in timeless time, before the disappearance into a chasm of unutterable doubt. No answers were forthcoming, nor have they been ever since: ever since we met; ever since successive moments thrown into memory's relief by the recollection of a piece of music; ever since I asked that stupid question in Paris on an almost too perfectly beautiful morning; ever since a letter was to be found waiting at your piano one cold wet winter's night; ever since ... no, I find it impossible to say, just yet, even though the sentence completes its phantom self in the absence of its framing, the absence of my ability to offer it completion, even silently. Ever Since. One has to learn to live with the ever since, ever since how and where became ripped violently apart by the impossible why, the callous, indifferent, ruthless absence of why. *Only connect*, you had read once, in a book. *Is that a hope, a desire?* You had asked, to which James, at the time for some reason best known to himself was balancing a coffee mug on his head, replied, *a fool's prayer*.

But that day, that morning, when I asked you that question *how*, I had, then, never expected an answer. I knew better then, knew more than I do now. You knew that, you knew I was not really looking for an answer, you told me. You knew me, you see; you knew I always liked the question that resided, full moon in an opaque halo of undecidability, I always searching for the heart of the onion, your blue eyes refulgent in the morning of the world, that Parisian Sunday. But you did say over breakfast that morning that the *how* and the *here* were as inseparable as you and I, or either of us from the others.

— Oh, we're in Paris, let's get philosophical, dears!

Shadow looming, large distension over the table distorting, comical, though even in silhouette, James's voice, no, more fundamentally, his tone, mocking but in on the joke, identified him before our eyes could adjust.

— You've stirred then; where are the others?

— Kate's just wandered over to the Abbey to take a few snaps. Graeme wasn't answering when we knocked, so I left him a note. He'll never find us, you know he'll get lost and we'll have to call out the police.

— Oh James, Graeme is not helpless…

— …No, he's a drummer, that's worse.

— *Quatsch!* Have some breakfast your royal baldness. Kate, Kate…

Kate had appeared behind James making rabbit ears for him, without his knowing, without his ever finding out.

— …Kate, I want to play a solo song tonight, convince these two…

— Excuse me, I don't need any convincing, not usually, it's Captain Slap who always wants convincing, don't you Judge?

— Has to be a reason for everything; no, a purpose, there's never a reason for anything.

— *Meine Güte*, now who is being philosophical? *Le philosophe, malgre-lui—le bassiste, le violoncelliste, le cynique musicale!*

— Entschuldigung, gnädiges Fräulein.

— Come along kids, what song?

— Now Ben, don't say anything, it's the one I wrote you for Valentine's Day.

— That's why you thought I'd need convincing; well, I'm not going to say anything, just don't dedicate it, okay? And—no, and, I get to play 'Little Wing', and I will dedicate it, that's the deal.

Before this day, I had resisted, wanting to keep this song to which Anna alluded private, not from selfishness but because its naked sentiment, delivered in the gentlest of Annagreth's voices, was always too much. I found it unnerving, had thought myself undeserving, this song too

knowing of me. But now, having given in to recognising
the impossibility of knowing *why here and now, why how here,*
I said yes, already anticipating Graeme's nudges, winks, and
the touchingly delivered, *bugger, she loves you; don't know why,
buggered if I do.* A smile, the chin pushed a little forward then
retracted, to say in the teasing gesture, *vielleicht,* as Kate, her
face framed, dark hair down, hennaed red reflecting brightly,
a beaming mirror image of Anna's dimpling golden laughter,
gave away the set up that this clearly was. What James said
next told me he too was in on the con.

— Well, Fritter my Wig! That's all you needed to say, Anna,
you only had to tell us it was 'Deep in, Lost'. And you've just
proved me wrong you see, it must be something in the coffee,
there is a reason after all.

~~~

*Chasing the rain today, into the west. Another show, 21 people. Playing
last bus, that first feeling over again. I had not thought you would have
achieved the tune. It didn't matter. What I said—you will never know
this—was, James's phrase, in jest. Yes, jesting. I was yours. Always, from
the first day I saw you. Writing now, you are asleep. Another new song
played, how much we like it. Played in the hotel room, Graeme with pill
bottle, shaking it, Kate a dinner knife on a bottle, Judge with a camera,
falling off the bed. Home soon.*

~~~

That evening, a sound check. There you are, silent movie,
black and white, the film, you. Black dress, white cheesecloth
shirt, or linen perhaps, collarless, open over the dress. Playing
the piano, on your own, you tuck a wayward strand of hair
behind your ear, as you alternate a higher Tonic C major
and a transposed F major below, the root note the high note
of the chord, not the lowest. Though there is no sound, I
know from the positions your hands assume the tune you are

playing. Your lips move, verse, chorus, verse, chorus doubled
in length though the words are not repeated, alternating
major to minor back to major again, all concentration,
gathering yourself as you reach the final chord sequence,
the right hand playing ever more intricate figures, dancing
arabesques against the regularity of the skipping, metronomic
left hand, emphasis on the first and third beats, in 2/4 time.
Your elbows gather to your sides, holding yourself compactly,
as I might do were the arms mine, and you sway, slightly, your
head looking down, though not necessarily at the keys, for
you know the piece so well. Your head tilts, toward your right
shoulder with its slight forward incline, as you lean into the
music, inclining your body to the right.

Play it again, screen the memory once more. Watch over,
the details taken in, seeing you there, on the screen, seeing
you as I would have seen you then, but seeing you in closer
detail, seeing now as I never could then, the camera's eye
zooming in, then out, moving slowly round you, your face,
three quarter, from the front, your hands in close up, pull
the focus, in, out, in again, precisely. Hand held camera.
Hand held. The thing I can no longer do, hold your hand,
have you hold mine; to hold you in my hands, your face in
my hands. Watching, a third time, this run through, a song
for me, written about me, a gift from earlier in the year,
played now for the first time in public, then, here, there, a
small basement café bar, no more than a dozen tables, check
oil cloth memory tells me were red and white, though the
film says otherwise, everything here only black, only white,
whitewashed the walls, bare stone, large rocks, without the
regularity of brick, but placed into wide spaced, white plaster;
your hair; yes, even your hair, white blonde, white golden
in the black and white world of the screen, though nearing
the neck, underneath, closer to the ears, within the thicket, a
density of hair, loose piled, somewhat disarrayed, chiaroscuro
darkening, framing, setting in relief your face brightly lighted.
As you sing the high notes that end each line, your eyebrows
raise, small arches overhanging your deep set eyes, oyster

ovals almost on occasion perfect rounds set in the larger
oval of your face, wide to narrow, top to chin, nose perfectly
straight.

And then that strand escapes your ear, your head
forward another falling in front of your face, but still, the
concentration never goes, does it? *Mein kindisches Haar, mein
Kind über's Haar, meine Tierhaare…unberechenbar, unwägbar!* All
the things, these and many more, you had said at different
times, childish, child, animal, wayward, imponderable hair; *I
am, yes, I am, don't argue, I am going to have it all cut off one day! I
will teach it a lesson if it cannot learn to behave. It is, what is that book
we read? It is a bad child that costs me a world of…of, of, no do not
tell me, of scolding! Yes, I remember, you see!* Reaching a point of
absolute fuming frustration one night, you said this before a
show; then, seeing my face, you returned an evil grin, *if you
are ever bad, I will cut it all off, just to teach you, haa!* But you never
did. And so, once more, perfect composure, absolute focus,
you wait, there on film, to return in that cellar to the simple
chord left-hand rhythm, your right reaching for your hair,
your head inclining once again, how many times, how many
years had you done this, I ask myself, to tidy, temporarily,
away, those possessed tresses?

The silent song continues, you linger over a word, which
though I cannot hear, I see you form, and hold, lifting your
heard slightly. Your hand, controlling with futility your hair,
you control nonetheless the music, as you give yourself
up to the end of the song, an instrumental passage, small
imitations, echoes, brief ghostly figures suggesting Chopin
on the one hand, Satie on the other, as you pull your
shoulders up, while your hands open wider; that F chord,
now augmented, busier, sounds under your left hand, fingers
fanned, thumb and little finger playing an octave, first finger
depressing B, second and third, lifting or lowering, alternating
above and onto the black and white keys. You sit there, in the
illusion of the freeze frame, black and white, piano clothed,
and your face…what does your face tell? For the merest
seconds, eyes closing, you face is haunted by that of your

ten years' old self. Seeing you like this, I hear all that cannot be heard, all that the film withholds, as if it had been made to be only ever silent, deliberately; as if the image could not bear the weight of the sound. As your hands become busier still, your arms tucking ever more tightly into your sides, your body sways more, head tilting increasingly. The camera closes in on your hands, those long fingers, nails short, left hand holding a chord, third finger of your right hand pressing D, thumb playing F, the other fingers arched, poised, a canopy or frame for a sound as yet unplayed, or the phantom aftershape of an arpeggio recently finished; impossible to tell which, I notice on your wrist one of those coloured elasticated bands which held your hair in a tail, in looser overflowing folds.

And the music ends. Concentration, tension releasing through your lines, your body uncurling, you are out of that place the song had sent you. Arching slightly backwards, a smile, a pursing of the lips, almost a look of embarrassment, self-consciousness at having been so serious, appears on your face, as you scratch the top of your head in what appears a self-deprecating gesture. That sour lemon mouth, as you called it, signalled you thought the playing could have been better, *it's only a sound check*, Kate had once half-seriously responded, when you had criticised your playing on another occasion. But she knew what you meant, as did we all. And then, and then, finally, it is matter of seconds, I know. I rewind, replay, two three times that instant, it is a question of two, three seconds at most, a gesture captured, made artificial, but tracing nonetheless that strange beautiful communication between grace and awkwardness, a discomfort not in body, never in your physical motions, but revealed for those of us who knew how to see you, seeing where you stepped out, your hidden self emerging from that public carapace, to see the real you inside the performer, a self-consciousness at being the sole focus. In those seconds, your hands flee the keys, hiding themselves in your lap, in the folds of that black dress, you begin, laughing quietly but aloud in recognition of being seen, to bury your chin into your neck, as, hair falling

forward, yet again, this time much more, your hand sweeps
all backwards, and you look up, laughter ever more present,
visible. *That's that over!* Your face seems to say. But of course,
I cannot hear that on the film. No one can, there being no
sound. The words appear to come back to me, as the video
ends. But who said that? The echo of a laugh, laughter of
relief, never recorded, but, yes, recorded elsewhere, left in me,
leaving its inerasable trace.

You left your autumn laughter in a foreign town with me
that evening.

Film, fading black, the last image of you fading too,
disappearing slowly from view, but for the outline flicker in
the mind's eye. I have paused the replay at the last moment
of fade out before the world turns black, before that small
basement is lost in the inviolate nightshade, the last star
faded. There you are, I see that interrupted gesture, as,
leaning on the stool, you touch swiftly, hand to breastbone,
then, head turning aside to escape the gaze of the camera,
your other hand grasps the edge of your shirt, lifting a little,
pulling forward. Surprised at your own embarrassment it
appears, you disappearing.

~~~

*Light, from Old English— līhtan, to lessen the weight, morning lessens
the weight of night. You lessen the weight of darkness.*

~~~

Diaries do not reveal everything. They offer snapshots, small
histories more or less. Do diarists think posthumously? Do
they write, in advance anticipating the time to come, the time
after, when writing will have stopped? Some do, it seems,
writing with an eye to their historical memorial. Such diaries
are ghoulish because they aim to have a voice from beyond

the grave. There is something gravely comical in wanting to control one's legacy, even to believe in the idea of a legacy is absurd. To have a word after the last word, to commit words to what ought to be a private, and an intimate archive, for the purpose of revelation, speaking from beyond the grave. Only those diaries written without the intention of publication, the imagined legacy in ink, are honest. That other kind is obscene. I would not betray your words, never that.

What has made me think of this? In searching through memories, those various excursus, the apostrophe to oneself, or no one, I'm struck more than ever by an anxiety over fidelity. On the one hand, your story, our story, our stories, this, these are the ones I finally know I am telling, even as I speak to you, as I did on certain days, in the pages of diaries, notebooks, and journals. We kept so many, and, as if there were not enough space, I find, as I have done regularly, surprised by words, notes in the back of books, volumes of poetry, novels, always in these in pencil, never in ink; *unforgiveable*, you had once said. Sudden thoughts, the experience of a meaning or a pattern unfurled from a need to expose, if only as a reflection, a mood, or otherwise, you told me, *something I want you to find when you don't expect to, when you are not looking, waiting to hear.* So now, I tend the diaries as I would a garden. Your gardener. This is now my role. I tend the plot, but leave the weeds, knowing you hated fussy order. You would like this image I believe, the gardener at work. Ever since that evening at the cottage when you asked, and I named for you all the flowers, though that garden was kept by another. So, I weed, I train, I look for ways to encourage growth, from the seeds spread across the pages, germinating, waiting in the dark. In the spring, shoots will begin to appear. April. Perhaps you are directing me, in the absence of your voice. Perhaps you are speaking to me after all, you have been all along, haven't you? *Yes, here I am.*

I have never opened your last diary. In its ochre leather cover, the threaded thong tied as you had left it, it remains silent, even though, knowing it was never finished, the end of a year not to be reached, stopping in April, it speaks nevertheless…what? Should I complete the obvious, do you think? Is it as silent as the grave? Does it speak volumes? Perhaps the clichés are best after all, they keep you hidden, they hide us away from view, as if we were ourselves entries for the other's diary, to be read on the occasion of. We stay, closed on ourselves.

I wonder what you would think if you knew I abandoned diaries and journals afterwards? At most, notes are hurriedly scribbled in margins, largely as a professional gesture, notebooks filled with ideas, phrases, copied, again a professional tic. Once used, the pages are torn out, destroyed. If I were to keep diaries, I would want to tell you things. I would want you to understand, to *appreciate* what I have to say.

~~~

Sunday. 21 Sept. No James last night. No word still today.

~~~

Other autumns. The diaries prompt once more, as on different occasions do those postcards, purchased for no reason, except as a key for memory a souvenir or ten, prompts for Mnemosyne. Turning to 1979, sifting through the evidence, the cryptic phrases, the minutiae, the mundane, and the occasionally inexplicable, I come to a Sunday, in Annagreth's diary of that year. The page is marked by the insertion of the radio listings from a newspaper, *The Times*, I think, from the layout. And then, in Anna's hand, short statements, terse, stark, an incident I remember all too well.

Having a quiet couple of weeks, back again on the Island, we had still a small number of regular gigs. This Saturday, we had arrived at Ventnor Winter Gardens for an early soundcheck, Anna and I in Waltraud, collecting Kate on the way from her house, to drive south and west following the coast; Graeme, the van loaded still from the two nights before, coming from Cowes, cutting across. Though not yet five, the time had been dictated by our having to fit in with everyone else, this being a competition evening. *Battle of the Bands* the posters read; less a battle though, more a friendly evening of rivalry, joking, verbal sparring between friends and acquaintances. The musical equivalent of sledging at a Test match. We had entered not from any particular desire to win, but as an excuse to socialize, to catch up with people, having spent more time away. None of us had seen James since the previous show, he having assured everyone he would make his own way, but in a manner that, at the time, caused Graeme, always a barometer of advancing storms, to ask Kate during the intermission between sets if she thought everything was alright. If Graeme noticed something, it was best to pay attention. Though nothing remarkable had happened during the show, James had been more than typically inside himself. It was not just a question, I said to Anna on hearing Graeme's question, of being away with the music, something else was noticeable. His usual grim hilarity was muted, no, absent. James had excused himself without explanation, not returning until right before the beginning of the second set. Afterwards, he had cried off from helping with packing up, saying that he had promised Leila he would drop by and didn't want to make it too late.

Having no contact with James on the day after was nothing out of the ordinary, only worthy of remark after the fact. When he failed to show in Ventnor at four, as everyone had agreed, nothing much was said. Forty minutes later, we were due for the check and, no sign of James, we decided it best to go ahead rather than attempting to rearrange. Morphy would be at the desk after all. We had played here before, several times, and the acoustics were not an unknown quantity. Anna played bass pedals or the bass keyboard to fill out the sound, as we ran through two cursory versions of tunes from the four we had chosen for the evening, and from which we would eventually decide on three. No James, yet,

and Morphy asked if I would just run through a line or two
on the bass, to take a rough level. Matters were simple there
being no double bass, no cello this evening, nor any trumpet
or saxophone, and only backing vocals for James. Finished
up, not dissatisfied, we left the building.
— Is there any point in calling the cottage, or do you think
he spent the day with Leila?
— Does anyone have her number?
— Not with me.
— Well, he knows we were going to head over to the Spyglass
for the rest of the afternoon, so we can see if he hauls up
there. We'll get concerned…
— Or annoyed…
— If he doesn't show by seven.

Seven came. And went. James had been known to vanish,
but never before a show night. Considerate even in his
obsessions, or when driven by whatever compulsion called, he
would be sure not to inconvenience others, if he could help
it. Sitting at the Spyglass, overlooking Ventnor Esplanade,
there was to the sea front a slightly dishevelled, disreputable
air. Plastic tables and chairs, left out more in hope than any
reasonable expectation, pooled water on their surfaces, or
were occasionally caught by the increasingly strong winds,
making as they moved a sharp scraping, plastic on concrete.
The Channel appeared equally unwelcoming, bereft of boats
or ships. Fish pie or macaroni cheese ordered, a round in,
we had found ourselves a table before French windows,
surrounded by pirate memorabilia, straight from a fifties
B-Movie. Further back a trio, guitar, fiddle and flute had just
begun a set of reels and jigs, taking our interest a little. We
were due to play shortly after eight, about twenty minutes, no
more than that. Having considered alternatives, *can you take all
the bass parts on pedals, or on the Fender? For sure, but it will leave the
sound a little thin; what if we choose other songs? Can't do that, if they
don't require bass, there's another part in there that James plays*, it was
then that Kate's face shaped itself in that way that announced
that, there being no other sensible alternative, she had already

thought of a solution, which when all else was found to be
impossible, whatever was left, however improbable was the
only answer.

— We'll do the set as we decided. I'll play the bass. I know
James's lines fairly well, I can always simplify them a little.
Mind you, some plasters would be of help.

The evening over, there was still no sign of James. Kate
had more than coped with the bass, the songs that night
being simple enough for anyone familiar enough with
stringed instruments, though *that thoughtless sod owes me,
any more of that and I could ruin my fingers without practice*. We
discovered nothing until the Sunday evening. Kate having
cycled over, Anna and I were cooking for the three of us,
when the phone rang just after six. Graeme had said, had we
not heard anything by four he would go around to see Angela
and John that evening, living the nearest, in order to inquire.
We had agreed this better than calling cold. John had already
left for London, to be in court the following day, but Angela,
keeping Graeme at the door, informed him that her son was
in St Mary's. *Alcohol poisoning, she said. Someone had found him at
a bus stop in Cowes passed out; made me feel like it was my fault, she
did. Anyway, I went straight round to Leila's, see if she knew anything;
apparently she's been seeing someone else, didn't know how to tell James
as it had started when we were away last month, she finally told him
Thursday night, after we'd played. He must have been drinking all day
Friday. I went right round the hospital; I'm phoning from there now;
wasn't allowed to see him, lost my rag a bit I'm afraid cause I couldn't
find anyone to tell me anything, this nurse got shirty with me. Still,
after I apologised, she did say he was going to be ok, they'd pumped his
stomach, and they'd probably release him in the morning. I said I'd
collect him.* Annagreth interrupted, Kate and she listening on
an extension, telling Graeme to bring James to us tomorrow.

— Anything else, Rog?

I could hear the grin, through the wires, Cheshire cat
at the other end, expanding with his face, relief and that
irrepressible quality all his own.

— I got a date.

— You never told the nurse about George?
— Always works, bugger.

~~~

Frightened witnesses, rejoicing—the voyage continues—we're making a
crossing but we cannot see the other side.

~~~

1980

Home became increasingly important, as time away from it
became, if not more extended, then more frequent.
— I feel like Mole, you know? Sometimes I can just smell it,
and there's nothing I can do.
— I know. Time passes, we do what we want, but we sometimes forget the things we have to do.
  Sitting one afternoon in a small café, October well
advanced, past the midway point of ten days, ten nights
away, Germany and Denmark. A rare gap in the itinerary,
a day without travel, without performing; just to hang out,
lingering, sightseeing, such luxury, such joy. *What's that word*
for in German? Sehenswürdigkeiten, Besichtigungen. Across from
the café, a foreign square, two small children played with a
ball, while in the sky suspended, passing, an orange train,
faces at the windows, ours, theirs, so many strangers, stranger
still for having been seen; the hidden lives of others barely
glimpsed. Always stranger in a foreign town the everyday that
is unobserved at home. *If I see someone three times,* Annagreth
said, *I say hello; I mean, what are the chances in a city?* Kate had
just coffee before her, foam dried, chocolatey residue, last
remnants of whipped cream being gathered by a spoon and
then, as if not precise enough a tool, the finger, moistened
with spittle, wiping carefully the edges of the bowl. James
worked at a torte, plum, with berries, assiduously, not from

hunger but as a means to focus on a crossword. Something was shifting, taking place. Graeme, restless, already twitchy from too much Coke, pulled on his parka, and set off to join those two other children, possible playmates, or to retrieve a football from the back of the van. Graeme was adamant that Morphy join him. Three more days before home. None of us were giving anyone, or anything our full attention. Incapable of that, vague, distracted, not exactly tired, but not fully awake either, we existed for now in this German town, strangers partly to ourselves, estranged and pulled to inertia by ennui. Time passing, acquiring a viscosity that dragged us along with it.

— Kate, what's on next, after this trip, I know I should know, just can't remember.

— We've got ten days with just three nights, two back at the Harbour Lights, one over at the Buddle, an evening of acoustic music. It'll be nice to be unplugged, somewhere small and familiar. Then first week of November we're booked in at the Solent.

— My eyes hurt; all this white light, low cloud, its endless.

— *Ja*. We suffer.

Anna had said this, giving everyone pause. Even James hovered over filling in the squares.

— I say! Steady on, not as bad as that old girl.

Launching into those anachronistic idioms he loved so much, they appeared in the air surrounded by their own invisible speech bubbles, so spontaneously as to sound parodic, calling from Kate and I, *hold hard, steady the buffs, cheese it*, followed by a weary laughter.

— No, seriously, we suffer but passively, from *ennui, vielleicht*, of course, but also *Sehnsucht*. You don't have a word in English, that is why you people are always so disgruntled, no poetry for what you feel, not really. *Stimmt das? Das stimmt!* Right now, we are all missing something intensely, and we call it home, but is that it? I do not know;. Perhaps we are just addicted to the yearning. It is this, perhaps that drives us, makes us play, even though we feel we miss something. We have a longing towards joy, but it haunts us because we never find it.

Nods, barely articulated grunts, sighs of agreement, acquiescence. If Kate could say with certainty the way things should be, James could push towards what he knew to be just right, Graeme capable of restoring order, offering the jester's equilibrium in a sometimes too serious world, Annagreth always had the words for ministering to the soul's sores, her voice a balm, medicament for what ailed, deep down. I knew this, had done for four years, but the others had found this out also. You could feel time shudder, the air being sucked from the room. Anna was right. We enjoyed the longing, the want of place, to be in a place, but not to stay, to arrive only to depart again. In the square the children had gone or were at least nowhere to be seen. The fishbowl world—or were we the other side of the bowl? Hard to tell now.

(I find I have paused. Your diary has in it on that day a dried leaf, a sketch, two hands at the piano, I recognise the ring, mine. Taken aback for that moment, I search for a connection between the drawing and the memory of the café. Nothing comes.)

Inhabitants gone, the world beyond the window empty, clouds hanging low over a stage set from which the actors had departed, or were yet to arrive. Between performances, then, the audience uncomfortable in the silence. Shifting in our seats, waiting for the next act. Feeling as though we had turned up on the wrong day, or that the event had been cancelled, nobody bothering to announce this, no one to confirm or deny. Perhaps the venue had been shifted, and no one thought this worth bringing to our attention. There was something, slightly undefined, not quite out of earshot, taking place unseen, just below the radar of immediate perception, but drawing, pulling nonetheless. Looking up, I saw James looking at me, returning my quizzical expression, a light in his eyes, his scalp as alive to whatever we both had noticed, not knowing exactly that we had, as a dog's nose in pursuit of a rodent. Annagreth was straining to see beyond the windows in every direction. Almost immediately, Kate asked, rising from her chair, pulling at her coat without waiting for an answer,

— Do you hear that? It's Graeme, it must be, it's coming from the direction where the van's parked, what's he up to?

Hurrying to settle up, I followed the others, turning to the right. At the far end of the street at the edge of the pedestrian area, in amongst the benches, near a fountain, surrounded by municipal shrubs, there were the two children who had been playing ball, green and orange coats, one a trailing scarf, the other, brightly blue flecked bobbled hat with earflaps dangling, brushing the ground, swinging to a rhythm. Around them, first I saw their mothers, but also, seven or eight other people had gathered, drawn, brought to a pause by the percussive sounds. There were Graeme and Morphy, Congas, bongos, various other bits of kit hastily set up on a carpet Graeme always brought with him to keep things from slipping, sliding or bouncing around. Kate, ahead of the others, peeling off her coat, was clearly going to join them. They were playing. Simply because. Because they wanted to, because they could, because it was, after all, what music was about sometimes, and too often forgotten. Just for the joy. Her violin retrieved from Waltraud, Kate began. By now, James was scrabbling around in the back of the van looking for something, his saxophone case. And there, heading back towards me, Anna, Annagreth. There you were, your hands out, taking mine, hurrying backwards, quickwalking in reverse, confidently, *come, come,* tugging; *come* you said, *let's play, just because,* said Annagreth, Anna, her face, your smile, radiant, never more alive it seemed than in that instant, starting that old, of late forgotten fire in me, with the warmth, the glow of joy at the idea of making music. The world had once more righted itself, the realignment initiated by Graeme's moment of inspired magic.

~~~

I still feel your absent body. The ghost weight of your always absent body. Contrary to what some might say, I do not like to waste words. Love is unpresentable. It is unrepresentable. To represent love is to sully it. Make it corporeal, reduce it to physical form, you lose the inexpressible. A ghost: this is love. Not even a noun, just ghosting. *No negotiating with a ghost. That sudden rush of sorrow? When you believe you have exorcised the ghost for ever. Do not be sad though. We will never rid ourselves of our ghosts. They love us too much. To be haunted. Is this not love?*

~~~

Autumn 1981
— No, you really must stop doing that with mics, Kate; keep it up, we'll be calling you Roger.
— Bugger off, that's my name!
— Roger, Roger.

Summer into Autumn: motion in light, frozen attitudes for which the camera legislated, an advocate of suspension in the midst of flight. Impossible as it is to tell the music, to convey in words those myriad intricacies, beautiful brutalities of sonorous implication, there is still the memory of motion, fast, slow, interrupted on film, in print. How memory imitates the camera, conjuring less the completeness of the sound, but opening onto shafts, shards, flows and fluctuations. In memory, sound is shimmer, resonance and echo, glancing blows, intimate touches, a shiver down the back, along the arm, evanescent, revenant, to which the image stands poor testimony, but all there is. Substitute, supplement, stand-in, archived prosthesis of a fugitive medium. Music though, what is that in memory but pure recollection, the trace of a felt perception? Virtual but real, so close yet at an impossible remove. If I sing the tune, hum it or whistle, it is still not that. Perception of music in the memory is an echo without the original. Memory of music is a reminder, a souvenir of the impossibility of ever staying in that moment where we feel ourselves most alive, most absolutely living, with, in, for another. The touch of the beloved's hand, her lip, her tongue, not flesh at all but the scintillating course along the invisible pathways of who we most privately, and endlessly become, but who, in the moment having past, we have to abandon, moving on, leaving us with the memory of a perception of an experience, lost, never to be regained, and felt doubly. Twice in the delight, the anguish of that memory and the loss for which it comes to stand. So we remain having to make do with the supplement, the replacement, the impoverished carbon copy. We are sealed off from what we desire the most, the then, the there, the briefest brightest burning of our consciousness. The indirect image, recollected feeling of a memory of an experience is everything, it is nothing at all. We plunder it, we treat it like the whore of all emotion. Believing its cheap replacement to be the real thing, lying to ourselves, trading, grasping time back, or pretending this is what we do. But it is nothing. What lies beneath, and why there are those nights we feel so alone, so cold, so dead afterwards: there is where the music, just one word for something that cannot be said, music, the real matter of memory remains, hidden, protected. Guarded, it guards our better selves, our purer being. In return, we are granted brief insights, thrilling inspirations, when, in the second that crows rise from a copse, or Bach calls us to tears, glimpsing witness to the eternal and ineffable, we receive this small gift, this little gift in the instant's wound, before it closes up, sealing itself within us.

Summer had been taken up with our usual routine of a summer season, several trips away, and, for the first time European festival appearances. The small stages, to be sure, those to the side, away in another field, in amongst the vendors, but playing nevertheless before more faces than we would normally play in a year, or so it seemed at the time: Landgraaf, Roskilde, Stockholm. It had been a summer

where we played in full sun, out doors, Morphy trying to
capture shows direct from the desk onto the Revox, as always
having to do too many things, fixing, making do, mending.
Running repairs. Lives lived from suitcases, backpacks, damp
clothing barely drying worn again, smells of must and musk,
patchouli and perfumes unidentifiable, bags not always to
be opened without preparation or precaution. White jeans
had been a mistake, one from which I failed to learn. Kate
playing bass now, four, five tunes, more and more wearing
simple, sleeveless short dresses often black, her newest
instrument liberating James, insisting that summer, whatever
the temperature on tuxedos, formal suits in which to play,
for horn, trumpet and saxophone, spiralling solos floating
away over late afternoon skies on lengthy jazzy workouts
structured from, extended out of basic tunes, 'Cortez the
Killer' or 'Calvary Cross'.

Or our own compositions, reinvented over the years
from improvisations: 'Angel' with its dithering, echoing cross
rhythm guitar pattern, 'Apple Quark', another title inspired
by the countless cheese jokes that had become part of our
own shared language, this an instrumental with the organ
as its heart, its focal point, its virtuosic, often furious focus,
wave on crashing wave of psychedelic Bach inspired lines
descending, ascending, crossing; kaftan tops, multi-coloured
stitching, a silver sequined mini-dress, nothing but sparkle,
shimmer and shine, golden hair increasingly down, swung,
thrown back, trance motions, before reaching a climax
until, that afternoon in Denmark, as Anna traded patterns
and runs with James, a white evening suit beer stained, or
rhythmic stabs and punctuations with Graeme, bumble bee
striped, aviator goggles, absurd moustache, tombstone grin,
she began, holding a chord, to climb aboard the Hammond,
first one foot on the keys, then the other, as the collective
noise became increasingly, insistently bludgeoning. Or,
playing more rhythm and blues, James taking second guitar,
the wigs appearing; Kate once again on bass, faster, slower
blues numbers, I usually singing, that summer for the first

time Anna, coming out from behind her barricades, short white sleeveless dress, counterpoint to Kate's midnight figure, intricately, brightly bejewelled in small arabesques across chest and back, firing brilliant in spotlight or sunshine.

But Kate singing the blues, a voice larger than the stage, older than she could possibly have appeared, no instrument, untrammelled by other duties, freed to work stage centre, working the melody with improvisations, working the crowd with encouragements, handclapping. Picking one face in a sea, bending over the foldback monitors, appearing to single out a solitary figure, singing in that moment just for that bright shiny sweaty face. Or the unoriginal, but always crowd-pleasing trick with the microphone. Stockholm, and then home, summer coming to its slow end: we had just come off stage. Despite the elation of coming off from two encores, there were burly stage hands, roadies, technicians, men looking as if they'd be more at home in a biker gang or a chapter of the Aryan brotherhood, scowling, muttering, and one or two cursing in Swedish. Still.

— I catch it most of the time.

Watch this. Follow. See the flight, describe the arc. Middle of a song, guitar and organ trading solos, Kate dancing in her own world. Something by Bessie Smith I think, Judge could tell me for certain. The improvisations build, and so the circling begins. See it in slow motion, as you would the oncoming car crash, the train wreck, the Hollywood flashback, slow fade to reveal. Focus in on…on what? Where? Tight focus pulled on Kate's right hand, shallow depth of field, a cable, black, extending from her grasp. Pulling back, the wrist is working circular movements, causing the microphone to swing, circle after circle. In the photograph it becomes either a blur of wheeling play, lines a child's imitation of movement, or else frozen, time's cycle captured perfectly, without admitting the reality of ineluctable onward passage. On film though, the circle would be seen. Pull back further as the cable is played out, Kate working ever greater circumferences, hypnotising the crowd. Will she release, won't she, if not now, then when? Sound has simplified into rhythm for the audience, subsumed within their individual and collective locomotion. Is it drum and bass driving them, fuelling them, or are they being wound up, by Kate's twist and turning clockwork wind? And then…and then…and then up, away, released the cable no longer tight, straining, but a scurrying, twitching watersnake, eel among the currents of the air, mic in flight, aloft into the sky, swimming in this alien medium for a time. Before the pull of earth promises to punish hubris. Her head straining backwards, confident of the trick performed many times before, Kate had never done this in daylight hours, out of doors. She had failed to account for the sun. James and I both knew the fielder, out there at cow corner, or running at long off head back over shoulder moving forwards looking backwards, arching, straining, would never take the catch, the ball lost in the midst of the blinding light, to come crashing down. So the microphone, Kate blinded for the second, flashbulb frozen for the instant, as if the image had itself been recorded, *I never saw it*. Into the monitor, suicide dive. And the crowd roars!

Relived too many times for her to take with any equanimity between that midsummer madness and the autumn, Kate took her revenge the first week of September. Chiefly, this was the fault of Judge and Graeme, Morphy guilty by association, the three perennial seven year olds who could never let go the cat's tail, a joke too good to abandon so easily, regardless of the eventual cost to themselves. So it was, the last day of August, having gathered at the barn for our by now usual winter planning session, shows entered into diaries, other dates sketched out, Kate handed round small forms, A5, to be filled in by each of us.

— What's this, then?

Graeme's simplicity could be touching, genuinely, the more so in hindsight, in the afterglow that knowing the punch line can deliver. Kate explained, her glances telling me that she and Annagreth were, once more, in on the plot together.

— I've entered us in a charity volleyball competition next

week. On the beach at Ryde. Other musicians are taking part, SG, Geoff, Phil, no not that one, Truckel, they'll be there; Rob told me about it a while back, it'll be good fun. It's fancy dress, and I've chosen the costumes, they're here. Judge, Rog, Morph, you'll all be dressed the same, dad's helped me get hold of what I wanted, and mum's adding the final touches.

Eleven days later, three wet-suited angels appeared as in a holy vision. Wet suits, to which were affixed stiffly projecting, horizontal tutus, from which depended bells. Viking helmets, souvenirs of the summer's trip, were mandatory, as were swimming goggles, and to complete *le tout ensemble,* bright red and yellow clown shoes.

~~~

That final diary taunts me. It reproaches me for cowardice. What could I possibly read that I do not already know? Too much, not enough. So it stays with me, a mirror in which I avoid looking every time I notice it. Without an autumn, mere spaces, creamy, their blank pages implying reproach at abandonment, calling up the ghosts of guilt once more, an impossible guilt for there is nothing I could have done, everyone has told me this, this broken off journal incomplete, not yet properly itself, never to be so, sits on my hand. There is, I see, how have I never noticed this before, sticking from its pages another piece of paper, rougher, thicker textured, torn from somewhere. Feeling, the touch and nap different completely, without untying the bind I pull it free, unfolding. I see at first a date, *March 30, '83.* As if called to it, answering some unheard voice, I read, in your hand

> *she stands at the water's edge thin clinging cotton of her dress clinging to her here and there it touches as the breeze gusting from the sea lifts once more at an angle she is turned to me but partly away always out to sea*
>
> *what does the wind carry?*

*Her hair raised
and dropped by invisible fingers clumping at her shoulders before
separating again watching a mime acting out the tide withdrawing from the rock pools at her naked feet her ankles washed free
of sand absolved shoulders bare smooth moulded rocks round
shaped warmed marble he will want to touch unable to resist
run your finger over the curve and before them their own pools
dipping below the collarbone hollowed evacuated either side the
column of her neck exposed then obscured as hair is gathered a
futile repetition backward by both hands then twisted to caress
hair encompasses neck pliant fold on firm column that dress,
horizontal hoops bands of colour she is a glass figure filled with
different shades of sand souvenir memory no sound*

*do we hear
in dreams?*

Or do we just imagine that we hear?

*Despite the wind everything including the observer I realise this
is me I tell myself*

here   you   are,   watching,
looking at yourself

*we are all becalmed I am watching myself, watching, watching
her slender wrists forearms to touch he likes*

Where are you?

*Light down invisible unless seen up close or touched secret on
the surface reach up I reach I lift her arms she points she calls
one delicate finger pointing another the other hand beckoning
something there is something that I cannot grasp arch of back
foot turned out always toward the sea*

Why?

Is she me?

A stranger to me a large balloon floats into view along the shore head reflecting light shining dome, and in that crown a plate metal on bone I want to stir clockwork monkey wound begins to drum its teeth to chatter play monkey. rust intrudes already eating at the mechanism from out the water this is not clear another steps watery kelp instead of hair green brown green polyp and bladder then a voice

My violin is on fire

I turn again to where I stand to where she stood but now facing sea again knowing

what do I know?

There is no one there the circus is deserted the clowns have left run home children quickly getting late leaves blowing winter coming faster young ones before the dark

Who?

I am

am I you, or was that me there standing waiting at the margin between land and sea at the table in the corner between

what was there and what is there no longer?

Who speaks?

Not me though it is my voice I know it is not me my lips do not move they will not move and I want to call you

O will you save me?

Here I am

I hear a voice opening my eyes I had not realised them closed I see her you she you I we are stepping from the water Venus in Pierrot's costume white faced smiling sad

My hair is quite gone

you say

Cut off cut you cut it off I did this and now I am sorry

hollowed the sand has drained away just this white listen you will hear the echoes trembling inside me cold so cold and I in turn am cold too your voice not your voice

how can you be speaking when a butterfly stops your mouth?

Another, at each ear, around your head aurora if it were morning shadows retreat as you open your eyes all breath held gone the waves withdraw there is only the beach as far as the eye can see and your words come back your stupid question dumb questions that make me laugh faded sound ink on a page torn from a diary my diary is broken

where is my bicycle my beautiful red cycle?

Stop asking

if there is never any water does the beach become a desert?

Never stop returning my love, with the sea never to return I will come to you

………..

What had you imagined? Was it really a dream or were you shaping an idea, a whimsical fantasy? Smaller than usual, miniscule, your writing covered a single side. Having read it again, not understanding, I turned the page over to look for any clue, seeing first this

yes I will come Love interminable fidelity

Then, this, I knew it at once, Rilke:

> *Und so drängen wir uns und wollen es leisten,*
> *wollens enthalten in unsern einfachen Händen,*
> *im überfüllteren Blick und im sprachlosen Herzen*
> *……...*
> *Also, vor allem das Schwersein,*
> *also der liebe lange Erfahrung—*

Autumn is over. You are back home once more, Anna. Annagreth, you have returned, safely. I hear you again. Every time, that unique intensity, to love for always. It's ok, you say, go on, even if you think you cannot go on, go on. Don't mourn. Love me. I will not abandon you, do not abandon me. I have always loved you forever. Do not worry. Here. Here I am. I will never again go down into the depths, without you. The water will not close around me alone any more.

We continue. *We abide.*

11. Moving (1982)

Where were you? I have been waiting.

Three nights of uninterrupted sleep, slowing down I thought,
feeling as if I were catching up with lost time, not making up
for it. No longer drowning in tiredness, dragging, treading
ineffectually, beginning to surface. Sleepwading. Then, just
tonight, a dream. There you were. The overgrown paths
cleared away, bracken hacked back. *Come and see my garden, it
has never been so beautiful, so much hard work, but it is worth it, no?*
There was still so much work to be done, all the roots to be
killed. No time to count the cost, the house needs clearing
before April arrives. Cream lace billows from open windows,
unfurling outward, escaping the frame. That sense of danger
lurking beneath the banal. *Careful, mind your step. It has been a
long time, why have you not been here before? Did you lose your way?
Always like you to stop, lose track.* Yes. I lost track. I lost the path,
as well as the time. Someone, not me, must have answered,
speaking on my behalf. He had not known the way, how to
get here. It had been difficult to leave, it proved increasingly
difficult to get away for a long time, the longest time and
when he had, the directions got lost, as did he. *The longest time.
This always feels so brief. Until we realise.* Out of the woodland we
step. You are already ahead of me, I find with some surprise,
having thought you just there on the terrace. Breadwhite
balustrade, large rough formed pots, planted out, fern tendrils

337

uncoiling, escaping between posts.

And we sit in a room I cannot describe, though to be sure I have a sense of its shape, of light, unburdened white walls, wooden floors dark polished, and somewhere off stage, a window. A wall, with an unadorned arch, a disappointed doorway, divides the room. I sit in the corner, facing the aperture, looking across the diagonal of the square to where you sit, a glass in my hand. Red wine. I think. I remember the taste though I seem unable to see, or lift, to taste or smell, so as to verify. I am proceeding, without moving, entirely by sense. No, it is the memory of sense, all senses otherwise departed, abandoning. You are there, across the room, sitting, legs tucked beneath you, just the other side of the arch, a low, simple chair, geometrically severe. Wearing an oversize white shirt. You hold a glass, this is how I know I have one also I reflect, the realisation taking a moment. We talk about Germany. That is where we are, somewhere north. *Yes, it is such a large country, there is so much to see. All the way to the south, so different there than here, in the north. It is more than hour to drive to Hamburg.* I lost sight of you for a while. Could I have forgotten? Forgotten what? You? That hardly seems possible but the sensation, inchoate, irritating, assures me that I must have. I was careless. I lost you. Most careless when closest. You slipped I think. Into the unseen of the everyday. The invisible familiarity. A smile, slight, hovers just beneath your face. You seem to want to say, or to have said, that *everything is all right.* Dressed in black now, no, the darkest, deepest grey, a thin, crocheted scarf wrapped round your neck, *yes, you are right, how clever of you to remember. I made this one autumn, my sister had sent me the yarns, such pretty colours.*

Then I notice. Your hair is short, very. Smiling, dimpled. Ears exposed, the simplest silver earrings, the shape, it appears, of coffee beans. Did we buy those together? Did I purchase them for you? It is hard to remember, but I feel released, at ease, relaxed, just to be here, a place I know but am not familiar with, being, just being, with you, in your company. I realise that your face is in close up. Depth of field so shallow that only eyes and cheeks below orbits are in focus. Everything I see is your face, but most everything is unsharp. Very still, you sit. There is that smile, just, at the edge of the surface, seen from above, playing below, your lips pursed, eyes, heaven blue, in on the secret you look as if you are about to share, looking at me steadily. That most delicate of dimples, *my kiss dimple*, appears adjacent to your still closed mouth. *You know the story, don't you? Once, when I was little, I don't remember but* Mutti *has told me this so many times it is like I remember, she said that the angel who sent me to her sent me off on my way with a kiss, just here, leaving this, what do you call it, impression, ja, yes, a stamp to guarantee delivery. I had been, what is the word,* franked, *ja.* Your face, my sight, the one filling the other, light falling from the left, stage left, your right. You are you, but older you. The time is now. There is no time. But no lines. *You're just saying that to be sweet, of course I look older. How could I not?* No, I know that you are your older self, but up close, you haven't aged, you are still you, you are still who she was. She is there. In you. You are here. Though I have the memory of your words, your mouth has never once spoken all the time we have sat here, waiting for I don't know what, though I have the feeling all will be revealed soon. The light is that of brightest day, though I tell myself it is evening. What a lovely day, such a happy day, a day like no other. Winter light, though I know it to be summer, late summer it is true, but still summer, just, nonetheless. My thoughts return to give full attention to your older, though unaged face. Dimple deepening, knowing look, known so well, on the verge of the secret given away, and silent, mischief of the most loving kind, just beyond the door. Nothing moving, no one moves, the merest flicker around, in, your eyes. We remain. In each other's eyes. Forever.

~~~

— We need to move.

Winter was hard. The year had started deceptively, but then settled into what seemed at the time an endless chill too cold to be called that. Frozen did not begin to describe the latter half of January. The world relented in February, coming out of mourning but vacillating, a general sense of everything mild, cloudy, and damp. On and off, back and forth: the winter months saw us in and out of Solent Studios, short frantic bursts of activity around the Island, two or three nights away, then back, only to leave once more. Grabbing time for a trip to Germany, just Annagreth and I, so much to and fro, so much work, so little home. The basement apartment appeared to assume an air of neglected resentment, or as if its residents had departed all too hastily. December had seen the beginning of what were to become an interrupted set of recordings, new material of our own remaining incomplete skeleton keys, caricatures of themselves until March. Most of the concentrated studio time, virtually living in the bunker, had been taken in January, winter at its sharpest, the heavy hand of cold slapping with an eye watering painfulness. We were recording an entirely instrumental collection, ranging across our tastes, our styles, some of these a commission, but then developed further through the desire simply to play some of our favourite things, keep them for whatever posterity we might anticipate having: memory archived. There had also been much group improvisation developed out of themes and motifs as a project, to be sold at shows as cassettes, for charity.

We had found a way of producing musical forms, structures that could take flight unexpectedly, out of improvisation, with a starting point of little more than nothing, so comfortable were we by now with one another. In principle, everything was easy, and yet in the studio matters could escape our control. *Simplicity isn't that easy to achieve*, Mike had once remarked after an especially difficult two hours. Making the sound simpler in the studio, this had become a concerted goal though. *I say, I think we've got it; we have an aesthetic,* James very Rex Harrison, mugging as Henry Higgins. The pompousness of the affirmation aside, and he was right, notwithstanding, we were endlessly stripping back, down, refining but searching also for an elegance in our sound. February, season of fogs and damp, we returned once again, to the tunes we had begun to track in December. Between then and now, those songs played on a number of occasions, had grown, evolved. On hearing the playback, we were not always satisfied with our initial efforts. We heard others playing our sounds, and were displeased. *It's too cluttered, too busy, take that part back some more in the mix; no, the problem is with the take, you're doing too much, too soon.* James's birthday a week away in March, a party planned two days before we started a road trip of fifteen nights, *leave the baked beans, Rog; seriously, there are other things you can eat if you're really vegetarian,* we were going through the motions of planning a party at the barn, for the fifth. *Well, whatever we're doing, no one will be able to pull a stunt,* James said, perhaps with something of disappointment, mixed with just a little relief, in his voice alluding to a birthday surprise, on stage, the first night of January for Anna. *You should have seen your face,* Kate broke out full beam; *I was watching from the kit, could see everything; you were just frozen. I don't know,* James contributed, as everybody warmed, again, to the subject, *whether it was watching you as you watched Ben climb to the top of the gantry, and getting up on the PA tower, or the sight of the banner, which surprised you more. Both, du Arsch,* came back the stage indignant response, already well known for having been played out on several previous occasions, for successive friends and acquaintances over the past weeks; *I still didn't miss the chorus though, and I hit that high C.*

Anna, helpless in having been the victim of the night, had a very public birthday announcement before two thousand cheering faces two months in the planning, everyone in on the secret. Support to a band far too important to do more than acknowledge our existence in passing, and told by their road manager that on no account were we to overrun our allotted time, we were, thanks to Morphy's eternal good nature, able to convince the crew to allow us the use of a large banner bearing the logo of the band. Designed by Kate and Anna and made by them with the help of the members of Cuboid Goat, a folk trio of old school friends, Prudence, Angela and Jenny. Hung from a frame, some fifteen feet high and the same across, our standard, as James insisted on calling it, was positioned at the back of the riser, behind Graeme. For this particular occasion however, it had been replaced with a flag of equal size, but with the words 'Happy Birthday, Anna', which, Morphy had had the idea, would not be displayed for the entire show, *Anna will never agree, it'll make her really mad.* Instead, claiming it to be damaged or stuck once erected, the release would be to hand, rigged as part of a spare bass drum pedal, *I can do that, bugger, no problem.* We would save the surprise till the last song, 'Last Bus'. At an agreed moment in the guitar solo, everything building to a climax before the return of the chorus before the end the song, drumming concentrating on the toms, driving the count over four bars with increasing intensity, so Graeme would trigger the release, for everyone to see. Afterwards, waiting for the ferry, I somehow became the chief culprit, the result being that Anna didn't talk to me till the next day. *Yes, and I still would not talk to you!*, I said as we sat in the studio that Sunday evening in February. *Yes, and I still would not talk to you!*

So we talked, back and forth, all but the last couple of parts laid down, in the kitchen, the last February evenings in the studio. This had been a quieter time, fewer friends dropping by, hanging around. Rob had been by to hear whether we were doing the same old difference, though admiring we knew, what he called *the vibe*, a word he knew inadequate but standing in as a word for that which had no words. A brace of Phils had been called in, one with 12-string guitar, the other with a fretless bass, to add a third bass line 'live' rather than Kate or James dubbing the extra part, in a string section written by Annagreth for three bases. Mike, Dil, Morphy were all present, Fred there too, having come along for the ride on several days, so much had he missed Kate, and behaving suspiciously well. In general friends were though beginning to drift away, their own lives placing them in their particular orbits, school long past, college or university by now over. No Pete this time, moved away, to London, playing himself in a band, freelancing as a photographer for any band wanting promo pictures. No Damian either, though this was very much a curate's egg of a blessing, mostly good we felt. In truth, we saw him less and less, particularly since he had, a surprise to some given that he bore with him his own universe of chaos, mayhem and disorder, misrule and eccentricity in equal measure having to them no discernible internal coherence or logic, joined the navy. *He'll end up a rear admiral,* Graeme had joked; *do you mean up a...; stop right there, Judge,* Kate had commanded. *Full steam ahead or a full head of steam, it's all much the same.* Half-heartedly, Morphy began to whistle 'In the Navy', only to fall silent, having been looked at by Annagreth. There were still the other musicians we saw in passing, at pubs, at the Guitar Centre, or at infrequent social events. Once, there had always been a party, somewhere. Now, now there was an air of retreat. Gradually, we were coming to realise that what we thought of as our world was beginning, inevitably, in its growth outwards, to distance us from those who we had felt near to us, or to take them away, as they grew into lives of their own. Small losses barely noticed, until one or other of us would begin the by now familiar litany: *have you seen...?*

— We need to move.

Without being aware of it, a silence, and with that something of a gloom had settled. Sea smoke without over the Solent, a gradual, creeping thickening of the atmosphere within. Her usual forthrightness pulling apart the cobwebbed opacity of our collective pause, Kate cast her statement. Fishing fly or hand grenade, it was too early to tell, but her words settled amidst the murk which had crept off the water, over the curve of the land, a sleeping body as yet unaware of any intruder, through cracks of which no one was conscious, to feel, to insinuate its way inside each of us. The short, brumal days, sloughy solstice, moist and clinging, weeds of dead men, searching out the fractal patterns of our existence threatened with a quiet more menacing than any noise, forced us that evening to confront what had been poised, lingering, behind us for the last few months. Cheerfulness betrayed through being over-forced, the laughs not a little hollow for having been replayed just once more than was healthy for them. Irrational discontent settled, out of all proportion to our situation. Kate's words had been the spell, letting the genie out of the bottle. The seal broken, it would not go back in. Was it that, earlier in the year, Ozzie Osbourne had bitten, by accident rather than design, the head from a live bat while on stage or that he had, less than a month later, been arrested for urinating on the Alamo? *All of it? Bugger.* Or that John Belushi would turn up dead at the Chateau Marmont, the day of James's party a few days from now? Our shared malaise, realised in Kate's statement, found further expression in the cover of James's copy of *The Economist*, which he said he read *because I'm always on the lookout for new material.* On the cover was a cartoon of Ronald Reagan as Snow White. Or, as the cover had it, *Right: Snow Right v. Europe's Dwarfs.* For some months we had felt as if we were steering a different route, but with no particular purpose, except for the, always, shared sense that this is who we were, this is what we did. The feeling began to creep upon us that, having become, having realised our own direction, we were unsure as to where it might lead us, or where we wanted it to take us.

— Well? Am I the only person in the room who can hear me? Or have I become invisible?

— No more than the rest of us, Kate.

— It's dead men's bloody fingers. They're tugging at the sheets and we have to leave soon or it will be too late.

Nothing else was said, for now. I was avoiding Kate's gaze,

knowing that, between she and Anna, clearly this was already discussed, probably decided. Graeme looked blank, rubbing his fingernail back and forth along the table surface. Morphy was busy making more tea, shutting himself out of the conversation that was not happening, but which sat expectant a raptor in attendance on a not quite expired body. Mike put his head round the door, are you coming back? In a minute, came the reply in a manner that indicated it would accept no counter-argument. The door closed. James, flicking through the pages of his magazine, made great play of getting to the book reviews.

— *Sawdust Caesar. The Wider Sea.*

Then turning the page,

— *How Voters Decide. Life Itself.*

Whether this was avoidance or an oblique commentary at the crossroads Kate insisted we face was unclear. I imagined, lack of sleep a contribution to my stranger interpretations, in addition to being more than familiar with James's more oblique commentaries, that in various scenarios, the titles were deliberately chosen. This would be 'just like Judge'. I felt the quotation marks, having heard the phrase with metronomic regularity, usually from Kate, over the past six years. In a style refined during that time, but encountered, defined from the very first moment the three of us had sat that school afternoon eight years before in Fowlers. Never acrimonious, simply the sparring dance a ceaseless ritual between people closer than lovers, I and everyone else knew the steps, expecting James to take the next, inevitable measure. Which always led to a bravura performance, her logic, Kate's will, as inexorable as her argument was coherent, a carefully shaped improvisation of ideas, the pieces of which had long ago been rehearsed secretly, played through, given variation, returned to its initial premises.

— All right, and we're on the clock, mind, and, and, remember, we can always continue tonight after we're done here, but why we—need—to—move?

Each word was spaced, heavily emphasised, doled out

with an equal temperament, suggestive of James's insight into everything that stood behind the pronouncement. I felt like a child at a panto expectant of the harlequinade: old enough to have been before, but not so old as to fail to feel, however many times I had previously been taken, the tremor of that expectation, the dizzying delight signalled in the dimming of the house lights, the darkness hung from tenterhooks, filled with the acceleration that pushes the heart in the seconds before the lights make the audience instantaneously squint-eyed.

— Because…because, because, oh bugger it, man, you know exactly why and if you don't then you've been masquerading as someone much more intelligent for the past eight years. Perhaps that's what it is, just feline cunning, you're not really smart at all, you just play the game, pretending after the event to know what everyone, especially me, has been thinking. But I can see I'm going to have to explain, if only for your entertainment, and stop smirking right now, you glib sod, if you don't want to spend the next half hour picking this coffee mug out of your forehead. Because Jill can get us work abroad—and I'm not talking about moving to the mainland, here at least is home, is bearable, however claustrophobic, is insulation against all the crass, dull-headed stupidity of the larger rock—as she has done, and it's so much easier; because when we do go there, and we do it more and more, there's a reason for the move right there: by and large we get audiences who really appreciate what we do beyond the usual run of rock and rhythm and blues and pounding. Don't get me wrong, I love to get sweaty with the best of them—do not, Rog, or I swear—but we do so much more, and we' so good at it, we really are. I haven't finished, wait…

…this interjected as a response to what Kate took clearly as a shaping of the face on James's part, readying himself for a reply,

— …Because we all know we are in danger of being forced here into being that pub band, and finding ourselves fifty or sixty, doing something that will sound equally as absurd as

'My Generation' beyond a certain point. You know, throw the monkey some nuts and watch him do the jerk dance. I'm just not sure whether the monkeys are us or the lot who stand out there making whooping noises. There's the danger, I'm beginning not to be able to tell. We're still not there yet, but it creeps up on people; look at some of the bands who trot out from their day jobs on the island, cleaning off the instruments once or twice a week if they're lucky, playing to thirty people and a dog, if the dog's deaf and they are particularly lucky, getting out of work, probably having to get the ferry back from Pompey or Southampton, to go play a set of covers. We still choose the covers we play, when we want to, and yes, I know, we've got a great crowd here, more than one audience, and they're very loyal. They're also very needy, they have to have new material. We always have to keep ahead of them, because any punter is fickle, can't help it. It's why we introduced the request box, it's fun but it's a gimmick. Can the performing monkeys learn a new trick by next week? I still love it all, it's still fun, serious fun, but I don't want to find, and I'm not the only one, that I'm pitching up one night and I don't remember why I do it. If that happens, we either cling to one another in desperation or end up loathing each other. God knows, it's bad enough with Rog's baked beans already, twenty more years of that, no thank you.

— But I like beans, and they don't do other vegetables in tomato sauce.

— Have you ever thought of ketchup and fresh vegetables?

— I...

— Because, and here's the last because, though you know, Judge, you bloody well know, just like you know I've got more, we'll never get a contract; what with the way things have been the last few years we wouldn't want one anyway, that'd just mean everything becomes a larger, sweatier version of the twenty-year stretch of rhythm and blues. We need to move, and we need to move to Europe. Germany makes the most sense, and we have to decide to make the jump before we find too many excuses not to. Anna knows I'm right.

— Talked about it already, then?

The smirk returned, the bald head ducking out the way, James avoiding the imagined hurl Kate began to mime, a frustrated pace bowler aiming to shy at the stumps in burlesque anger, the batsman opposite not deigning to recognise the might and natural superiority of the bowler, refusing to be bowled, caught, or stumped. Graeme's face still taking everything in, his resemblance was nothing so much as to a baby who, having learned how to stand, started to realise he was about to fall over in surprise at his own independent verticality.

— Well, I don't mind. I mean, I want to keep on playing and I'd rather play with you lot than anyone else. There's no one else. Anyway, they've got good sausages, cake and beer.

— You're a vegetarian right now, remember?

— That's cause I can't get wurst here, bugger. I've never been the same.

— Oh you can always get 'worst', Rog; sorry, no, I know, that one was beneath even me, so...

James looking at me, I catching everyone's eye, Annagreth sitting silent, looking everywhere but in my direction, the dimple near the corner of her mouth starting to deepen, eyes now turning down, every effort made at containment.

— I had no idea, I swear, I'm always the last person to find out.

— Of course. Has he figured out you're in love with him, yet? Do you want us to send him a post card?

James to Anna, Kate visibly unwinding as he spoke, clearly happier now everything was said, having carried the day in that effortless fashion, her own mix, as Mike had once said to me, well out of earshot, of vision and a division of heavy artillery. We had not discussed the details, how to achieve this, where we would live, how any of this would work out. We had no clue. But, as with anything Kate would say, the inevitability of agreement was a foregone conclusion. Her will would carry the day, ensure we saw it through. I still felt excited, open countryside instead of a cul de sac appearing at the bend of the road.

— So, I suppose that's it. Well, I'm game. Just what I'd been thinking in fact, but I didn't know who'd go for it. I can't see Thatcher going anywhere any time soon, and I don't know what I hate more, her or the people who keep voting for her. We'll do it. We've been told the why; we have no idea about the how, but we can discuss the when later back at the barn, spring rolls on me, let's finish up these recordings for the day.

~~~

— It's all got so much worse, y'know.

— Since when, the invention of the grand piano, or one Wednesday afternoon in 1572?

— No, no, popular music, the last seven, eight years, when, Ben, when did we meet?

— September, seventy-three.

— Nine years then, almost. I mean, in nine years we've gone from *Tubular Bells* and *Dark Side of the Moon*, just to take the most obvious examples…

— You must be really drunk, bugger, you're never so obvious.

— Sod off, drummer boy; as I was saying…

— Yes, Rog is right, why not say Amon Düül, Soft Machine, Magma?

— You too; and they only prove my point…

— They're not so bad, if it a little obvious too…

— All of you, let me finish, at least in Europe those bands are still there in one way or another, every reason, once again, why we should move, why we have to move; where was I?

— Same place as you always are, sooner or later, don't we know it.

— Can I continue, can I finish?

— We don't know, we've no evidence you can, you may, if you want, though on past history it's very unlikely, and like we could stop you in any case, tell us something we don't know; pray, continue, chunter away…

— I feel like I'm listening to some tape loop and I can't turn
it off; we could use this for a minimalist piece, something
serial, play each phrase over and over, add the next part piece
by piece, to build up to the inevitability of aural bludgeoning.
— As I was saying, to take the most obvious examples, we've
gone from Floyd and Oldfield, to the B-52s and XTC, and
Magazine. Phil Collins should never have left the drum stool.
— The old ones are the best ones, change the record; the
views of the bass player in no way reflect the views of the
management!
— You know I'm right.

The diatribe continued, a stream swollen, its banks
having burst, Judge was on a marathon this night, intending
to outlast *The Mousetrap*. Everyone gone home, save the
six of us, the litter of a party everywhere in evidence, our
presents, easily chosen, old copies of Wisden's, plugging gaps
in James's collection. Fred, indifferent to everything except
whatever food had been left and which was, therefore, his.
Late, late; how late, too late, everyone feeling an exhaustion
that would not fully kick in for a day or two more, James's
party had ended, the first in five years not on a stage, not
snatched between venues, celebrated in a small, makeshift
way. The topic, the decline and fall of popular western
music, a favourite theme for Judge, sober or drunk, straight
or stoned, was always an excuse to vent, to rail, to unleash
a dyspeptic disquisition with copious illustration, examples
carefully dissected. In truth, *truth being anything a jury will believe
given a consensus of stupidity, juries inevitably being a fool's cabal*,
his father had once said, a sentiment James was fond of
wheeling out as the occasion chanced. This particular strand
of hauteur, this sustained incident of bilious venting *de haut
en bas*, had started and was sustained in the winter, during our
time in the studio. Judge always warmed to his subject given
the least opportunity, unwary opponents left in evidentiary
shreds, *no, let him go*, Kate had once remarked, no, let him go,
I responded, *he's been wound up and it's fun sitting on the side lines*.
James would never admit that there had always been the bad

with the good, and that the dross far outweighed the gold. We
were usually wary of taking this particularly well-beaten track,
littered as it was with the evidence of equine flagellation.

But the old familiar tune, the same old refrain had raised
its hoary head when Steve and Judy, infrequently seen those
days, but stopping by Solent this one time, shortly before
the decision had been taken that we needed to relocate for
the sake of our collective musical health, they inquired of
me, thinking James out of hearing range, if there were any
albums he might like as birthday gifts. I had tried, too late,
not obviously enough, to eyeball James's appearance in
the doorway behind them. So, it had begun, but had been
sustained, developed, improvised upon in interesting ways, a
lengthy solo, breaking the forms, moving into new harmonic
areas, following no regular pattern, its strongly pulsed
rhythms varying wildly over the course of the days, and,
inevitably nights, cycling in strange inversions of diatonic
structures, altered dominant phrasing *accelerando* or *ritardando*,
to create the impression of something moving in waves, *like
peristalsis, but in reverse, here comes the flood.* This last had been,
as was typical, an observation of Kate's, referring knowingly
to a song of Peter Gabriel's included in some shows since
I had wanted to do it, on a whim after having heard Fripp's
quietly insistent, plangent sonorously sculpted version,
bringing out, I thought and said to anyone who would stand
still long enough to listen, the real work within the song, in
lines and loops mournful in their soft force, full of grace and
melancholy in equal measure. A guitar near to hand, James
droning on, going for gold, I reached over, fingering slowly
the chords following Kate's remark.
— Well, I don't know about anyone else, I'm going home, got
a lot to do tomorrow before we leave. Night all.
Graeme leaving, Kate decided bed was also a requirement,
Zebedee's calling, James realising he was holding court with
an audience too tired to care any more, too familiar with the
turns of his argument. A little unsteadily, he found the energy
to raise himself, Morphy coming forward to steady him;

preparatory to anything else, James had to be handled into the car somehow, his legs neither willing nor able. Anna and I looked at one another.

— You and Morphy help him outside. I'll bring the car nearer, otherwise we'll be here indefinitely.

Once in the car, setting off for Seaview, James managed the question, *who wants an ice cream?* before drifting off. Reaching Embankment Road, the harbour still, the water strangely, unseasonably gelid, disquieting in appearance; tricking the eye, reflecting darkly, without definition the massing cloud armada hovering with a sinister patience across the sky's canopy. A still night, a moonless night, a very quiet night; solitude and stillness at sea, solitude and stillness in the sky; solitude and stillness on the land; silent the houses, silent the road, silent, more silent than silence itself, with the creeping silence that attends all natural places, Knowles Copse, the windmill unturning, sentinel asleep; clouds casting their grey ghost bloom on all below. A stranger, having returned to earth after long absence or death, would have found the world ashen; without distortion though disfigured in its stillness, its solitude; boats, dinghies, yachts, yawls clustering thickly, nothing murmuring, so still the flow; away and rising the fields either side the water, green to grey to darker shades, grossly delineated in being undistinguishable, a wilderness of oblivion and forgetfulness, sleeping disregard. Morphy's voice broke the silence, the dropping of a crystal vase on flagstone.

— I won't be coming. Not away next year, I don't want to move. No don't say anything, please. This is hard enough.

Anna could not drive. Pulling the car over, she turned the key, all sound dying. All at once the car's interior felt too intimately confining, coffin close. Leaving James to sleep, as yet unaware, happily ignorant in his bovine, chemical aided stupor, apishly lumpen, we got out.

— warum? Why, it is…

I placed my hand on Anna's arm softly, signalling the need for silence in return, and with that the space to

speak. She pulled away. Turning to look at her, I saw a
look I had seen only rarely before, never one directed at
me, but a look unmistakeable nevertheless: inmixture of
shock, dismay, disbelief and a something approaching
anger, as if disappointed by a trusted friend, a friendship
broken, betrayed, belittled: a face uncomprehending at the
announcement of the impossible, the unthinkable. For some
seconds nothing was said. Morphy rubbed the ball of his
foot back and forth on the edge of the kerb, hands tucked
into pockets, arms tucking themselves into himself, his head
down, then looking away across the harbour, looking without
expectation that any ship should arrive. Then, clearing his
throat, he looked up. I realised Anna had taken my hand,
squeezing it tightly, in need of aid.

— Look, I know, I know this isn't a good time to say this. No
time would be, would it? I've been thinking about this though
since that evening in the studio, and everyone's been so gung-
ho about the move, I haven't wanted to throw a bucket of
water over your enthusiasm.

— You didn't want to tell Kate, you mean.

This, less accusation from me than acknowledgement of
some people's limits.

— That too; I know you both…

Morphy paused, to look pointedly at Annagreth; looking
between them, I had already felt her shivering, tears starting
to well.

— …you'd be the most reasonable, and could help me tell
the others. I'm happy, no, more than that, I want to keep doing this till you leave next year. I'll even keep on the cottage,
once Judge moves out, after all it's not like it costs. Then
you'll always have somewhere to visit, right?

— I don't know what to say, really, have you got plans; I
mean it's all sudden, but do you know what you intend to do?

— I'm not going to work for other bands, don't worry.
Wouldn't feel right, Ben.

— No, and it wouldn't matter anyway.

— No, well, the old man's been asking if I'm ever going to

get a 'proper' job, and I've been thinking some kind of course in electronics; I know it all anyway, but, well, I could contract out, work for myself.

Then Annagreth spoke. Finally, a quiet voice. A small, a lost voice.

— But why?

— This is home, it's all I want, really. I love getting away, and, I know, I complain more than most when we are here, about the grockles, about the yokels, about what a right pain it is getting back and forward to the north island sometimes, but I know everything here. Nothing ever changes. I wish nothing ever changed sometimes, that we could just all be us right now for ever. I'm sure there are other reasons, but I can't, no I won't, I'm not able to say exactly. It's just home, Anna.

Taking a decision, I said, returning the pressure of Annagreth's hand on mine,

— Don't worry. It's alright, really. I know, I understand. And if it's not with any of the others I'll make it right. But they'll be ok after the initial moment of wanting to flush your head out. Just the way I felt when I moved here, when I left London. Makes perfect sense. We're the mad ones, and why should you be touched by our insanity? Look, don't turn up for the meeting tomorrow, there's a bunch of stuff, supplies, I've got everyone's lists back home, I'll drop them by in the morning. I'll say I asked you to get everything in and ready for when we go back out, the day after; then I'll get everybody to see this is right for you.

— No, Ben. *We* will. We will convince everyone. And we'll see you tomorrow evening at home, as we'd already planned, with the others, for dinner. Come here, stupid, you have ruined my evening but I love you.

Releasing my hand, Anna stepped forward, gathering Morphy in her arms, holding on to him tightly, as if by force of pressure she could keep his imprint, the memory of him with her forever.

~~~

Notice the world. Look around. Pause to take in all that is so familiar we have long forgotten to reflect, thinking it would always be there, and so allowing it to fall into heart's neglect. Remember familiar tracks, the old paths walked before, and woods that, welcoming, remind us of those we love the most. So long, too long the times away, our motions in acceleration, no looking back, no longer glancing sideways, outwards, focused only inwards, keeping going, following the road ahead, white line in the night, vanishing point in the on rush. Stop.

End of the night, the last of winter well past, time to slow down, take notice of everything inconsequential though important, everywhere around us; everything surviving. Not without cost, we survive, we continue. Early in the day, sun not yet fully awake but in front of us, appearing unclouded. Almost, not quite summer, nearly there, two weeks away, here is Spring: *Frühling, vår, printemps, vere*. Words like flowers freshly gathered, clustering in your arms, on your lips. Everywhere vernal freshness, the land becoming new. Starting over. Beyond our carefully contained, preciously preserved, well tended, if off-kilter garden, celebrations for the coming summer had begun. Margaret Thatcher had declared war against Argentina over another small island. *Perhaps the French will invade here*, was James's remark. *We can only hope*, came a reply. Canada would that day be granted full political independence. James had been looking for signs of the consequences of the previous month's syzygy in these events but came to no definite conclusion. We were where we always found ourselves, in the oddity we called the everyday.

Here we were again, home once more, moved on. The world's clock had turned, rewinding itself. Not yet adjusted to sleep, awake before dark, Annagreth insisted it would be a beautiful, a *resplendent* day, rich, the perfect picnic day, a day ideal for doing nothing. *Kate's expecting us for breakfast, but let's walk, we can leave soon walk, it's not quite six, we'll be there when we said, near to eight.* Passing Priory Woods, skirting its edge, heading south, following the road, here and there a

fox heading home, avian call, chorus and cry, we followed
the road. St Helens Green, quiet, a few dog walkers, old
men moving slowly, anticipating their daily papers. Taking
Lower Green road, curve and camber away from the longest
side of the triangle, then somewhat steeply down Latimer
Road. The harbour reached, sun risen ahead of us, the curve
of Embankment Road displayed the horseshoe harbour,
opening narrowly between dunes onto the Solent, revealing
greyly Hayling Island, tucking itself, nestling between
Portsmouth and Selsea, Thin gauzy strip of land, a mist of
rock, no more, supine, horizontal. Just giving itself to be
seen. Spring supplicant. Breaking free of the road, we sought
to shorten the journey working our way between the trees,
Coming at the barn, not from road side but on this newly
picked morning up from the bay, clambering hedges, into
the copse, accompanied by wood pigeons, a crow here and
there, perhaps jackdaw or magpie, further sounds of hidden
snuffling, scurrying, busying in shadier corners, surreptitious
before our alien presence, or here and there a red squirrel.
The fields belonging to Harry in sight, a rich swathe of
cornflower blue, a violin voice reached us, something richer,
more exotic than any ordinary fiddle, lamenting, celebrating,
singing in the little births everywhere. Kate, we heard as
we moved over the incline, hardly hill, before seeing her.
Appearing once more in the unadulterated sun, the strings
spoke, sang, slight harmonies half thought, abandoned,
a melody unearthed within. Sounds, more than one,
improvisation for bowed instrument and birdsong.
— It's the new instrument. Let's listen!

Her finger to my lips, her other hand halting me, Anna
closed her eyes. Feet over foliage silenced we paused to hear
the Hardanger, a present from Annagreth, in anticipation
of Kate's birthday today, just over five weeks after James's.
The haunting sympathetic echo of the understrings,
resonating beneath the melody, lilt and lift, drop and turn,
double stopped or quite alone. Eight strings in troll tuning,
Hardingfele droning through its four notes, greylighting,

admitting the morning already underway. Kate already
coaxing, feeling out the instrument's voices, its spirit,
seducing it into surrendering its memories, its secrets.
— She is calling us, she knows we are coming, hurry!

Laughing, taken in the tune, drinking in daylight, off Anna
ran into the sun, bouquet gathered in the walk held tightly.
We were at home. We were home. Back home, we had been
for six days, the winter's recordings completed, a lengthy
excursion also completed after this, our plans, vaguely shaped,
taking form, the anticipation tempered by considerations,
reflections, discussions more, then less, sober, in preparation
for moving away. Harry had contacts, of course, the
inevitable. Jill had thought this sound, her word, a sound
idea, makes sense. A sound idea, James had joked, that's what
we were, but more than one, many ideas, sound notions. We
would, it was finally concluded, be here until the end of the
following summer as we had initially thought, then make the
move. Anna and I had told Heike of our plans during our
previous visit to Germany, she agreeing enthusiastically to
help. New territory, uncharted waters, terra incognita: all the
stock phrases, clichés perhaps but then, maybe, just maybe
that was why they were such, already familiar talismans, way
markers, linguistic buoys to hang from our tongues guarding
against, while guiding us toward, and through the unknown.
Everything unfamiliar, we could still rely on the stale comfort
of words. We would head north, knowing there was always
the barn, always another home, our old shared home, a fixed
point, a constant.

As Annagreth ran I watched, thoughts surfacing. As she
ran over the field, denim jacket undone, brown and red, long,
vertically striped pinafore dress gathered in your free hand to
prevent you tripping, I paused before continuing.

I pause now, recalling you as she ran, with that spontaneity
you always had, which had, I know now as I never knew
then, so attracted me to Anna, to Annagreth, to you? Why,
when such things happen spontaneously, in what we call too
easily real life, does this all seem natural, inevitable, but when

seen in a film, there is something cloying about the image, contrived? Is it the capture of that which should always be seldom seen, the spontaneous ossified into representation? Older, cynical, now disappointed repeatedly, I find myself pulled unwillingly toward the saccharine of some climactic shot, panning, in a musical of the most appallingly sweet kind, when I know that, at the time, it was not like this, I would have not seen it in this way. Where does the distance come from, and why? I ask myself this now, as my memory wants to make of this a cinematic moment. Am I protecting myself without knowing? Does it not bear the weight of narration, of the representation? Or was your vitality, your overflow of joy simply unrepresentable, not to be captured? In screening it now, am I betraying the memory? Have I betrayed you? What would Anna say?

You are curiously silent on this, and knowing what led from this brief pause, a pause suspended with an unnatural length in memory, I am tempted to think, no, to believe, and so trust to your silence on this matter, that, in saying nothing, you tell me exactly what you think. You tell me gently what to think. As I was to do that morning, and I always did, I arrive after you. I lag behind, and you wait, always patient, always gentle, kind, a little sardonic. For, as with the impossibility of describing music, so it is with our most expressive gestures, those little nameless acts of simply living beyond mere existence, the mundane tick of the everyday. All I know now, having had to work through the problem as if it had been an equation requiring solution is what I then knew without having to think the matter through, making of it a problem it had never been. I simply felt the pleasure in seeing you thus. Everything felt right, feeling was everything, and all the rest was, and is, and remains silence, in the very same way that once Kate had said we need to move, everything felt right about this decision. But for now, here was where we were, this home ours, our safe home, Kate had called it, referring to the barn, but also the Island. We had, each, found each other, every one of us arriving just at the appropriate moment, whether or not any of us had known that, in those moments, when each of our needs was at its greatest. Committed to each other, committing ourselves, each to the other. The Island had made this happen, this small world, this little stage, strange place all its own, not quite real but more than merely real: Island time, Sidereal, surreal, out of time, offbeat, the land that time forgot, time's orphan. The isle has such sweet sounds, the words floated to me, with the hedgerow birdsong on that morning. How ever far we travelled, I thought looking around, back toward the copse, imagining the bay, hidden beyond, then turning toward the fiddle, seeing Anna, passing over the gate, toward the farm, and just beyond the bright red barn, freshly painted. However far we moved, however far, not matter how far, we would, we could, never leave here; here was where we were, together; here was who we were; no, we could never leave, the Island would never leave us. We will never have left here.

The sky, bare painted, rich burying cupola, blue golden blue, flaking, diffused as if something almost tangible hung with fragile apprehension for the morning, the air not yet fully clear, nearly invisible motes, stirred from fields, lazily falling to the stubbled greens, browns, earthen hues a haze diffracted over the horizon's curve, returned to me the thought of you, of us, cleaving, delirious. Then, I was taken by a memory vignette, conjured by the golden light. Annagreth the previous summer, surfacing, golden hair breaking the bluer surface, darkened by the inland waters on the shore at Travemünde, the beach on Lübeck Bay, and afterwards sitting, silent, still, far away her eyes, but near at hand, looking out toward trees clustered further along the shore's bend, as if waiting for someone to sculpt her; as if a statue just come back to life.

Why that vision, now, this morning? Was it the light? The tremor of the day, swelling into itself, filling out, expanding? No, here the daylight had a bluer clarity. Travemünde was always cast in a yellow daylight, blissful summer days remembered with the rarity of a first meeting, the filament touch of the beloved's fingers or lips on cheek or neck when, still half asleep, you are drawn by the surprise toward wakefulness. Here the sea was always that colder grey blue, the steelier tone of the Solent I reminded myself, looking back toward the harbour, and beyond the open channel.

And then I remembered, as a gull passed overhead adding its throat to the Hardanger's notes, to which, I realised also was added Anna's voice, singing a traditional Swedish song: that other morning the previous summer, you had been singing this song, a tune from the north, quietly to yourself. We had been sitting far away from others, as far as it was possible to be given the popularity of the spot. Away to our left, an abrupt, precipitous rockface, boulders and lime, beyond that a wooded hillside, beneath and stretching around the finely sifted sand, smooth and hard. A lotus land in memory where it was always afternoon, Travemünde that day was gently animated, peaceful in bestowing the illusion of isolation on us, bringing with its benediction the joy of the seashore, untrammelled, unconditional. How, I thought, could anyone touched by the magic, learn to live without the sea. Waters lapping, whispered against the rocks, light green waters cresting, foamed with the clarity of crystalline glass diffusing the yellow day. Blues touched with green, both having a lemon lightness to them, warmth with just a hint of brooding presence. Small shells sifted through my fingers, dull or polished by the intimate abrasion of sand, the consistency of castor sugar, shell caught in the tug of water. There was a hushed peace, enclosed within a faint murmur of rhythmic waters, bearing up the softly sounded melody, a high clear voice lifted into the air, words taking flight north across the water toward their home. Enchanted, the air bore with it an apprehension of eternity. Stopping abruptly, Anna had turned towards me, saying, here is beautiful, I love this, hardly anything could be better; but the Island has a magic, of which, I do not know, but a feeling, yes, I have this feeling it is not quite completely good, not benevolent, that is a good word, yes; no it seems it is not this all the time. It will never leave us, it is always there, but it does not want to let go.

Months after, the winter following, on a snow plagued night in Hamburg, before reaching her parents the following morning, as we lay, almost at the point of light, watching large flakes hurl themselves through distant street lights, say Lanternenpfahl for me, please, say it, it sounds so funny when you do, like you are five; Annagreth lifted herself onto her elbow, hair falling forward onto, over my face, to pull it away, saying, I miss our flat, I know it's lonely; such a lovely apartment and we spend so much time away; it doesn't like that. I know, I am being silly, I know, tiredness; Ich bin müde—Jag är trött. Summer, Winter: Memory so vivid, all at once so odd, unaccountable on this, another more than perfect day announcing a place at the edge of seasons, made me shiver. Seasons in alignment, like a planetary arrangement, opposite though in conjunction yoked together, and through them, what caused me to find myself halted, the thread of your, of Annagreth's words. I felt somehow chilled, at my back the slightest sense of consternation, an imprecation, dead men's fingers. Someone walking over my grave. Consciously shaking myself, forcibly to pull away from the touch of unseen cobwebs, I walked on, cheering myself with the thought of breakfast, taking to myself the welcoming glow of an already bright morning. Picking up the pace, I began to run. Knowles Copse, I knew, was receding; but it remained, that dark hand over the brightness of the day.

~~~

We sing our lives in songs, the words of others telling us with a truth greater than any we can share ourselves.

~~~

By the time I had got to the barn, my mood had reverted once more. At least the darkness had been cabined for now. I see this clearly, recalling the joy on your face, Kate's also, a special day. Another special day. And I ask myself now, what am I remembering, what comes back? Memory is fickle, a tricky thing. Do I recollect, as I think I do, or am I telling myself stories, from the images I seem to recall, from the eternal idea of them, slight imprints pressed into, raised from some substrate that hides as much as it recalls? Is it you I hear saying the kettle's on? Is that you I see spilling crumbs on the bed? It might be just that I am giving myself now a kind of prescience in the moment then, to protect myself from what came after. Screening myself then from what happened a year later, almost a year to the day.

But no; I do not believe this; and I refuse to believe it for a reason. Until the instant when I wrote just now those fatal words that take my breath, threatening, I can feel the tightening in the chest, a brightening of the eyes making it difficult to focus, the white of this paper over which I am scurrying so quickly to cover with words, giving shape to, making sense of, but I cannot write quickly enough, my hands shaking, I am going to drown in anxiety, overwhelmed, overflowing, losing all sense. All is not, I know it is not, I will not let it be, belated realisation, assigning to the inconsequential frisson the death by water that we describe as the weight of significance, as though significance were not equally a featherweight, the lightest breath. It is only I who give significance a weight. Things happen all the time, and I will not believe, I cannot accept that I am the one creating in this instant of unbearable burden the significance, any more than I believe, or accept the stupidity of predestination, fate giving off its signs like so much corpse gas before the victim is even dead. Roadkill, all we are then? Taking the path, stepping off, driving with the windows down, there is that smell, that stench announcing a not recent mortality. There is no other scent like it. Filling the nostrils, like the stalker who, unseen announces himself with that violence, that imposition from behind of hand over mouth and nose. We smell his sweat, his fear, your face feels the coarseness, the calloused palm of heavy hand, ludicrously sausage fingered, close around us. Always there's that moment, stepping outside yourself, you find the circus clown in the monster, the monstrous in the comic. So near, impossibly proximal, crushing. Yet, that aroma is far off still, it is merely its phantom in the nasal passage that fools us into thinking it on top, inside us. The impression of proximity is all.

Calm. Be calm Breathe in. Pause. I pause, and, in pausing, letting my fear take me, I just let go. And there: I see myself again.

I stand there, just beyond the copse, not yet having run. The memories of you have arrived, you on the beach, that smiling face in Travemünde, southern end of the Baltic coast on a summer's day. Your hair ornately wavy, released from heavy braids, held back by that Turkish scarf, reds on white, golden dots among the peacock feather pattern. Early morning, hair haloed from the outside lamplight, a winter moment in a shared bed borrowed from another, in another's apartment, pausing on the way north. There you are, tent to the left, Waltraud to the right, a morning image, impossible July orange, gold, bronze brass, shining summer, leaning on an elbow, half smile half squint, laughing questioning, mouth filled with food. All these are real, and if I felt that instant acutely in pausing beyond the copse, above the bay, on my way to the farm anticipating birthday celebrations; if, as I believe now, I felt that moment, it was in the realisation dawning on me as if for a first time, how impossibly precious you were to me, how everything that morning, midway through April, everything I had, everyone I had and who had me, who held me safe in their hearts, their affection, and for whom I did the same in return: all this I wanted to remain the same. The Island made that seem possible, it promised the possibility of the impossible. This was what, I believe now I realised then, was what you had been, in your own way, seeking to tell me those other times, in summer, in winter, in

Hamburg, in Travemünde. They were Island stories you told, and you are here now to tell the Island stories once again. All stories meet in the memory of you, this is true, but all stories come to me from your memory, the memory I have of you, the many memories, told, untold, those unspoken inside those written down, hidden and in full view all the while. Yes, yes, the memories of you, but also your memories, those that, in every minute where you found yourself reflecting on your happiness, there would creep on you the melancholy of realisation, the moment passing as soon as it had given itself to you; *tristesse*? Afterglow? *Sehnsucht*? Words for other words, words for which there are no words. Or simply, the songs inside, beyond the words, standing in for the music we could hear but which we always had to trust that each other could hear in the silences where words would never be enough, never enough, where words would merely fall, faltering, inadequate, limping lame footed, stray, wanton, homeless: shadow starvelings hungry for scraps, mere scraps themselves, the detritus, dead flesh of all that could be felt, and which only the salt sharpness of a memory could access, which only the sweetest, most poignant, haunting music, touching us unawares, not with a mugging, but lovingly, so that we found we had been touched in those seconds that have to pass, as, coming to the surface, but remaining as yet without distanced realisation, perception opens onto all we cannot name, but which we find we love, cannot do without.

Yes, what I know now, what I felt then, what I know from having known and loved you, what he felt, from loving Annagreth, Anna, was, no, is, and remains to come: what I know as I felt it then is that all the stories meet in the memories of you. Yours is the story I have wanted to tell. my story would not exist without yours, without you. There is no story for me without you, without your story, your memories, your music.

As I write this, I realise that your music, what I call your music, is to me many things, not least the music that you made, music to which I am listening this evening, as birdsong fills the still, soft quiet of the crepuscular air, singing in the night. Blackbirds accompany your playing, ghost fingers moving the keys, moving the hammers; moving me. You are not there, yet there you are, speaking to me. Things you showed me. This plays, those words the title for a song without words. You move, *little ghost dance with me*, toward the final bars, those minor chords, repeating slowly, over the final seconds, counting down, as, in the background... What was that? A bowl? Yes, a singing bowl, its voice returning, passing again, or seeming to. Play it again. No, I have to let it end. It is enough that you are there in the ringing of the bowl's voice. Your stories remain. Memory has not betrayed us. You have not betrayed us. I will not betray you, your memory, or your music. Remaining with me, I remain to tell your story, to tell what remains. There you are, even if I am not ready for the end, not yet ready to end. I will never have been ready.

— No, do not weep. It is not yet time for tears. There is still summer to come. That last summer.

~~~

We are insignificant in everything but our passions, and love is our whole existence, if we have significance at all. This is our one reproof against the obliteration history forces on most of us. Memory, wherein we live more than the everyday, wherein we dwell, even as those we love continue to dwell in us, is our bulwark against such anonymity. The stories we tell ourselves, about ourselves and others; the stories others give to us, their songs, such stories without words, stories in the image, the vision, where a picture is not worth one hundred, one thousand, not even an infinity of words; for the vision strikes my eye and calls me in a manner that makes of words a joke, a poor device. History is proof of this, all phoney objectivity, all fact and causal sequence falsely read too late. Memories, those ghosts we call our own but which, in truth, own us, are, like music, just the sequence of our feelings given shape but unrelenting in their refusal to be governed by the constraints of historical slavery. Facts are bullies, the tattoos of a vicious gang, signalling tribal allegiance to an unloved shadow figure, hidden behind some curtain, wanting to believe the levers he pulls make everything happen after the event. History roams the streets looking for its victims. Vision, memory, these protect us from the night time fears history repeats as the only truth, when the only truth history has to teach us is that there is no truth, just more words, masquerading as fancy dress to hide the pox sores of a world lacking imagination, fancy, passion. It is easier to see the world in a grain of sand than it is to find a truth untrammelled for the heart, in all the facts of history. History is the spawn of Satan's strumpet, chafing at its iron collar, and punishing the rest of us for its embittered servitude, its craven, fawning supplication to the masters and mistresses it serves.

— What are you writing?
— Just idleness. I've been thinking about birthdays, about last days at home, not away. You know.
— Yes. Everything that became abandoned. Everyone just walked away.
— What else could they do, once you'd gone? James couldn't bear the cottage, Morphy either; or the village; did you know Kate went to South America? Had a baby, called him Jésus; Baby Jesus! You were the glue, you know.
— That was my word!
— I know.
— I am sorry.
— For what?
— That I went. I had to, you know. I had no choice, no say in the matter. There was no why, no time to ask.
— I know, I wasn't speaking from any sense of wanting someone to blame, least of all you. If anyone, history, I find, is to blame.
— You still cling to that overgrown schoolboy, don't you. I know, I am not teasing, much, it, he makes it that little bit

easier for you. History had nothing to do with it though.
— I know, yes, but sometimes, today, whether it intrudes
itself in between the pages of our lives, forcing its way in like
a small child who can only think of the prize turkey in terms
of his own size, or whether it demands, requiring of me that
I go back, 'check the facts', well, I hate it, I hate the needy too
clever child, but I have to see whether the haze surrounding
the outer edges of my memory is significant after all.
— You have been going through the papers?
— Yes, I keep making post cards of them; posting them,
trying to diminish history, cut it down to size; perhaps it's
because I need to keep my rage going just a little longer
against them for obliterating you. You never had a chance,
you weren't even forgotten, just never remembered. Perhaps
I'm going through them too because we used to. Do you
remember?
— Of course. In the kitchen of our basement, or with the
French windows open, 'thrown wide', James used to say,
a silly phrase sounding as if it wanted a home in a story
somewhere, looking out over the garden; you would sit there,
reading stories, making fun of the headlines.
— I don't do that any more. I haven't since then.
— Why?
— Everything reminds me that the world continues much
the same, indifferent to your disappearance, your loss. My
loss too, everyone's loss. I still read, on occasion, the cricket
reports.
— Because they are the one thing in the papers that never
change. Despite the different names, statistics, scores.
Everything just the same, the same for ever. An eternal
afternoon.
— You remembered!
— Of course. That man whose book I found one day in that
little dusty shop in Bath. Cardew or...
— Cardus.
— Yes, Ja. Absolut. Exakt. Genau. Stimmt. Eternal
afternoon...

— Can we get back there?
— We will, soon. One day. I promise.
— You never broke a promise to me.
— I promise. Come. She's asking for you.

~~~

Summer. A last summer. August: a lost, a last breath, thin air. What was that summer? I find it hard to recall. Was it what the weathermen call a singularity, one of those odd points where, by virtue of the time of year, certain unseen confluences, weather patterns repeat themselves with an uncanny precision? I don't know, though August proved unsettled, unsettling, too much heat for too little time, too many too short thunderstorms that cleared the air hardly if at all. Coming home every time that summer leading into intemperate, vacillating August, the world felt troubled, temporary. There had been a royal baby. We had won, we were told, the Falklands War. The World Cup, usually an event assuming unreasonable emotional involvement for James, Graeme, and Morphy, seemed lacking in its glamour or appeal for them, had those of us on planet normal cared. *What is it with boys and balls?* Annagreth had asked, of me as much as Kate, apparently with no sense of irony. *I'm sure I don't know*, I said, *after all, it's not cricket.*

After a time, doing the same thing in different ways, or doing different things the same way, it all comes to seem the same and yet not the same. I lose focus, but not intensity. After six, no nearly seven weeks away, back. Despite diaries telling me, heaven only knows how many towns, clubs, motels, strings changed, laundrettes tracked down, brief aimless wandering in and out of shops and cafés, the killing time, discovery of some souvenir, some novelty to sustain interest beyond the night's work, all too infrequently a museum or some other point of tourist interest. Back home, hanging on, to a thread, for dear life, out of one of life's folds into another, one rhythm for another, substituting, crossing

back and forth, déjà vu, the visible and invisible crossing
lines, getting wires crossed, recrossing, uncrossing. Helter
Skelter. I felt myself paper thin, blown, tissued. Back at the
Harbour Lights we would be, *here we are—again,* James's face
a grin to rival Olivier's on the posters of *The Entertainer,* all
close-up, teeth, and pancake. Three nights from the fifth my
diary tells me. Then the end of the month, Ventnor Winter
Gardens, before spilling into September, autumn arriving.
The last Friday, Ventnor once more, several small shows,
followed by the long weekend at Puckpool Park, what turned
out to be the final *Wight Rock* though no one knew at the
time: *The Gentry, Big Swifty, The Mechanix, The Pumphouse Gang,
Last Straw, The Confusers, The Monitors, The Waltons, The Choir,
The Nightwatchmen,* Rob and Ian rigging the stage, cursing the
musicians, a voice, Welsh, coming from off stage shouting
'shut up, boyo!', Tony, Morphy, and Baz making sense of
sound and light, Terry stealing everything that wasn't nailed
down. Beginning on a Friday afternoon, followed by two
full days of live music the advertising said, announcing as
if to celebrate, the end of summer; a month late, Kate was
heard to say, *that's Island Time for you.* The circus back in town,
our characters make their way across the stage: Arlecchino,
Brighella, Pedrolino, Pierrot, Pantalone, Colombina, the
Innamorati, Scaramuccia, Pulcinella, La Signora.

The diary is only a partial record though. The facts are not
all that are in the case, the Harbour Lights and the Gardens
bookends, marking the space between without giving away
what was sandwiched, shoehorned, stuffed in there. Nor
do the diaries remind that you, Colombina, one evening,
on a whim Noël Coward's 'Parisian Pierrot', followed by
'Pierrot's Serenade', by Bohuslav Martinů. Nor will giving
away the titles—go ahead, look for recordings, listen, if
anyone believes it might help—do much to complete the
scene. Facts are like that, aren't they? Deceptive, for all that
they announce what they stake out as their own local truths.
The truth is though, and this, *the truth is*, not a phrase I've
ever used without a sense of irony, knowing it to be wielded

as some mace of usually bigoted opinion, masquerading
as authority; the truth is so much more, and so much less.
Truth is not the truth, but instead an indicator, a mark on a
dial, line of script as recorded measurement. Nothing more,
nothing less. Something from which we start, not where
we end. A truth, like a fact, allows us to begin from there,
setting off to something larger, greater. A gatekeeper, or
the gate itself, a fact, written as a truth, the entry in a diary,
a bare name, that of a person, place, or event, suggestive of
all that a diary cannot allow, because the space is cramped,
confined, but onto which it gives access; this little jotting
holds its own story, simply, without fanfare. At most, the
name, the descriptive shorthand, see here, read, *Lights, Cowes,
first of three.* This offers what? There is a poetry of sorts,
skeleton scansion, scaffolding from which can be built the
more wayward, generous, rambling edifice of a tale. Interests
make strange friendships A diary can give us pause, can cause
us to reflect, remember. or it can remind us that we do not
recollect. The gate locked, access barred, we are thrown back
on our own resources. The diary closes itself, leaving the
reader with that mere, naked poetry of the scant phrase.

My diaries had little more than *facts*, an agglomeration
of sequential pronouns and place names, daisy chained
across the days, hung on dates. Annagreth's, always more
detailed, more evocative, even then, record the incidentals.
Seeing them again, as if a first time, I find they seem less
diaries than a form of musical score, each entry a complex
orchestration, arrangement, variation, or when brief, so many
grace notes, accents, adjectives alone tending to tone, tenor,
directed emphasis, posthumous instructions for someone
to come after. Everything a little commentary, instructive,
helping the performer in deciding how to play, where to place
the emphasis. Comparing Augusts, I find you had written,
here it is, *Aug 3. Home a day. Hallo Island! Reading at the beach
this afternoon.* Then this, underlined five, six times: *Shell-snails
copulate. Apricots set, & swell.* I am lost, at a loss.

And then I remember. A book you had found, old, the

pages warping from a century or more of damp, found
just a few days before, a must-laden, dustheap of a junk
shop in Bath, the place held together by good will and the
sloughed skin cells of thousand upon thousands of the
dead, over the decades accumulated, to leave indelibly their
own particular legacy on the objects now for sale. A large,
battered, leather-bound volume, given as a school prize; oh,
look, Ben, your elongation of sounds made me semi-precious
on your tongue, something brightly shining in your mouth,
oh look, so süß, and you read aloud, your feet shifting slightly,
accompanied by the creak of well worn, often trodden
floorboards, *to Daisy Simkin, 1st in class, Head Girl*, followed
by the date, tidily inscribed, steel nib scraping at that page,
teacher's hand carefully rehearsed, 1902. And in the top
right-hand corner, small, faded, barely there and somewhat
smudged, *this must be Daisy's writing*, a pencilled signature, and
with that the drawing of a flower. Turning the page, I saw
the book was *The Journals of Gilbert White*, whose house we
had visited two years, no three before, on a whim, early one
spring, after I had talked, endlessly, the others told me, of
the idea of writing a set of music, instrumentals inspired
by White's writing. The *Journals* purchased, they became a
constant source of fascination over the coming months,
Anna reading aloud random phrases, memorising others,
selecting a number as the lyric for a tune, or simply copying
out entries, as they struck her, as they caught her imagination.
Shell-snails copulate. Apricots set, & swell, must have been one of
the first entries copied.

Looking back at the entries for the August of that last
summer, I am struck by the sparseness of further remark,
the absence of more detailed entries. Had we been just too
busy? Had everything sped up, in preparation for a gradual
deceleration? The previous winter saw us, with the help of
Harry, make the effort to book many small gigs all noted,
names, times, here and there, an afterthought, addition, *Gt
nght, not that version, packed, tired*; around the Island, a veering,
places we had not played in some time, every venue we could

accommodate, could remember, could cram into the month, six, seven weeks. Barely a day without, the poetry of public house names, most hiding their own particular charms or memories in the anonymity of often used, much repeated names. Back and forth we would go, over the details much as we were to travel over the roads, decisively, having decided, committed ourselves to playing local places once more, one more time, from the top, where it all started, repeatedly. *Who says you can't go home?* Kate had asked, to which the only reply came from James, his usual fatuous, self-mocking seriousness: *Hail, the Conquering Hero Come!* Returning to where we had started, returning to repay debts, beginning the process of saying goodbye, a long goodbye, a last, good Friday stretching over the months through autumn, into winter, a planned extended visit to Mike, the studio come January, and from there the spring of the following year, once more into summer, a year's leave taking, until gone.

First however, the end of this summer, moving between a groove and a rut. And in there, Graeme's birthday at the Winter Gardens; *you can choose the set list, Rog. Good. Can we do a new tune, it's not one of ours, but I've wanted to do this for a while, and I want to sing it.* Silence fell like a plague of cows falling unexpectedly from the sky, all at once, synchronized free fall, the impact of this statement as if more than one hundred had landed, legs in the air, simultaneously, and we were standing in the midst of the downpour. Anna was the first to speak.

— Which song?

— Well, 'snot really a song at all, but the drum breaks are mad, and it's got something for everyone. It was one of the things in the request box we've never got around to. But I know Ben can play it.

Kate and James looked at me, mystified. Shrugging ignorance of the whole matter, there being lots of things I played, played around with, wandered in and out of all the time, I hadn't the least idea.

— So?

— It's that Focus number, the fast instrumental.
— Hocus Pocus?
— That's the one, bugger.

The grin appeared, appearing ever larger, bright white beacon in fading evening, the air visible as the world turned away from the sun. Graeme had been feigning forgetfulness, fooled us all with what some might have taken for anxiety over introducing the topic, when in fact bravado, something Graeme managed to produce at key moments, was the motivator. The song or tune, not quite instrumental, not really a song, such much as a hurtling, hurly burly ensemble workout, flashy pyrotechnics and virtuoso soloing in equal measure, 'Hocus Pocus' had all the qualities of manic, breath-taking jazzy melt down in the form of a rondo that we found so exhilarating. In so many ways it announced itself to us with an inevitability that evening, as we sat at the Vine, as quintessentially an end of summer bravura set closer. That night, too hot to sleep, too close once more, the evening pressure unrelenting, giving no relief, Anna scored the various parts for next day's rehearsal, turning up at the barn the next day with the breakneck version for playthrough, taken from the Dutch band's live album. Sitting at the Wurlitzer, impertinently orange still, headphones shutting out everything that was not the music, she concentrated, hair loosening, dishevelled, small patches of damp on forehead and nape, the night's moisture, insect close; tired eyed, I worked, fingers over frets, in imitation, silent mimicry, occasionally we came together, then apart, hands on keys, fingers, thumbs, full octave stretch. Transcribing, transposing the key to suit Graeme, whose yodelling capabilities had never before been a matter of note, interest, or even knowledge, a dark secret he seemed suddenly to bring out of some dodgy closet into the full glare of the spots, we spent that humid afternoon working through arrangements, with accordion, without, as an acoustic piece, slower, faster, more or less stringy, but coming back finally, shortly before supper, to the heavyweight juggernaut brutality of the recording at the Rainbow, in all its sublime, lunatic majesty, a Silverback on a sled, taking the Cresta Run by storm.

Graeme had remembered 'Hocus Pocus's sheer, hard edged force ever since, two years before he had asked about the tune, on seeing the title, as he'd recollected in a, then, recent innovation, the request box, a gimmick we had introduced one night to appease all the 'why don't you' and the 'I know what I like' punters, all those audience members who, ignorant of the difference between a fret, a stave, and a coda, had, nevertheless firm opinions about music; many regulars in our audiences when playing the Island had been happily appreciative, genuinely supportive, but the whynots, the whatabouts, or the canewes, as they were christened by Kate, were, without doubt, something else. Less a breed, certainly not having evolved into a species, lacking either the *jejune* charm of the average tech-spec obsessive or the self-inflicted bite marks of the tribally inclined, *always noticeable, the way in which they don't talk to one another, merely grunt, nod, and shuffle on*, the *canewes* were squinty, runty pleasure defilers. Their one question and its variations, *caneweplay, doeweknow, betewecan't*, which with subtle twists in those of their ilk with what might pass as higher neural functions could become *howabout* or *whatabout*, was issued not from any enjoyment of music, but with a rodent defiance in the face of those not like themselves, *to wit, humans m'lud*.

One too many had been encountered after three years of playing regularly, causing James to turn up at the barn one evening with an old crisps box, recovered from a pub, covered in foil, a slit in the top, and the sign, big bright letters, REQUESTS. *It's simple*, James announced, *so simple, it proves I'm a genius; it will shut the canewes up, catch 'em on the back foot at least, get 'em on the defensive. Put this on the bar, first set, anyone wants to put a song down, slip it in, great. We'll pick one, and then, second set, announce what we're going to learn for the next time we're wherever we happen to be that night*. And he was right, boringly so, to the point afterwards of becoming for a time insufferable, more than usually, smugly pleased with his own ingenuity. *It's not the wheel you have invented, James* Anna had sighed one night when James had let us all know again, having pulled out of the box the scribbled title, *oh look, they can't spell, sweet!* Of something of more than usual appallingness from the current top twenty. *So kiddies, what's the arrangement to be, all strings, a tango version?* What had begun a simple joke, spiralled incrementally, exponentially, into a constant test of our inventiveness, our ability to produce a version that outshone, showed up the tawdry pop sensibilities of a song as commercially successful as it was bereft of musical originality. Once in a while however, when blue moons were back in season, a nugget, a gem, appeared, amidst the dross. 'Hocus Pocus' was one such jewel.

Graeme's suggestion tried out at rehearsal, the initial shock of the drummer singing over, *he'll be wanting to walk upright soon, we'll have to let you out on your own,* Morphy offered from behind the desk, making to duck before the drumstick took his eye out, we had a new number, one clearly too long neglected. Losing energy, losing will, we all agreed to call it a day for business matters, though it was, as yet still early, for us. Morphy set about working through necessary packing, the afternoon's touchy warmth wearing on us, the clouds beyond the barn's thrown wide doors menacing, muscular contours of discoloured woolheaps assuming bruised shades in anticipation of what would prove to be a sustained percussive light and sound show; *looks more like* sturm und drang *than* son et lumière, *eh?* Kate observed, having wandered to the door, before turning back, pulling at her hair as though she wished to be rid of it all, its weight made more unbearable by the treacling dampness of the air's density, the close quarter unwelcome attention of late summer's pestering intimacy. James took the chair, little energy for banter.

— Let's decide what we're doing, when; Rog, you come up with your birthday set over the weekend, and when we get together after the Harbour Lights—when does anybody want to do that? We've got three days clear after Sunday, before we head over to Arreton.

— Why don't we just get to Arreton a little earlier? I'll work on the folk sets, Anna and Ben can come up with the jazzy evenings, and we'll use that as the basis, with the Harbour Lights lists, for the next few weeks up to Ventnor. Graeme, you just make sure you've let everyone know who you want on the guest list for the 24th that Morphy's looking after their tickets, alright?

Kate had taken charge. This had always been so, James's authority merely a means of setting in motion business as usual. Sets decided for the Harbour Lights, different each evening, though with particular points of reference, musical co-ordinates for an evening's orienteering, the nights presenting the small challenge of pleasing and surprising old familiar faces in equal measure, I had begun to toy with a riff, familiar, not much loved, but persistent, in that aggravating but irrepressible way of bugs on a summer's night, the whining children of dilatory parents, and scabs, sore but demanding the intrusive worrying offered by a finger nail in an idle moment; an itch unscratchable.

— So, what's on for this evening?

James sounded a little lost. Kate, perhaps a little too quickly, with too much edge, said,

— not the pub, again, Judge, no. Absolutely not. I need a night in.

— So do we, mate; sorry,

I added, having caught Anna's eye. It was, we both knew, a matter of who said something first. James looked as if he might crumple, his head less a balloon than a slightly deflated football. We were not there yet, not quite, but constant performance came with its own negatives, most noticeable of which was the addict's withdrawal, that febrile, restless rapid eye motion energy; unable to settle, twitching, a pulse coursing underneath a calmer exterior, the inner life at odds with what remained visible to everyone else, though threatening, no, promising to break through at any time. It's that point when indifferent expressions threaten with

a troubled hint at barely containable anger or frustration
for no good reason, nothing other than seeking something
else, to bring back the reminiscence of a life not lived in
the perpetual twilight, the constant greys and beiges of the
endless same; when wanting pain is preferable to realising
that nothing is felt at all. With James this had always been a
very recognizable problem, his forehead becoming crumpled,
folded leather unnaturally creased, his neck seeming to swell,
a red beacon, warning light, looking for anything, alcohol, an
argument with a stranger, which suited his purpose, a means
of purging, exorcising, simply feeling life again, feeling life
once more. James bore in him his own darker plagues, figures
of a folklore surviving at the fringes of the most primitive
cultures. He could be rescued if the signs were spotted,
and we all knew them. We all knew James could be dragged
back from the brink of whatever precipice he chose to build
himself, seeing, happily for all of us, only infrequently, if he
could survive the fall without a safety net. Graeme, clearly
still pleased with his choice of a new track, stepped to the
crease, the night watchman believing he can win the day, see
out the final session.
— Why not come over the farm for supper with the folks,
bugger? They've been complaining they've hardly seen
me, and later, if you're up for it, there's a double bill on in
Newport, *Blade Runner* and *The Thing*, late night show; we can
pick up some chips from the Chinese.
— Can I come?
Morphy's interest sealed the pact, diluting the charity with
the patina of enthusiasm.

~~~

— It is so nice to be here, just with you; it seems like so long.
All tomorrow too, then three days. I miss just us sometimes.
— Yes. I know. We're always together, but hardly alone. We
need to find time for a picnic soon. Anything. What do you
want to do tomorrow, other than nothing, with me that is?

— Let's go to the beach, if it is nice. Priory Bay. I love it there.

— Yes, of course. If it's fine.

12. A Letter and a Party (December 1982)

There you are.

I see you. I see your lips beginning to form a shape, beginning to give life to the thought behind the eyes. And, seeing, I hear you, hearing again what you had said one winter's morning, words for which, on a winter's night, I was so grateful, grateful for the agreement, the pact we had bed morning made.

— We should write to one another, all the time we should.

This said with a certainty I had come to know, against which there was no counterargument, no defence. Only willing compliance. Your certainty had in it the inevitability of appreciating what was right. And you continued,

— Not to wait for absence, being separated, apart for any reason. Promise, promise me, please, promise that we will write to one another every week. I will give to you letters, cards, and you must do the same.

I did, that day, I promised. And I did, in the days after, on the days that remained, not every day but many days, as did you, notes everywhere, on any occasion, for no reason, for every reason.

— In that way, we will each have a souvenir of the other, we will still have something there, then we will never have to say again, I miss you, because writing will be there for each of us to read, when we cannot hear each other speak; but we will, won't we? We will hear each other, and I can say to myself, there you are. There. And so will you.

I hear you now. There you are. There, a letter from you. Your pen behind the words, hand behind the pen. I am led to you, the visible now, the invisible then.

~~~

December 1982

Älskade Benedict,

Du är min älskling, min käraste man. Jag älskar dig mer än alla stjärnor i himlen. Det snöar inte så mycket. Jag kommer till dig.
  Vad skulle du tycka o matt ha en bäbis?

Puss och kram,
Din kärleksfulla Annagreth

~~~

— Really?

There is a silence that falls when news so unexpected is received that nothing comes to mind. What is there to say? Everything is poised, waiting for what is to be said next. There someone sits, not yet having spoken, about to speak, about to respond, the news already transmitted though that person had never said anything directly on the subject until this point. The information received so unlooked for, the enormity of it impossible to take in immediately, one might as well have woken from a sleep to find a sudden talent had imposed itself. A new language say, never before spoken, the ability to tap dance, or, imagine it, the gift of telepathy. A flourish is required, trumpets heralding a change of scene, a harlequinade ensues, the entrance of someone who sweeps us off our feet. Instead of which, there is this exchange of the eyes, each pair daring to outstare the other, while the lips are pressed tight shut, forbidding exit of any lesser observation, any possible truism, banality. Eyes widen, brighten as lips tighten, mouths giddily incompliant, wanting to turn banana shaped, up at the edges, as if to join the eye widening that curves inevitably downward, each face forming itself, mirror of the other, into a circle of delight, surprised and responsive variously; really? Yes, yes; for sure? Yes, of course. So much is being said without being spoken, so much in the circles that circumscribe eye to lip to eye. Faces turn to bubbles, fit to burst.

The second week of December I had spent Monday and Tuesday in London, returning Wednesday afternoon. The eighth it was. Though I remember this clearly, I have the proof of this in the form of a letter, a letter I keep but which, of all the notes, cards, photographs, souvenirs, scraps, fragments, hastily scribbled, cryptic comments on restaurant napkins, a quickly devised verse, a joke, some doggerel, the occasional single word, perhaps two, in English, in German, French, Swedish, one or two in Latin, across and between the tongues, passing and repassing through the years, too few, so short, so rapidly disappeared. Of all these, and all the others, everything kept by me, by Judge, Kate, or Graeme, this remains the hardest to read. Returning home, it was near six, I felt submerged in water, wet through with that feeling that never again could I get dry, jeans sticking to legs, water working its way through, in between, the heavens torrential, the day as dark as night. Water weighing, pulling everywhere.

No lights on, no one home. An emptiness close to loss settled, turning me inside out, causing me to sink inside myself with every step along the path toward the steps and then the door. I felt as if I did not want to put the key in the lock, to know with certainty that no-one was there. It was not unreasonable that Annagreth would be out, in fact she had probably spent the afternoon with Kate, as this had, by then, been something of a custom for at least three, no four years, the habit of close friends, baking, knitting, sharing secret stories, laughing. And always tea, more tea, a gallon, an ocean of tea, all manner and taste of tea, with milk, without, with lemon, herbal infusions, spices, home brewed experiments, ingredients coaxed from hedgerows, fruit flavours, winter berries, *Schwarzer Tee, Grüner Tee, Schlechtwettertee mit Himbeerblättern, Apfelstücken, Walderbeerblättern, Pfefferminze, Sonnenblumenblüten.* Kate loved to learn the names of the ingredients, as Annagreth loved with a birthday excitement the arrival of packages from the north, the aroma seeping, escaping through cardboard, cellophane and wrapping paper. Here was home, therehome, in that scent, so strong a call long before brewing or taste could pull homeward, reaching in with its scented fingers to unravel memory's skein, threading through its private archive, unlocking doors, opening drawers, and letting out every *you* that you, Anna, had been, all of which had gone into the making of you, so many flavours together poured into Annagreth, Anna, you.

Hard edged, sharp shaped metal sitting in the barrel, after some difficulty in the dark, my own shadow darkening more the already hidden lock; and then the turn, the tumble, feeling in the wrist, that momentary lag past, the falling into place, so slightly behind time with the motion widdershins, that the bolt might be withdrawn. Unlocking, committing to entrance. Perhaps, if I locked, turning back again quickly in the other direction, and then, turning around, back down the road, knowing James, just left, also dispirited, equally vexed, would have the kettle on already, the cottage now welcoming, but as yet a little cold; perhaps, and then come back a little later, in a while; Annagreth might have returned. But no, not wanting to delay, just wishing for anything other than empty rooms right now, at this very moment, I went inside.

The door closed behind me, I stood for some seconds in the dark, not moving, not reaching for the light switch. Still hovering, that indecisiveness that could exhaust, frustrate, leaving me doing nothing, avoiding doing anything, working hard at prevaricating, too many times in order not to convince myself of something so much as to put beyond the reach of possibility a certain action, if only so as to be disgusted with myself. This particular goblin was already hovering, looming in the shadows. Pushing through that, leaving my coat, pulling at shoes sodden without unlacing, kicked off in the hallway, I walked through first to the kitchen, lights on, putting on the kettle, then back to the living room to start a fire. The air had the damp raw petal fleshy feel of graveyards at the end of too wet autumns, no lingering late summer's days retarded by a reluctance to give the world over to its melancholy weeds. Then it was I noticed a small lamp already on, the smallest in the room, on a shelf in a recess in the wall by the piano. Tucked away, it would be hard to notice in passing. Rain racked the window frames, made rattle the glass like chattering teeth. Paused, something made me turn not to the grate, but toward the piano. As I reached it, looking down, I noticed the lid up, keys exposed untypically, but on them an envelope, tidily posed, secured with a ribbon and on the reverse a wax seal, the letter K embossed therein. Turning back again, in that fine script were the words Read Me. Reaching for the lamp in the alcove, lifting it to place it carefully on the top of the piano, I settled myself on the stool to read.

The kettle began to call from the kitchen, shaking itself to attract attention, as if the whistle were not enough. I would have to fetch a dictionary in any case, the letter being in Swedish. Leaving the letter on the piano, I went first to make tea, then bringing back pot, mug, milk and spoon on a tray, placing these on a side table, went to the room nearest the front door, which we had in the past few years transformed into a small study, deliberately out of touch with the modern, resembling a heritage production stage set for a Victorian melodrama, or perhaps AmDram Ibsen, lacking nothing, not even period antimacasars, and other curios, knick-knacks, gewgaws and *divers relics*, James so self-consciously studied in his expression, of another century washed up in various alleged antiques shops during periods of travel, being away, on the road, *what a bloody awful phrase*, wherein often the only thing genuinely antique in such places was the owner's cat or the owner's halitosis. Old words for old things, everything delightful, everything *contretemps*, and so, in being homeless, in harmony, in sympathy with everything else. We had even, in a spirit of parody, acquired an aspidistra, which that evening, as though in sympathy with the world and my mood, had wilted unbearably. Everywhere in the apartment, a dampness, the cold of the day. Feeling, unreasonably, a chill on the verge of shivering, phantom prescience of nothing comprehensible, no reason for the perception except my own weariness, that dispirited exhaustion at another fruitless attempt to find professional interest from record companies, *it just doesn't grab me, where's the single? Ten years ago, lads, maybe…, you do too many things, you need a single style, something we can market,* I returned to the living room, dictionary at hand. Determining to light the fire, having poured a large mug of tea, I set to work.

Not that there was much to do. Annagreth had laid the grate already, newspaper, kindling, it just remained for me to get it going. The satisfying crackle of paper and thin wooden sticks, that sudden leaping of flame, a kind of life licking larger logs, produced a beneficial response in me. Things would be all right. Record companies, what did it matter? Leave. Walk away from it all. We earned, we played, we still enjoyed what we did. We had an agent who got us plenty of work, especially in Europe, small clubs, the odd festival, the occasional support on the leg of a tour. And we had the freedom that no contract could countenance, of having choice to play still in places we wanted, where people knew us. There was a lot to be said for obscurity, as long as it paid. When we had gone to town to meet with the A&R men of several major labels that week, James had prefaced the trip with the remark that *of course, we're only doing this to convince ourselves we're completely out of step, irrelevant, and that's what we like, isn't it?* He had, as usual, been right; there was a perverse, wilful joy in the idea of a jazz version of a Hendrix tune, playing an evening at an arts centre as live accompaniment for a modern dance company, thinking of inventive arrangements for standards, and most of all writing how we wished, as the fancy took us, without the commercial constraints of expectation leading to the production of more of the same, conveyor belt constructions, hook, top line, and sinker. What had left me with a sunken feeling, I realised as I began to thaw, was the sheer cynicism of the business end of things: middle aged drunks, alcoholic legover merchants, men whose nostril linings were in a terminal state of dilapidation for the most part, ensconced in tasteful Conran sketched offices, all leather, chrome, the obligatory Altec speakers, the Revox and stereo systems the cost of which was in inverse proportion to the musical equivalent of baby food spewed back as flavour of the week. *Only notes those buggers understand are pound notes*, Graeme had said, wryly, on another return from a previous trip.

Had the business always been the business, hanging like a suicide from the imaginary meathooks of invisible quotation marks? Probably so, what from the outside had seemed to have happened for a brief six or seven year period from the end of the sixties through the early seventies was an anomaly of sorts, something which, over time, would become distorted, bloated with reminiscence, either too willingly excoriated as self-indulgent, pretentious, or else given a nostalgic patina, a mere by-water reimagined as a golden flood, a torrent of creativity given free rein. There had been a few good men and women, there must have been. There always were, regardless of whatever the creative medium. People who, if not visionaries, at least knew how to make the most of those who were, or who had, a slight or great talent for seeing just differently enough. Hallowed names such as Tony Stratton-Smith or Peter Jenner sprang immediately to mind. And Jumbo of course. But in the darker waters, just below the visible depths, there swam the schools of predators, eyeless and razor toothed, glutting themselves in feeding off others who just happened to float by, all optimism and a three-chord trick. No, all in all, it was probably better that we were inedible, our sell by date, had we ever had one, having passed some time before, probably even before we had got started. No, I reflected, my second mug of tea almost gone, it was better to be an anomaly, a collective anachronism.

Then I remembered the letter. Having sat before the fire, encouraging its blaze, holding paper before the grate so as to catch the updraft, I had for a brief moment become lost in my own thoughts. Grabbing a couple of larger cushions bought from Oz, all purple and orange, stitched in glittering threads with Moorish patterns inset with mirrored sequins, I placed these before the fire, to make another pot of tea, some toast, returning with all on a flowered tray, and to collect the still unread letter, making myself comfortable in the fire's glow. Anna's letter being in Swedish, this was doubtless of great significance, what it had to say to be taken with a purpose of attention, reserved only for the most special of communiqués. Some of the words were to me recognizable. Though I had made no real effort to learn the language, I had picked up words, phrases, here and there, letters combining in now familiar ways that, if not legible exactly, nonetheless had about their alien life a certain predictable motion before the eyes, which revealed their half hidden meaning. Over five years though, this had become a game between us, one in which the note or letter arrived unexpectedly, as a challenge, playful provocation to find me deserving of the sentiments expressed.

As always with such letters it was the parts that framed that drew my attention initially, the address, the greeting, the salutation, *how silly, no wonder no one says this any more, did they ever? Only when talking about the parts of a letter*; then the complimentary closing, the signature. That first word, *Älskade*, 'dear'; but it could also mean 'beloved'. The choice was mine to make, a decision for which I was wholly responsible, the writer unavailable for interrogation. Then, in closing, a phrase that could be merely conventionally affectionate, and, therefore, not really affectionate at all, insincere inasmuch as it was convention: kiss and hug, this followed by *Din kärleksfulla Annagreth—your loving Annagreth*. This short letter took me in, opening and closing around me, making me subject to its affectionate embrace, beginning and end, *beloved* and *loving*. *Loving*, that was the word, *kärleksfulla*, or just one translation in any case, also tender, amorous. Filled, overflowing, adjective, but also, I knew I could read this, a gerund: endless in naming, Annagreth naming herself, giving all herself in this word that named her again, but which, before me on the page, knowing what I could read there, how to read her signature to me, knowing, having the absolute belief that her name for me already told me that love, spoke to me of that unending giving of love, in her name. Her names for herself, at once on display, but also private, something remaining out of sight, yet in plain sight, in full view, silent but louder than any pronunciation spoken aloud. *Kärleksfulla Annagreth*: everything was there on the page, just for me, the same number of syllables, the same softening rounding, last small breath, -a, a final sigh, exhalation, a release almost, to be heard just between us, as when the beloved in the lover's arms sighs submission, completion, surrender, a final sound that whispers the desire to be held closer, *let me die in your arms so the vision may never shatter*. Not pronounced with a hard, cold, English K-, I knew, *kärleksfulla*, not the K of *kill*, *kiss*, or even *Anna*, *Annagreth*, Anna; not this pronunciation, but *tsch-*. *Tscherr lecks foolla*. One sound hidden within the sign of another. Something sounding softly, with the shaping of the lips as if to kiss, at odds with the shape, to an English eye, on the page promising but not delivering the stop. While the English sound was produced by obstructing airflow, dictionary definitions insisted, its more affectionate Swedish counterpart, *my tongue is sweeter, more loving than yours*, breathed communication, encouraged connection rather than forbidding it. Anna and I had spent an increasingly drunken evening talking in mock pedantic seriousness about such matters, about consonantal tone, velar plosives and the like, finding the formal definitions unaccountably hilarious.

In the secluded quiet of the fire lighted room barely disturbed by the insistence of winter weather, I worked my way, word for word, through the few lines, too few, not so

many, saying so much, too much. Some words understood
more readily than others, the import and effect of the whole
was not hard to grasp exactly; merely of such an unlooked
for enormity that my first thought was that I was, if not
exactly glad, then relieved in the instant of comprehension to
be alone. I was glad that I had had to work at understanding,
translating the news. The lines of the letter did not follow.
There was not a logic in any obvious manner. To the eye,
everything there was, was there. Yet more, playing with
me, teasing, across the lines, obvious phrases, private jokes,
*here I am, giving a little away, not too much, a little reserve, just to
pretend.* The heavy wooden cased clock on the mantelpiece
marked time with a marionette's foot strike while, at the
windows, the rain beat, incomprehensible semaphore, tapping
a message in an unknown language, awaiting its recipient,
its only translator, the one who could make of pointless,
irregular percussion, a night dance, a winter dance. *The snow
is not so bad, not that heavy; I will come to you.* Understanding
the words without being able to take in everything, my eyes
began to well up. The more I saw, the less I could see. Seeing
everything, gradually, I saw less and less around me. Blinded
I saw. Everything then floated free of its moorings; nothing
was seated properly. Chairs, the flames, photographs in
frames blurred at the edges, lost their focus. Seeing beyond
what I saw, what I could no longer see; and hastily, I wiped
the edge of the letter, a tear having dropped onto the paper,
threatening to make the ink run, once again, so that the
words might, themselves in sympathy with my view of the
world then, also become smudged. In the tears I saw through
what was merely there that evening, through the gaze veiled
by tears. I neither saw nor did not see, indifferent to blurred
eyesight, perceiving instead that to which the script, elongated
graceful curves dried, gave birth.

The last thing I wanted then was to speak; curiously, the
only thing I desired was to hear Anna make music, feeling
behind the notes the weight and pressure of finger on key.
Had she been here, Annagreth would, I knew, have found,

inside the broken rhythms of rain on window playing against the regularity of clock, and with the occasional small explosions, cracks and hisses of the fire, another slighter, more minutely accented rhythm, from which to say, listen, and then to begin to play, line over breaking line of improvised figures. If she had shown herself countless times a selfless and devoted auditor, encouraging confession, purging doubt, Annagreth had also shown how to listen when there appears no music, and to encourage out of its hide the strangest, most touching, wildest and most subdued phrases that found their way beneath the skin, raising the hairs, or pulling at the heart. Alone, pleased for this instant of time on hold, I nonetheless wanted to hear her playing. Music that marked time, played with time, but in its playing suspended time, excused itself from time's motions, from the coarser counts. A waterway separated from the main stream, the tidal flow. Ecstatic. It was Anna's music that came to mind, music as yet unheard, but there, surrounding me in the spaces opened by its anticipation. I wanted to say nothing, to ask everything, to have confirmation, to see that nod, and with it a smile of affectionate affirmation. Yet did I not realise I had these already? Was I not by now familiar with every little gesture, the turns of the head, the glance, the way it was possible to say so much, to share effortlessly between two without the obvious, without words? In five years, with little effort, we had accustomed ourselves to each other. Without her, what? I realised the madness of subtraction. Anna's absence left me with an appreciation of what stating the obvious would coarsen. We existed with, for, in one another, in the spaces, between the lines, in those instances before and after speech, in what took place endlessly, with the others, before an audience, in private, travelling, at home, wherever we were.

Were she here right now there would be no need for me to want. Need would vanish. Anna had taken herself away understanding with that keen appreciation behind which my own comprehension had always lagged. She had departed temporarily, absented herself as old-fashioned books would say, books we read together, read aloud, I reading, she knitting, before the fire, in order that, having before me just this trace of her, her writing, her voice but not her voice, the sound alive for me in my imagination, I would come to know that everything on which either of us counted was only there, poised, on the verge of disappearing forever, or on the edge of rushing back in to consume the vacuum. In that absence, this cold, this rainy, this windy, this haily night, oh let me in the soldier cried…, the world did not continue. It could not go on. I had to go on, I had to choose what next to do, from second to second, and yet, there was nothing decisive to be done. To do…what, exactly? What was there to do, not to do? How could anything be decided when what had become so quickly five years ago the norm, the every day, the inevitable was now so remarkably missing?

— Why aren't you here?

I said this aloud, laughing a little as I said it, sighing with exhaustion, a smile beginning to make itself known on my face despite myself. My eyes had dried, feeling dehydrated, tight, slow slight burn along the rims, toward the outer edges. There was that prickle heat that comes after tears when one can see again, but sight is restored at a cost, to make it the more appreciated. The taken for granted world was returning slowly, but on the understanding, on the condition that it was to be taken less for granted for a while at least, just for a time. Or that the taken for granted be understood as special in itself. All the little gifts. Expressions thoughtlessly uttered between two people, familiar with one another to the point of invisibility, a caring comfortable, sharing invisibility of action, gesture, thought and word. Here the unique, the absolutely irreplaceable, with all its irrecusable evidence was realised for me in the interruption, the more so because I could not say with any certainty when the interruption would cease, the waiting over, the wound healed. Laceration, lesion in the fabric of the normally unthought real; a graze, a gash in the everyday; *do you want me to kiss it better, I will kiss it away,*

the promise in words spoken to a child, impossible magic
healing nothing but giving comfort nonetheless. Impossible
illogic would win out every time. I wanted the kiss to make
everything better, to make everything go away, but to be left
with what was there in outline, behind the lines of the letter.
I began to shiver, though so near the fire, remembering
my clothes, particularly my jeans, still had about them that
mildew dampness, cadaverously clinging, a wraith dogging
the living, hanging on, not quite there, not completely gone,
refusing to be dismissed. Tangibly discomforting, realising
nothing to be done, I decided to shower, to change, and
wait, begin to force the normal back into place by preparing
supper.

— Hallo. You are steaming.

There you were.

— There you are.

— Are you sure? You look as if you had seen a ghost.

— I…oh, sorry, no, I mean…oh

— Silly man, such a stutterer!

That smile, wider than a cloudless July day. Clearly
amused, you, Annagreth, standing in the doorway, still in her,
your coat, the grey, with large felted buttons. You looked
entertained at my perplexity as much as she had that day,
that overheated summer's afternoon at Cowes High School,
shortly after I had come off stage and had been confronted
by a silhouette, a voice, a hand. Nothing had changed.
Everything was different, but nothing had changed. Anna
still had that special power to surprise me, to creep up on me,
take me unawares. Something I always loved in you, about
you. Something I always love.

—Well? You look wet.

*Still, the smile, fishing, waiting for me to bite; or hav-
ing bitten, you were reeling me in, playing me, playing the line.
Annagreth had, yet again, shown me how frangible was the
world around us. Travelling in the unremarkable medium of*

the everyday, we took corners without thinking, often giving insufficient attention to the ordinary, caring less for our own mortality than for hurrying to the end, unaware of whatever might be coming at us, from around the curve, hidden to the headlights, emerging too late from out the darkness of the mundane, so that in the sudden contact, the haphazard collision, things fall apart. Looking again at the letter, then back at Anna, I began to uncoil myself, stiffly, damply, uncomfortably, to rise, to stand.

Once more, at the letter, then,

— Really?

— Yes.

— Yes?

— Yes, yes.

Laughter now, first Annagreth, louder, amused at me, then me, realising my own foolishness.

— Yes, *Sjåpig.*

— For sure…?

— Of course, ja, O Benedict, yes, for sure, yes, of course.

— A baby, you're pregnant.

— Yes. yes, yes, yes, yes. Let's get you changed, you don't want to die of pneumonia before the baby arrives.

~~~

— Play that again, once more, please. Play along this time.

An old 78, the sound of grit upon sawdust in a rutted road, a steel rim rolling, starting into life again, the ghosts of the song. An old disc found in an antiques shop in Shanklin, one rainy afternoon some months before, the tourists departed, squalls from the Atlantic bringing with them gulls and the anticipated, precipitate desolation of long wet winters.

— Ok, silly. Put on the record.

> *...after the ball is over*
> *after the break of morn*
> *after the dancers' leaving*
> *after the stars are gone*
> *many a heart is aching*
> *if you could read them all*
> *many the hopes that have vanished*
> *after the ball...*

~~~~

Does the world become more irritating, does the majority of its populace really become more stupid, less bearable, more venal, less engaging, more facile, less challenging? Or do we simply grow less and less tolerant the older we become? Is it others or ourselves who force us to simplify, shut down our own possibilities, ignore more and more, through that ever present, ever more closely pressing insistence that there is less time, less quality to the time we have, all those other paths, other potentialities, which once we thought would always be there, in those half-remembered always sunny, always snow covered days, when we lived our lives as if we were immortal? Do we just settle? Settle for, settle down, settle in, settle upon? Do we find accommodation, compromise, as each little disappointment, every little death, eat away at our optimisms, our humanity, our intangible and necessarily vague half beliefs, those moments, ever evaporating, of hope, longing, and, well yes, call it what it is even if we cannot define for ourselves or others what we cling to, and which, for want of any better word seems not unlike faith? Not *faith* in any thing in particular. No, nothing so absurd as a deity or other transcendent myth such as humanity. Both those options were never really that, never on the table, up for grabs, never susceptible to any worm-eaten cliché, or any fly-blown, moth-worried fumble, an attempt at naming, an effort at saving the day, winning the game. No. Faith itself. That which is in the music but not the music. Just something that was barely recognised, merely motion, small, a stirring of the heart, keeping things turning, but for which, though it might be felt on occasions, was never to be pinned down, given object as excuse for definition. So it is, we become cruder, more roughly hewn, as we realise, to ourselves, if not to others, that though we never gave in, never compromised, faith, like a dying lover one is incapable of saving, slips away before one's very eyes.

Slips away. What a stupid figure of speech. For there she is, lying there, eyelids barely moving, a ghost dance imitation of pleasure's flicker, in a cruel souvenir of other more intimate moments where there was a share in the pleasure. Now, that brief, half motion is merely shallow pastiche haunted for the one observer who feels the cruelty of significance and memory mocked, even as she doesn't slip away, simply dies. A final breath, laboured as if unwilling to go, unwilling to let go, unwilling, unwilling, but unable to hold on, too much being damaged, too much irreparably transgressed, torn, turned and twisted about. No, no 'slipping away'. Small movements, impossible and unbearable, tiny instances of bodily synecdoche, signifying the intangible, the unnameable, every...what? everything? No, not thing, but everything that disappears save for that which though neither nothing nor something exactly remains if at all only as the memory for whoever loved, whoever survives, whoever can only hear in private the faintest echoes, the slightest intonations, brief accents; or for whoever, in being the one burdened with bearing witness, might just be able to convince himself, fool himself into believing that, yes, yes, there is that merest sense of the memory of a touch, a breath upon the cheek, the imprint of a hand in a hand, on a face, cupping the head; that folded finger, through which came the beloved, just tissue, simply flesh, but crooked and gently wiping away a tear. If anywhere, there is faith, faith in what that memory might cause to be felt. Felt in the heart as it was once felt on the skin.

I had asked you once about faith and you had replied simply, *listen. It's in the music. You know that. Really, hear. Schubert. Bach. You know, of course you do. Because you feel it, no, not all the time, those special times that creep up on you, when you catch your breath, stop, pause, look around. Yes, yes, then you realise, don't you? And not just the notes either. There is nothing remarkable in playing the notes. All one has to do…*

— …is hit the right keys…

— …or the right frets, or the right strings…

— …now you're mocking me; yes, let me see: 'all one has to do is hit the right keys at the right time and the instrument plays itself'. That's not you, that's Bach.

— *Ja, natürlich.* Why try to say anything after Bach…

— The immortal god of harmony.

— Now, you mock…

That playful mockchild's pout, head tilting, before, in the instant after, that sudden thrusting forth of the chin, and with it, the smile, that smile, which confessed faith in everything and everyone.

— …but, no, yes, oh, yes, it is, it is in the music; and in the spaces in between, in the silences; the best music is always in the silences, because it is in the silences that God speaks. Papi told me that when I was very small. Annagreth, he would say,
…

and your face would take on a serious aspect, an elder's persona, all stern brow, not from displeasure but in the moment before speech, to signal import, head tucked, the turtle half in, half out its shell, brows gathering, eyes focused, the blue a greater intensity for being so precisely locked on the invisible, on memory itself, lips pressing slightly forward holding back for that second alone the force of truth about to emerge

— …Annagreth, silence in music is everything. For it is in the silences that we might be able to hear God. There is where he puts his lips to our ears and our ears alone. He is not for everyone to hear, even though he is there for everyone. And I remember this very clearly. I was five, it was just after my fifth birthday. We were in the cathedral, my church you know, we were listening to Papi's assistant playing the organ. Yes, and I remember, little Anna remembers for me. She asked Papi why there was music:

> *Dem höchsten Gott allein zu Ehren,*
> *Dem Nächsten draus sich zu behlehren.*

— For the glory of the highest God alone, and from which my neighbour may learn…

I translated.

— Not so bad; it is the, it is from Bach's Orgelbüchlein, the, oh, what do you call it, at the front, the…the…

Searching for the English, I knew you were thinking the German, hearing the word I had, I believe, already guessed, anticipated, but knew you would not want me, certainly would not thank me for finishing off your phrase, the search sometimes being everything, the journey more than the arrival. Always better to travel hopefully, James was fond of saying, half mangling, half hanging out the bait of a quotation, daring anyone to correct and or finish it for him.

— …*Inschrift, Sinnspruch…*

I couldn't resist.

— Epigraph.

— *Ja, Epigraph.*

— But that's what it is. Epigraph is, well, it's epigraph.

— You are making fun.

— No, it's the same.

— But that proves my point. It is between the two isn't it? In the silence between the two words, English and German, there is everything, what we cannot hear but which means so much, between one word and another. For God alone, and for us to learn.

There. There and not there. There you were, once again,

in that realisation, in telling the story, you reached that recognition of what the silence bears, of what can be heard when there is nothing to hear, of what might be seen when nothing remains visible.

I am waiting to hear from you.

As I always do.

~ ~ ~

— Shall you mind? Being a father?

Frost and Ice everywhere, night tipped white in otherwise blacked out streets. Dark lanes leading into the past and future at the same time, one possibly misremembered, the other, uncertain, moments to be anticipated, though their arrival not necessarily guaranteed. Driving back from the barn, carefully, a little too much food and alcohol leading to incaution, overconfidence, largely rural roads, touched here and there by signs of settlement, newer life, habit drew the eye to the invisible, to times older than it was possible to imagine, save for sympathy with those who, moving by the stars, had experienced the same inkstain midnights, dense rather than merely dark.

— Mind? That's an odd way to put it.

— You know what I mean. I know you want to be a father, now this little one is happening. I know you like the idea of being papi, but shall you mind?

You were, as ever being you, being Annagreth, sage, serious beyond your age, more serious than any age could give a place to. It was always in that sententiousness of hers, in Anna's sudden appearing suddenly unworldly, as if come from a place not appreciably dissimilar to where the rest of us inhabited but somehow different, a place where people asked profoundly unanswerable questions, the tone of unexpected, because seemingly dispassionate, interrogation was at once playful yet with a purpose or significance not to be fathomed.

Just two weeks. Just over two weeks since the news. How

could I tell? I didn't think I would *mind*. We had already spoken several times of the changes, and what would result, all future anticipations, imagined situations given a German turn. It was as if a child, a baby, the future, was the natural consequence of the planned relocation, the much anticipated, barely to be waited for move to Hamburg. That had been taking up much of our discussions, late evening at the barn, with everyone involved, even Morphy, though he remained resolute in not wanting to leave, wishing to remain. In between the talks, the planning, the jokes, endless enthusiasms intermingled with a desire to escape predictabilities already ossifying and which we had all felt inevitable in our present situation, there had been shows, gigs, performances, longer booked than change announced, but now given something new, different, something added, knowing these to be *amongst the last*. That had been James's turn of phrase, surfacing nine nights ago. Unannounced to the rest of us—we had not yet decided what we were going to say to *our adoring public*, as Kate had put it with an irony not wholly forced—James introduced a new song one evening by including those words.

— This next song, it's new. Sort of, well, we've been kicking the tune around for a while…

…his description of a way we had developed through closeness, musical intimacy shared by us all, of following an idle moment of doodling on the piano by Anna, during a break in the studio,

— …So this is a first, and a last time you'll hear this; this'll be amongst the last evenings we play here, so this might be heart rendering even if the tune isn't. The song's called 'Where is that Baby?'

Reactions, visible, audible, faces turning to one another, questions, half mumbles of surprise, puzzlement. Had they heard correctly? What had he meant? Were the band splitting up? Were we just working through the last of our bookings? Had there been a quarrel, a falling out, or, cliché upon cliché, irreconcilable musical differences? Kate and I had exchanged glances, knowing that there would be questions as soon as we had finished that evening. More generally however, there had been an intangible, though felt difference in the shows since the realisation and revelation of the pregnancy. This had given to our performances certain grace notes, as we had thought, as well as slightly different, more immediately perceived, somewhat urgent rhythms in the playing. There was much in passing made of this or that, a fleeting moment half realised rather than fully apprehended in the manner of a delivery: a solo, some particular improvisation, a lilt or dying fall on the end of a melodic run. It was as if the baby had sealed the compact. A small demiurge had announced itself, playfully, during the wettest, bleakest of winters, blowing the woods awake, and crafting in the process a world opening before us, for which we thought we had planned, but which, until that time, had not been felt by all of us with an equal intensity. This infinitely small existence, as yet unreal, and all the more magical for its being so, had made imaginable, materially at hand in a way not all the organization, discussion, or anticipation could, the move to Germany.

She has arrived to show us the way, Annagreth had said earlier in the evening at the barn, before the disingenuously idle question of my 'minding' had issued from the dark warmth of our bed, appearing in those brief eternal passages definable as neither sleeping nor waking, but savouring of both.

— *She...?*

Came the immediate response from Graeme and James, one of the few moments when they had been not completely in time with one another, disbelief occasioning the rhythmic hiccough in the certainty expressed, no, felt in the tone of Annagreth's voice, a surety of delivery usually reserved for the articulation of displeasure or mild annoyance, when accompanied in that stern child's voice, and in third person as if she were her own ventriloquized mannequin.

— *Ja*, of course, *da stimmt*! How could she be anything but a girl, I mean, don't be silly, boys.

And that was that, the end of the subject. But this little, little fish, swam from the icy north, feeling the currents of the Baltic already along those miniscule veins, to wash sleepingly on the shores of her mother's body, was already making her presence felt, announcing her intentions, that yes, really, no question, *how could it be otherwise*, we were moving, moving, heading north, together, without pause, less than a year from now. And yes, she, she, had arrived to tell us we would soon be gone, to begin, once more, all over again. This was the spirit in which we played, we had found ourselves performing, the familiar all become fresh, a renewed vitality coursing through the trainline tempi, gathering momentum in every piece.

Tonight had been a rare evening at this time of the year without performance, a Monday, Christmas passed, just, today an extra holiday for some, Boxing Day falling on a Sunday. Tomorrow was to be a private party, Swainston Manor, and from there on toward a New Year's Eve, at the Ventnor Winter Gardens. Another last, the last of the loud blues-based, out and out, full tilt, over the top, take no prisoners, the last of those evenings of what the British music press, with stunning unoriginality, called either 'high-octane' or irrelevant dinosaur guitar centred rock, depending on where, journalistically, one stood on fashion and anachronism. This was not to have been the last, but the news of the baby had made us reconsider, despite obligatory protests from Annagreth that, *no, don't be stupid, I am fine for a while yet.* James, Kate and I had, however, made the decision, Graeme going along as he always did, but on this subject especially, his knowledge of the practical aspects of gestation and pregnancy limited to large four legged animals that gave milk. January and most of February had already been scaled back somewhat, in anticipation of the eventual relocation, and in order to work on material seen collectively as who we wanted to become more completely, how we saw ourselves develop.

Tonight though—our own solstice celebrations, quiet,

low-key, reflective without being sombre, the band, close
friends, all acknowledging what was gradually becoming
broadcast further abroad. Soon we would be gone, *departed
from these shores, an idle memory, remembrance of which should cause
a tear to drop, a glass to pause, a lip to still the voice.* This, Damian,
his own ponderous, purple efforts at poetry summoned
as a toast, everyone wanting to say something, anything,
to acknowledge endings and beginnings. We all avoided
knowing glances, smirks or smiles. Damian could mean well
we knew, even when he failed spectacularly. Especially when
he failed, as he did, so often. Even failure for Damian was
a glowing triumph of the will, ineptitude and overarching
self-promotion their own successes, excess of overkill,
overdoing it to such an extent that we all admired what Tom
Goodchild, the metalwork teacher and cadet corps instructor
back in Sixth Form had once called Damian's infinite cock-up
capacity. Tonight though, tonight was different, and we were
happy to allow the imperfections, the failures, along with all
the other lesser sprites of domestic, daily disappointment into
our circle. These also were part of what belonged to us, and
to which we belonged.

~~~

Ice freezes memory. It is said that we remember winter's
coldest scenes, as we remember those of summer, because
the frost is at its most intense, as summer's heat sears the
shapes, etching into the mind's eye, those scorched images.
As summer is all wheaten gold and brown, lips dried,
chapped, skin slightly sticky to the touch, the world before us
accordingly parched, amber turning to terracotta after those
earlier days of deep blue clarity have passed, so in winter,
we find ourselves at our other bodily extremes, fingers, toes,
ear tips and noses having been touched, with a near fatality
of intimate immediacy, burned by the bite that tells us, here
is winter. We know such a touch because it is a memory of

the feeling we have lost. Some would have us believe that winter is monochrome, but that is only because they do not see. Or rather, it is that they see only with the eyes, rims of lids already tight from light and cold. Therefore, they see nothing. They, whoever they may be, do not see; they do not feel winter. They fail to live its strictures. Lacking imagination, winter is reduced to absence, lack and death. Yet, crystalline, skeletal, stark, touching on the perception of eternity, an eternity with us all too briefly, before it withers into soggy disappointments, the compromise of mud and puddled soil, winter holds in place, with its rimy fingers framing the view, all that, were we to realise it, we hold most dear. For in winter, with the ice comes a fragile beauty, appearing but only as if to remind us of other beauties we hold closest to us, within us, stilled in the sudden snapshot of memory's archive.

When I think of summer, it is always the Island, always what seems to me now that first summer, a summer of introductions, encounters, chance, change, transformation and all the possibilities under the sun of a potentially infinite world. When winter returns, out there or in here, in me, then it is the winter of other places, never English winters. Or instead say this, English winters are small dark cosy holes of comfort, retreat and refuge, winters of interiors and familiar faces, all those glowing, rosy, embossed with a Pickwickian sentimentality, aureoles of refulgent bonhomie. Those larger, darker, more expansive winters of memory, these belong to the North. Winter is Germanic, winter is Nordic. It is Scandinavian. Winter is the world gone quiet, the sharp crack of blackened branches giving before the insistent weight of snow, piled pillow thick beneath the feet, mirroring the scudding wrack in ice-blue skies, already dimming in the early afternoon where, at particular minutes, there is a special silence, the silence of that which lies within music, that which remains underneath the surface of the rhythm, the counterpoint, the melody and harmony. The winter comes to recall the silence, drive away all noise, irrelevant and irritating chatter, sound and every utterance small humans make to fool themselves that life is theirs, that it continues forever, or that they are immune from the travail of that long, darkening road.

I once told you, you must remember, how I thought you had taught me such ways of seeing. You had merely laughed, called me silly for imagining that. You told me, with a smile impossibly tender, that, no, no one could teach such things. All you had done was very little. You said this as if it were a matter of fact, of record even, a law written somewhere, not to be contravened or countermanded. No, silly, all you had done was show me in the mirror of your eyes what I already saw, what I already felt, but hadn't known. If you had a gift, you remarked, it was that, to show people what they know, even when they don't know it. Nothing else. Everything was always there, if we could only learn how to see. Everything was there, and there you were as always right, it seems now in the retrospect of a winter's memory, if only we could hear, if only we saw with the winter light, if only we heard the silence.

~ ~ ~

Pete had brought 'home movies' with him, his name for the various recordings at different times, in diverse places, preserved, more or less, in different formats: our own ghosts, the spectres of ourselves speaking to us, even when there was no sound, from a sheet hung from one side of the barn, or played back on TV and video machine borrowed from the farm house. Everybody sat, growing quieter, as Pete's footage spoke in different ways, telling us who we were, who he saw us as, the kinds of stories he had made from our unthinking everyday lives. Concert footage for sure, indoors, outdoors, at home and abroad, larger, smaller crowds. All the shadows in motion, sometimes slow, Super Eight a novelty of deliberately antique appearance already, its softer colours lending the patina of nostalgia to what had been work. There was the whale outfit, Judge clowning, a circular dance, arms outstretched. A whale? With arms? No one remembered, or cared to remember why. Those who were there for the evening but not belonging to the inner circle, Steve, Judy, Teresa, Leila (now forgiven), Rory, Guy, Menna, Garry, Tim, Mike, Harry, Sue, Debbie, Rob, various assorted Phils, Harry and Rosemary, all wondering the comic enigma of the bass player's melancholy prance.

— Where was this filmed?

Whose voice this was mattered hardly, as everyone not knowing sought, you could see in their film light, flicker reflected, illuminated faces, the question, the puzzle, the enigma. Pete's voice, reluctant to give too much away, always taciturn, admitted to the building being part of the old County Workhouse, long disused. He did however add the footnote that on the day we had filmed around there, a newspaper dated 1877 had been found with the headline, 'IDIOT STARVED TO DEATH IN THE ISLE OF WIGHT WORKHOUSE'.

— Damian, mate, must be a job going for you.

— Has anyone checked the villages over the West Wight lately?

— Rog, how is your brother?

Voices quietened once more. What had begun midway through the long winter night, well past Solstice but still having about it the darkness of lost ages, the evening enfolded our retreat, protecting our...what could we call it? Farewell? Not yet. Party? Hardly. We had no word for what we had wanted to host, but instead told friends and close acquaintants that simply this was our 'not a farewell party' soirée, absurdity and pretension balancing one another with a certain meaningless equipoise, meaningless phrases covering like the clouded night the absence of any meaningful definition that might have been assigned. An excuse to get together, one more time. From the top, with feeling. Everything was in what was not said, once again, everything in what was not to be seen, not heard, as darkness and time went hand in hand, the darkness of concupiscence,

Judge had observed. Tosser came the affectionate reaction. Pulchritudinous prat was the only riposte he would offer.

People had been asked to turn up as early as five if they could, ask to leave work early, on the promise of a long evening. Kate and Anna had made presents for everyone, James, Graeme and I contributing in one way or another. Chris we had asked to choose from our recordings his favourite pieces, enough, I had said, to fill two sides of vinyl. Peter had ventured a photo album with his preferred shots, refusing to consult us, as we would just become overly precious, too picky, and generally annoying, his original idea being that friends should be able to write something in the book. At around 7.30—the evening had to be scripted, Morphy insisted, organizing chaos, as was his gift—home movies began. Pete offered very little by way of introduction, preferring the film and video to be its own commentary, to serve as the visual equivalent of the music, moving images in so many ways, a mute speech with the power of incarnation. At first, the film show had appended to it occasional commentary from its subjects and other members of the audience, often flippant, sometimes glib, not infrequently embarrassed,

— Oh crap, I wasn't really doing that, what was I thinking?
— I can see your knickers, Kate
— Keep looking, arse, it's the closest you'll ever get. Actually…
…here it came, duck for cover…
— They're your mother's; she's never got them on anyway.
   …a line that cued howls and hoots, the barnyard zoo asylum shrieks, *she got you, bugger, and good*; but this subsided, as concert footage gave way to moments 'on the road', at cafés, even a hotel room, shared by everyone, and all captured by Pete whenever he had had the chance to travel with us. Our lives were slipping by, away, receding, frame upon frame, imperceptible the joins, the edges, no frames visible, all that motion, hardly time to catch breath, so intent were we on catching fire; a brief still point, or no, two it was, a last

performance, a capella, 'Woodstock' perhaps. Then, not a still but so idle as to appear from the other side of a tableau vivant: still life on the road, ennui setting in, tired eyes, red rimmed weary, barely the movement of a head from anyone, sitting on flight cases, in the back of the van. Kate leaning into the back of Waltraud, searching silently for something unremembered. Annagreth, early morning, a Danish camp site, talking with joyous intensity to a small curly haired child. Then Morphy's face up close, breaking the moment, out of focus, filling the frame, the lens, mugging for an unknown audience, ghosts the other side of the camera, waiting to arrive for the show, instances of passing time their flesh and blood counterparts never witnessed.

From here came the archive of memories, unguarded moments, one or other of us caught unawares. At this flat, or that cottage; by the sea, on the edge, at the shore, in the park, in a garden, arm in arm in arm in arm up Union Street, snow falling to silence the world, great coats, overcoats, fake fur and leather coats, hair damp, straggled, stray and lightly blown; or a woollen tam Rasta floppy, with tassels covering baldness. Again, the arms conjoined, though summer now, Cowes High Street, moving as a wave through unsuspecting tourists, looking alarmed, perplexed, startled, at some local Hydra-headed mythological creature emerging from the depths, though whether of the Solent or the undiscovered places of the Island, no one seemed quite sure. Our world was filled with white and wonder unexpectedly, when Anna, Annagreth, appeared in a park, in the snow, firs and pines sentry straight, an apparently breezeless winter day.

— This is last winter…

I was surprised at seeing this.

— Ja, Hamburg. *Planten und Blomen.*

The film ended. No one knew quite what to say, a small pause, filled with an entirely different silence. Then, Annagreth,

— Pete, you will teach me how to use a video camera, we will film the little one, all the time, watch her grow. Then when we are old, or when she is too wilful, too grown up, too independent, we will show her film and say, remember when you were so small and so sweet. Yes, and we will use it to embarrass her in front of her boyfriends!

— It's a deal. But I've got one more piece, the most recent. Hold on everyone.

A videocassette at hand, before anyone had moved or had a chance to refill glasses, turn on lights, it began, dark, handheld, with sound this time. Anna, once again, this time, at the apartment.

— Two weeks ago, I had that dreadful cold; Annagreth NOT pleased!

And it was a new song, quiet, playful, a cheery 2/4 waddle of a tune. None of us had heard this before, save for Pete. I wanted to ask, but had no words, and turning repeatedly, to the screen, to Anna's profile, close to my face, a smile, her gaze trained resolutely in front of her, refusing to acknowledge my look. Began with the simplest of chord patterns, little embellishment, then gradually, with each refrain, the verses and choruses linked by ever increasingly complex curlicues of sound, weaving in and out the metronomic regularity of the left hand bass, the musical box tune came to its final arabesques, triplets descending, chasing one another. The last notes dying, fading, falling away, seabirds disappearing beyond the cliff's edge, Annagreth withdrew her hands from the keys, placing them in her lap. Looking briefly around, down, anywhere but the camera, as if she had dropped or forgotten something, or was slightly embarrassed; then suddenly, her face turned directly towards us, a smile breaking, as if to say, 'this is all too serious, here I am again', and with that sudden so familiar gesture of the neck and chin thrust forward, the eyes and smile widened, before the film faded to black. I felt breath on my ear, a whisper. Für dich.

~~~

When I fall asleep, I disappear. Where do I go?

This had puzzled you at one time. Such questions came around every so often, from somewhere, causing us to pause, whether 'us' were you and I, or, choose who you wish, any permutation of Kate, Pete, Graeme, James, Morphy, you and I. Everything would stop moving, the world slowing down, or otherwise carrying on, as we, whoever we were at the time, found ourselves in a situation, a social evening, at home or with friends, at a rehearsal, in the studio—wherever. Once at the studio, just after ten in the morning, one backing track completed, such a question had arisen. The discussion continued until eleven that evening, at which point, recording resumed, the track completed three hours later. No one can hear that gap, a space in the song, but everyone knew it was there. Four minutes and 54 seconds of sound, followed softly, a Thuggee's silken rope around thirteen hours of what, to all intents and purposes, is a silence: unheard, unrecorded and unrecordable, but there, all the time, the pressure silently behind a dam wall built from the completion of the tune.

Today had been the day though, when you asked, knife poised unexpectedly in mid-air, glinting edge, silhouetted blade, against the brightly streaming sun

— When I fall asleep, I disappear. Where do I go?

We had been preparing a meal for the others, but not, as you liked to say, the other others. Who the other others were was always ill defined. They hovered, on the edges, shy ghosts in the grey of the morning on the verge of absence, dream figures sometimes disappearing too quickly, and at others, vanishing not soon enough. This evening, the meal was for Morphy, for his birthday, so we were going to fit into the flat about fifteen people, so many pieces in a puzzle, resembling something larger but often variable, the solution to which only we, the five of us, knew.

People, you had thought, were like songs. Who they were should never be known completely, could never be known completely, not even, especially not, to themselves. People were made more of turbulence than simplicity. People, you insisted, had 'holes'. James's voice, Graeme's voice, these were already imaginable. Looking at one another we smiled slightly, my eyebrow raising, your eyes creasing into that recognition of the remark unsaid but there nonetheless. Hearing the response, the childish humour, though not spoken, was all too easy, and we stopped, more, before continuing. No, you said, people had holes. It was only right, the way a good song should have holes, not to be fully understood. So a song should never be didactic, never obvious, at least not obvious in what it was doing elsewhere, underneath, in secret, in the silences, while all the obvious was going on, all of what you described as the obvious obvious.

There were, you wanted to give me an example though this was unnecessary, the words about not missing a bus and finding a box, the sound of a dog somewhere in the dark, but that was not what the song was about. There was the hole, right there. We had had this conversation before, were to have it many times. But it always returned, because the conversation had no final point. Like an improvisation it continued to move, to expand, to shake loose, get tight, pull itself in different directions, exploring all the tensions, the counterpoints, traversing as it did the smallest area of a potentially infinite spider's web of fragile, impossibly convoluted, secretly patterned threads, filaments and clews, this archaic word you had confessed to loving, because, as you said, once you had discovered it, it went in several different directions at once: back into the past, forward to whatever futures in which it might become accommodated. Or, you imagined, it was itself a thread. It acted out, as the ravelling of its own being, that most imperceptible of connections between the literal and the metaphorical, yes, yes, that was it of course. There was the enigma in plain sight, all the time, right before our eyes, the hole already in place, not some final answer, never a solution, end of story, conclusion to the matter, but one more mystery.

Realising you had wandered away from your topic, *I've been following the clew*, you said, smiling as a defence against any possible accusation of not sticking to the point, you restated your assertion that people were like songs, and that songs, like people, were not finite, definitely knowable, but had holes. The good ones anyway. Perhaps not everyone you conceded, only the best, only the finest, the most beautiful. There was no hole in, oh what had been on Radio One at that moment? 'Rasputin', *Meine Güte!* No, no 'hole' here, not as in Bach, but the Bach of the *Magnificat*, the cello suites, not the Bach, well not as much, not the Bach of BWV 1079. You could never resist showing off your knowledge of the numbering system that identified Bach's compositions, could you? *Bach-Werke-Verzeichnis. And why should I not use them? After all, Bach was so, so, mathematical,* you had once defended yourself, playfully, when Judge had, on playing the Suite for Unaccompanied Cello Nr. 1 in G major, responded to your jumping excitedly, clapping and shouting *BWV 1007,* by making a sarcastic hooting noise, coming from somewhere between Frankie Howerd and a quite camp owl. *Get you, dearie,* his other reaction, covering the fact that clearly, he had met someone more than a match for his own musical snobbery, worn lightly, but taken seriously.

But no, you said, people had holes. Songs, pieces of music, the good ones, had holes, and it was up to us to place ourselves in the space, to understand, to appreciate, to feel as it were from inside the hole whatever the mystery of the hole might have been. Even Wagner, you had been forced to admit, yes, even Wagner, the great didactic monster with all the myths dancing to his direction, jerking as he worked the levers, forming a truth from a children's tale. Why yes, even Wagner gave us the Tristan chord, perhaps the greatest musical black hole ever. Such gravitational force. Of course, you quickly would follow, every time this subject arose, others had already used the chord, and so, knowing it would get no one any nearer the mystery, you would reel off, with that charming child's face of knowledge retained, the names: *Guillaume de Machaut, Gesualdo, Bach—natürlich—Mozart, Beethoven.* But knowing the music would still not solve the riddle of the hole, the enigma of the silence, that one, special silence. This would not, of course, give us any certainty, no answer. Experiencing or perceiving the hole and being unable to say any more about it, other than knowing you could feel but never say. Well, that was the point, there was that special silence again, the ineffable capable of overawing, overwhelming, beguiling, and yes, yes you had thought, perhaps even seducing. *Ja, and love too, of course.* You didn't have to say any more, did you? I knew, had come to know, to perceive as if you and I were inside one another how love can dislocate, disorder, make our limbs unworkable, cut our puppet strings, calling a halt to the habitual routines of forgetfulness and well oiled, strongly schooled rhythms of the everyday. Love takes away our joints, our hinges, and we collapse, as if we had been filleted nimbly, with the sharpest, the truest of knives, delivering us over to the other, the beloved, all rectitude gone, and we become left with a spineless, amorous idiocy.

And when such questions came from nowhere, whenever you reminded me of the hole, the silence once again As when you asked that sunny afternoon in the kitchen of the flat on Fairy Road, *When I fall asleep, I disappear. Where do I go?* I had no answer. Or rather, I did, but that evaded all words, leaving them orphans, bereft, redundant.

~~~

Early in the evening, before most of our guests had arrived, I felt as if I had to say what it was needless, because known, to say, as we carried food from house to barn, crates of beer, courtesy once more of Steve, accompanied on this occasion by Marty, bottles of wine, placing all around the trestle tables borrowed from the village hall. As we shifted amplifiers against the walls, moving instruments and cases in order to clear a large, central space, lifting, I paused, to look Morphy in the eye.

— It's not too late to change your mind. About staying. It'll never be too late, you know that, don't you? I mean, it's not going to be the same without you.

— That's right, we'll have to carry things for ourselves and get our own drinks.

Judge, ever the glib opportunist, moved in.

— James, shut up…

Taken by surprise he looked around, as did Morphy, to see Kate, who, silently, emerged from underneath a table, only to bark a little too sharply.

— Thanks, no, I know you mean that, I know you all do, really. It's just, well…I've gone over this lots since I made the decision, and I don't know if it's right or wrong, I can't see any reasons why it's not right. I don't know, I think I'm, well, this is comfortable, it's all known. And, what I mean, it…it's not about me, about wanting or not wanting to do this, not being afraid of the move or anything like this. How can I put it? The band is about here, Old Time Hockey belongs to the Island, I know that sounds stupid, as soon as you put it into words of course it does, but, we'd lose something, moving away. Just this feeling I have; we'd be the same but not the same, d'you know? And I know, you've all avoided asking me about this, you've all kept silent, and I appreciate that. Going, well, it's just wrong. If I'm wrong, I'll admit it, and I'll happily come out, but I think it would…it's something someone says in *Lord of the Rings*…

— Oh bloody hell, Tolkien, that's all we need. Anyone seen that copy of Bo Hansson around here?

— Don't make me hit you…

— …someone says something about diminishing; we'd diminish.

— You think we do not know, how could we not? *Komm*…

And there we were, as always, and captured, as always, Pete's camera now seeming to have a prescient will all its own: Group portrait with dog, our very own *Commedia dell'arte*. Each in their, our roles, suddenly transposed. No one who didn't know, would ever know what was behind the image, though, those of us who knew, who still remember, those of us who are in the picture, understood that the person and the mask are often inseparable: Brighella, Arlecchino, Pedrolino, Pierrot and Pierrette, Colombina.

Looking at this now, I recognise the moment. I hear the voices. I see in the faces each personality. Behind each face, stilled briefly in that silent witness of the print, there they all are still. There we are, each of us, us and them, small, ambered, caught in a slice of Island time, out of time forever, gone but there.

There we were.

There we are.

~ ~ ~

— You haven't answered? Are you asleep yet? I am not going to allow you to fall asleep until you answer.

— Sorry, what was the question?

Fingers reaching for ribs, half pinching, half tickling, playing annoyance in the half dark, searching for the keys, to play a tune, coaxing one more melody in response, an instance not to be gainsaid, or deflected. Through the laughter, that interrogation arrived again.

— Shall you mind being a father?

Does one mind? Did I mind? To mind suggests that one thinks actively about a situation, from which comes a possible objection. A hypothetical now real, I sought for the right formula, as the answer to such a question should be carefully phrased. No, of course, I didn't mind, but as yet this event had not taken place, this condition of being a father not yet fully realised. I began—do you remember? But naturally you do, no question about that—by pointing out that the question demanded a careful rethinking, according to how you, how she would have defined, would have understood a father. She, you, Annagreth, Anna, knew what I was going to say, replying that, yes, she was, you were, aware of the distinction I was making, and no, a father was not the one who happened to have a hand—I thought better of suggesting that hands really had little to do with it—in the making, but yes, being a father

413

came later, for a long time. While Annagreth was always capable of seeing everything in the blink of an eye, I had to begin with the obvious, worrying at the question or problem until it began to reveal its intricate structures, down to the microscopic level. In this moment however, we had arrived at an accommodation between us, agreeing with some celerity as to our nocturnal subject.

There. No way out through prevarication, which, you do know, I can feel you telling me, that of course, of course, we both understood I had no hesitation here, but, and here was the nub, the crux, the heart of the matter, the question was not concerned, not really, with minding, but with allowing this third person in, being always welcoming, always open, never jealous of a presence that would change forever how you and I saw one another, how you and I were to one another, for one another. How could it not? I can say all this now. At the time though, I only felt that. After all, what I am saying, all that I am saying is not very much at all, hardly anything. What I thought of this situation, not yet quite imminent, I could not have said. Perhaps the matter had not become real as yet, the pregnancy still in the earliest stages, the management of the move to Germany consuming many conversations, the air of dawning finality in beginning to plan the gradual diminution of activities locally signalled only in letting, on a strictly need to know basis Kate had thought, those who were asking know whether we would commit to various future bookings.

Though Kate had not asked any similar question, James, Graeme, Morphy had all expressed opinions, asked those questions most obviously signalling their kind incomprehension as to what any of what having a *nipper*, as Graeme had cheerfully put it, might mean. Anna and I had considered the suitability of the boys as parents at a quiet moment. Graeme, yes, Morphy too, no question, *the best of fathers, I think*, Annagreth had remarked; both in their own charming, guileless ways, were ducks looking for a pond on which they could alight, without consideration for testing the depths, or being overly concerned with what creatures might be swimming about in the weeds, out of sight. James though. No. This was an image impossible to conjure, much less contemplate. As conjectures went, it was a fiction beyond words or images. We had fallen silent at the mere idea. When later, we mentioned this to Kate, her one remark was that we should imagine her impersonating Graeme, single word, two syllables, sounds like 'mugger'. They all proffered help though, when the time came though without specifying what help or when that time might be. With the exception of Morphy. Always skilled with his hands, he had already, he said, imagined a cradle, on rockers. He had already been to the library, found some photographs, knew what wood he wanted, how he would shape and craft it, and have it ready long before the event. Pete had said nothing beyond congratulations, typically, everything said in the enormity of the smile with which he said the little he thought fit. Chris, equally pleased for us, equally taciturn, had said nothing beyond announcing that he would be ready to attend a baptism or christening anywhere. This was, in itself, a remarkable statement, given Chris's well-known reluctance to travel off the Island. All our friends had made the conventional, the usual, well-meaning remarks. Damian's thoughts went in every impossible direction at once, all circling back to the role he could play. *He would certainly*, John observed, *put the loco in the parentis.*

But for now, I could no longer distract myself by thoughts of recent weeks. The question hovered, in the dark, an unwelcome third squatting gnomically in the moonlight at the foot of the bed. What, I asked, should I mind? To what could I object? How was it possible? Oh, yes, there would be small day-to-day differences, all of which, I felt certain, would be inconsequential. I had no doubt. But no, I should not mind, I would not mind, I could not, even if I would.

Night's quiet settled in again. Tomorrow would be another day. No, today was already that other day, already here. We had planned a day around Yarmouth. Harry, having heard that Reed and Snow Buntings had been seen, thought it a good day to go in search of birds. Possibly there would be Black-Tailed Godwits, Goldeneyes, Shovelers, Curlews, and Egrets to be seen, did anyone want to come along, he had asked, as the evening had begun to conclude, knowing perhaps that there would be few, if any, takers. But no, on a whim, with a laugh in her voice, Annagreth had volunteered our presence.

— Of course, Harry, Ben and I will come; I shall bring cake. *Toscakaka*

This would be today. Today would be just ours alone. For now, this was enough; it was all we needed.

~~~

> *...after the ball is over*
> *after the break of morn*
> *after the dancers' leaving*
> *after the stars are gone*
> *many a heart is aching*
> *if you could read them all*
> *many the hopes...*

13. A Lost Breath (Spring 1983)

The nearer I get to the end, the more I find I am left with fragments. All the photographs are here, the notes, scraps, journals, diaries. Even paper napkins, hasty scribblings in cafés, cryptic coffee Baedeker. Shreds. Patches. All the bindings gone, nothing holding this exploded archive together.

Nothing but you, now. I can't help you get to the end, but I am waiting. I am still here.

Small pieces all around me, spread out on the floor, across the desk. I have resorted to the tops of books on shelves, spreading out, no order, but as something takes me, the sad detritus of an absent life. it is as if, as if, if I could just find the proper arrangement, the appropriate orchestration of these traces, then, closing my eyes, I would open them to find you there or, at the very least, me with you. If it were possible through some conjuration of tale and photograph, to find us, back on the Island... would the Island's older magic still retain its power? I find I have grouped the photographs chromatically, not chronologically, colour a key. Everywhere they surround me, suggestions of memory I seek to sew back together, making a pattern, which I tell myself was already there. I know, too, I avoid saying the same things, for the sake of saying something.

Mostly though, reaching towards an ending I have not yet

started to know how to begin, I dread using your stories as a means of prolonging this ghostly afterlife, by which I come to keep you just that little while longer. I won't detain you I promise, though you know, don't you, I only want to keep you here, with me, forever. Please don't mistake this for the churlish sentimentality and greed of the cheap sentimentalist. It is anything but, though you know how words can coarsen, you more than anyone.

But, what's that? Yes, I know. You will always be there, you have always been there, waiting, listening, telling me. It's my fault that I've failed to listen in the past, not heard you as I should have done. You tell me what needs to be said, I realise that, and I know as well there is no point in the tale told simply for the tale's sake. Of course, I imagine you saying, in telling the tale there will be many who just don't get it. That is not to be helped. Telling, not telling, letting go or keeping hold. The secret remains the same, whoever chooses to hear, whoever misses the point. Nothing to be done.

Then, there are all those other moments, we both know I will never share. Yes, you're right, I've said that already, I do have a penchant for repetition, don't I? But of late this has become something of an orison. *The more you tell, the more you want to keep secret, to keep safe, isn't that so? Just a few hints, like our music, notes inside the rhythm, the hint of another tune, if only those listening know. If they hear, that is all right, because they would understand, they would appreciate us.* Keeping the secret then, keeping the everyday, the little unremembered things of no consequence, except that they were, and so remain, between us.

With this in mind I skirt the edges, I walk to the border, on my own. Standing at the edge of the sea, remaining, taking shelter in the lee of memory's island, waiting for the tide. *Did you know, did I ever tell you, Tide, this was one of my words, a favourite, it comes from old German, of course, what does not? You see, I still remember how to tease; no, tide, it is related to time. So, that stuffy phrase, James's father used it once,* Time and Tide wait for no man; *it is a nonsense, you say the same thing twice, time and time, tide and tide.* Time and time again, yes. All time, every time, always there, flowing through other times, of course. You have never really been gone at all, you remain. You abide. I appreciate that you are here. So I wait. For the tide. I hover, feeling the tidal pull, ebb and flow, the current waiting to guide my direction. The only thing to do, standing before the interminable waterway is to wait for the turn of the tide, in this brooding half light of memory, picking through the fragments washed up at my feet. I only have to wait for the neap, paused, idling here, this slack water time. *The sails come down.*

And once it takes you? us? Let us go then. Where it doesn't matter, only that certain duties have to be carried out, the offices of memory, others to be remembered in between us, part of us, before the end. Let us go, where, no matter where, to the movies, to a show, to do nothing, doing everything in the nothings that we shared, all those little times, nameless, unremembered, something in the nothing because it was with you. Let's go. There will soon be no need to wait any longer, recalled time and again to my purpose, I have, I swear to you, never forgotten, I could never forget, that look upon your face, the knowing smile, slightly impatient, indulgent nonetheless. *I know. Ja. It is good.* You were always ready ahead of me, as I dithered. Dither, a word, another of the words you collected, it comes to me as if you had held up to my ear a shell in which to hear myself, in which I hear the turning of the tide. It's just that I dread that moment the most, because in admitting it, I know *there,* there you are in the loss that is at the heart of me, when I feel my own life, my solitary existence the most.

~~~

Early morning sky, soiled with grey, dirty wisps discolouring. A hush, air vibrating long after. Memory hints at whispered conversations, one voice questioning, correcting, interrupting, the other. Back and forth, sound of laughter, quietly, before the fall of silence, again, as curtain, lace, lifted as a sigh borne away on a stronger, though still sleepy breeze. To touch; touching: a touching proof, no longer the night time exile, in momentary blindness lasting an impossible time, coming back from that immeasurable invisibility. To wake; waking: being there, once again, cool against warm, pressing close with a lightness that promises to float away. Fleetingly, so swift, as to seem involuntary, but with an indefinable weight so lacking as to feel it a phantom across that surface just above oneself, neither there nor not there, another stroking caress, brushing buoyant. Soft tickle waking touch. Absence of voluntary movement, refraining from deliberate reaction, while, outside, somewhere near, song. Whistling chirrup full-throated, melody holding off time's commencing, notes, complex weft of trill with shift of pitch; impossible to see, though weighing down, a pleasant, a luxurious oppression. Silence is a space, an emptiness to be traversed, though holding us in our appointed places; but with no appreciable motion beyond, flocculate inertia forms all around, holding everything in place, resting, reassured in proximity, dampness, hand cradling a new-born's head. All the love, all the endless care and joy. The world feels vapour, nothing but everywhere notwithstanding. To stir; stirring, slight, barely movement, butterfly motions around the eyes. Today. What? Today?

Yes, today.

A picnic, yes.

Today.

~~~

And for my next trick, I'll jump from the seventh floor.
I'll sail the Atlantic, on a broken-off car door.
I hope that you get it, if not, there's no more.
No more.

Two months of studio time, more. Fifty recordings, two more versions of ne me quitte pas, several traditional Swedish

songs, much improvisation, and, with a brief visit from
Heike, a recording of a Schubert song, two versions, 'Der
Leiermann', one sung by Heike, the other by Annagreth.
Out on the lawn, Fred joining in at the sound of the
accordion. We, no, Anna had convinced Mike, *really, it will not
rain, bring the old eight-track, bitte!* Her child's voice appeared,
and how could he resist? Out to the deck, this rare mild
Spring afternoon, Dil and Fred, mad circling on the lawn,
play snapping, seeing, hearing everything beyond a human
range, cutting crazily, shapes in the drying air, the world just
touched with the mildest, merest warmth. Morphy and Mike
arranging mic stands, baffles, pop guards, leads and cables
tucked and tidied across the deck, extension cables for the
Rhodes to be powered, a small amplifier, *mic or DI, Anna?*
The other instruments, acoustic, mic'd, a table brought for
a hastily organized console stand, basic mix, and then, Kate,
the accordion, 'Apache', drifting toward the Solent. Or, late,
the following evening, last of the recordings, Anna held up
her hand, to signal a pause: *I want candles, I must have candles.*
Mike looked mystified, *where on earth, at this time of night…?*
Tah-Dah! Came the reply. Here you go, Matey. Morphy had
been in on this all along. Holding a box aloft, he revealed the
desired light source. Mike, sighed, knowing resistance was
futile. So, studio, lighted with candles that final evening, for
the Schubert, Anna's arrangement, *no, no need to play all the
phrases, each of the measures, Kate, James, just these, and here, and,*
pointing to the dots, *here; Mike, can you loop these, please, für mich,
bitte?* The smile, through the glass, face pressed against the
pane, kissing through the glass; *no, the timing doesn't matter, just
let them play, in and out, ja, and bring them up, fade them in and out.*
And she played. There were no words, there are no words.
Listening, now, she is there, I am there, sitting in the darkened
room, moved but unmoving, silent on the floor. No, there are
no words. All the rest is silence.

These two recordings stand out for me still, remaining as
radiant, touched with a rarer quality impossible to define, but
felt still, after all these years. Our two month residence was

marked by endless, tireless, unstoppable work, Annagreth disregarding any suggestion that she not work quite so hard, that she take things a little easier, Kate concerned that the days need not be quite so long, and being, with that loving care that existed for, between, them, rebuffed. Each of us pushed our own limits, the limits of one another, Anna and Kate in particular driving each other on, in the most circumspect, the quietest of passages, or fierce bursts and wistful refrains, improvisations become structures for infinite variation, sound weaving. Stranger songs, more and more folding in upon themselves, pushing toward pure music, pure sound. No one knew what pure music was, except perhaps as an idea we had not yet heard, not discovered, but knew somehow there, in us, with us all the time. But strangest of all from all those sessions, uncanny in its fearful confessional drive, beautiful in its bleak despair, 'I am Nothing', which built and built, a noise punctuated, pierced by a mournful voice. Fantasy of emptiness, music Annagreth's, words mostly hers, a few verbal fills from me to round out, accent, her strong, unerring music breaking in on all of us. From everyone's faces during playback I could see each felt, Kate, Graeme, James, but also Morphy, even Mike; everyone had been taken out of themselves, but with this disquieting sense that the music did not return us to where we had begun; instead, we were left, somewhere deeper, darker, somewhere, the heart of all things incomplete, abandoned. We stood facing an ocean, preparing to be drowned.

In between the original material, storing up mostly ideas for the coming autumn and winter, once we had moved, *once the baby's arrived,* Kate couldn't help repeating, already knitting, every spare moment, at home, the barn, in the studio. There were some other 'covers'; a Tim Buckley song, stretched and pulled; yet another, even more unearthly version of 'Black is the Colour', *the sound of Faerie* was James's description, so ethereal its sound might simply have evanesced, vanishing in the instant of its performance, leaving nothing but the trace of a memory, were it not committed to tape. Titles were equally vague, obscure, suggestive of nothing but the indefinable, an experience of what words could not capture, experiences for which there were no words, but which got under the skin the more for being so ineluctably there; or else titles hinting at the secret, the confession again, affirmations of desire, need; or just words for images, significant only in their being anchored to a sound, teasing clues to a possible meaning never revealed, because not wholly apprehended.

— What's that you're playing?

— Ben heard it last night, on the radio. It is beautiful, no? The last day of mixing, the final, impromptu recordings of the Schubert, two takes, piano, with some minimal looped cello, violin and viola; taking a break, sitting near to the piano, I had begun to play a song I had felt compelled to learn from hearing the first notes, a descending, legato line, double bass leading in guitars and fiddle, brushed drums. Writing as quickly as I could that previous evening, *Anna, quickly, the words, get the next line,* we took down alternate lines, I hoping our approximations were nearer rather than further away from what we were hearing. A song I had to play, we had to play, *we just have to play this.* It called with what I thought an unattainable perfection in my own writing, giving me an apprehension, a distillation, of where we had been heading musically, collectively, even though this could not as yet be fully realised for most of our performances. We had never been happier together, having come through the prolonged, sustained exhaustion of the previous year, but our music was changing form once again; shapeshifting, it was assuming a more interior, darker, open ended life. This once heard song touched a nerve, in both sound and words. Kate spoke once more, as James had wandered back in.

— Play it again. Please. No James, refrain.

— How can I refrain, don't know what the refrain is yet.

— Leafrain? What's that then when it's at home?

Graeme had now appeared.

— Not leafrain; you've been hitting things for too long;

refrain, refrain!

— How can I, when I haven't started

— Hah bloody hah, never let the same joke go by twice. Go on, Ben, play it.

And I did, Annagreth joining a harmony, a descant in the chorus, following me back into the verses.

> *Salt water to a thirsty man*
> *Was all we had to give;*
> *We ran aground, we're scared to talk about*
> *The will to live.*
> *Somersaults on a rainy day,*
> *Sails went down;*
> *Am I allowed to mention why I talk so loud.*
>
> *And for my next trick, I'll jump from the seventh floor.*
> *I'll sail the Atlantic, on a broken-off car door.*
> *And I hope that you can get it, if not, there's no more.*
> *There's no more.*
>
> *We'll join the circus, we'll travel the world,*
> *Everyday will be fine;*
> *A clown waits inside the walls of everyone's mind.*
> *I've let you down I know this inside,*
> *Let me just try,*
> *I'll wear my face with so much pride,*
> *I hope I'll make you smile*
>
> *And for my next trick, I'll jump from the seventh floor.*
> *I'll sail the Atlantic, on a broken-off car door.*
> *And I hope that you can get it, if not, there's no more.*
> *There's no more.*
>
> *Even Christ fell by the wayside,*
> *Yes, even Christ cried.*
> *I tried to start my broken down car*
> *While they passed on by.*
> *Please will you watch me now, I'll startle your mind;*
> *Pick a card, I hope it's number ten,*
> *Sorry not this time*

And for my next trick, I'll jump from the seventh floor.
I'll sail the Atlantic, on a broken-off car door.
And I hope that you can get it, if not, there's no more.
There's no more.

By the time I had finished, opening my eyes, I saw Kate,
violin in hand, James, his double bass ready; Graeme brushes
poised. Still the same, six years on. Everything as it had
always been, each face a smile, eagerness, ready to start one
more time. The song knew us, had found us in the night,
had arrived in time to remind us that we were about to
begin, once more. James spoke first, announcing what was in
everyone's mind.

— Let's try it, we can add it, night after tomorrow.

~~~

— A picnic, yes. It doesn't matter about the weather. Let's
explore. We will remember the day we find a name. Then,
tonight, we tell the others. We will celebrate.

The rains came earlier than expected; by midday, the world
had turned to water, all that could be seen occluded, driving
made more difficult through water blindness. The Island was
hiding itself, disappearing into the heavens' welter. Venturing
up on Boniface, Ventnor Mountain, parked, we walked
wetly through the gusting sheets, silver grey stinging needles
encouraging shivers, trembles; your eyelashes, droplet heavy,
only your eyes, their blue, that special hue, remained that day
radiant, defiant of the natural world, and its unseasonable,
unnatural downpour. Absurdly bright cagoules, mine yellow,
yours orange—what else?—hoods up, we appeared to
ourselves, odd flowers torn from the soil, pushing against the
wind; rain seeped in, insinuating dampness, damper chill than
the cold of water, at sleeves, around the edges of the hoods,
blown off now and then, if we turned too suddenly, dripping
into, and around our necks. I observed that I could just hear

my mother right now, *ja, you'll catch your death! Death, where are you, I don't see you, come out, come out wherever you are; no not today.* Laughing, realising that we were no match for this mad March day, we admitted defeat, headed home, jeans heavy with their gathered rain, drenching, sticking, clammy clinging.

Home, just after one; *here, get out of those wet things.* We said it, not quite together, a heartbeat separating by only the thinnest of walls, the shared thought; let me dry your hair; and I will dry yours.

Later, we decided that the picnic would go ahead, just as we had planned. *We have gone all the way to the other side of the island, in order to get home once more,* you said, pausing as if, in making this remark, something had struck you. And then, *that is how we have been, no? All the time, we leave, to come back, we always return here. I am always happy here, here, with you, it is never winter. I am hungry!* Food. Walls turned acquaint, shadows rivuleting down in imitation of the streams that snaked their way down the windows, sunlight, white, a troubled light, illuminating drops. Setting out our picnic in the living room, the chairs pushed back, a chill taking the air. *Let us have a fire,* you said. Such extravagance in March, so exorbitant, *just a small one.* Cake, cheeses, biscuits, fruit spread across the blanket stretched, some wine, *not too much,* I had said, and was told not to fuss.

— So, a name.

On the previous day, March 16th, *not the fifteenth, no,* you had said emphatically, explaining to me after it was the Ides, nothing good would ever come of doing anything important on such a day, we had, together, visited the hospital. *Obstetric Sonography,* such big words for something so little, you had thought. We both had to know, *we are just like each other, impatient children, all the time, now now now. I was always this way at Christmas; not Heike, no, she was the good one, the patient one, I could never wait; and anyway,* you justified for me our shared impatience, *my parents will love to know, and we'll be there, it will be a September baby.* So we went, and were told.

— Well, Annagreth, everything looks just fine. You're sure you want to know the sex? It's a girl.

Driving home, we had already moved from 'it' to 'she', this small life found, discovering us. She will do this, she will do that; I want to teach her to play the piano; Papi always wanted granddaughters, I shall do something before Heike! Talking late into the night, you had already begun to think about a composition, a birthday present, and we must phone Kate, James, Graeme, you said, Morphy too, I interjected, of course, you replied, offended in tone at the implication you perceived on my part that he had been forgotten, omitted, *we must phone them, we must let them know, we have a little party tomorrow night;* but then, as we lay, only pale moonlight illuminating the bedroom, our tiredness, you remembered just two weeks before, when, finishing at the studio, the last day or two, Heike still there, staying with us another day, there had been that softly pulsing instrumental, which had appeared to grow from next to nothing, from idle lines trippingly coaxed from the piano, then made more formal, simplified, played on the synthesizer, sonorous bell resonances, echoing discretely. We had been at a loss as to what to name it. *It sounds like a lullaby.* We had looked up, surprised at the source of this statement: Graeme; agreeing to leave the title for the moment, it remained just a sound; until that night, *that's the title, Vaggvisa för...*

The afternoon of the picnic, we chose a name.

— I hope this doesn't take as long as it did to find a name for the band.

— Stupid! Of course not; anyway, we are not asking the others, it is just us.

— What do you think, then? Shall we make a list?

— *O Benedict*! This is not a set, we're not going to decide on the running order. Meine Güte! Sometimes you can be just like the other boys, you know?

I apologised, admitting to the flaw in my character, and asking for leniency.

— Just for that, you can go and make tea. Hurry, I am thinking.

As I stood at the range, watching the patterns of rain form and dissolve, rearranging, the grey beige clouds beyond thinning, light turning a pale, unwashed white, words appeared to me, and it came to me I was singing softly, *somersaults on a rainy day, the sails gone down.* Then I realised, Anna was playing this, a spare arrangement, fingers I imagined lifting tenderly from keys. Returning with the tea tray, I was greeted with a comprehensive, 'I have the answer' smile.

— Well? You clearly know.

— Yes, I clearly know, don't I? As I always do. I always know what's best; I am wonderful that way!

— Yes, yes, you are, but I wouldn't be too smug about it; there's nothing wrong with a little humility.

I returned, smiling back.

— *Oh Quatsch*, so English of you!

And you, she, Anna, Annagreth, began to play, pulling in her chin, assuming a mask of martial seriousness, Land of Hope and Glory.

— Okay, I give in, you win; I would never disagree with a pregnant woman, and I know there's no point disagreeing with you. You are, after all, always, always right. So, what's it to be?

— Our grandparents' names.

— I don't think Sidney or Andrew would work too well.

— *Arsch!* You know what I mean, grand*mothers*.

— Well, you know one of mine was named after Kaiser Wilhelm, and look what trouble he got everyone in; no, definitely no to Wilhelmina, I'll go with the others, for sure.

— There, you see, it's decided. Amalie. Sofia. Juliana. *Vaggvisa för Amalie.* And Kate can be godmother.

~~~

— What are you reading, *Schatzi*?
— Eliot, T. S., not George. *The Waste Land.*

~~~

Salt water for a thirsty man…

Where does it all end, history? When do the big facts stop coming? Respite, if only just so very little. Why do they not stop, pause for one moment's grief, one instant of mourning, a time, infinitely short, infinitely long? History is a monster, obliterating our smaller worlds, smashing with its iron clad feet and with a barbarity it calls justified, everything delicate. Arbitrary in its choices, its decisions, what it chooses should be remembered, what gets written down, it nonetheless causes in myriad and infinite ways chance conjunctions with ruinous outcomes, and then on it goes, uncaring, unceasing. History is the driver on the motorway, who, turning off into unlit lanes, sees not too late, but not caring to slow or swerve, the rabbit, badger, hedgehog or fox in its path. This is the world in which we live, the one we make, too frightened, too needy to unmake what we have so impetuously, recklessly wrought.

What is history? Who gets to decide? I never got to say, to have a say, neither did you; scant consolation that I get to speak for you, now, now you are no longer here. But history. History is a feckless thug that tramples, despoils, mugs personal life, holding it cheap. It never sees, never perceives, never anticipates. At any given point, something is about to happen, while recent events are consigned to the archives where something is only to be remembered for a few months, or forgotten about for years until another context insists that the forgotten is important. Klaus Barbie had been arrested in January. Who cared? Aldo Moro's assassins, members of the Red Brigade, had been convicted in Italy in the same month. The Wah Mee massacre had taken place the following month in Seattle, Washington, and, oh yes, M*A*S*H had aired its final episode. That's history, in a nutshell: crime, terrorism, acts of atrocity, organized on greater or smaller scale, and underwriting it all mordant comedy turning sentimental at the last. Life's small accidents, the little incidents, the suffering the ordinary and unremembered have to live on with, none of that counts. We suffer, you had once said. As always, you were right.

History is a brutal bastard beating us with its own belligerent self-importance, demanding that we submit to its stories, its tales, while we're left bleeding, in pain, crying at the sheer, random, impossible injustice of everything that is said not to count. But we know, I know it does count in every countless, thoughtless accident, because it happens, every day to those we love, to those who loved us, and therefore to those of us who have no right to survive, on a whim. I let you down, I know this, I could have done something. I am trying before we all are forgotten, because we are unwritten, survivors on remand. For you, for me, for all the unwritten.

Everyday ordinary events take place, little anonymous acts, all the time, inconsequential or building to a pattern revealed only after the story is told, when someone claims to have seen the signs all along. Someone turns a corner, and the world changes. That day when everything changed though few people noticed, and fewer cared, taken purely in an historical perspective. The bombing of the US Embassy in Beirut had taken place. History fails to mention though that we had, on a whim, gone to see John Martyn, on a Thursday. Returning, on the last ferry, Waltraud parked not far from Ryde Pier, ready for our late night drive home, we stood on deck, singing together, softly, though not without causing one or two other solitary passengers to look at us askance, 'May You Never' and 'Solid Air'.

A Friday. April. Playing much less frequently, quieter performances, shows at which we sat, or moved hardly at all. Fortunately, there had been several private parties, birthdays, Fleur's out in Rookley at the family farm, particularly memorable; other anniversaries. That particular Friday

night in April yet another birthday performance, a friend of
Graeme's father, a fellow farmer, a party for his wife. James,
Graeme, Morphy to meet us there, Kate coming to Fairy
Road, around five that afternoon.

A Friday.

April.

The morning, fresher, clearer, the sky promising a blue
to match Annagreth's eyes, light to complement the gold of
her hair. Four months' pregnant, your stomach rounding,
smooth belly, skin tightening, Amalie now about the size of a
grapefruit, the doctor had said when asked. *My grapefruit belly*,
you said, returning from the surgery. You looked pleased,
Anna appeared delighted, no clichés, no stock phrases from
the guides to pregnancy too much, or adequate enough.
That Friday. April. We had stopped off in Puckpool Park,
once a fortification battery intended to guard the Solent.
Walking slowly, Anna asked whether invaders might possibly
think to come another way, catching all those soldiers off
guard, looking out at nothing except passing sea lane traffic?
I thought it entirely likely, history proving the anticipation
ridiculous. The crazy golf range was open, little Easter Island
figures, mouths open waiting to receive, no one around, no
signs of tourists this early in the year; it was ours, just ours,
Annagreth wanting to play; *I still beat you, my grapefruit won't
get in the way.* Finished, we went to the café in the adjacent
and rather grandly titled tea gardens, its tired, clown sad
dilapidation comforting, cheery even, something old, loved
for its imperfections, tea always too strong, or too weak,
orange squash too sugary, as were the cakes, but Victoria
Sponge nonetheless a must.

The weather dry enough, the temperature mild enough,
we sat outside. The clouds, thin, high, pale sheep off-white,
scudding, imitating the few yachts tacking on the water,
here and there the sun, not yet a summer brightness, shafts
belonging to a painterly illusion cast down, to disappear over
the ineffectual curving hillock, back toward Ryde.

— Are you looking forward to the move?

Somewhere, a tinny two stroke engine buzzed, hummed, a radio playing, not loud, just enough to make us aware of something from the top twenty, dreadful, dreary synthesizer bleatings, programmed drums.

— Yes, but I am looking forward to the baby more.

We hardly spoke. It was unnecessary. Between us silences were always understood. This thought, that passing observation. Around us, we felt unseen motions, as if in preparation, for another summer, another season, more visitors, tourists, day trippers from Portsmouth and Southampton, Grockles, I could already hear the same old joke, trotted out one more time, James would be unable to resist, or, as he was pleased, to change words in song titles, *here's a particularly heart rendering number, by Budgie, just for all you holiday makers, it's called 'haemorrhoidal, suicidal';* Graeme would be grinning, chortling behind us; yes, that's what he did, he chortled; the anticipation of the remark, the joke, the chortle, this coming summer season, for which we had agreed, we had all insisted, Kate having laid down the law, with a more than usual emphasis, that, *no, Anna, listen, pretend I'm your mother— Oh, I never listened to her—that explains a lot—Judge, button it; no, really, you can come along, not all the nights, we can manage a four piece, we used to—yes, I know, I was there, I told Ben, you needed glue—stop interrupting you bad child, you can play one or two nights, but you're not going to overdo it—ja, Mutti, cluck cluck cluck.*

Elton John came past on the back of a golf cart, a gardener arriving with tools to tend the flower beds, another sign of summer's coming not that long away.

— Shall we go? I feel like a little sleep.

— You don't look like one.

— Ha ha, funny man. So many bad jokes.

— It's why you love me, isn't it?

— Yes. And because you know about trees. Tell me, again, about the trees.

~~~

You slept that afternoon. I joined Anna for a while, until her breath shallowed, becoming a rhythmic sibilance, suggestive of peacefulness. Quietly, I lifted myself, with a conscious deliberation, from the bed. Time to change strings, make out set lists, an entry in the diary; little, if anything, of consequence, nothing after this time that makes much sense, phrases imagined, remembered, and, incomplete, always holding out hope, a sentence without an end: *my turn, this time, to*

It halts, just like that. Was I distracted, had there been some noise? I do not recall. Today, all this tells me is that it remains, waiting to be completed. Whatever happened, whatever, even if nothing had happened, you could not have told me, Annagreth was asleep, I decided to read for a little.

~~~

— What are you reading, Schatzi?
— Eliot, T. S., not George. *The Waste Land.*
— When should we leave?
— In about half an hour, an hour? Kate should be here soon anyway.
— That's fine.
— I'm going out; we have no aspirin.
— Do you want me to go?
— No, that's fine, I'll be extra quick, I'll cycle.
— Ok, be careful…
— Ja, I know, and *don't talk to any strangers!*

~~~

— There you are
    The door.
    Leaving my book, I walk into the hall, turning.
    Kate stood there.
    Kate is standing there in Annagreth's place, where Anna should have been, Ashen, ghostly drained, already trembling. In the doorway, shaken. I knew. I know. I see it.
— an accident, Oh, Ben

Coda

Where am I in all this? Telling the story, I realise that I appear
like a ghost. How to tell the difference between this me who
is telling the tale, and the me about whom the tale is told, at
least in part? I am, I have to confess, not certain. I do not
know whether that person was left there, speechless thirty
years ago, or if I am still that person, never having left that
spot, when everything changed. What would he have to say?
How would he tell this differently? Are we the same person?
Are we continuous? Or does he dog my footsteps, the rise
and fall of the pen, the stroke of the keys, like a stray dog in
search of home, of comfort, warmth, light?

Or, is that simply me, and this the reason for telling the
tale?

I have this feeling that I want to come home, to go home,
but have no sense of direction any more; if I ever had one
that is.

Back then, I was happy to drift, simply to be, not choosing
a way of saying who I was, just being that person. Going with
the flow, caught on the tide, taken further out, or brought
back in. Today, I hesitate over choices, and react, respond,
when a call comes, when something is asked, or demanded
of me. Making a choice always implies getting it wrong. A
fear, really. Terrible, debilitating, impossible. What would he
think of me? I do not know what to think of him. I hate him
often enough. And then I find I long for him. I only know I

wish he did not have to go through what happened, having it all to live through once more, as each word I write moves him closer to that point. But then, that's it, isn't it? He had no idea, and I do. He would never have thought it necessary to tell the tale, I think it impossible not to, my compulsion fighting still with the desire for silence and secrecy. He could never have imagined a world, a time, where the story, this story, had become a story, where there had been a moment, irreversible, for life to pass into story. He would not have known how to frame the thoughts, the passions, the feelings, emotions, ideas. Unhappily, I do, I have the means to spell out what he felt intuitively.

It's rather like the before and after in the history of an idea. The idea, all its little parts, everything that makes it take place, exist. They just do not have a name. Imagine, a world before something assumes a shape and that shape takes on its own signature, becoming visible as that very idea, the notion, the intangible thing we call this, or that, or something else. Once we step over the line, once we give it a name, there is no going back.

This is not to say he did not think, he did not have ideas. It is just that he had not yet had the experience I had, and so nothing had taught him how to speak the name, even what the name was, or how to become the place on which that signature was written. He was not yet hustled across the border, from one land to another, deported, no right of appeal, the passport taken away, with no chance of return. Exiled. Yes, that's it, exiled. Cast out, outcast. To wander, and in the end, alone, to be forced to take responsibility. Not for what happened. Even though the guilt he felt, a guilt which became mine all too suddenly, too imperceptible the shift, was never his, strictly speaking, nevertheless that led him to me, to realising, every day, little by little, but over far too long a time, too far removed, so that the responsibility arrives for me. A responsibility for him, to him, as much as for you.

Do you see what I'm trying to say, Anna? I can. How much I hate the irony. I can speak to you now in a way that, then, he never could have. At best, at some utmost limit, he could say the things I say in an implied, simpler form, so that you, as you always did, comprehend, appreciate, and for that we both loved you, love you still; and to say these things so that you could fill in the shape he sought to outline; in order that you would come to colour in between the lines, making the picture whole, allowing him with that good grace that was always yours, with which you touched other people's lives, as if a breath had woken them to life, to seeing for the first time the world as it actually was; yes, allowing him to understand, to appreciate what he felt, but for which he had no names, until after you were gone, until after he became me, or I abandoned him. I left him standing in that doorway that day. No going back. But I never abandoned you, you have always been with me, but him, I simply let go. You tell me that yes, that's ok, really, there was nothing I could have done, doing anything would have been wrong, inappropriate. I guess you're right, as you always were, as you always are, for you always knew, always seemed to know, you, Anna always know, she, Annagreth, always knew the names for things, as well as knowing when silence was the only possibility that remained.

O Benedict, I hear you say, O Ben, it is ok, it is all right.

Yes, it is all right. I know. But it is a pity. Oh such pity. It is a thousand pities that, for all that now I know the names, I cannot prepare him. I cannot save him. He will always have been bereft. What I know is belated. And, really, whether he knew them or not, knowing will not save him. It never has. Knowing the name is just a party trick, a picture frame, something in which to give a place to everything else that took place, so that now we feel comforted by standing outside the window looking in, or, on the inside, locked away, we watch the world go past. Standing in the doorway that afternoon. The moment after, when a voice that is familiar, a voice belonging to a friend, has to tell the news. The instant after. In the door frame. A bright day, life resuming for everyone else. Birds sing, blackbirds mostly, away, a car, having taken a corner, accelerates, the noise then dying away.

Why do we say noise dies? No noise ever dies, it merely becomes quieter, its waves spreading further, less and less audible but there still, rippling through space. Like children's voices, laughter, home from school. Have you left your sound moving through space, through time, on the tide? But that's all going on over there, not here, not where he is. Adrift, aground, stranded, the sails down, mast broken, no one will ever leave the island. No one ever leaves. No one ever gets away from the Island.

Aground, belated, overtaken by darkness, bereft. I find comfort in words. Finding in them something else, on the surface but buried nonetheless deep down. Words will not connect, the name will not save, but they offer consolation after a fashion. Or, if not that, then I find there are games at least, to distract, to busy the idle hours. All those idle hours, so many, so long, to fill them in, finding diversion, distraction, in the small hours, the dark days, the long years.

Did you know that bereft, an old form of bereaved, means to be deprived of something? Or that, and this is where the word private comes from, that *privare* means single, individual, withdrawn? Completely single, withdrawn, away, always completely removed. Language doesn't die any more than sound, does it? It just leaves, even as it withdraws, this little filament of itself, this small clue, tiny sibling of its greater form, less lively, but surviving, impoverished and withered, the tiniest piece of itself, hidden, private, suffering privation, but going on; private, deprive, bereave, bereft. Or just reft, reaved, robbed. Had he had a name that day, he might have felt himself robbed. Had he cared to give, that day, a name to that feeling for which there are no names, he might have said, were I to put words in his mouth, that he had been robbed.

Some reaver. Some reaver riding by. Some reaver, wantonly. Some wanton reaver riding by, has...Yes, you know this don't you? I cannot fool you. He could never fool you, not that he ever tried, while today, I try to find an amusement for us both, a game at memory: do you remember this, when did we read this, do you remember that night when you read this aloud to me, or I to you? Some wanton reaver riding by, has stolen, stolen away, leaving a boundary wall in that place where you were, in the instant, belated, overtaken by darkness. Belated, bereft. We stand, either side the wall, the reave, a terminal reave. We reach across, straining to touch.

I know.

I know, I am wasting time. Ben, I know this one, of course: I wasted time, and now doth time waste me. For now hath time made me his numbering clock: my thoughts are minutes; and with sighs they jar their watches on unto mine eyes; so sighs and tears and groans show minutes, times, and hours. Our games, those games we played, with words: entire conversations in quotations, breaking off a sentence, expecting the other person to finish it, or continuing, until we could no longer go on, from laughter; or charades, playing out a phrase from a book, picked at random. When we drove, at home, at the beach, waiting somewhere, always waiting, so much waiting between one place and another, so much away from home; waiting to leave, waiting to arrive, waiting to return; wherever, there would be those word games, constantly being reinvented, toying with language, between languages, the different tongues, German, French, Swedish, Latin; even Latin.

Why, do you suppose, do others have the words for the things for which there are no words? Or is it that they need anything rather than the silence? There are those who cannot bear a silence, any silence, however short. The space silence occupies terrifies them. But there is always, if not a space, then a place between people. That's how we know one another. I see you, I recognize you, I know your needs, I answer you. You do the same for me. Lighthouses. Silent music. But he stands there, out of time, time continues around him, unspeaking. There are no words. He had no words. If he had no name for what happened that day, at least he was right to remain silent, and to be true to you in that. I, on the other hand, am trying to fill the space with words, but also in order to be true to you, my beloved other. Speak or remain silent. Both fail, either risks everything, succeeding on occasions. I cannot avoid choosing. Even evasion is a choice. To be true, to be faithful, this is what counts, no matter how much the odds are stacked against me. So I waste time, as time runs down, bringing me closer to you. He could not have waited. I can. I will wait, relishing the space between us. Waiting, speaking, not speaking, I will wait, looking at others, peering into the spaces between couples for the place where you might yet be seen again. Time, I find, has started once more, since that phone call from James, since a visit to a Berlin café, eating strudel and vanilla sauce, since… But this is irrelevant. There you are. You are there. Wherever someone loves or is loved. I leave him to his own place, leave him behind, paused indefinitely, infinitely. He has to wait at the threshold because, while he does not have to have the name, while there is no name, and only silence reigns, he has to wait, and, in waiting, to learn how to wait for you. I know you will come. All in the silence. Whenever I become aware of a space opening, wherever silence descends, there you are. We are together once more. Let us leave him to his silence. Let us leave him in silence, you and I. Let us go, then.

For me though, what? What was that you had once said? It all ends; we all end. Ready or not. You had told me this, comfort or consolation, just recognition of the inevitable to which I could not reconcile myself, to which I will never be reconciled. In our ending…? I do not know. I cannot tell. The idea of an ending with no subsequent beginning seems, has always seemed particularly cruel. But then, it's only cruel if there is a design; one that is limited and flawed, but a design nonetheless. Randomness and chance, absolutely. They appear equally ridiculous. Little stories that lie about the nature of stories in order to hide from themselves the brutal realisation that they are stories.

It is growing dark. I am tired now. Almost done. Too many sleepless nights in shepherding these charges to their home. James exists in a world all his own. Kate stays away, in a foreign town. Graeme is gone, suddenly.

Are you there though?

Are you waiting?

Oh, my love, my love. I know. Yes, I know.

Getting darker; can hardly see any more. I don't want to turn on the lights though. Enough artificial light, no more of that. Outside there are no lights. It is a starless sky, a moonless sky, a sky forsaken, emptied, voided. Just this grey, shading darker by the minute. Everything slows. Somewhere, not that far away, a sound, sounds. I seem to hear the last notes: of curlews, dowitchers, and godwits.

You always knew such silly names. Silly things, and their silly names. Such a silly man.

Or had I been reading of them, fallen asleep, then woken, imagining them out there, at the water's edge, on the sandbar, silhouetted in the dusk?

Straining to listen, hearing nothing now, except the sounds of my own shallow breaths, a last tide drawing away, a shingle song.

It all ends. Soon enough, not soon enough, the tempo right, all ending together. Thank you, and good night. Darkness indecipherable. Are you there? Are you coming soon? Almost, soon enough. Ready or not. I am ready, I think. no, I know, I believe. The readiness is all. It will be light soon. The snow is not so bad. I will come to you. Trembling. Must be cold. I sense a movement elsewhere, near at hand, but unseen. All at once: a shadow? Is that you? Did you call? Everything seems to go back to the beginning. It will be light soon. Such brightness, you there, a silhouette. Hallo. Time to go. She waits, waiting. Who is that, though? Another shape, and in the silence a voice

Papi, here you are.

Encore: Morphy

I had gone already before the end it seems. Not left or separated, but beginning to move away from the others. Someone once asked if I had an inkling of the end, but no. I make no claims to special insight.

This has been a good summer. We don't seem to get them any more, not until this year. Days have been long, hot, dry. Not like that summer you understand, not like that endless summer, a first summer Ben might have said. But it has been a good summer. And now, there is that slight back to school change in the air, when the gulls sound less and the crows sound more, when the light is less golden than blue, less warm than cool, and when clear skies seem to welcome night. I wish I'd thought of that. That was Anna. I remember her, the first autumn, saying that, *look everyone, the sky begins to welcome winter, it must be autumn now.* But that's another story.

I've been asked to say something at the end, this one now. Not very good at this, I have to confess, so I've brought a small silent movie with me. Watch the film. Pay attention. What do you see? To begin with, look at her eyes. Look into them. Her eyes, they do not quite settle, there is a fluttering of the eyelids, more nervous than flirtatious. She appears uncertain where to look, or perhaps the motion is one of adjustment. The light, too bright, requires but a second or two. Well, no, somewhat more than that, fourteen to be precise, if the counter is to be believed. A brief glance; note that, down, diagonal, to her right. Then…then notice also the breathing. It is a little, what might be the right word, pronounced, yes, pronounced. As if adrenaline were flowing, as if there were a sensation akin to nerves as, already greeted, having responded, in a tongue not her own—*Klaviermusik* the only word to pass her lips not in English, let me hasten to add—, there is a slight concern. Did she try too hard to be accommodating, allowing her interlocutor an ease and a familiarity through a response in his tongue, following which she could not follow? Perhaps. She was always too ready, too accommodating, not eager to please, no, never think that. But there was, how shall I say, a readiness to be welcoming, open, in order to give the appropriate due to whoever was the one to arrive, to speak first, to ask questions, or make inquiries. With a politeness beyond mere formality, she could appear welcoming to all, to everyone in turn, to make them feel important, special, the only ones who counted while she gave them her attention. The mouth is a little dry, it would seem. Can you see that? A slight pressing of the lips, and with it, in opposite motion, the separating of tongue from the roof of the mouth. This is what there to be seen. I imagine the feeling, practicing, moving my mouth thus, again and again. And then, the head tilts toward the right shoulder, just slightly, ever so, and with that motion too, a turn in the neck. The lips part and the head, crown to forehead, inclines toward the unseen guest who speaks. Her eyes widen, the gaze fixes in concentration, and, as if to aid the comprehension process, her right hand reaches to her hair, the face more seriously attentive, giving full weight to what is being asked or spoken, as those long, tapering fingers so used to the intricacies and intimate involvements of Bach, Schubert, Chopin, Debussy, scratch in short bursts, half combing hair, before, the hand surrendering, the head tilts backward at the nape, the chin elevating, thrust a little forward. And there, the smile appears, that smile, the one that says, yes, yes, I have you now. I know your purpose, I feel more comfortable with what it is you are saying, are going to say. I am ready.

Ben wasn't ready for what took place. None of us were. Rob said afterwards, we were talking about valves, wires, amplifiers, anything but that; and he paused and said, twenty-three, it's no age to lose someone, no fucking age at all, you're just not ready. You're never ready. But Ben. How do you say what happened? He went on. He went away, decisions made quickly but with a certainty that wasn't to be argued against.

I've been reading about grief. Those clinical definitions of trauma or breakdown are wide of the mark if you want to understand what Ben stepped into through those weeks of unbearable sorrow. He hardly knew what was happening himself, we certainly didn't, though at the same time there was a grim sense that he was watching himself go through various necessary motions, actions needing to be taken, after the accident, a word he later came to realise, he told me, he detested, as he would the word trauma in middle age. Everyone uses it, he said, they throw it around for everything from the loss of mobile phone content to the shock of seeing something unexpected in a newspaper. People devalue words. It could make him quite angry. He explained the anger to me. At some point, he rationalized, everything and everyone could, for the media, in a world of twenty-four hour forensic obsession, be traumatized. It was that simple, trauma was an app to be employed, like finding a restaurant, getting directions, looking at your phone to see if it's raining instead of looking at the sky for clouds. Our world though, a small world in which there was no email, no texting, none the endless, nauseating narcissism of public gaze victimhood, and pointless self-announcement; none of this existed.

Grief seemed all the more real then, and felt the more deeply, because it had not yet become tradable. No one had assumed that they could 'feel' another's loss or, what's that phrase you get in movies from the 80s and 90s, *I feel your pain*. As a result, Ben's closest friends, all of us, but I think Kate most especially, suffered all the more greatly because, not yet knowing that empathy was the great lie foisted on the unsuspecting who, finding themselves to be, in some manner, jealous of what another felt, needed also to be a victim, a sufferer, to have a by-proxy, a virtual look at me, aren't I brave too, aren't I sensitive because I am displaying what another feels so much do I empathize with that person. Feel for me too, please, such behaviour says, virtual grief is just as real as the real thing. Indeed, there is, no longer, any real thing. We all just indulge in stealing one another's ghosts.

But no, the world in which such indecencies occur had not yet made itself virtually present, ubiquitous. 1983 was not yet such a time or place, whatever its myriad faults. Don't think I'm being nostalgic, don't mistake this for a sentiment-honeyed exercise limned with false desire, smeared through the dubious witness of a myopic, tear-filled eye. No hypocrisy here, none whatsoever, I assure you. There are cultures of appalling behaviour, of self-aggrandizement, whole epochs of mass attitudes that range from faintly embarrassing to unbelievably awful. No, Ben's world was no less dreadful; it was just unpleasant in different ways. But what was different was that until very recently, and for several years before that, Ben had found a home, a safe harbour. His world had been in another, in the band certainly, but in Anna for sure, and in the music they played; and from there, beyond what was always seen, jokingly from within, disbelievingly from without, a magic circle (we were really all just circus clowns without a big top), a broader series of widening ripples caused by lesser friends, less close friends, acquaintances, and those who came to hear, to watch, to dance, to share in something, as if through such rituals and repetitions the larger and the uglier worlds could be held at bay. Which they were for a time, though of course every so often there were cracks, fissures through which nastiness seeped, rumours of dark clouds, storms and trouble on the way.

But then. But then; but nothing; nothing and everything; something, not very much, which would, by historians, sociologists, statisticians, and those who took the long view,

saw the big picture, dealt in events the ripples of which were
already of a far greater magnitude, count as nothing; would
not be counted.

There you have it. There it is.

But I need to tell you about an evening. Bear with me a
while longer.

And there it was and there it remained, inside Ben. Kate
knew. She told me recently. One evening, as we sat on her
porch watching as the sun went down, the smell of barbecue
coming from somewhere on the beach, near the lifeboat pier.
The wind was calm, the sun was sinking low, as if about to go
out suddenly, touched by a gloom anticipating the turning of
the tide.

Kate knew all too well she said, returning with another
gin and tonic for herself, a beer for me. She knew all too well
for she had, in coming from Bembridge that day, arrived at
precisely the wrong time, at what the police like to call the
scene of the incident. If ever there could be a wrong time,
that was it. Incident is such a neutral, careful word, so much
less committed, and yet so much more an indictment than
accident. She described what she saw to me once, everything.
I won't repeat it. I can't, I haven't the heart. But one thing
has stuck with me. The slightly folded bicycle wheel was
still turning a little; so close upon the heels of the incident's
occurrence was Kate's arrival. It was Kate who was the first
not to say, but to give everything away in a face twisted in
with more than horror: hysteria, grief and disbelief were the
lineaments of the mask she wore that day, and most likely the
impossible weight of the news she already knew she must
bear, not just on that day but ever after. Much later, when
it was too late, years after, Ben had in moments of thinking
not of Annagreth, thought of Kate. He had imagined how
terrible her burden. He managed to compound his own sense
of guilt in burdening himself with not having thanked Kate
sufficiently. To have been the witness and the messenger, as if
in a Greek Tragedy. That had been Kate's role. This was how
Ben described it to me; to speak as though impelled, having

no other option; to be the one, the one who...Ben suffered doubly, but then already he had begun to become silent.

There was in Ben a sealing up, the start of an autism of the heart, brought about through the enormity of loss. No one is ever prepared for the loss of a loved one, of the love of one's life, as the saying has it, but to lose someone who had so effortlessly, with such charm and simplicity arrived to replace all those childhood abandonments, as Ben had felt them, of father, aunt, grandfather, in short succession, less than two years. How is it possible to bear such terrible pain? Ben needed family, but had family taken from him repeatedly. It takes its toll. Sooner or later the losses can no longer be added up, it isn't a question of number, they just become too many.

Ben found a family with us, with James, Kate, Graeme, me. We knew it at the time so didn't need words. It's only when you lose things, you need words. Words are there for what exists no longer. Like Annagreth, Anna. All the time they knew one another, Ben would often speak both names, in rapid succession when talking with her, of her, especially when asking her a question, wanting verification, needing her certainty; never settling on one name; it came to seem she had been named twice. Golden, calming, serious beyond her years but with a sense of such fun, Annagreth was someone who could and did unconditionally give to Ben all the safety, all the love, all the care he had never known he needed, with a desperate aching and emptiness. She took away his restiveness, the fretful energy that counterpointed the periods of intense stillness and quiet, the non-stop fretting that others who were never allowed so close mistook for neurosis, a lack of balance.

Fathers told sons of Anna that she was just the sort of woman they should seek out. I remember hearing just this one night at a pub we used to go to regularly, not far from Seaview. I was already there, at the bar, chatting to Steve. Ben and Anna arrived. Typically, he opened the door for her, she in front, he behind, her smiling, taking in everything

and everyone, her golden hair bright against the collar of
a crimson coat, Ben, his head down, face obscured by that
mop of his, a leather biker's jacket to hide inside, pretending
to be someone he wasn't. Seeing Annagreth, Steve's father,
the publican said just that: that's the kind of girl you want.
Kate's father, on first meeting Annagreth, had spoken of her
afterwards as 'our lovely girl', a phrase that had remained with
us all. Annagreth had made a world, a home, a final and a
perfect family for Ben. Our lovely girl gave all of us a home,
a family.

Then she was gone. Six years over. Just like that. At
twenty-three, a mere month younger than Ben. Twenty-
three: too young to die, too young to lose someone. Yet it
happened.

So Ben began to shut himself up, to close down, to
speak less, say little to others of his feelings about anything,
without realizing at first that he was doing this. Unless in a
torrent of tumbling emotion he blurted out in frightening
moments, little insanities escaping uncontrolled, some half
formed expression that gave word to pain, he said little, when
he spoke that was not fact, measured and controlled. Or he
engaged in moments of what seemed like sophistry.

The night now having completely arrived, Kate told me of
one such other night, when a storm arrived unexpectedly less
than a month after the 'incident'. On the night of the storm,
Kate had seen to it that that Ben was tolerably calm, before
leaving for home. Ben had wanted to take up a conversation
about the meaning of an expression that had, he said, been
bothering him. This was all said quite slowly, with a certain
assumption of disinterest, as though Ben had been reading
a study of cross-pollination, or the hybridization of apple
varieties. Kate, for once in her life, had no ready response.
She remembered how she had remained silent, beginning
to stroke Ben's head, a single tear making its way down
her cheek to tickle the corner of her mouth. I could hear
darkness in her voice. Realizing the tear itched, she resisted

nevertheless wiping it away. A watery insect, it moved in the near silence of early evening, slowly and as if with purpose. The sensation of slow descent, drying in the deceleration captured how time felt in those days.

Kate wondered at the time when it might stop feeling this way. Would time heal? Would it heal Ben and her? Would time heal itself up, leaving nothing except the merest scar as an occasionally too dry reminder?

The evening had begun with supper.

Mushroom soup. Some stale bread. Outside cloud upon cloud, the sky a turbulent ocean, discord and gathering darkness, an early evening in spring. Kate watched Ben, saying nothing. Slowly, spooning, spilling, spooning again, shivering as he did so, Ben watched the sky, watching the clouds, and, talking more to himself than to Kate, he observed, grey on grey wisp moving beneath the greater blanket with the density of a deathly pillow, smothering the life of the world. Kate felt the need to engage Ben in some manner, but no longer noticing her in the room, he continued to talk, fugitive translucent stained and sullied sky moderately dull broken only by brighter haloes of luminescence where sunlight struggles for small dominion everywhere darkling an impermanent magenta apparently malignant mass, tumor in the heavens Benedict believed, seeing in the clouds, Kate thought, the sky held all that was suffocating, stifling, choking his heart.

As suddenly as the wind had returned, day turned night once more, and with that rumble of thunder unnervingly near. Ben rushed from the room, chair falling backwards, soup bowl pushed violently away. So rapidly had he moved, in contrast with the torpor by which he had previously been gripped, that Kate could hardly respond, feeling for the first time since Annagreth's death, genuinely, desperately scared, not for herself but for Benedict. Following along the corridor, she was already too late. Ben had locked the living room door. Kate heard the key scrape. Calling his name, first softly then more loudly, Kate heard first faintly clicks of clasps. Her mind searched on its own as she began to call, more insistently, begging to be let in. Between cracks of thunder, Kate's increasingly urgent voice was counterpointed by her hands hammering more frequently on the door. The world was no place for silence that afternoon, silence was the enemy, it allowed too much thought, too much feeling. There was no place for feeling, it had to be drowned in noise, in a welter of clashing, strident disharmony, spastic atonal percussion, as if some prelude to end time, the safe world, the small world, the world of known things were being quartered, torn bodily apart.

We continued to sit, another drink or two. Long pauses, silence accompanied, save for world of woodland and water's nighttime whispers.

Ben had, finally, unlocked the door. It was not so much a case of tidying up as clearing away the signs of destruction. On entering the room, Kate saw what Benedict had done. Pieces of guitar were everywhere. He had broken their bodies into unplayable shards, wreckage the outpouring of grief resurfacing yet again, as it had so often done in the past few weeks. Kate could not help imagining Ben first opening, then stamping down on, and finally, pulling at the already splintered bodies with his hands, hands she had seen were extensively cut from wood and strings. She could imagine, as she began to tidy, the measured way Ben had gone about such destructiveness. The ruined instruments, their necks awry but strings still attached, either to a partial top, the bridge still intact, or otherwise hanging in confusion, looking for all the world like dream abandoned puppets brutally unloved. Ben had piled wood into the fireplace, as much as would fit. There having been nothing with which to start a fire, the sight was a particularly sorry one.

Typically, Kate told me she thought at the time, Ben had been careful enough, even despairing, only to damage that which was his, as though the guitars were extensions

of himself. Which of course they were. Kate continued to
clear, to gather the fragments. More than that, Kate knew,
the guitars were his voice so much of the time, Ben always
having been reserved, quiet, turned in on himself, whether
in company or when playing. Don't get the wrong idea,
please. Ben was not maudlin, never that, he wasn't one for
playing the suffering poet. Rather, those who knew him
understood, his was a slow, vegetable world of reflection
and consideration. Not one given to the expansive outbursts
that were so much James's hallmark, or the raucous gleeful
madness of Graeme, Ben was never mercurial. There was
nothing of quicksilver about him, save occasionally that
strange, often comical dervish dance to which he succumbed
at the end of sets, as returning to the stage for an encore
before the others, he would begin some rhythm work,
intricate but never flashy, and, the rhythm building, it would
call upon, releasing something in his heart.

And then she thought, pausing in the telling, of Ben's
smile. His smile, Kate reflected, herself now barely a voice,
nothing else on the verandah, as she continued to clear away.
Ben's smile had been slow in appearing, embarrassed, rarely
given full measure, as if so much of him was uncomfortable
with being just simply who he was. From the earliest days
of rehearsals, first as a trio, then a quartet, Ben had been the
last to offer an opinion, make a point or stake a claim. He
had always been happy to let James and Kate steer, direct.
Suggestions came, but in a deferential, not to say hesitant
manner. While she and James, and subsequently Graeme had
always been busy, loud, expressive, expansive, and, she had
to admit in James' and her own cases, dogmatic, Ben allowed
everything about himself to appear in the songwriting, the
playing, the manner of his accommodating himself to an
arrangement. While they spoke readily, socialized willingly
at gigs, Ben was happy, in those strange periods of nervous
languor between soundcheck and show, to sit, with a drink, a
book, and a notebook. Or otherwise he'd wander off, hardly
noticed in his absence, with his camera, which I remember

he always had with him. Later, Kate said, he would show us photographs of trees, or churches, graveyards and shoreline.

I seem to be rambling. If I'm getting away from the point, it's because I'm not sure I have one. I think Kate would have been better suited to speak here, now. I think that's why I'm deferring to her voice at this point.

Annagreth had brought out in Ben a more visible aspect of his happiness or joy with everything. Without trying, her mere existence, her gentle and loving proximity had caused him to smile more readily, to laugh a little less shyly. Everyone, even Graeme, had seen and commented, over the six years, how more open Ben had become. The transformation effected by Annagreth had been one that was both immediate and gradual. But then, Annagreth had shone, that was the first word that came to mind, the only word for it. She had shone, a face of silver, a heart of gold. Though never publicly except once, on her birthday, Ben had demonstrated a remarkably untypical moment of spontaneity by playing for Annagreth, in front of several hundred people, Neil Young's 'Heart of Gold'. The audience, a local and regular crowd knew. Even those who only nodded acquaintance saw and knew. There had been those who had joked, but not unkindly, Rob, Garry, Ian, Tony, Steve, Jack, Jon, Tim, Stu—who had christened Ben and Annagreth 'the duffel coat twins', for their habit of arriving at venues in this most un-rock n roll clothing—Keith, Ron, and other musicians who made up the other bands of the Island; they had joked about the pair being joined at the hip, Ben and Anna, Anna and Ben being twins separated at birth, being two halves of the same person: all the usual things someone says about a perfectly paired couple.

And they were, thought Kate, someone for whom relationships never sat easy, who had abandoned the idea a little too pragmatically, a little too swiftly, but with that certain energy that always marked her out.

Kate had almost completed restoring what order she

could. Furniture, accidentally knocked over, had been righted, the last of the fragments of wood and what remained of the distorted bodies, the necks and any other incidental tokens of the irreparable damage stuffed inside cases, which were closed as well as it was possible to do. There had been loose pages of music, and a book of Schubert pieces on top of the piano, mute testaments to a time irretrievably gone, still close and yet already distant.

Lady Marjorie and her husband had, in those days following, been very understanding, not at all impatient about the various comings or goings, or inquisitive come to that. Immediately, there had been the village policeman, a doctor, then family, first Kate's, then James's mother, Graeme's father George. By some unspoken agreement, Kate had assumed various roles, Ben being incapable in the first days of doing anything at all. It had fallen to Kate to contact Annagreth's family, telling the news a second time, immediately to Heike, whose burden it then became to inform her parents. Walter, Sophia, Heike, Heike's boyfriend, Volker, arrived. Kate acted in all of this tirelessly for Ben, for the family, helped with all the necessary arrangements, aided by her parents, Harry and Rosemary. And after it was all over, Kate had continued to be of use, to be available, to be around, as unobtrusively as possible.

Almost at the end of tidying the room, Ben now wrapped in a hand-knitted blanket, curled in a chair, Kate came upon a postcard. The strange, unworldly, old fashioned and formal turn of phrase; the fountain pen inflection of the line was immediately familiar. The voice remained intact, though only dried ink being left, this seemed a very personal and cruel souvenir. There was no date, no clue as to when this had been written.

The card itself was a cartoon of sorts, French, from the gift shop of Victor Hugo's apartment, in the Marais district of Paris, the flat in the Hôtel de Rohan-Guéménée, on the Place des Vosges. In French of course, the card announced that if you stared at Hugo's likeness for a while, afterwards, on taking your eyes away a ghostly image of the author would appear before you. I have a copy of this, we all thought it quite amusing: *Regardez fixement l'œil de la silhouette dans un endroit bien clair, en comptant mentalement jusqu'à 80 ou 100.*

This must have been bought the autumn before the end, on a brief trip to Paris in late September.

Another autumn. Always autumn, always spring or winter, never summer any more. Here though, now was this card, whimsical and yet also earnest, with its own ghost.

And there she was, Kate thought, Anna, Annagreth, appearing through that very German hand, just visible beyond the ink line.

Kate wept.

Acknowledgements

There are always debts, those the most real the ones that remain unpayable.

For permission to quote, I would like to thank the following, whose unreserved enthusiasm was without measure:
Peter Hammill, for 'Vision'.
Hugh Lupton, for 'Bleary Winter', and Chris Wood for his wonderful music; there are no words.
Iain Morrison, for 'Broken-off Car Door'
Richard Thompson, for saying 'go for it', although I never used the words in the end.

Thanks to Russell Richards for cheering me, cheering me on (and keeping me running).

And the good readers, however far they travelled:
Christine Berberich, John Brannigan, Doris Bremm, Stefanie Caeners, Torsten Caeners, Johanna Hallsten, Ruth Heholt, Kate Hext, Jackie Jones, Dragan Kujundzic, Robbie McLaughlan, Hillis Miller, Ken Womack.

And for the Nightwatchmen.

About the Author

Julian Wolfreys is Professor of English at the University of Portsmouth. His band, The Nightwatchmen, is based on the Isle of Wight and plays music that mixes the eccentric and the whimsical from the English underground tradition of the late 60s and early 70s with its visions of a lost, surreal rural England and a darker Northern European sensibility that takes in cabaret, chanson and various folk leanings.

His research covers the nineteenth century and English modernism, with particular interests in inter- and transdisciplinary approaches, while also being informed by continental philosophy from Kant to the present day, and with a particular philosophical interest in phenomenology. He has published on Romanticism, Victorian literature, Modernism and postmodern literature and culture, with particular interests in questions of identity and subjectivity, the politics and poetics of urban representation, the rural subject in English culture, perception in literature, and the relationship between language, music and that which cannot be expressed directly.

He is currently working on four books, a study of Victorian poetry and the influence of German Romanticism, a phenomenology of loss, the relationship between subjectivity and loss in the context of Englishness, from John Clare to Virginia Woolf, and the question of place and dwelling in novels of the late nineteenth and early twentieth centuries, from the perspective of the concept of "dwelling".

About the Publisher

Triarchy Press is an independent publisher of alternative thinking (altThink) about government, finance, organisations, society and human beings.

Its Fallen Arches imprint also publishes an occasional series of altThink fiction by serious people of impeccable standing. The main criterion for inclusion is that the writing should be very good indeed.

www.triarchypress.net/fiction

Lightning Source UK Ltd.
Milton Keynes UK
UKOW04f1001121114

241480UK00006B/70/P